ACTS OF CONTRITION

WILLIAM HEFFERNAN

NAL BOOKS

NEW AMERICAN LIBRARY

NEW YORK AND SCARBOROUGH, ONTARIO

Publisher's Note

This novel is a work of fiction. Names, characters, places, and incidents either are the product of the author's imagination or are used fictitiously, and any resemblance to actual persons, living or dead, events, or locales is entirely coincidental.

Published simultaneously in Canada by The New American Library of Canada Limited

 NAL BOOKS TRADEMARK REG. U.S. PAT. OFF. AND FOREIGN COUNTRIES
REGISTERED TRADEMARK—MARCA REGISTRADA
HECHO EN CRAWFORDSVILLE, INDIANA, U.S.A.

SIGNET, SIGNET CLASSIC, MENTOR, ONYX, PLUME, MERIDIAN AND NAL BOOKS are published in the United States by New American Library, 1633 Broadway, New York, New York 10019, in Canada by The New American Library of Canada Limited, 81 Mack Avenue, Scarborough, Ontario M1L 1M8

Library of Congress Cataloging-in-Publication Data

Heffernan, William, 1940–
    Acts of contrition.

    I. Title.
PS3558.E4143A63   1986   813'.54   86-8671
ISBN 0-453-00513-6

Designed by Leonard Telesca

First Printing, October, 1986

1 2 3 4 5 6 7 8 9

PRINTED IN THE UNITED STATES OF AMERICA

ACTS OF CONTRITION

Other books by William Heffernan

BRODERICK
CAGING THE RAVEN
THE CORSICAN

For Karyna, Cheryl, and Alisa,
three young women of whom I am extremely proud

A special thanks to Maureen Baron
and, as always, Gloria Loomis.

PROLOGUE

November 1, 1984

JOEY GAMBARDELLA CLIMBED the front stairs of the refurbished brownstone, inserted a key into the heavy oak door, and stepped quietly into the partially lit foyer. He hesitated, eyeing the staircase ahead, then moved quickly up it. He was a small, slender man in his mid-thirties with a sharp, narrow face and coal-black eyes that, in the dim light, made him appear predatory.

At the top of the stairs he instinctively unbuttoned his jacket to provide easier access to the automatic tucked into his trousers at the small of his back, then moved down the hall to another door, which he opened without knocking.

Across the room a heavyset man with white hair sat behind a large partner's desk. The only light in the room came from a brass desk lamp, and behind the man at the desk, Gambardella could see the other, younger man standing in the shadows.

"Come in, Joey," the man behind the desk said, beckoning with one hand, then gesturing toward a leather visitor's chair.

Gambardella moved slowly to the chair and sat, carefully adjusting the crease in his tan slacks. He was wearing a dark blue shirt, open at the collar, and the light from the desk lamp caught the reflection of a thin gold chain around his neck.

Paul Levine stared at him from behind the desk, as though studying Gambardella for some flaw. Paul was in shirtsleeves, but his necktie was still drawn tightly to his collar, and it seemed to emphasize the bulk of his body.

Gambardella ran a hand over his thinning black hair. "You said it was important, Paul."

"At eleven o'clock at night it usually is," Levine said. He watched a slight tightening in Gambardella's thin lips, an almost imperceptible rise of his pointed chin. "You look nervous, Joey," he said.

"Not nervous, Paul. Just curious." He glanced at the other man, who had turned his back and was staring out a window.

Levine sat back in his chair and folded his hands over a protruding stomach. "You know we've had a problem. A serious problem."

"I thought it was all taken care of. That we fixed it," Gambardella said.

Levine smiled without displaying his teeth, causing the folds of his face to bunch up until his eyes were only slits. "So did I, Joey. But it didn't happen."

Gambardella nodded and watched Levine lean forward, his elbows on the desk, his heavy shoulders still displaying a bulk of muscle beneath the fat. Even at sixty he looked powerful, Gambardella thought.

"We've tried everything reasonable," Levine said. "But now it's a question of survival." He hesitated. "*Our* survival."

Gambardella drew a shallow breath. "What do you want done, Paul?" he asked.

"I want our problem to disappear." He hesitated again. "Permanently. But neatly this time."

Gambardella's eyes drifted to the other man standing in the shadows, and Levine, noticing, swiveled in his chair. "You agree, don't you?" Levine asked.

Gambardella watched the other man step into the light. His face was drawn and tight, and his eyes seemed to hold a hint of pain as he said, "I agree."

"When do you want it done?" Gambardella asked.

"Tonight," Levine answered. "And come back here when you're finished."

Gambardella nodded, then stood and walked out the door.

Levine leaned back in his chair. "He'll do a good job," he said without turning to face the other man. "It's the type of thing he does well."

The other man was quiet for several moments. "Yes, he'll do it," he finally answered.

Outside, Gambardella stopped on the sidewalk. It was early autumn, but it was already getting cold, and he wished now that he had thought to wear a coat. He glanced at his watch. Eleven-fifteen. With luck he'd be finished by twelve-thirty. One, at the latest. He hunched his shoulders against the chill and started down the sidewalk toward his car. With luck, in another hour the woman would be dead. And, if necessary, the man as well.

CHAPTER/ONE

April 1984

JENNIFER BRADY LET out a long, tired breath and stared into the open closet. Damn, she thought, there really wasn't much choice. Half a dozen designer originals stared back at her, dresses she had bought at one fancy charity thrift shop or another. The dresses had been worn only once by their original owners, then donated to a good cause and quickly snatched up by Jennifer, who could never afford the initial prices. She drew another long breath as she studied one dress she particularly liked. It was a filmy, blue silk by Karl Lagerfeld, and she knew how much she would like to wear it. But not tonight, she told herself. Tonight's party would be elegant by anyone's standards, and the risk of finding herself face-to-face with the original owner too great. There was only one dress that would qualify, and she had worn it for the first time two weeks ago. And with the same man.

"Oh, well," she said aloud. "Newspaper reporters aren't supposed to be rich, anyway."

She reached into the closet, pulled out the dress, and

held it out for inspection. Basic black, she said to herself, and more than half a week's salary at Bergdorf's. She smiled slightly at her irrational disappointment at having to wear this dress. When she had come to New York two years ago, she had known little about clothing, little about how to approach the problem on a limited budget. But she had learned, had developed her own style, mixing and matching, until she had become comfortable in almost any setting.

After carefully placing the dress on her bed, she turned to face the full-length mirror. She was naked, and except for panty hose, that was precisely all there would be under the dress. Better to see you with, my dear, she told herself, then tried to remember if Little Red Riding Hood had had red hair as well.

Jennifer studied her body in the mirror. Not bad, she thought. At least there's no fat. The breasts could be larger. But then, as her mother had always pointed out, that wasn't one of the blessings bestowed on Irish Catholic girls.

The image of her father rushed to her mind, the way she always thought of him, just standing there, swaying drunkenly in the doorway of her room, screaming at her, calling her a slut, telling her she looked like some whore on the street, then staggering toward her and roughly wiping away the makeup she had applied to her face secretly.

A shiver went through her body, and she pressed her arms against her sides to stop it. "Damn." She spoke the word aloud. Twelve years and you still shake whenever you think about him. You're twenty-five years old and you still let the thought of him upset you.

She shivered again and was immediately angry with herself. Her father had left her and her mother when she was twelve, had deserted them for some woman he had met in a bar. And she had been glad. Glad then and glad now. She closed her eyes, squeezing them together. No. She hadn't been, then or now.

You'll never amount to anything! Never in your whole damned life! He had shouted it at her again and again, every time she had tried to do something. Bastard, she thought. I'm a lot more than the drunken barfly you turned out to be.

She turned away from the mirror and sat down at the vanity facing the small, round, makeup mirror, encircled with a ring of tiny light bulbs. Picking up a tube of lipstick, she saw that her hand was trembling. She put the lipstick back on the table, exchanging it for a brush, which she began to pull through her red hair.

It had been a bad day in the newsroom. That's what had brought it all on. Marty, the bastard—her city editor— had asked her out again, implying with all the subtlety of a horny goat that dating him would be in her best interests. She wondered how he would have explained the late night out to his wife and kids.

Jennifer tried the lipstick again, and it worked this time. Nothing like thinking of Martin Twist to make you feel cool as ice, she told herself. The eye shadow, liner, and mascara went on without difficulty, and she concentrated on the blush, trying to hide as many of the freckles as possible. You grew up in Boston, not on some farm in the Midwest. So why do you have to have freckles? She batted her dark blue eyes at the mirror. Just as cute as a button, she told herself. Except buttons aren't what's selling in the big city.

Jennifer stood and slipped the tight-fitting black dress over her head. Stepping in front of the full-length mirror, she studied the result, turning to inspect one side, then the other. Ravishing, she told herself. Freddie will be walking around all night with an erection, hoping he'll finally find his way to your bed. "Not tonight, either, Freddie, dear," she said to the mirror.

From the top drawer of her dresser she removed a string of cultured pearls and a delicate dress watch, the lone pieces of decent jewelry that she owned. Basic black and pearls, she told herself. Your sense of the original is overpowering tonight. She fastened the clasp of the pearls, then affixed the watch to her wrist, noting the time as she did. Seven o'clock. "Damn," she said. It was already time for Freddie to arrive.

Jennifer moved quickly out of the bedroom and began sorting through the mess she had not had time to clear from her living room that morning. A dirty wineglass and a soiled dinner plate, along with an overflowing ashtray, were rushed out to her tiny kitchen and dumped into the sink. She hurried back to the living room and straightened the pillows on the sofa, rearranged the position of an occasional chair, picked up the bedroom slippers she had left on the carpet, and tossed them through the bedroom door.

Stepping back, she studied the room, searching out any remaining flaw. Not bad, she thought. Not a Park Avenue co-op, but not bad at all for a kid from the wrong side of Boston.

The buzzer of the intercom sounded, and she moved to it, pressed the button, and listened to the doorman announce Freddie's arrival. A ransom in rent every month for the safety of a building with a doorman. Pure extortion and absolutely necessary. The only way to keep Godzilla from your door.

Jennifer hurried back to the bedroom and consulted her mirror again, then quickly moved back to the living room for one final inspection. Well-appointed and tasteful, she told herself. And reasonably clean if you don't look too closely.

The door bell rang, and Jennifer fixed a smile to her face as she walked toward it.

Tony Marco leaned back in his leather swivel chair and waited for three other men to work their way through a typed agenda. Absentmindedly he glanced at the nails of one hand, then took a cigarette from a box before him, lit it, and watched the smoke rise toward a heavy brass chandelier that had once graced the main salon of the *Queen Mary.*

While the others continued to sift through the agenda Marco turned his chair in a half circle and allowed his eyes to take in the room. It was large and imposing, something he had always appreciated, and the dark mahogany paneling gave it an aura of austere power. He turned the chair again, completing the circle. Along three of the paneled walls, spaced at precise intervals, lithographs of cargo ships hung in lifeless tribute. On the fourth was the portrait of an elderly man who seemed to stare across the room with unforgiving eyes.

Marco and the three men were seated around a conference table in identical high-backed leather chairs. In the center of the table a round, brass disk bore the emblem of Local 302, of the East Coast Brotherhood of Longshoremen.

Marco stubbed out the cigarette in a heavy brass ashtray, then rested his forearms on the table and waited. At thirty-five he was the youngest of the four men there. He was ruggedly handsome with finely chiseled features beneath wavy black hair that lacked even a trace of gray. His eyes were light brown and could appear harsh or gentle, depending upon his mood. Now they seemed slightly tired or perhaps even bored.

As always he was impeccably dressed—today in a custom-tailored gray pinstripe and a pale blue shirt with white collar and cuffs, set off by a silk necktie in light gray. He carried himself with an air of success that belied his years, and the men he represented often joked that their union president wore more on his back each day than they earned in a month. Marco knew they were usually right.

"I don't understand this item."

Marco turned to the sound of Paul Levine's rumbling baritone. The union's sixty-year-old organizational director sat hunched over the agenda, looking like an old bear appraising some morsel of food.

"What is it you don't understand, Paul?" Marco asked.

Levine raised his fleshy face to Marco. He had a thick neck, and his custom-tailored suit seemed to hang from his bulky body, rather than fit it. Yet he had the manner of an articulate businessman, something he had learned with difficulty in recent years.

Levine smiled. "What's this about a political contribution for the governor? I didn't know he was running for anything this year."

"He's not," Marco said. "It's for the democratic presidential primary. He'd like it to come from us, through him. He wants to curry a little favor."

Levine gave a short, snorting laugh. "I'll bet he does. How much favor?"

"He'd like five thousand dollars now, for the pre-convention campaign, and a pledge of ten thousand for the general election," Marco said.

"Do we get to know who he's supporting?" Levine asked.

Marco smiled without warmth. "The front-runner, Paul. The governor's a very cautious man."

Levine returned the cold smile. "Is he offering *us* anything?" he asked.

"So far, no quid pro quo has been mentioned," Marco said.

Levine studied Marco's face and noted a hint of amusement in his eyes. He looked down at the agenda. "Well, it can't hurt your own political plans," he said.

Marco leaned back in his chair, the look of amusement still on his face. "My political plans are greatly exaggerated, Paul."

"There's been a lot of talk, Tony. In certain quarters. And we haven't heard any denials."

Marco could feel the eyes of all three men. Very clever, Paul, he thought. I'll acknowledge my plans, and then you can organize a palace revolt. "The talk is good PR for the local, Paul. We've spent the last six years trying to improve the image of this union. And that type of talk shows how successful we've been."

Levine offered a smile of defeat, stared momentarily at the agenda again, then back at Marco. "That's a good point, Tony. As far as I'm concerned, the contribution is up to you. But I'd still like to see a little quid for the union, before we hand over the quo."

Marco nodded. "It's just what I've been thinking, Paul." He turned to the gaunt, rawboned man on his left. Like the others at the table, Vincent Albanese had spent his early years on the docks. Now he was the local's vice president, a job he had assumed six years earlier when Marco had become president. Marco studied his weathered face. There were still some rough edges to the man, although many had disappeared under Tony's tutelage.

"Have you made any progress with that British shipping company, Vince?"

Albanese ran a large hand across his balding head, then pulled on his nose with his thumb and index finger as though thinking with it. His square jaw tightened, and his lips moved slowly, almost imperceptibly as he spoke. "I'm getting the same answers," he said. "The representatives here say the new managing director in London will only continue our agreement if we promise not to support any future strikes in Britain."

Levine snorted again. "I'll bet they do. And I suppose they want us to kiss their blue-blooded backsides as part of the bargain."

Albanese shook his head. "I've tried everything I could think of. I've even talked about reprisals. But they seem to know that's not in our interests right now." Albanese raised his hands, then let them fall into his lap in a gesture of frustration.

"You did everything that could be done, Vince." Marco smiled at him, trying to ease the disappointment.

"Maybe we should let them see just how rough things could be. If the men started having a few accidents and started losing some cargo, they might get the message."

Joey Gambardella's high, grating voice cut into the quiet tone of the conversation, and Marco's eyes turned sharply toward him. He had warned Joey about such suggestions, but it was like talking to a wall.

"We don't do things that way anymore, Joey," Paul Levine said, cutting in. "Using force openly is counterproductive. There are better ways to get what we want."

Marco stared at Gambardella through steepled fingers, then lowered his eyes and shook his head. Six years of effort and they're still the same, he told himself. They go to better tailors and they've stopped using four-letter words in public, but their attitudes haven't changed. And now they're an even greater liability to you.

He looked up and allowed his eyes to roam the table. "I thought we might find a way of putting these two items together. The governor, and our problem with our British friends."

"Sounds interesting. How would you do it?" Levine asked.

Marco looked at Levine squarely. "Politicians don't like

to have labor disputes in their own backyards during national elections. Especially international disputes that might
prove embarrassing to their candidate. I think the governor might be persuaded to arrange some shipboard inspections that could prove inconvenient and expensive for
our British friends," Tony said. "If it can be arranged, and
if it happens often enough, this new managing director
might find our old agreement to his advantage. If not, I'm
sure his board of directors will."

"You think you can persuade the governor to do that?"
Levine asked. "I know you're good, Tony, but I didn't
realize you had that kind of political clout."

Marco allowed a smile to come to his eyes, acknowledging Levine's none-too-subtle assault. "I can try, Paul. In
any event, I expect to see him at a cocktail party tonight,
and I'm sure he'll at least hear me out."

Levine inclined his head. The boy wonder strikes again,
he thought. He forced another smile. "Who knows," he said.
"You just might be able to pull it off. So why not try?"

Marco turned to Albanese, who nodded, then to Gambardella, who simply shrugged. "Any problems with anything else?" Marco asked. Greeted with silence, he turned
to Gambardella. "Indicate in the minutes that the agenda
was unanimously approved *without discussion*." He emphasized the final words and noticed Gambardella's jaw
tighten under the rebuke.

Marco placed the agenda on the table and started to
rise, but Paul Levine stopped him with a beefy hand on
his shoulder.

"There are one or two things I'd like to talk to you
about," Levine said. "Unofficially." He glanced at the
other two men, then waited as they collected their papers
and started for the door.

Marco returned to his chair and leaned back. When the

others were gone, he turned to Levine to ask, "A problem, Paul?"

"A potential problem," Levine said. "Two potential problems, actually. And a little advice."

Marco sat forward and gestured for Levine to continue.

"First there's Maxwell, the shop steward in Red Hook."
Levine paused, awaiting Marco's reaction. When none
was forthcoming, he continued. "He's getting ready to run
against you when your term's up next year. I've been
around this local for more than forty years, and I've seen it
before." He stared at Marco. "You haven't noticed?"

"I've noticed," Marco said. He smiled at Levine. "It's
his right, Paul. We're a democratic organization."

Levine wagged his finger. "Take this seriously, Tony.
This could happen unless we're on top of it." There was an
edge to his voice, barely perceptible, but Marco had learned
to watch for it.

Marco leaned back and folded his arms across his chest.
"Maxwell has no organization, no power base, outside a
handful of ambitious clowns who see themselves sitting in
our chairs. The only thing he can do is run a negative
campaign, and there's nothing negative to run on."

Levine's eyes hardened. "He's running a *personal*, negative campaign against all of us. He's making broad hints
about corruption on the executive committee. He says we
all live too well. He tells them about the tailor you go to
for your fifteen-hundred-dollar suits while they're scraping
to get by."

Marco chuckled softly, then, noticing the color rising to
Levine's face, put up his hand in a mollifying gesture.
"I'm only laughing because *I* was the reform candidate six
years ago. But if you think it's trouble, I'll look into it."
He paused. "Besides, the suits only cost twelve hundred."
Without warning Marco's face became severe. "And I
don't think the men object to that. They know I came

from the same place they come from; they know my mother and sister still live in the old neighborhood, and that *I* still live here in Brooklyn." Marco leaned forward, bringing himself closer to Levine. "And they know this union has never been better run, and that *they* have never had it better." Marco's face changed again, as quickly as it had before. It appeared relaxed, confident once more.

Levine drummed his fingers on the table as he took in Marco's change of mood. The man's confidence was justified. He did have support from the membership.

Levine forced his voice to become warm, fatherly. "I'm not saying it's going to happen this time, Tony. We'll win the election, one way or another. But even if he makes a good showing, that's bad for us. He's going around to the men and making accusations, and we have to let him do that. But if he does it, and makes a good showing, too, then next time around somebody else will do the same thing, and sooner or later somebody will win." Levine shook his head. "Christ, in the old days nobody would have dared say the things this Maxwell is saying. And the men know that."

Marco looked past Levine to the portrait that hung behind him. Moe Green, his mentor and father-in-law. The man who had founded the local and who had run it like a private fiefdom until he had died six years ago. No, Marco told himself, no one would have dared speak out when Moe was in control. If they had, Moe would have had something heavy fall on them. And Paul Levine probably would have dropped it. Paul had always been Green's right hand, a member of the family and the union's heir apparent. Then he, Marco, had been brought into the union and, later, had married Green's daughter. Marco studied Levine's face for a moment and wondered, as he had before, just how deep the hatred went. Deep enough, he decided.

He leaned forward again, trying to simulate some degree of intimacy. "No, you're right, Paul. In the old days no one would have opened his mouth, at least not publicly. But even Moe knew that had to change. The publicity had been too intense, too adverse. That's why he put me in a position to succeed him when he retired. It just happened sooner than he planned." Marco waited for any animosity to show itself. Levine remained impassive. "You made the change, too, Paul," he added. "And you did it because you knew it had to be done." He kept his eyes on Levine's. He had been forced to keep him on the committee six years ago. But he had boxed him in; filled the balance of the committee with his own people. "It was either that or have the Waterfront Commission camping on our doorstep," he concluded. "Now that's not a worry anymore, and the public sees us in a different light."

"It could still happen if this type of talk continues," Levine said, and raised his hands, warding off an anticipated objection. "Not now. Not yet. But you have to stay on top of it," he continued. "Get down to the docks more often and let the men *know* how good they have it." He hesitated again. "And please, not while you're wearing a twelve-hundred-dollar suit."

Marco turned his chair slightly to one side, paused to light a cigarette, then glanced at Levine out of the corner of his eye. "I will, Paul. And I'll borrow some of your old clothes before I go."

Levine laughed softly, but the humor did not carry to his eyes. "If you do that, they'll vote you a raise."

"Only one more thing, Tony," Levine said. "Joey Gambardella. He's a hoodlum, Tony. And he's going around talking like one in public. That's not good."

"Talking about what, Paul?"

"Maxwell. This British problem. Tough talk. Much worse than what he started to say at the meeting today. If he keeps it up, somebody's going to pick up on it." He watched Marco's features harden. "Look," he continued, "I know you two grew up together and that you brought him into the local. Hoodlums have their places, but I think he's pushing too hard."

Only because he's my hoodlum, not yours, Marco thought. "I'll take care of it, Paul," he said.

"I think you should sit on him, Tony. Hard," Levine said.

He had to admit Levine was right. Tony knew he never would have brought Joey into the union if his own mother hadn't begged him to do so when Joey was released from prison.

"I said, I'll take care of it." Marco stared at Levine.

"That's good enough," Levine said. "I thought you should know." He drew his papers together and rose. "So you'll be seeing the governor tonight?"

"I should," Marco said.

"Good luck with him." Levine started for the door, then stopped and turned. "And enjoy yourself. You've been working too hard."

When the door closed behind Levine, Marco pushed back his chair and stood, hesitating a moment as he looked again at the portrait of Moe Green. It was a good likeness. The artist had captured the slender hawklike face, the cold blue eyes, and the thin lips that seldom had been known to smile.

He stared at the portrait's rigid features. What would you think, Moe? Marco wondered. What would you think if you knew I was planning to chuck your empire for something better? Chuck everything. Even your little girl. His lips parted in a cold, involuntary smile. "You'd cut my heart out. Or you'd have Paul do it for you."

Marco turned abruptly and walked to another door that led to his private office. All the trappings of power were there: the richly paneled walls, the leather furniture, the deep-pile carpet. Framed diplomas attesting to his B.A. and law degrees hung alongside political photographs and plaques citing his work for various civic organizations. All the expected bric-a-brac, he thought wryly. And you're still just another labor leader from Brooklyn.

Marco reached out and picked up his private telephone to dial his home. The phone rang several times before it was answered by a voice he did not recognize.

"Is Mrs. Marco in?" he asked.

"No, she's not," the voice responded.

"This is Mr. Marco. Who are you?"

"Oh, hi, Mr. Marco. It's Suzan. Mrs. Marco asked me to baby-sit for Josh."

"Did she say when she'd be back, Suzan?"

"She just said it would be late."

Marco swiveled in his chair and stared out the window, drawing a deep breath. And who are you sneaking out to meet tonight, Shirley? he wondered. "Would you please give her a message, Suzan? Just tell her I'm going to be very late myself."

"Sure, Mr. Marco."

"And Suzan, how's Josh?"

"He's fine. I was giving him a bath. That's why it took so long to answer the phone."

"Okay, thanks very much. And don't forget the message."

Marco placed the receiver back in its cradle and stared at it for a moment, his face offering no hint of emotion. He ran his hand along his cheek, feeling the stubble of beard that had grown since morning. He glanced at his watch, decided that the barbershop down the block would still be open, and headed for the door.

Outside, the spring air felt light and cleansing as Marco bounded down the steps of the large Brooklyn Heights brownstone in which the union's offices were housed. He drew a deep breath, glad to be out of the building, then moved to the curb and leaned into the open window of a black Chrysler New Yorker to speak to his driver, who was slouched behind the wheel.

"Pat, I'm going to walk down to the barbershop for a shave, then head over to Foffe's for an early dinner. I want to be at Mrs. Mobray's house by seven-thirty, so pick me up in time."

The driver nodded, and Marco turned and headed down the block. Most business offices had just closed for the day, and the sidewalks were crowded with people eager to be elsewhere. Marco moved through the crowd, his six-foot two-inch frame weaving between passersby with an easy grace as he enjoyed the same sense of release from the day.

From a second-floor window Paul Levine watched Marco walk down the street, his eyes following each step. When Marco moved out of view, Levine's jaw tightened, his eyes narrowing. He turned slowly and walked to his desk. He picked up his telephone, punched the intercom button, and dialed a single number.

"Joey," he said, "I'm glad I caught you. Look, why don't we have dinner tonight. We could go into Manhattan to that place you're always telling me about in Little Italy." He waited, his smile broadening. "Good," he said. "I'll meet you in the reception area in ten minutes."

Levine reached into the breast pocket of his suitcoat and withdrew a cigar. He held the cigar in front of him, staring at it, then drew it under his nose before biting off the tip. His face hardened again, and he spat the remnant of tobacco across his desk, as though discharging something foul from his mind as well as his mouth.

CHAPTER/TWO

JENNIFER BRADY STOOD to the left of a large marble fireplace and surveyed the guests who filled Anne Mobray's East Sixty-third Street town house. The two middle floors of the impressive four-story structure had been gutted and modernized to accommodate large parties. The second floor was now one oversize room with a spiral staircase leading to a balcony area that took up half of the third floor. The fourth floor undoubtedly held bedrooms, and there was a converted attic above for servants' quarters. On the first, or garden floor, she knew, was a dining room and kitchen.

At the rear of the room in which she stood, a wall of glass doors led to a balcony overlooking an English rose garden, and just inside those doors Jennifer could see the governor speaking to a well-known investment banker, who several years earlier had helped save New York City from financial collapse.

The room was a virtual gold mine for her, except for the fact that any attempt to use it would find her instantly ostracized. She smiled at the idea. Very few there would be pleased to learn that a reporter for the *New York Globe* was in their midst. They might even decide that the man who had brought her there, Frederick Norton III—Freddie to his friends—was no longer worthy of their trust and friendship. The idea irritated her, and she glanced at Freddie, who was standing a few feet away, seriously explaining the economic philosophy of his father's brokerage firm, for which he worked.

Freddie had warned her not to divulge her occupation, and she realized he had taken some risk in bringing her, even if it was largely a ploy to lure her into bed. Poor Freddie. Tall and slender and blond with an aristocratic face and lips that barely moved when he spoke. Yale, 1974. Completely typical and delighted at being so. And to these people, so much more acceptable than she. But he needn't worry. She had no intention of committing social suicide. She had looked forward to attending a party like this for too long.

A maid passed with a tray of champagne, and Jennifer took a glass and sipped it slowly. Across the room she could see Anne Mobray moving among her guests. Stopping and chatting, flattering each person in turn; showing off her femininity with an affected toss of her shiny blond hair. She was a beautiful woman. Newspaper reports gave her age as thirty, but she appeared younger. She was approximately five foot six, Jennifer guessed, an inch shorter than she was. Anne's willowy body gave her movements a touch of elegance that seemed to match her blue eyes and perfect teeth. Someone definitely to the manor born, and now, it was rumored, estranged from her husband, one of the country's most prominent steel executives. Some people have terrible crosses to bear, Jennifer told herself.

Freddie arrived at her elbow. "Enjoying yourself?" he asked.

She looked up at him and smiled, aware that her smile was her most attractive feature. "Very much," she said. "I've just been watching our hostess, and I've decided I hate her."

"My God, why?" Freddie whispered.

Jennifer leaned toward him and affected a stage whisper. "It's simple. She's five years older than I am and she looks two years younger." Freddie laughed, and Jennifer glanced up at him, amazed to find that he could even laugh with pursed lips.

As Jennifer looked back into the room she saw Anne Mobray move quickly toward the door to greet a late-arriving guest. He was tall, strikingly handsome, with athletic shoulders and an engaging smile. He seemed about Freddie's age, or a few years older, but any similarity ended there. The man carried himself with an easy sense of confidence, and from the body language that exuded from Anne Mobray, Jennifer knew he was much more than a favored guest.

She turned to Freddie. "Who's the new arrival? The one our hostess is fussing over?"

Freddie looked across the room and arched his eyebrows. "Ah, that's the revered Anthony Marco, noted young labor leader and current favorite of the liberal set."

The name clicked with Jennifer. She had read about Marco and even seen pictures of him, although none of them, she decided, did him justice. "The waterfront union," she said, almost as an afterthought.

"The same."

She turned back to Freddie. "It sounds as though you don't approve."

Freddie stared past her. "It's really not a question of approval or disapproval," he said. "It's just part of a continuing cycle. In the sixties, during the civil rights movement, the Black Panthers were in vogue. Then it was Jane

Fonda and her anti-Vietnam crowd. Now we're into liberal young labor leaders."

Jennifer forced another smile, wondering how Freddie would describe her to someone else. She looked back across the room, again taking in Marco's striking good looks. Beats hell out of Jane Fonda, she told herself.

Anne Mobray slipped her arm into Marco's and guided him toward a group of guests. She leaned close to Tony and whispered, "I was beginning to think you weren't coming." She turned her head to smile at passing guests. "It wasn't easy getting all these political power brokers in one room," she added. "And they *are* here to meet you, darling."

There was no criticism in her voice, but Marco squeezed her arm against his side to show his appreciation. "A few last-minute problems," he said. "But you needn't have worried." He looked at her and smiled. "I'm free for the night. All night."

"Delicious," Anne said as she pulled to a halt in front of a small group of men and began introducing him.

Marco greeted each of the men, indexing their faces and names in his mind. As the conversation returned to politics he allowed his eyes to roam the room, looking for his secondary objective of the evening, the governor. His eyes stopped on a woman across the floor who was staring at him. She was tall, slender, and had exceptional legs. A redhead with striking blue eyes that seemed even more brilliant against her milk-white skin, and a hint of freckles along her nose. He smiled at her and she smiled in return, then looked away. The girl next door, come to the big city, he told himself. Not the type of woman he was usually attracted to. But this one had an intenseness that fascinated him. She stood out from the socialites around her and he was curious. Not something you can afford to let show, he told himself. Not this evening. Not here.

Marco's attention was drawn away by an arm slipped around his shoulder, and he turned to find James Giuliani's familiar smile confronting him.

"Tony, good to see you here tonight," Giuliani said.

"Good to see you, Governor."

Giuliani raised his eyebrows. "Formalities between friends?" he said. The governor turned to the other men in the group, greeting them each by name, his arm still around Tony's shoulder. "You know, I met this bright, young rascal when he was a student at N.Y.U. Law School. I was an assistant district attorney in Queens at the time, and he came out on an internship program." He turned to Tony and smiled, then looked back at the others. "It scared the hell out of me when I found out he was already a better lawyer than I was."

The other men laughed politely. One, Walter Johannes, a state senator, urged the governor not to tell that story should Giuliani be chosen as the candidate at the upcoming national convention.

Giuliani grimaced in mock displeasure.

"There has been talk," Johannes countered.

A small smile formed on Giuliani's lips. "Walter," he began in a deep baritone, "Mrs. Giuliani had only one son, and it's said he was always a very bright lad. Too much so, I think, to take on the present occupant of the White House." He paused to enjoy the laughter of the others, then cocked an eyebrow at Johannes. "Besides, Walter, I promised the voters I'd serve a full term as governor." He winked. "However, I may not make that promise next time around."

Johannes raised his hands, indicating defeat, then joined the laughter of the others. As the governor let his arm drop from Tony's shoulders, he grasped his elbow and squeezed it lightly.

The governor excused himself, explaining that he needed

some air, then squeezed Tony's arm again and moved across the room and out onto the deserted balcony. Tony followed a few minutes later. Alone in one corner of the balcony, Giuliani lit a cigarette, exhaled with genuine pleasure, then cupped the cigarette in his hand, hiding it from view.

Tony smiled at him. "Still trying to keep the voters from knowing you smoke on the sly?" he teased.

"You'd be surprised how many antismoking fanatics there are who wouldn't vote for someone who did." Guiliani laughed, then shrugged and said seriously, "It gets crazier every year. Everybody's becoming a zealot about something. Christ, unless you say you want to abolish abortion, you have to say good-bye to that whole group of voters, no matter *what* the Supreme Court has ruled. You know, last month the pastor of my own parish denounced me from the pulpit, just because I said I would enforce the law on abortion."

Tony paused to light his own cigarette, keeping his eyes on the governor's face and wondering why anyone put up with the insanity of elected office. "I hope you kept your hands in your lap when the collection basket came around."

Giuliani snorted. "What I'd like to have done is tell that aging celibate just what I think of his expertise on the subject. But that would have cost a few thousand more votes." He shook his head and drew heavily on his cigarette. "If you get that appointment we discussed, you'll find out very quickly that success in politics depends more on what you keep from saying than on anything you *do* say."

Tony leaned against the stone balcony rail, his back to the garden. "From what you said inside it seems it'll be another four years before I have to learn that lesson."

Giuliani dropped his cigarette and ground it out underfoot. "You can never tell. That's part of the mystery of the

game. Anything could happen in the next few months."
He moved next to Tony and looked down into the garden,
breathing in the scent of the roses clustered beneath him.
"Hell, I never thought Carter would be denied a second
term. Then that bearded bastard in Iran pulled the rug
out from under him." He turned to face Tony. "Still, if
that rescue mission hadn't been botched, he'd probably
have won another term." He shook his head slowly, almost sadly. "All you can do is position yourself and be
ready when the time comes." He glanced toward Tony
and smiled. "And then pray that nothing disastrous
happens."

Tony extinguished his own cigarette, then turned to
face Giuliani. "Were you serious about taking the plunge
yourself, four years from now?"

"If the fates allow," Giuliani said. "And if I make it, you
won't have to worry about who'll be the next secretary of
labor." A smile spread across his broad face. "Two Italians
from New York City. Christ, I can hear the jokes now.
The boys on the bus will have a field day."

Tony studied the amusement in Giuliani's face. He was
slightly shorter than Tony, with a broad, athletic body that
had only begun to go to seed, and a homely, comforting
face that made him seem like someone's favorite uncle. A
good face for a politician, Tony thought.

"I appreciate that, Jim. I'll settle for under secretary
this time around." He paused. "If we get lucky."

"You're in a perfect position for it," Giuliani said. He
waved a hand toward the crowded room. "Our friend,
Anne, certainly knows how to bring the right people
together. You're lucky to have her in your corner."

Tony nodded. Speculation about his relationship with
Anne had been rampant over the past two years, but it
was something no one had been bold enough to raise

directly. "I know I am," Tony said. "She's been a good friend."

Tony studied Guiliani's eyes to see if he, too, was speculating, then decided to move ahead with business. "While we're on the topic of position," he continued, "I want to talk to you about that contribution you mentioned last week." Tony paused and allowed himself a small smile. "It's all arranged. The executive committee approved it this afternoon."

The governor brought his palms together in a light slap and began rubbing them together. "That's what I love about you, my friend. You're always one step ahead of the game." Giuliani hesitated, then raised a cautioning finger. "Now, if you can begin to start distancing yourself from the union, *you'll* be in a perfect position."

Tony nodded and turned to face the garden. Giuliani, and others, had made that suggestion before, warning that the union's past—no matter what changes had been made—could still prove a liability. "I'm moving in that direction, Jim. But it will take at least a year." He turned back to face the governor, noting the hint of disappointment on his face. "I've got to be sure the right person takes my place. Otherwise, the changes I've made could disappear overnight." He looked at the governor levelly. "And I've worked too hard to let that happen." And personally paid too high a price, he added to himself. Tony watched the governor nod in agreement. What Tony had not said was that any return by the union to past practices could produce a stigma that even those who had stepped away would not escape.

"Well, none of us wants to see a return to the old days," Giuliani said. He looked at Tony more intently. "I suspect this means you'll have to move some people out."

Tony nodded. "That's another reason it will take a year. There's a union election then."

Giuliani gave a slight shrug as he said, "I wish I could help."

"I wish you could too. I could use some muscle." The governor laughed at the idea, and Tony continued. "There is something you could help with, though."

Giuliani raised his eyebrows in surprise. It was unlike Marco to ask for favors. Normally he preferred to grant them and build up his line of credit.

"We're having a nasty problem with a British shipping company we have an agreement with. It could result in a wildcat strike if we can't pressure them into being more reasonable."

"What can I do?"

"A little governmental pressure, by way of some safety inspections in port."

Giuliani's eyebrows rose. "Would we find legitimate violations?"

"Jim, there's hardly a ship in the world that could pass a thorough inspection. All the inspectors would have to do is stick to the rule book on things they normally overlook for practical reasons."

"And you think that will be enough?" Giuliani asked.

Tony smiled without warmth. "I'll make sure it is."

Jennifer Brady watched Marco and the governor move back into the room. She had noticed them together on the balcony and found herself tempted to go out there herself, to see what snatches of conversation she might overhear. Her city editor, Martin Twist, would have mocked her for not doing it, but then, he mocked most things she did. She pushed the thought away. No sense ruining the evening thinking of that pompous . . . A bit of hushed conversation that had included Marco's name drew her attention. The two men she was passing were older and overly reserved, and they, too, were watching Marco and the governor intently.

A maid passed with a tray of champagne, and Jennifer took a glass, using it as an excuse to stop and linger, staying close enough to another group to make it appear she was part of their conversation. She watched the two men out of the corner of her eye and saw one lean his head closer to the other.

"Unless I miss my guess, our young labor genius has just moved one step closer to a future cabinet post."

The second man looked at the first for several seconds before replying. "First we have to win," he said. "And then our young friend has to keep his goons scandal-free through a Senate confirmation hearing."

"He seems to have done rather well so far," the first man said. "Although, I have to admit, it's not the kind of monkey I'd care to carry on my back."

The other man appeared about to answer, then turned his head slightly and noticed Jennifer within hearing distance. Without any noticeable change of expression he took the other man by the elbow and began moving slowly across the room.

Damn it, Jennifer thought. She wondered what more she might have heard if the men had remained within earshot. She followed their stares and again found Marco standing near the doorway that led to the foyer. He was with Anne Mobray and two men, one of whom she recognized as an influential Democratic congressman who represented an ethnic stronghold in the Bronx. She moved quickly to Freddie and, after apologizing to the couple with whom he was speaking, drew him aside.

"The man talking to Anthony Marco . . . not the congressman, the other one. Do you know who he is?"

Freddie looked at her with mild amusement. "You seem inordinately interested in Mr. Marco this evening."

Jennifer offered one of her best smiles. "It's an occupational disease."

Freddie nodded knowingly before turning his attention to Marco. He looked back at Jennifer and arched his eyebrows. "Rarefied circles," he said. "At least among politicians."

"Who exactly?" Jennifer asked, a little more sharply than intended.

"His name's Saltzbury or something like that. Very high up in Democratic politics. He's supposed to be here in New York gathering support for the presidential contender of his choice, whoever that might be." Freddie winked like a man who knew more than he should. " 'Tis the season, you know."

"What do you mean?" Jennifer asked.

"The time when things are bought and sold," he said through a smirk. "Cabinet posts, ambassadorships, whatever. Those who join the right side with the most, and at the right time." He hesitated, as though enjoying the humor of the situation. "Well, those people simply have the best chance to get what they're interested in getting. You might say Mr. Saltzbury is here on a selling trip of sorts."

"And what would he be selling Marco?"

"Heaven knows," Freddie said. "More political clout for his union, I would say, although I don't see how they could need any more than they already have."

"Could they be selling him a spot in the new administration?" she asked.

Freddie winced at the idea. "I would hope not."

"Why do you say that?" Jennifer asked.

Freddie pursed his lips. "Mr. Marco may be considered the bright young liberal, but the union he represents has quite a disreputable past."

"But he's the person who cleaned it up," Jennifer said.

Freddie offered her a rueful smile. "Yes, indeed," he said. "But he was also a minor official under the old regime. And the man who ran things in those less halcyon days just happens to have been Mr. Marco's late father-in-law."

Freddie waited for some appreciation of his inside information, but Jennifer only nodded vaguely and turned her attention back to Marco. The congressman and Saltzbury were just leaving, and Jennifer took note of a special warmth there seemed to be in their farewells. They treat him as though he were something special, she thought, and immediately found herself wondering how they really viewed him.

Well, I damn well want to find out, Jennifer thought. She could feel the journalistic juices bubbling. She recalled snatches of information she had learned about Marco while reading clippings for other stories. Anthony Marco's name constantly appeared in social columns and was invariably connected with fund-raising efforts and charitable causes. The bright young star of the liberal labor movement; the reformer of the corrupt waterfront union. But was he really? And if he was, could he live down the past he had fought to change? Live it down all the way to a cabinet post? Jennifer chewed her lip. This was the kind of story that could send a career soaring.

She looked across the room at Marco again. So smooth, so self-assured, a vision of what the successful male of the species was supposed to be. And now with the possibility of a huge leap into the political arena. She stared at him intently, and the more she did, the more she found herself intrigued by the vision. She knew something of his background. A poor family from Brooklyn and an uphill struggle to become something more. It was not unlike her own background, although that was something she kept closely guarded. Here he was, moving in circles he could only have imagined as a child. Jennifer knew she had to get closer to him, talk to him. Perhaps find a way to arrange an interview that would give her an excuse for an even bigger story.

She turned back to Freddie. "This is a wonderful party," she said, stepping closer to him. Her mind was moving rapidly now, and she wanted Freddie as distracted as possible. She intended to meet Marco and talk to him. She would let him know who she was, promises to Freddie be damned, and take advantage of her presence at the party to eventually get an interview with him.

Freddie was prattling on about something, and she responded with an occasional nod or murmur, hearing nothing. A chance like this might not come again, and she had no intention of missing it. Freddie paused for a moment, and she reached out and touched his arm.

"Freddie, dear, you're going to have to excuse me a moment while I go powder one thing and another."

Freddie offered a small bow with his head. "Powder away," he said, glancing around quickly. "There are some people I should speak to," he added. "Would you mind finding me when you're finished?"

She nodded. "Don't worry, I'll find you."

Tony Marco ended a conversation with one of Anne's uniquely boring guests and turned to find himself facing the red-haired woman he had noticed earlier in the evening. She was even more attractive at close range, and the freckles on her nose gave her a natural touch he had not found in any of the other women he had met that evening.

"Hello," he said, as his eyes warmed to her automatically.

Jennifer hesitated. The man had an aura about him that she found disconcerting, yet appealing, at the same time. She fought it off.

"Mr. Marco, my name is Jennifer Brady, and I've been looking forward to meeting you."

Marco's face broke into a smile that seemed almost

boyish. "My God," he said. "Do we have to be so formal? I'm Tony."

He had put her off-balance, and she felt a touch of color rise to her cheeks from the ease with which he had done it. "No, of course not," she said. "I've just heard so much about you, I decided I didn't want to miss the chance to meet you."

Marco feigned mild surprise. "You certainly don't look like someone who follows labor unions." The humor moved to his eyes. "What would they call that? A labor groupie?"

Jennifer laughed, and some of the tension drained away. "No, I'm afraid that's not it."

"I didn't think so," Marco said. "At least I hope we haven't reached that stage. It might be hard to explain to our members."

He was flirting with her now, and Jennifer felt the advantage slip slightly in her favor. "No, it's simpler than that. I'm a reporter for the *New York Globe*—a feature writer, actually—and I've come across your name so often in clippings, I thought I'd see if you'd let me impose a bit"—she paused for two beats, then continued—"and let me talk you into an interview for a feature story sometime soon."

Marco studied Jennifer's delicate features, and the attraction he had felt earlier returned, but he forced himself to remember it was not the right time or place. Still, the idea of an interview intrigued him. He smiled to himself. Not just the interview. What it might lead to.

"I'm afraid there's really nothing worth a story right now. The only time I'm newsworthy is when I'm about to start negotiating a contract or find myself in the middle of some dispute. Right now everything is going so well, I'm afraid I'd bore your readers."

Jennifer issued a hollow laugh; she hoped it sounded differently to Marco. "That's not at all what I had in mind,

Mr. Marco. Excuse me . . . Tony. I wouldn't even begin to know how to cover a labor negotiation." She watched Marco's eyes harden slightly and realized she was going too far with her feigned innocence. "Oh, I'm sure I could do it. But my assignment right now is more human interest." She added a hint of humor to her voice. "And frankly, Tony, from what I've read, you're a very interesting human."

Marco laughed again. "The gentlemen in the shipping industry would disagree with you. They think of me as a very uninteresting subhuman. You should talk to them before you make up your mind."

Jennifer felt herself thrown off stride by the suggestion. He seemed to be directing her toward a story solely about the union, and that was not what she wanted. She wondered if she should raise the question of his political future and immediately decided against it. No, don't scare him off, she told herself.

A maid came up to them, and Marco took drinks for himself and Jennifer. When he turned back to her, his features remained relaxed and friendly. "What exactly did you have in mind, Jennifer?"

She paused, sipping her drink, to buy a few moments. She decided a businesslike approach was best. "You have a reputation as a reformer, the man who cleaned up your union and gave it a sense of civic consciousness. I'd like to start from there and then go into some of the problems you faced doing it, and what problems, if any, you still face."

Marco looked away for a moment. His contacts at the *Globe* would allow him to check on this woman, to find out what she really planned to write, and possibly to scotch it if it proved necessary. He also knew a favorable story in the *Globe* might work well for him now. On several fronts. Besides, an interview would allow him to see her again.

"Well, reformer, yes. But even that's been a bit over-played. Or perhaps *exaggerated* is a better word." He looked at her levelly, as though about to confess some secret. "The people I succeeded weren't corrupt. They were rough, and they didn't always use the best judg-ment, especially where public relations were concerned. But you have to remember where they came from. And what labor-management battles were like in those days." Marco shifted his weight and changed the pace of the conversation with the movement. "Don't misunderstand. I'm not saying they were angels. My predecessors fought fire with fire. It was something that worked for them, and the union, and some of them just couldn't adapt to doing it differently. All I did was reorganize and put the union on a more businesslike basis. It was never a case of facing threats of violence, or fighting off gangsters." He offered another boyish grin. "I wish it was more romantic, but it wasn't."

Jennifer fought the temptation to push further. That, she decided, would come later, after she had done her homework. She allowed herself to look eager again and said, "It sounds even more interesting than I thought."

"It could be," Marco said. "Providing it's not romanti-cized. . . ." He paused and allowed his eyes to harden slightly. "Or villified," he added. "The thing for you to do, if you're really interested, is read the old articles with the idea that things weren't quite as sensational as they were made out to be. And also, keeping in mind that the docks, by their nature, are a pretty rough place. Our job is to make them less rough, less dangerous from a safety standpoint, and to see that the men who work them are taken care of in the best possible way."

"You make it sound so . . . altruistic," she said.

Marco laughed softly again. Far from it, he said. "As far as the members are concerned, we're completely pragmatic. And we'd better be, or we'll find *ourselves* out of work." He glanced around the room and found Anne staring at him. Precisely what he wanted to avoid. He turned back to Jennifer. "I'm afraid there are quite a few people I have to see here tonight. But why don't you give me a call. Perhaps we can have a drink together and talk about it further. And I can tell you how wonderful we really are."

Jennifer laughed, but beneath it she felt tense, almost excited at the suggestion. "I'll look forward to it," she said. "And I'll take your advice and read the clips."

Before Marco could say anything more, Anne Mobray swept in, confronting Jennifer with a cool smile. "You must forgive me, but I have to steal Tony away." She paused, then said, "We met when you arrived. You came with Freddie Norton, didn't you?"

"Yes, I did." And that definitely establishes me as part of the "B" list, Jennifer thought. Not an invited guest, merely the guest of an invited guest. Wouldn't want Mr. Marco to be confused, would we?

Anne Mobray had already turned her attention to Marco, effectively dismissing Jennifer from further consideration. "Tony, there are some people who say they have to meet you before they leave."

"Of course," Marco said. He nodded to Jennifer. "It was nice meeting you. I hope we'll talk again."

"I'm sure we will," Jennifer said, offering her best smile, more for Anne Mobray's benefit than Marco's.

Jennifer watched them move toward a group of middle-aged men at the opposite end of the room. Anne Mobray had Marco firmly in tow, and it gave Jennifer a sense of satisfaction that the elegant Ms. Mobray had found it necessary to snatch him away from her.

Jennifer moved slowly across the room toward Freddie, still keeping an eye on the possessive body language her hostess displayed with Marco. If she's not already sleeping with him, she certainly intends to. Jennifer looked at Marco again. He was trim and had a very physical look about him, and she found herself wondering what he'd be like in bed. He'd probably screw your pants off, she told herself. She looked toward Freddie. The comparison was ludicrous. Too bad, she thought. Yet, not a bad evening. A chance for a story any reporter would kill for, and . . . She let the thought die and forced herself to concentrate on just what she might learn about the intriguing Mr. Anthony Marco.

CHAPTER/THREE

ANNE MOBRAY SAT at one end of a long white sofa, her legs tucked beneath her, a snifter of brandy cradled in one hand. She still wore the Halston original she had worn during the party, a delicate blue silk with a full-length skirt that managed to cling with each movement. Beneath the dress she wore nothing, knowing that the combination of the silk and the nakedness made her very good body all the more appealing.

She looked at her watch. Twenty minutes had passed since the last guest had left. She expected Tony to have returned by now. Probably waiting for the servants to retire, she decided. She glanced around the room. It was still in disarray from the party, because she had sent the servants off with instructions to leave the cleaning until morning. You're being too eager and you're allowing it to show, she told herself.

She realized she was still annoyed about the unusually long time Tony had spent with Freddie Norton's little friend. Her lips tightened. Dressed in basic black, obviously off some rack somewhere, and an unimpressive strand of cultured pearls. And so *damned* attractive.

The sound of a key in the front door pushed the thought away, but Anne remained where she was, determined to mask the need she felt. Marco stopped at the foyer arch and stared across the room at her. He looked enormously appealing, Anne thought.

"Recovering from the party?" Marco asked.

The question struck an unpleasant cord. "Why? Do I look especially tired?"

Marco caught the slight edge in her voice and was certain he knew the reason behind it. "Not at all tired. Just exceptionally comfortable." He walked toward the bar, inclining his head toward it and accepting Anne's nod that he should pour himself a drink. "It always surprises me . . ." he said as he placed ice in a glass. He allowed the sentence to fall away.

"What surprises you?" Anne asked.

He poured a small amount of malt Scotch, then looked up at her. "You," he said. "Or rather, the fact that you can go through an evening like tonight and still look as though it hasn't even begun."

Anne's eyes warmed, and her lips formed a slight smile. "Practice," she said as she raised the snifter. "Could you bring the brandy when you come?"

Marco removed his suitcoat and loosened his tie, then moved slowly across the room, the bottle of brandy dangling from one hand, his own drink in the other. Anne thought it a very erotic image.

He refilled her drink, placed the bottle on the table next to her, then sat beside her and kissed her lightly on the cheek. She felt an urge to turn to him, but she resisted it. Her annoyance at him still gnawed at her, and she knew she would have to resolve it first.

"It was an interesting party, wasn't it?" she asked.

Marco nodded and sipped his drink. He was familiar with Anne's roundabout method of reaching unpleasant subjects, and he decided to let her accomplish it in her own way.

"I thought Victor Saltzbury was very impressed with you," she continued. "He commented on the obvious interest you received from the governor. He seemed quite pleased by it."

"I wish the governor were more impressed with Saltzbury's chances of getting his man elected," Tony said.

Anne's lips tightened again. "Well, that has nothing to do with the fact that he was impressed with you, Tony."

The edge was back in her voice, and Marco wished she would simply get to the subject of the *other woman* and get it over with. "I'm just trying to put it in perspective," he said. "I liked Saltzbury, by the way. He seemed very straightforward."

"He could do you an inestimable amount of good. A word from him could be one more step toward a post in the next administration."

"When the Democrats next win," Marco said.

Anne propelled her breath in a display of annoyance. Had she been standing, Marco thought, she probably would have stamped her foot.

"If not this time, they'll win next time," she said. "And if you let me help you cultivate the right people, you could very well end up as under secretary of labor. And from there . . ." She let the sentence fall away, then continued. "Everyone knows cabinet members move on before an adminstration ends. They simply can't afford to give up the earning power for that long."

Marco laid his head against the back of the sofa. He had heard Anne's own scenario for his future ever since their affair had begun four years ago. And he had seen her manipulate her government and political contacts to help him gain every advantage possible. But tonight he was too tired to review it all again. He reached up and stroked her cheek. "Let's talk about it another time," he said.

"Sometimes I wonder, Tony, if you really want these things to happen," she snapped.

"You know I want it," he said, fighting to keep the irritation out of his own voice. "And you know I'm working in that direction. I'm just tired. It was a difficult day."

Anne sipped her brandy. "You seemed quite capable of conversation earlier. Especially with that woman you spent so much time with." She instantly regretted the remark. It was not how she had intended to broach the subject. But it was done, and now she turned and looked at him coldly.

Marco smiled and stroked her cheek again. "You know I'm always polite to the press."

Anne stiffened. "The what?"

"She was a reporter for the *Globe*. Or feature writer, actually. Her name is Jennifer Brady, and she was looking for an interview."

"Damn Freddie," Anne snapped. "He knows I never allow those people at my parties. I'll burn his ears for this." She looked at Tony sharply. "Besides, it's too early to allow anything to be published about your political ambitions."

Marco expressed agreement, then reached back and massaged the back of her neck. And another crisis is over, he told himself. He cradled his glass in his fingers and swirled it in a circular motion, listening to the ice rattle against the sides. Anne had everything he wanted; everything he had always wanted. But her juvenile jealousies were maddening. They were something he had to endure, however, if he wanted the things that went with her. "Actually, it could work to my advantage. The right kind of article, I mean."

"If you can be sure it's favorable and doesn't reveal too much," she said.

Marco took a cigarette from his shirt pocket without withdrawing the pack, lit it, and blew out a long stream of smoke. "I can make sure it's favorable," he said. "And if not, I'm reasonably sure I can see it isn't published."

Anne tilted her head and regarded him. "Your secret little ways of manipulating things always surprises me."

"There's nothing surprising about it," he said. "You just do large favors for people in the right places. Then, when you need them, you call in small favors in return."

"You never ask for large favors?" Anne asked.

Marco shook his head. "I try to avoid it. They create debts, and debts are always dangerous."

"And what about me?" Anne asked. "Don't you consider my favors large?"

Marco leaned forward to kiss her. "With you I like to live dangerously. It makes it more interesting."

Anne gave him a coy look. "It's also dangerous to flirt with little newspaper reporters."

Marco allowed a touch of mischief to enter his eyes. "It's just that the timing was right."

"What timing?" Anne asked suspiciously.

"For a barrage of good publicity," Marco said.

"Barrage?" Anne's eyebrows rose.

"Next month *Manhattan* magazine is doing an article on the twenty brightest young men in New York. I was told yesterday that I'll be one of them."

Anne seemed to swell with pleasure, then she caught herself. "Twenty is too many. They should cut the list to ten."

Marco leaned his head back and laughed. "There are a few other bright people in New York."

"But they don't have your other talents," she said.

Anne reached out and took the glass from his hands and

placed it on the table. Then she turned and moved against him, pressing her mouth to his.

Marco ran his hands along the soft silk dress, feeling, as he knew he would, the absence of clothing beneath. Even after four years Anne's blatant sexuality, the aggressiveness of it, still amazed him; aroused him more than any other woman he had known. He moved his hands over her breasts, gently stroking the nipples, feeling her breath catch, her back arch with pleasure.

She reached down and began running her hand along his inner thigh, stroking slowly upward until she could feel him growing beneath her hand, the sensation heightening her own excitement. She drew down the zipper of his trousers and quickly took him in her hand, feeling him throb under her touch. Anne leaned back, still stroking him, and stared at him, her face flushed with pleasure. Then she attacked his mouth again with her own, moving her tongue wildly, her breath coming in gasps.

"Take me now, Tony. Here," she breathed, her mouth still against his. "I've wanted you all night. Do it now."

He raised her dress and placed his hands beneath her buttocks and moved her gently beneath him, entering her almost at once, hearing her groan with pleasure, once, twice, then the shuddering of her breath as she reached what he knew would be the first of several orgasms. He thrust himself into her slowly, rhythmically, drawing the minutes out, gradually intensifying the pleasure and the speed until she finally cried out again and began to claw at his back. Almost as soon as she reached her second climax she began thrusting against him again, searching for still more pleasure. He arched his back, lowered his head against her shoulder, and began to pound himself into her in a near fury, until their bodies hung on the edge of control. Within seconds he felt her begin again and, no longer able to contain himself, threw his head back and felt himself explode inside her with a force that seemed to drain him completely.

He collapsed against her, his uncontrolled breathing matching her own, unable to move, unable to feel anything but his own exhausted sense of pleasure, every muscle in his body limp with the satisfaction of release. Slowly, weakly, he stroked her still fully clothed body, his head turned so he could run his lips softly along her neck.

When his breath had begun to return, he raised his head and brushed his lips against her ear. "I'm going to be afraid to marry you," he said, his voice still weak and shallow.

"Why?" Anne asked, her own voice little more than a hoarse whisper.

"Because, if we live together, you're sure to kill me in the first six months."

She let out a panting laugh. "Unless you kill me first," she said.

"I wouldn't even know how to begin," he said.

"I'll teach you," she said. "And we'll practice every night." She drew her arms around him and pulled him closer. And I'll have you, she told herself. No matter what it requires, I'll have you.

It was four in the morning when Marco left Anne's town house. He had sent his driver home when he had arrived at the party, and now he walked wearily toward Fifth Avenue, hoping to find a taxi for the twenty-minute drive to his Brooklyn Heights apartment. He had showered at Anne's, but the blissfully hot water had only brought him closer to sleep. He stopped to light a cigarette, hoping it would revive him, then continued on, silently praying it would not be a long wait for one of the scarce cabs that worked the early-morning hours.

But it would be over soon, he told himself. A few

months, six at the most. By then Anne's divorce would be final and he could begin on his own. And he could also step away from the union. If a political appointment was not forthcoming, he would become an executive in the manufacturing plant Anne's family controlled. Marriage was what she wanted for him—it was something she needed to justify their relationship. And it was what *he* wanted as well. A chill spread through him, but he knew it wasn't from the night air. He had fought too long. Struggled and scratched for too many years. Even as a child. He could still remember the looks he had received, looks that had told him he wasn't quite good enough, that he had lacked some intangible asset that others had been born with. But not anymore. He forced a smile to his lips. Under Secretary of Labor had a nice ring to it. But it was something, he knew, that would come only with difficulty out of the docks of New York.

He reached the corner of Fifth Avenue and breathed a sigh of relief as he saw the yellow glow of the taxi's roof light moving slowly toward him. It gave him a rush of confidence. Your luck still holds, he told himself as he stepped from the curb and raised his arm.

As Marco climbed into the rear of the taxi a dark sedan pulled away from the curb and moved slowly toward Fifth Avenue. When it reached the intersection, the driver switched on the headlights, turned left, and began following the cab at a discreet distance. The driver of the sedan reached for the car telephone and punched out a number.

Paul Levine's voice answered on the second ring.

"He just left the woman's house," the driver said.

Levine turned on the bedside light and glanced at his watch. "The party just break up?" he asked, his voice fogged by sleep.

"He left earlier, then went back after everybody else

had taken off," the driver said. There was silence on the other end. "You want me to follow him home?"

"No," Levine said. "I found out what I wanted to know." He replaced the receiver and continued to stare at it. Slowly a hint of pleasure tinged the hate in his eyes. So, you thought you'd get rid of me, he thought. "But I'll bring you to *your* knees," he said aloud. "Right down to your knees. And then I'll bury you."

CHAPTER/FOUR

THE EDITORIAL DEPARTMENT of the *New York Globe* took up the entire ninth floor of the Globe Building on East Forty-fourth Street, with the center of activity concentrated in a cavernous room that housed more than two hundred reporters, editors, and photographers on the day shift, and slightly more than half that number on the night and lobster tricks.

By ten in the morning the city room was moving slowly toward the start of another day as editors passed out assignments to arriving reporters and took telephone calls from others who had been given theirs the previous afternoon.

Jennifer Brady arrived at her desk ten minutes late and found a handful of news releases she would be expected to boil down into one- or two-paragraph items. She dropped her purse into a desk drawer, slid into her chair, and stared unhappily at the unwanted work. So much for plans to reread the clips on Tony Marco, she thought.

The desks in the newsroom were arranged in nests of

four, with the fronts and one side abutting so they formed one large surface, across which four reporters faced each other. Two of the four desks in Jennifer's nest were still empty; the fourth, the one directly opposite her, was occupied by Joe Walsh, a forty-year veteran of the paper, who was staring at her with an amused grin. Jennifer looked across at him and arched her eyebrows. "Something tickling your fancy this morning?" she asked.

Walsh raised his chin, indicating the other two desks, which were free of any news releases, then looked back at the stack that sat before Jennifer. "Still on the shit list, I see," he said.

Jennifer offered Walsh an intentionally false smile and said, "Woman's work."

Walsh pulled on his long slender nose and shook his head. He motioned with his eyes toward the rim, a large horseshoe-shaped work area, from which the city editor, Martin Twist, and his assistants ran the newsroom. "For refusing, yet again, to have a drink with our great and generous leader," Walsh said, correcting her.

"Not on the best day of his wretched little life!" she said.

Walsh let out a gravelly laugh that matched his voice. He was in his early sixties with a painfully slender body, a thin face, an even thinner mustache, and rapidly thinning hair. His gruff, crusty demeanor was contradicted by gentle blue eyes that, to Jennifer, always looked slightly wounded. He had adopted her when she joined the paper two years ago, and she had quickly come to regard him as a favorite uncle.

Jennifer turned and looked again at the two empty desks. "Where *are* Lord Ha Ha and the Chief this morning?" she asked, using the office nicknames for Richard Amberly, a British-born reporter who played the pompous

Englishman for his own amusement, and Eddie Rogers, the paper's senior police reporter.

"Eddie had an overnight," Walsh said. "A press conference at headquarters. As far as his lordship goes"—he paused and shrugged—"he's probably at home talking on the telephone with the queen."

Jennifer tapped the side of her nose with her index finger, imitating an affectation Amberly favored. "Can't say too much," she said in a broad English accent. "Affairs of state, you know."

"The only affairs that palmy prig has is with the towel boy at his favorite Greenwich Village bathhouse," Walsh croaked.

Jennifer giggled. Amberly was not gay—he had a wife and two sons, to whom he was devoted, but Walsh enjoyed making the accusation. He also enjoyed accusing Eddie Rogers, who was a notorious middle-aged womanizer, of being unable to get it up, something that so irritated Rogers, he would threaten to tear Walsh's mustache from his face.

Jennifer watched Walsh as he began sorting through a thick research file he had been compiling for a story. It would end up, she suspected, like most of his projects, with a terse rejection from Twist. Twenty-five years earlier Walsh had won a Pulitzer Prize for his coverage of the Cuban revolution. But that had been at a time when reporters simply gathered facts, then turned them over to a rewrite man, who wrote the story. During the late sixties and early seventies, when reporters had begun to write their own stories as much as possible, Walsh had been unwilling to make the transition. Now, under Twist, he had been labeled a "dinosaur" and had been pushed aside, left to work on long-term projects that rarely found their way to print. When she had first learned of Walsh's status, she had marveled at the waste of talent. Other reporters had told her how good he was, and she had seen him work the telephones, gathering information, and had realized the others weren't merely supporting a friend.

But you've got your own problems, kid, she told herself, turning to her computer console as she prepared to struggle through the stack of drudge work.

When she had finished, she sat back and lit her first cigarette of the morning. It was nearly eleven o'clock, and across the room she could see Amberly making his way toward his desk. "His Lordship has arrived at court," she said to Walsh.

Walsh looked up and grunted. "Probably couldn't find any Boy Scouts to molest, so he decided to come to work."

Jennifer repressed a smile and took a long drag on her cigarette as she watched Amberly approach. He was moderately tall and slender with straight blond hair, cut in the style of British military officers. As always, he was nattily dressed, something he expected others to admire. This day's offering was a tan suit, blue shirt, and solid tan necktie, finished off with brown suede shoes.

Amberly bowed his head slightly, and Jennifer noticed again how his craggy face and slightly oversize nose gave him a striking resemblance to the British actor Trevor Howard.

"My dear children," Amberly said as he reached his desk. "And what are we up to this morning?"

Walsh raised his head, offered a gravelly, "Piss off," and returned to his files.

Amberly laughed and turned his attention to Jennifer. "I see Joseph is in his usual cheerful state," he said. "And what are you up to, my dear?" He paused a beat. "Ah, I see. Working on the big one."

His voice held teasing laughter, and Jennifer blew him a kiss. "Piss off, Richard," she said.

Amberly's eyes flashed mischievously. "My Lord," he

said. "I knew Joseph was going through menopause, but I thought it far too early for you."

Walsh raised his slender head, struggling to keep the amusement out of his eyes. "I'll give you menopause, you palmy faggot. What brings you in so early? The gay bars stop serving brunch?"

Amberly fussed affectedly with a folder he had placed on the desk. "Out gathering items for my column. The things people *really* want to know about."

Walsh rolled his eyes at the mention of Amberly's thrice-weekly celebrity column. "Wonderful," Walsh growled. "Now the whole world will know who threw up on their table at Elaine's last night."

Amberly sat up straight in his chair, offering his most imperious pose. "Can't say too much," he said, tapping the side of his narrow nose with one finger. "Must save it for my readers."

Walsh snorted, looked at Jennifer, and with his head, gestured toward Amberly. "His readers—his wife, his mother-in-law, and three aging queens in Soho."

Remarks about the column were part of a game they played, a game designed to mask pain that lay below the surface. Amberly, now in his mid-forties, had been one of the paper's finest feature writers. But he, like others, had fallen out of grace with Twist, and his punishment had been the column. Amberly dealt with the humiliation by turning it into an elaborate joke. Jennifer, Walsh, and Eddie Rogers played along with it.

"My troops!" The voice bellowed behind them, and Jennifer turned to see the assignment editor, Frank Falcone, swaggering toward them. He was short and overweight, and the swagger had a slight waddle to it but was countered by a sharp, cunning face and dark eyes that spoke of things learned growing up in the streets of Little Italy.

Falcone came to a halt in front of Jennifer. He was in

shirtsleeves, his tie pulled carelessly down from his neck. Jennifer thought his look was a bit wistful, but with Falcone it was hard to tell.

He handed her a press release with her name written across the top. "Noon today," he said. "The Central Park Zoo. Patsy, our favorite gorilla, is having her ninth birthday party."

Jennifer stared at the release, assuring herself it was not a joke. "Oh, shit," she said. She could hear Walsh and Amberly laughing softly as she looked back at Falcone. "Why me, Frank?"

"It comes from the man himself," Falcone said, indicating Twist. "Look, it's a sure thing for the bottom of page three, maybe even a picture on the front page." Jennifer began to object, but he stopped her. "Jenny," he continued, using a diminutive she allowed with no one else. "Believe me, there are worse assignments sitting on his desk. I've seen them. Take my word for it."

Jennifer gritted her teeth and stared at the news release.

"And listen," Falcone said, "get some good quotes from the gorilla. You know, the stuff people will be interested in."

Jennifer gave him a false smile. "I'll ask her if she's gotten laid lately. That should brighten up your tawdry little day." The smile became genuine as the laughter grew around her.

Jennifer telephoned Tony Marco's office the following day. It was a call filled with trepidation but one she knew she had to make, lest time and distance come between them. As she waited for him to come on the line she glanced at a copy of the paper's final edition. The photograph of Patsy the gorilla had made page one, with a story at the bottom of page three, prime space for the tabloid. She closed her eyes and silently prayed Marco had not

seen her byline on the story. It was not exactly the persua-
sive tool she needed. What can you possibly tell him? she
asked herself. Well, Tony, baby, I've done the gorilla.
Now I'd like to do you.

His voice came on the line, and she squeezed her eyes
shut again. If he's seen it, please don't let him mention it.

"I'm glad you called," he said. "I hope this means you
want to talk further."

Jennifer let her breath out, unaware that she had been
holding it. "I certainly do," she said. "Is there a time
that's convenient for you?"

"Well, I imagine you're as busy as I am during working
hours. How would early evening be?"

Jennifer felt a slight flutter in her stomach and tried to
force it away. "That would depend on the evening," she
said, then hated herself for the unnecessary coyness. It's a
story, damn it, not a date. "But I can usually rearrange
things."

There was a pause on Tony's end of the line, and
Jennifer realized she was holding her breath again. "I have
a meeting in Manhattan late this afternoon, and then a
dinner engagement at eight-thirty. I should be free from
six to eight-fifteen."

"Six would be fine," Jennifer said.

"Good," Tony said. "How would the Oak Bar at the
Plaza be?" He listened as Jennifer agreed. "I'll see you at
six, then."

Jennifer replaced the receiver, then stared at it for
several moments. There was a small smile on her lips, and
her eyes were filled with anticipation.

"You look pleased with yourself."

She looked up and saw Joe Walsh staring at her across
the desk. She allowed the smile to grow. "I am," she said.

"You want to tell me about it?" he asked.

"Tomorrow," she said. "I think I'll need to talk to you about it tomorrow."

Tony stared at the telephone, then closed his eyes and wondered why he was doing it, why he was angling for even more publicity about himself, why he couldn't just see the woman because she was attractive, interesting.

He sat back in his chair and opened his eyes. For the same reason you do everything, the same reason you didn't choose a simpler life, he told himself. It was ambition, almost to the point of lust. He lowered his head and pressed his fingers into his eyes. But it hadn't always been this way. At the start there had been lofty ideals; plans to make the union everything it could be. And when you saw that couldn't happen, you should have gotten out.

He swiveled in his chair and stared out the window. And do what? he asked himself. Your own law practice helping people solve their day-to-day problems? It would have driven you mad, and you would have hated yourself for doing it. And you have accomplished things. You have.

The Oak Bar at the Plaza Hotel always made Jennifer think of Cary Grant. Perhaps it was the subdued elegance of the dark, paneled walls, the understated but unmistakable affluence in which the actor had seemed to fit so easily. As she walked across the room toward the window table occupied by Tony Marco, she thought that he, too, looked as though he belonged there. She hoped the fact that she had rushed home and changed to more fitting clothes had helped her to fit in as well.

You're acting like a schoolgirl, she told herself. You'd fit in anywhere you chose. Her smile broadened as Tony rose to greet her.

"I'm so glad you could meet me on such short notice," Tony began as he returned to his chair. "I was hoping we might be able to finish the conversation we began the other evening."

Jennifer's mind flashed back to Anne Mobray's hit-and-run attack to snatch Tony away. "It was probably the wrong time to try to talk to you," she said. "Mrs. Mobray seemed determined to see you had equal time with everyone there."

Tony glanced out the window as though recalling the evening.

"I'm afraid all of Anne's parties are like that," he said, turning his attention back to Jennifer. "Unless people ricochet around the room, she considers the party a failure."

"She certainly knows how to bring political powers together."

Tony nodded. "The movers and shakers. At least, that's how they like to see themselves."

"And is that how you see yourself?" Jennifer made the question as neutral as possible.

Tony stared at her, studying her features, wishing he could tell her it was simply the trap he had fallen into. "Sometimes. But then, something usually happens to show me how little I can really move or shake and I'm brought back to earth with a thump," he said instead.

A waiter approached the table, and they paused to order drinks—a malt Scotch on ice for Tony, a glass of white wine for Jennifer.

"I'm sure you're being too modest," Jennifer said. "I couldn't help overhearing a great deal of speculation about you the other night."

Tony glanced out the window again. A hansom cab was pulling away from the curb, a middle-aged couple ensconced in its open carriage. "People are always curious about things that seem different or out of the ordinary to them." He gestured toward the cab. "That's why some people will pay an outrageous price to sit behind a smelly animal for a twenty-minute ride around Central Park."

Jennifer's soft laugh returned. "And that's how you think people see you?"

"Well, I hope not as a smelly animal. But as a curiosity, yes."

"Why do you say that?" She caught a wistful look in his eyes.

The waiter returned with their drinks, and Tony waited until he had left. "I'm thirty-five years old, and to most people's thinking that's very young to be the head of a large and influential labor union. And when you consider I've had the job for six years, that's even more difficult for them to understand." He sipped his drink. "I'm also well educated, and—I like to think—articulate, something that's also not the norm for people in my line of work." He smiled, more at himself than at Jennifer. "And the union I represent has a very colorful and very adversely viewed past. Everyone has seen *On the Waterfront*." He took the glass in his hand but did not raise it from the table. "But in recent years that same union has been out in front on social issues, charitable causes, race relations, and every other problem that affects the quality of life of the average person.

"And all those thing make us something of an enigma. And it makes me a curiosity, and people tend to speculate about things and people they find curious."

Jennifer toyed with her wineglass. "Some of the speculation I heard was rather lofty. Even talk about a possible cabinet post."

Tony steepled his fingers and hesitated. "I know," he said at length. "And I'll be honest with you, I encourage the speculation. It's good for the union's image." Not to mention my own, he added to himself.

Jennifer was surprised by the response. "You mean you wouldn't consider it if it were offered?"

"I didn't say that. It would depend on the administration. On whether I felt I could accomplish anything or not. And on what the situation was in my union."

"So your commitment to the union would come first?" Jennifer watched his face closely, especially his eyes, but they revealed nothing.

"I've made commitments there, and the people I represent expect them to be kept. I'm not saying no one else could carry them out. I'm saying I could never leave voluntarily unless I was certain they would be carried out."

Jennifer raised her eyebrows. "Is there some doubt about that?"

"There's always doubt." He smiled at her, pleased by her skepticism. "For example, we have a union election next year. If I were to leave, and if we didn't have a strong candidate to replace me on the ballot, a whole new executive committee might be elected. And their goals might be entirely different than ours have been."

Jennifer sat back in her chair and ran one finger around the rim of her wineglass. "Back to the old days?" she asked.

Tony didn't answer.

Jennifer waited, and when no response was forthcoming, she sipped her wine, then continued. "I took your advice—at least I started to—and read some of the clips about the union. Some of them painted a pretty sordid picture of the old days."

Tony toyed with his drink, watching her as he did. "Believe half of what you read and you'll still have an exaggerated picture of things." He stared across the table. She was wearing a pale blue silk blouse that brought out the color of her eyes and hair, and when she had entered the room, heads had turned to follow her. So far the conversation had been all business, and Tony realized he wished it had not been. But that's what you're here for, he reminded himself.

"I'm not trying to be negative, I'm just trying to understand. I didn't read very much, and perhaps what I read was just a bad period with the press. But the articles seemed to concentrate on violence on the docks, loan sharks, bookmaking, theft of cargo. Have those things been eliminated?"

"Curtailed, yes. Eliminated, no." Tony held her eyes again. "The docks, off and on, are a violent place. But it's individual violence. I worked as a part-time longshoreman while I was in high school and during part of my freshman year in college, and I saw enough violent behavior to last me a lifetime." He clasped his hands in front of him in a gesture that seemed to plead for understanding. "The docks are a hellhole to work on. Unbelievably hot in summer, and freezing in winter. And the holds of most ships are like climbing down into a sewer. The men who work there are essentially uneducated. People who grew up in rough neighborhoods and who tend to meet unpleasantness with unpleasantness."

Jennifer sat back, noting the way Marco discussed violence. He seemed able to accept it and yet remove himself from it at the same time. She stared at him, at the well-tailored blue suit, the white shirt, and silk tie. He had worked on those docks, and now he sits here exuding compassion and confidence and power and . . . She hesitated, then allowed herself to finish the thought. And sex. She pushed the idea away and, forcing herself to concentrate, asked, "And the bookmakers and loan sharks? They still exist?"

"I'm afraid so." He raised one hand, stopping her next question. "I don't want to sound defensive, but we're not

equipped to deal with felons. And if twenty-five thousand
cops in New York City can't stop them, how are a handful
of union officials going to do it?"

"But if you don't try, aren't you in effect condoning it?"

"I don't think so. Not any more than the city's newspapers
condone it by running the daily betting line on their
sports pages."

"Touché."

"I don't mean it that way," Tony said. "I simply mean
it's part of the human condition we can't control. We can't
dictate morality." He smiled at her. "If you went into any
store in the neighborhood I grew up in, you'd see a slip of
paper taped to each cash register with a number on it. It's
the previous day's winning number for the local policy
operator. The stores put it up as a public service, the same
way your newspaper runs the daily line. In that same
neighborhood, and every one like it, you'll find people
lined up at nine o'clock at night, waiting for the first
edition of the *Globe* and the *Daily News*. And they're not
there to read what you and your peers have written.
They're there for the race results and the next day's racing
forms."

"And we make damned sure the results are there,"
Jennifer agreed.

"I'd like you to do me a favor," Tony said. "When you
go to work tomorrow, find someone in your office who
plays the horses. I don't think it will be hard. And then
you ask him if there's someone at the paper you can place
a bet with. I'll bet you a dinner at the restaurant of your
choice, you'll find there is, and that your management
knows about it and simply looks the other way."

Jennifer stared at him, then nodded. "Will I find a loan
shark too?"

"I wouldn't be surprised, but I don't know. The people
at the *Globe* have steady paychecks. If some of them are

dealing with a loan shark, it would be the result of foolishness. For some of my people it's a necessary evil."

Jennifer's eyebrows rose. "Necessary?"

Tony nodded. "Again, I'm not condoning it, just explaining." He paused to sip his drink. "The men who work through us make a good hourly wage—fifteen dollars, to be exact—but it's not a guaranteed salary. And it's a dangerous job, one where injuries can put you out of work for substantial periods of time. Now we pay benefits, and they're good benefits by today's standards. But they don't cover much more than food, shelter, clothing, and medical expenses." He offered her a gesture of helplessness. "Unfortunately most loan officers are all too aware of that." He raised one hand. "Oh, they can get car loans or mortgages, because the loans are secured by collateral. But a personal loan? Never. These people earn a decent wage. But at the same time they live in an expensive city, and most have kids to support. So Christmas comes around, or a child is about to graduate from high school or college, or there's a family crisis. They need one or two hundred dollars. So they go to a six-for-five guy, because he's the only one who'll give it to them." He noticed her questioning look at the term and smiled. "Six for five. You pay back six dollars for every five you borrow. That's twenty percent interest, *per week*." He noted her surprise. "It gets worse. Let's say you borrowed a hundred on a Friday. The next Friday you'd owe a hundred and twenty. Let's say you didn't have it. So you pay only the twenty, or what's called the *vigorish*, the *vig*. Next week you still owe a hundred and twenty dollars."

Jennifer let out a long breath. "And how long do you get before some Neanderthal comes looking for you?"

Tony laughed. "That's only in the movies. These people are too smart to put someone in the hospital who owes them money. They want the money and they know they can't get it from someone in intensive care. If someone tries to run away and pay nothing at all, that's different. And there have been instances where automobiles have been signed over to satisfy a debt."

She sat back and played with a strand of hair as she studied Marco. Handsome and direct, with no claims of moral purity or righteousness. Honest? She wondered.

"If we agree on a story, to what degree would I be able to go into your personal life?" she asked.

Tony sipped his drink, then glanced out the window again before answering. "If you're talking about where I grew up, went to school, worked, I have no objection at all. I might be agreeable to you meeting my mother or sister, and perhaps my wife and son. But I'm careful about how much I allow my family to be involved in my public life. I'm very protective of their privacy. Especially my wife and son. It's what they prefer, and it's something I guard very jealously."

Jennifer sat back and nodded. But there was something that rang untrue, especially for someone who already had a public life and was seeking an even greater one. Something wrong at home? She wondered. Perhaps that was why he spent so much time with Anne Mobray. It was an interesting thought, and Jennifer immediately realized it was far more than that.

"I'd very much like to do this story." And to get to know you much better, she added to herself.

Marco leaned forward and smiled. "I'll give you all the time you need," he said.

Jennifer and Joe Walsh went to the cocktail lounge in the nearby Tudor Hotel the following day. It was a small, dimly lit room with intimate tables and, most important, one not normally frequented by members of the *Globe* staff.

They took a table away from the bar and ordered drinks, a beer for Joe Walsh, a glass of white wine for Jennifer.

"I thought you'd prefer a place where you wouldn't find yourself sitting next to half the staff. Besides, now you can tell everybody that you lured me to a hotel." Walsh winked at her in a paternal way. "So, what's up? Or is this just going to be a session where we sit and tell each other how much we're being screwed over?" He shrugged. "Not that I mind. It's one of my favorite subjects."

"One of mine too," Jennifer said. "But we'll save it for another time. There's a story I want to work on, an involved one. And I'm sure Twist will never approve it, at least not from me."

"That's no problem. You work it on your own time and lay it on him when you're finished." Walsh gave Jennifer a slightly wicked grin. "He's a rotten little bastard, and he'll hate the idea of you getting any recognition, unless you get it through him. But if it's solid, he won't have the guts to spike it."

Jennifer knew what getting recognition through Twist would involve, and she was grateful for the gentle phrasing. She also knew what Walsh meant by something solid. The story would have to be tight. No holes; no room for Twist to shoot it down. She wasn't sure it was possible.

Jennifer bit her lower lip. "Getting it solid is part of my problem, Joe. It's what I wanted your advice about."

Walsh shrugged. "You worried you're not good enough?"

Jennifer stared down at her glass, then back at Walsh. "Maybe."

Walsh grinned. "You're good enough. I've watched you work. And you've got the look."

"The look?"

"In your eyes," Walsh said. "I've seen it. An intensity. You don't like to lose."

"Nobody does," Jennifer said.

"You'd be surprised. Some people program themselves for it. It's why I drink too much of this stuff." He tapped the top of the glass. "So tell me about the story."

Jennifer stared at him, wondering about the impromptu confession, then put it aside. "It centers around Tony Marco," she said. "I was at a party a few nights ago. It was at Anne Mobray's town house, and everyone from the governor to a few national party bosses were there." She toyed nervously with her wineglass. "There was talk about Marco making a big move up the political ladder, maybe even a cabinet post if the Democrats win this year; if not now, then in 1988." Jennifer leaned forward. "So what I've got is this bright, young, attractive labor leader being considered for national prominence, who's the head of a union that has virtually been a synonym for corruption—a union that supposedly has now become an example of what every union should be. But at the same time—and I confirmed this with Marco, himself—the union still has serious problems. Bookmakers and loan sharks still prey on the men, something Marco says he'd like to stop but hasn't been able to. So, I think, the story is about a bright, young, charismatic labor leader who's turned a corrupt union around. But the union still has warts—serious warts— and this man, who may be the next under secretary of labor, has been unable, or unwilling, to deal with those problems. And I'm not sure which. I think it's a story. What do you think, Joe?"

Walsh took a long pull on his beer. "Half a story. And a dangerous one for you," he said.

A pained look crossed Jennifer's face. "What do you mean, Joe?"

"There's a lot of talk about Marco." He saw concern spread across Jennifer's face. "That in itself doesn't mean anything. Most of the people who do the talking would suspect the pope of running a whorehouse in a convent.

It's the nature of the beast. But Marco and the waterfront union . . . well, I don't know." He saw Jennifer about to object, but held her off. "Don't get me wrong. I've got a lot of respect for Marco. He's one of the sharpest pieces of work I've seen in a long time. But there are a lot of people who think the union really hasn't changed and that Tony hasn't done much more than produce a lot of glitz and glitter to make it appear that it has. If that's true and it comes out three months after you write a story favorable to Marco, what could have been a big breakthrough for you could become just the opposite."

Jennifer felt her stomach tighten. "So what do you suggest I do?"

"Find out," Walsh said. "Find out if Marco really did clean up the union and what it took to do it, both on a personal and professional level. If he did, you've got an outstanding piece of journalism about someone who beat back deep-seated corruption and is now being considered for a cabinet post. If he didn't, if the corruption still exists, you've got a story about a man about to step into a position of national leadership who's mired in corruption, himself. And that would be a blockbuster. But you've got to prove it one way or the other."

Jennifer felt an odd ambivalence. The idea of an even bigger story than she had envisioned excited her, and yet she hated the thought of discovering the man had clay feet. "If you were a betting man, Joe, which story would you put your money on?"

Walsh shook his head. "Hard to say, kid. But Tony has a couple of strikes against him."

"Like what?"

"First, Marco was an officer in the union during the last of the really bad days. Now that doesn't mean he was part of it. He could have been there trying to stop it, or at least curtail it. But it's hard to imagine he didn't know, or at least suspect, what was going on. Second, the man who ran the union in those days was a guy named Moe Green, and he made Jimmy Hoffa look like a Boy Scout. Moe Green was Tony Marco's father-in-law, and Tony took over the union when Moe died."

"Which way would you bet?"

Walsh shook his head slowly. "I'd like to think Marco's everything he purports to be. From what I've seen of him I like him. But who the hell knows? That's what you have to find out. And you're never going to find out about past corruption from Tony Marco."

"Because it would have involved his father-in-law," she said.

"That, and the fact that he was there. And people will always ask why he didn't go to the authorities if he knew about it."

"And put his father-in-law in jail," Jennifer said.

"That might have been the personal dilemma he faced. Interesting angle, isn't it?" Walsh said.

"So if there was corruption and it still exists, what would it be?" Jennifer asked.

"Kickbacks from shipping companies. That's what was suspected in the past but never proven. That's what you'd have to prove. Whether it happened in the past and if it's still happening now. And that won't be easy."

"How would I even begin?" she asked.

"To start, you'd probably need somebody inside. Some-body willing to talk. And that's a hard thing to get. Then, *if* you found that something smelled, you'd have a massive job of poring through public records."

"That's something I've done very little of," Jennifer said.

"That's something I can teach you. But there's no point in going into it until we know it's necessary."

Jennifer studied his grinning face. "Something tells me you don't think I'm going to find corruption."

"I told you, I admire the guy," Walsh said. "But I do think you're going to find one hell of a personal story. Maybe you'll find the other too. Who the hell knows. Your job now is to find somebody inside who will talk. Without that you've got nothing."

"I'm almost sorry I asked," she said.

Walsh picked up his beer and took a long swallow. "I know somebody who might be able to help. Let me call first, and see if he's willing to talk to us before I tell you about him." Walsh stood to leave, then paused. "He's a strange guy. When I tell him what you want, he might just tell me to go to hell. But he'll keep his mouth shut. He won't go running back to Marco."

Jennifer watched Walsh walk toward the hotel lobby and immediately began to speculate about whom he would call. He was said to have an endless supply of contacts: people who would only talk to him or, occasionally, to others for whom he vouched. Jennifer felt a twinge of uneasiness and wondered if she would ever be able to generate that kind of trust. Insecure, aren't you? she thought; it was something she could hide from everyone but herself. She stared at her wine and wondered if she had ever felt secure, if there had ever been a time in her life when she hadn't had serious doubts about herself, about her worth as a person.

An image of her father flashed into her mind. He was slightly drunk, as he had always been, and he was shouting at her in his heavy South Boston accent. Telling her how stupid or clumsy she was. Telling her how she didn't measure up. Jennifer felt a shiver run down her back, as it had when she was only seven or eight. The image changed, she was older, and her father was in the doorway of her bedroom, swaying slightly, his eyes fixed on her as she sat on her bed. He took a step toward her, swinging the door shut behind him. . . .

"He'll see us."

Jennifer's head snapped up at the sound of Walsh's voice. She sat back in her chair and exhaled heavily, and she could feel a trace of perspiration along her forehead. "I'm sorry, Joe. I was a million miles away."

Walsh looked down at her steadily. "Wherever you were, kid, it doesn't look like it was a good trip."

She forced a smile, the warmest she could manage. "I think your lecture about what's ahead shook me up," she said.

Walsh eased back into his chair and took a long drink of his beer, draining the glass. "Before you start worrying, let's see what my friend has to offer."

"You said he was a little strange. Who is he?"

"He's a homocide detective assigned to the Brooklyn D.A.'s office. Name's Pete Moran, and he and Marco grew up together as kids. Almost like brothers, I'm told. Anyway, when Tony went to college, Pete went into the service and ended up in Vietnam. Or, to be more precise, a Viet Cong prison camp. He escaped, but I understand he had it pretty bad. He came home carrying a lot of baggage, which is why you might find him a little hard to deal with."

"But if he and Marco are like brothers, how—"

Walsh cut her off with a shake of his head. "I said *were*. I don't know what happened between them—and I've never had the guts to ask—but Moran hates Marco like I've seen few men hate. I think if he had an excuse, he'd blow the guy's brains out without batting an eye."

Jennifer hesitated, staring at her wineglass for a moment, then looked back at Walsh. "If he hates him that much, how much can I trust his judgment?"

"He's a good cop. There are still a few around. But let's

not worry about that until we see if he's willing to help."
Walsh glanced at his watch. "We're supposed to meet him
at a restaurant in Brooklyn in half an hour."

Walsh started to rise, but Jennifer's voice stopped him.
"Just one more thing, Joe. Do you know if there's a bookie
working at the paper?"

Walsh looked at her curiously. "Sure," he said. "There's
a guy down in delivery. That's all he does."

"And management knows about him?"

"They'd have to be blind not to," Walsh said. "But if
they tried to do anything about it, they'd have a strike on
their hands. Why do you ask?"

"It's not important," Jennifer said. "Except I think I
owe Mr. Marco a very expensive dinner."

Monte's Venetian Room was located on Carroll Street,
only a few doors from the tenement where Al Capone
supposedly spent his childhood in New York. The restaurant was a favorite of cops, judges, and bookmakers, and
its parking lot was a peculiar mix of squad cars, Lincolns,
and Cadillacs. Inside, the decor was simple and relaxed,
staffed by older Italian waiters eager to offer their personal
recommendations.

Jennifer and Walsh stood just inside the door as Walsh
scanned the room before locating Pete Moran alone in a
corner booth. When they reached the table, Moran remained seated; he nodded to Walsh, stared at Jennifer
with hard eyes.

Walsh made a brief introduction, to which Jennifer simply said hello in a soft voice. Her normal smile was with-
held. It was something that would not work with this
man, she decided, as she studied his face. It was a
handsome face, in a beaten sort of way. Walsh had said he
was thirty-five, the same age as Marco, but he looked
older. The lines at the corners of his eyes and mouth were

deeply etched, and there was a distinct image of pain behind his hazel eyes. Unlike the younger police officers, Moran was clean-shaven, and his brown hair only moderately long and combed straight back. Moran's hands were on the table in front of him, large with long fingers more suited to a pianist than a cop, she thought.

They ordered drinks, and Walsh opened the conversation with small talk, hoping to ease into the subject. Moran listened impassively for several minutes, then abruptly cut Walsh off.

"You didn't tell me the reporter you were bringing was a woman," Moran said. His voice was soft but tinged with disapproval.

"Does it matter?" Jennifer said, before Walsh could answer. She kept her voice flat, fighting to conceal her annoyance.

Moran's eyes went directly to hers, cold and dispassionate. "Don't get in a snit, Ms. Brady," he said in a soft voice. "But if you're planning to go digging around the longshoremen's union, yes, it might matter a lot."

Jennifer's first inclination was to challenge him, but she rejected the idea, sat back, and simply asked why.

Moran leaned forward, his forearms on the table, and for the first time Jennifer noticed how broad his shoulders were. They seemed to be straining the material of his rumpled corduroy jacket.

Moran continued to hold her eyes. "It has nothing to do with competency. It has a helluva lot to do with the nature of the beast you want to confront." Moran paused, hoping his words had soothed the woman's ruffled feathers but not really caring if they had. "First of all, the people you'd have to talk to would have a lot of trouble trusting you, or taking you seriously. To call them chauvinistic is about as redundant as saying alcoholics drink." Moran saw a flash of anger in Jennifer's eyes that was quickly masked.

Feisty lady, he told himself, immediately raising her one notch in his mind. He decided to push it further. "The second problem is that it could be damned dangerous. I'm talking about the docks and the people who control them. I'm not saying it's no place for a woman. I'm saying it's no place for anybody who's not part of their little club."

He softened his words with a smile, a warm, pleasant smile, Jennifer thought, one that contrasted with his pained features.

"I'm a cop," Moran continued. "And *I* wouldn't feel safe poking around there alone."

"Are you telling me that Tony Marco might have me hurt if he thought I was looking into things he didn't want looked into?"

"I wouldn't put anything past Tony," Moran said. "But things could happen with or without his knowledge. Frankly, playing rough isn't his style. He's too smart to play rough. But even if Tony's as clean as the driven snow, you're still talking about poking around in things that happened in the past. And there are people there now who were part of that. And if you start poking around and show even the potential of causing them problems, they'd make your life a nightmare. And if they thought you could *prove* something"—he hesitated again, still watching her eyes—"yes, then they'd hurt you."

Jennifer felt herself pulled between apprehension and anger, but the anger won. He was doing what they all did to her, assuming she couldn't handle a threat because of what *wasn't* hanging between her legs.

Moran watched her, keeping his face impassive, not wanting her to know her reaction mattered. There was a glint of anger in her blue eyes, which seemed to have deepened in color, and the milk-white skin on her high cheekbones had shown a momentary flash of pink.

"I'm a big girl, Detective Moran—" Jennifer began.

"Pete," Moran said.

"Thank you. Please call me Jennifer." She drew a breath. "As I was saying, I've been taking care of myself a long time, and I don't frighten easily. No more than anyone else. I also think I'm smart enough not to get into trouble by thinking I have something to prove."

Moran turned to Walsh. "You weren't very specific on the phone, Joe. But you never are. What exactly do you think you have that makes Tony worth looking into?"

Jennifer watched Moran's face as Walsh explained Marco's political prospects. There was a slight narrowing of his eyes, an almost imperceptible tightening of his lips. Moran was good at masking his emotions, she thought. It's part of his job. But this is too much for him to take.

When Walsh finished, Moran stared at the table and slowly shook his head. "I knew Tony was ambitious, but I never guessed his ambitions went that far." He turned his attention to Jennifer. "And you want to look for the bad as well as the good. And you'll publish whatever you find." He spoke the words as statements rather than questions, almost as though issuing a challenge.

"That's right. It won't be a puff piece. And however it turns out, I think it will be a good story."

Moran continued to stare into her face. "You might find out more than you bargain for."

Jennifer kept her eyes on his, refusing to back away from the challenge. He wants it to be bad, she told herself. He needs it to be. "Do you think he's corrupt?"

"Let's just say I'd find it hard to say anything good about Tony Marco. But proving corruption is something else."

"Has the District Attorney's office tried?" she asked.

Moran tilted his head back and laughed. "Wake up, lady. Somebody would have to catch Tony sodomizing a

nine-year-old on the steps of Borough Hall before the
D.A. would even *think* about going after him."

"Marco's *that* powerful?" Jennifer asked.

"Not Tony. The union. It has a political action fund that
hands out a minimum of a hundred thousand a year in
political contributions. That's something Tony set up to
build his power base. And although the people in the
D.A.'s office would prosecute their own mothers if it
would advance their careers, they're not about to threaten
that kind of political goose." Moran's face broke into another smile. "Actually there's nothing I'd rather see than
you walking into the office and handing them a criminal
case against Marco. It would be a race to see who could
dive under his desk first."

"You don't paint a very positive picture," Jennifer said.

"We haven't even gotten to 'positive' yet," Moran said.
"First somebody's got to prove. And I'm not sure anybody
can do that."

"Perhaps there isn't anything to prove," she said. She
watched his lips tighten again, noticing it only because she
was looking for it. "Just being objective," she added.

"Maybe you're right," Moran said. "Maybe there isn't
anything to prove."

They were interrupted by a slender waiter in his early
sixties who patted Moran on the back with genuine warmth.

"Pete, it's been a long time," the waiter said. "What's
the matter, you don't like good food no more?"

"Just trying to keep the weight down, Al," Moran said.
"The older I get, the harder it gets."

The waiter gave an exaggerated shrug. "Heah, look at
me. You eat the right things, you never put on a pound."

Moran's eyes moved up and down the waiter's body.
"The book on you, Al, is that you only eat in Chinese
restaurants."

The waiter wrinkled his nose. "I wouldn't touch that stuff. They use cat meat, those Chinese."

"What do you recommend?" Moran asked. "Without cat meat."

The waiter jabbed a finger at him. "Veal piccata. To-night you're gonna get it like you never had it before. Unbelievable."

Moran glanced at Jennifer and Walsh and found them in agreement. "Three," he said. "And a bottle of wine." He watched the waiter scratch the order on his pad, then added, "And separate checks."

When he turned back to face Jennifer, Moran noted a hint of surprise in her eyes.

"The separate checks aren't necessary," she said. "It's a legitimate business expense for us."

Moran locked on to her eyes. "It's necessary for me," he said. "I have one rule. Never on the first date."

During dinner they dropped the subject of Tony Marco as Joe Walsh adroitly changed the conversation to more general things. When they had finished, Moran picked up his wineglass, turned it in his fingers, then replaced it. Jennifer noticed he had not touched the wine during his meal and apparently had no intention of doing so. It was simply ornamental.

Moran turned his attention to Walsh. "Okay, Joe. You've told me what you want to do. But you haven't told me what you want from me."

"I thought we'd feed you first," Walsh said, "but you won't even let us do that."

"Get to the point, Joe."

Walsh let out a long breath. "You're a hard man, Pete."

"I just don't have time for bullshit, Joe. So tell me."

"We need somebody inside, somebody close to what's happening in the union. And we need someone to point the way to that somebody." Walsh rubbed his chin with his fingers. "We also need somebody who knows the turf and who can steer Jennifer away from any trouble spots. I was hoping you could provide both."

Moran was silent, and Jennifer felt the story slipping away. There was no reason for him to do either. Unless, she told herself, he hated Marco as much as she thought he did.

Moran sat back, looking at neither of them. "It's a fool's errand." He turned his eyes toward Jennifer. "And you could get hurt, lady. One condition." He was speaking directly to Jennifer, his eyes hard. "If I tell you not to do something, not to meet someone, not to go somewhere, you *don't*. You cross me once, I'm history. Understood?"

Jennifer bristled inwardly, but she fought it, keeping her voice low and even. "I have to make some decisions on how to approach the story."

Moran shrugged and began to slide out of the booth.

"All right. Okay," Jennifer said. "Christ, you're a hard-ass."

Moran stopped moving and looked at her, as if surprised by her choice of words. "That's right. And don't forget it," he said. "I have no intention of attending your funeral. If you want to kill yourself, you do it without my help."

Jennifer held herself back; resisted challenging his statement as overly dramatic. She was certain he was simply trying to put Marco in an unfavorable light. But she needed his help, his expertise. And she knew she could lose both quickly if she didn't play the game his way. Or at least appear to.

"That's the *last* thing I want to do, Pete. You tell me where we start."

"With a guy named Maxwell," Moran said at length. "He wants to run against Tony in the next union election. He's a louse. But right now he could be your louse."

"Will he talk to me?" Jennifer asked.

Moran let out a small laugh. "Who knows. I'll try to set up a meeting, and I'll go with you. It might help. In the meantime you better use every free hour poring over old newspaper clippings. You have a month, maybe two, if you're careful. Because as soon as Tony realizes you're looking at the bad as well as the good, you're going to find doors slamming in your face. And even that wonderful smile of yours isn't going to help."

Jennifer stiffened. She felt the color rise to her cheeks, and she knew if she spoke, she would stutter over the words. She was saved by the return of the waiter.

"So, you enjoyed it?" he said, directing his question to Moran.

"As always, Al," Moran said.

"So then, how come you don't come more often?" the waiter challenged. "When you was a kid, you was here all the time."

"That was for leftovers at the back door," Moran said.

The waiter shrugged. "It was the same food. You come back. Front door, back door, what's the difference?"

A smile lingered on Moran's lips after the waiter left. Jennifer watched him, surprised that the revelation about his youth had not embarrassed him.

"Did you really come to the back door here when you were a boy?" She asked the question before she could stop herself, realizing it was intended to repay him for his own previous remark.

The pleasure in Moran's eyes faded slightly. "A lot of us did," he said. "It was one of the nice things about the neighborhood. If you really needed something, somebody always tried to help." He paused. "Sometimes Tony and I came here together."

The answer made her feel chastised, a victim of her own self-protective needs. She fought to recover, unconsciously beginning to smile, but stopped herself. "I hadn't realized this was part of the neighborhood you both grew up in."

Moran glanced at Walsh. He had known his past association with Marco would have been discussed, but he wanted Walsh to know the point had not been lost on him. Walsh smiled and shrugged.

"We grew up a few blocks from here," Moran said. "The neighborhood's different now. What they call gentrification. But there are still some of the old families left."

"I'd like to see it," she said. "Can we?"

"Why not," Moran said. "It might be good for you to see where the man grew up."

Jennifer and Moran walked the short distance from the restaurant, minus Walsh, who had begged off, citing his long ride home to the North Bronx. The lower end of Park Slope was still made up of tenements and commercial warehouses, with children playing in the streets and adults sitting on the stoops of the shabby buildings they occupied. Jennifer found herself reminded of her own childhood neighborhood in South Boston, and she quickly pushed the memory away. She tried to keep her eyes looking straight ahead as she listened to Moran explain that this portion of the neighborhood had, so far, escaped gentrification—the infusion of young, affluent couples who would buy old tenements and renovate them into one-family homes—but her eyes kept straying to the children in the streets and the dull-eyed adults who seemed anesthetized by their surroundings.

Jennifer adjusted the ruffled cuffs of her blouse, which protruded from the sleeve of her gray, tailored suit, assuring herself she did not seem part of her surroundings. She felt a twinge of guilt but rejected it. It's not wrong to want something better, she told herself. It's not wrong to try to forget the ugliness you grew up with. She glanced at

Moran; his rumpled corduroy jacket above neat chino slacks and well-polished loafers. He was wearing a checked shirt and solid necktie and still looked, she thought, very much a part of what he had come from.

"Do you still live in Brooklyn?" she asked. Moran glanced at her, then looked ahead, and Jennifer felt herself tighten, wondering if she had made another faux pas. Damn him, she thought. She wouldn't let him intimidate her. It was his size, she told herself. Six feet and muscular, the body of an athlete slowly going to seed. And the voice, the deep male voice, something that, to her, had always projected the possibility of violence. The two things that intimidated most women. Unless they fought it, as she intended to do.

"I live in Manhattan," he said, still looking ahead. "I have for the past ten years."

"Where?" she asked.

"East Seventy-second, between York and the river."

Jennifer's eyes widened in surprise. It was a better neighborhood than she could afford. She knew the buildings and they were far better than her own on East Thirty-fifth. "I'm impressed," she said.

"Don't be. It's only a remodeled loft, but it suits my needs."

They reached Fifth Avenue, the Brooklyn version, and the area was suddenly transformed into a cluster of small shops. There was a fresh-produce store on the corner, then a bakery, a pork store, a fish market, and a grocery store, each bearing the ethnic flavor of the neighborhood's Italian heritage.

Moran stopped and nodded toward a storefront social club. "The local mafia clubhouse," he said.

Jennifer stared across the street. Men sat on old kitchen chairs in front of the club. They were all middle-aged, or older, dressed in short-sleeved shirts that looked as though they had seen better days, and poorly pressed slacks. "You're kidding," she said.

"Columbo family," he said. "If you expected *The Godfather*, forget it. The Hollywood version is much more romantic. Most of these guys are low-level numbers men, bookmakers, and loan sharks, and most of them have trouble making a living. They drive Cadillacs and Lincolns one step ahead of the loan companies that own them."

"But not all of them?" Jennifer said.

Moran shook his head. "There are a few heavy hitters. And some young Turks, mostly my age, who are into narcotics. They have a big flash for three or four years, and then we usually find them floating in Jamaica Bay." He inclined his chin toward the men across the street. "Those are the guys they call 'buttons.' They do all the dirty work, and most of the prison time. They're just too stupid to realize they're stupid."

Moran took Jennifer's arm and continued down the street. At the corner of Fifth Avenue and First Street he stopped in front of a grocery store as a short, balding man with a white apron tied around his waist hurried through the front door.

"Pete," the man said. "Jesus, it's been a long time. Where the hell you been?" He grabbed each of Moran's shoulders and held them, dwarfed by the detective's size.

Moran made a quick introduction, but all Jennifer caught was the first name: Gino. Moran looked back at the smaller man and grinned. "I've been busy locking up your *gumbas*," he said.

"Heah. Don't do that. Lock up the niggers. You'll do more good for the city."

Moran shook his head. "You still try to keep the black kids out of your store?"

Gino shrugged. "You can't do that no more. You'll have

fifty ministers parading up and down with signs if you try." He shrugged again. "It's not like the old days."

"Nothing is," Moran said. He grinned at the smaller man. "You look good."

"*Così, così,*" Gino answered in Italian. "*Comé sta?*"

"*Bene, grazie,*" Moran answered.

"Heah," Gino said. "At least you didn't forget your Italian."

"How could I? You dagos beat it into my head from the time I was five."

Gino glanced at Jennifer, then rattled off another question in Italian, too fast for her to get even a hint at the meaning. Moran simply shook his head in reply, and Gino shrugged again.

"I always knew you weren't too smart," he said.

Moran laughed. "I'll see you later. Say hello to your wife for me."

"I will," Gino said. "And don't be a stranger, huh?"

He took Jennifer's arm again and started across the street, heading up First Street in the direction of Prospect Park.

"Why did he say you weren't too smart?" Jennifer asked.

"He asked if you were my girlfriend. I told him you weren't."

"Sounds like a smart man to me," Jennifer said.

Moran looked at her; there was a hint of humor in his eyes, the first since she had met him. "I'll tell him you said so."

A few yards up the block Moran stopped in front of a small apartment building. He looked up. "This is where Tony grew up. Third floor front, on the left side."

Jennifer's eyes climbed the building, stopping at the grime-coated windows.

"His mother and sister still live in the neighborhood,"

Moran added. "In a renovated brownstone up near the park. Tony bought it for his sister as a wedding present."

"Nice present," Jennifer said.

"He was always good to his family," Moran said. "It was like a religion to him." He turned abruptly and inclined his head to a three-story brownstone across the street. "That's where I grew up," he said. "Top-floor apartment." He turned again, dismissing the information as quickly as he had given it. "A few houses up the street is where Joey Gambardella lived. He was part of our little boyhood troika." He looked at her, his eyes almost severe again. "If you do this story, you'll come across Joey. He's recording secretary for the union now. Tony had him elected after he got out of prison a few years back." He smiled. "His political friends arranged to have Joey's record expunged."

"Prison?" Jennifer questioned.

Moran's eyes flashed humor again. "That's not an impediment on the docks. In fact, it's probably worth a thousand votes." He looked up the street. "Anyway, if you come across Joey, be careful. He was a rotten kid and he hasn't improved."

"Rotten how?" Jennifer asked.

Moran let out a soft laugh, one devoid of humor. "When he was a kid, he used to take cats up on the roof, pour lighter fluid on them, set them on fire, and kick them over the side." He stared up at the rooftops. "He called them Italian Roman candles. He never understood the redundancy of the name he gave it."

Moran was watching her, awaiting some reaction, but Jennifer fought to remain cool.

"Later," Moran continued, "after the first time he got out of reform school, Joey had a job working for a local glass company installing windowpanes. He was working in this house where they were stripping the plaster off a wall to expose the brick. They were using muriatic acid, and Joey was fascinated with the way it just ate the plaster away. He went out and bought gallons of the stuff. He told us he had found something that would be wonderful to use on an enemy."

This time Jennifer couldn't hold back the shudder. "Nice kid," she said.

"Just so you know," Moran said.

They continued on up the gradually rising street toward Prospect Park, crossing Sixth Avenue, then Seventh and Eighth, and Jennifer noted that with each block the houses became larger, more ornate, and more openly affluent. A few houses from Prospect Park West, which bordered the park, Moran stopped again and pointed to a large, four-story limestone house.

"That's where Tony's mother and sister live," he said. "You might want to remember the number. He's here every Sunday for dinner. For him it's like going to church."

Jennifer detected the veiled sarcasm in Moran's voice. "You don't like him very much, do you?"

A look of pain flashed through Moran's eyes, then disappeared as his features hardened. "There are people I like better."

"But you were close as children, weren't you?" she asked.

Moran's jaw tightened. "We had a lot in common then." He forced a smile. "Let's stick to business, okay?"

Jennifer stiffened slightly. Forbidden territory. "Sure," she said. "If that's what you want, Pete."

Moran indicated Prospect Park West with his chin. "We can catch a subway a block from here," he said. They started to walk again, not speaking until Moran broke the silence. "You get to work on your research," he said at length. "When you think you know the questions you want to ask, give me a call and I'll set up a meeting with Maxwell."

"You think he'll see me?" she asked.

"I'll see to it that he does. Whether he answers your questions or not is up to you. Just make sure you know what you want to ask. You may only get one chance."

Pete Moran stared down at the East River. He was seated in one of two wing-backed chairs, placed before a window that covered most of the east wall of his large loft. Behind him a scattering of furniture, clustered in groups, sat in darkness, the only light coming from the glow of the cigarette he smoked. He had not thought about Tony for months now. It had been a conscious effort, even to the point of avoiding news articles that mentioned his name. But now things were different. Now he had the opportunity that had escaped him for so long.

His thoughts drifted to Jennifer Brady. Beautiful woman. And smart. But there was no doubt in his mind she intended to write a story that would add to Tony's growing legend. Yet another piece of garbage about the brilliant young labor leader.

He crushed the cigarette in an ashtray. Below, a tugboat pulled a barge downriver, moving at speed with the outgoing tide. But she needs you to get the story, he told himself. And she'll move in the direction you take her. He rested his head back against the chair and again felt the pain he had experienced earlier when walking through the old neighborhood. There had been good days then, good days that had become tainted. And all because of you, Tony. All because of you.

CHAPTER/FIVE

December 1962

THE LIVING ROOM was shrouded in darkness, the heavy curtains drawn across the windows, keeping the morning sunlight at bay. Tony sat on the worn sofa, his eyes fixed on the battered linoleum floor. From the kitchen he could hear his mother's sobs, the comforting words of his aunts as they tried to console her, and the faint sniffling of his sister, Carmela, her head pressed against his shoulder. He slipped his arm around the seven-year-old girl, his gangly thirteen-year-old body moving easily within the oversize blue suit he wore. He swallowed hard, trying to think of something to say, afraid if he did speak, he would begin to cry himself. And he knew he could not do that.

A large bulky figure loomed in the doorway of the kitchen, dressed in black, the heavy-featured face rigid and determined. His Aunt Marie.

"We gotta go now, Ant'ny," she said. "You gotta stay close to your mother. She's gonna need you close to her, God help her."

Tony helped his sister up, then stood. He was tall for

90

thirteen, already five foot eight inches, and the suit he wore belonged to a cousin who was eighteen and away in the army. But the cousin was bulkier, and as he stood, Tony felt the suit would slip from his body if he moved too quickly.

He took his sister's small hand. "We have to go, Carmela," he whispered.

"Are we going to the church?" she asked.

"First we have to go to the funeral home. Then we'll go to the church, and then to the cemetery." He felt her hand tighten in his. Another long sob came from the kitchen.

"I don't wanna go," she said, her voice small.

"We have to go," he whispered, placing his arm around her again and bending close to her. "It's Daddy's funeral. We have to go to his funeral."

Carmela began to whimper, and his Aunt Marie took two quick steps into the room. "Shut up, Carmela," she snapped, her voice low, so it wouldn't carry to the kitchen. "Whatsamatter with you? You want your mother to hear you?"

Tony's arm tightened around Carmela's shoulders. "She'll be all right," he said. He brought his face close to his sister's. "Won't you, Carmela?"

The child nodded her head, then pressed her face against Tony's side.

"Come on," Marie said. "Get your coats on. We gotta get your mother to the funeral home. She gotta be there when everybody comes."

The Luchese Brothers' Funeral Home was only a block from the apartment, but Marie insisted they drive there in her aging Chevrolet.

"A widow shouldn't walk no place," she said as they climbed down the three flights of stairs. She glanced back at Tony. "You remember that, Ant'ny. You're the man in this house now."

They drove in silence, Tony in the backseat with his mother and sister, his two aunts in front. Nothing was said as they circled the block, guided by the one-way streets, Tony's mother staring straight ahead, one hand tightened around a handkerchief, the other clutching a pair of rosary beads.

Angie Marco gasped as they pulled up to the funeral home and found the long black hearse already parked in front. Tony placed his hand on his mother's, but she seemed not to notice.

"It's all right, Angie," Marie said. "Come on. We gotta go inside. People are here already." She turned in the seat. "You all right?" She watched Angie nod her head, then reached back and adjusted the collar of her black cloth coat. "Help your mother outta the car, Ant'ny," she ordered.

Tony felt his mother's body stiffen as he eased her from the rear seat. Her breath came in short gasps, and he held her arm firmly, then took his sister's hand and moved them all in one solid mass toward the entrance.

Inside, the heavy odor of too many flowers mixed with the scent of burning votive candles to fill the air with a sickly, waxen sweetness. The cloying odor struck Tony at once; he hesitated, his body resisting the room where his father's body would be laid out in a coffin. The odor also struck his mother, her silence erupting into a wail that began low in her throat, then rose to a shattering pitch that sent shivers down Tony's back. She pulled away from him and lurched forward, her short, stocky body swaying as her legs threatened to give way. Her sisters rushed to her side, grabbing her arms to support her, only causing her legs to become less firm, less capable of holding her up.

"It's all right, Angie," Marie said as she wrapped a solid arm around her waist, lifting her. "Let's go sit down."

The other sister, Antoinette, small, thin, and wiry, pulled up on the other arm with even more strength, propelling Angie forward into the room where several dozen friends and relatives had already gathered.

Tony watched his mother stagger ahead, his hand gripping his sister's so hard that she whimpered in pain. He released it and slipped his arm around her, pulling her to him.

Inside the room his mother threw back her head and called out her husband's name in an agonizing cry. The parish priest, Father Donato, and the funeral director moved quickly to her.

"Why'd you die, Joseph? Why'd you leave us like this? Oh, Mother of God. Send him back to us. Send him back."

Father Donato placed his arm around Angie Marco's shoulder and began whispering to her. The funeral director stepped to her other side but was quickly blocked by Marie and Antoinette, who refused to relinquish their familial roles. Slowly they guided Angie to a row of chairs just to the left of the funeral bier. Tony stood just inside the doorway, uncertain now of what to do. He looked toward the coffin and was struck by his father's waxen features, eyes closed, hands overlapping his midsection, rosary beads entwined in his fingers. It didn't look like him. Something about his face was wrong, some feature not as it had been in life. They had said his chest had been crushed when a cable had broken, dropping the cargo they had been unloading toward him. Maybe some of it had hit his face. Maybe it had hit more of him than they said. Tony stared at the lower portion of the coffin, which was closed, and found himself wondering if they had done that because the rest of him had been too badly crushed. He tried to remember other funerals he had attended. His Aunt Marie's husband, three years ago, had been the last, but he couldn't remember if the lower half of the coffin had been closed then too.

"Ant'ny." His aunt's harsh whisper snapped his eyes forward. She motioned aggressively at him, and he moved toward her, pulling his sister with him.

"Sit with your mother now," his aunt said in a low voice when he reached her. "You gotta greet people when they come in. And keep your sister quiet," she added. She reached out and stroked Carmela's cheek, looking into her liquid brown eyes. "*La bambina*," she moaned as she turned away and started for her own seat in the front row of mourners.

The words brought more sobs from Tony's mother, and he took her arm and leaned close to her. "It's okay, Ma," he whispered.

She brought her handkerchief to her mouth and sobbed into it. "What are we gonna do, Ant'ny? What are we gonna do without him?"

Father Donato came quickly to her and took both of her hands. "Everything will be all right, Angela," his soft voice said. As she lowered her head and began shaking it back and forth, he extended one hand to her shoulder. "He's in a better place now, and he'll be looking down on you, watching out for you and the children."

"I want him *heeere*," Angie said, the final word coming out in a long, jagged sob.

"I know, I know," the priest said, bobbing his pale slender face until his wispy white hair began to flutter. It reminded Tony of the angel hair they spread on their tree each Christmas to hide the bare spaces between the branches. "We'll say some prayers in a few minutes. It will make you feel better." He turned his eyes to Tony. "Comfort her, Anthony. You have a big responsibility now. For her and your sister." He looked to Carmela. She had taken a small child-size rosary from her tiny purse, and it made the priest smile. He patted the hand that held the rosary. "What a good child," he said.

When the priest returned to his place by the door, Tony looked at the mourners for the first time. There were many more than he had realized. All the chairs were taken, and people were standing at the rear of the room, and through another door that led to a smoking lounge he could see still more. Some of the faces were strange— people who had worked with his father, he supposed— mixed in with others from the neighborhood and relatives, some of whom he hadn't seen in years. His eyes stopped briefly on Joey Gambardella and Petey Moran. They were seated together, still wearing their zippered jackets even though the room was stifling. His mother sobbed again, and he looked away. He felt as though he was on display, as though everyone was watching him, waiting to see if he would do the right thing. He wished he knew what that was; what was expected of him, and he wished his mother wouldn't cry so much and make people look at them.

A shadow passed before him, then stopped. He looked up and found two men standing before his mother. The first was short and thin with a hawklike face and cold blue eyes. The man's lips were pressed together in a narrow line. He was in his early forties, Tony guessed, but there were deep lines at the corners of his mouth and eyes that made him seem older. The second man stood slightly behind him, bull-like in a blue suit that seemed identical to the one worn by the first. He was slightly younger with a beefy face that made his eyes little more than slits, and Tony noticed that the knuckles of his right hand were scabbed over as though he had used them on someone recently.

The first man introduced himself as Moe Green, and his companion as Paul Levine. Tony knew the name. Mad

Moe Green, his father had called him, the president of the union's local. His father had always shaken his head with what seemed to be a sense of awe whenever he mentioned the man, and Tony was surprised to see how small he actually was.

Green spoke quietly to his mother. "I'm sorry for your loss," he said. "Joe was a good man, a hard worker, and we're going to miss him." His mother began to sob again, and Green stood there making no movement toward her, patient with her grief. When she looked up again and mumbled her thanks, he bent toward her. "Don't worry about the cost of the funeral," he said. "I spoke to the funeral director and he understands that the union will take care of it." Tony's mother began to thank him, but Green made a slight gesture with one hand, indicating it wasn't necessary. "We'll have someone come to your house and help you fill out all the benefit forms. If you have any problems before then, you call Paul." He paused. "Don't forget. Any problems at all."

Green took her hand and patted it, then straightened up, and leaned back toward Levine. Tony heard Levine whisper his name in Green's ear.

Green stepped in front of Tony. "You must be Anthony," he said. "Your father was very proud of you. You make sure your mother calls us if she has any problems." He waited as Tony nodded his head. "How old are you?"

"Thirteen, Mr. Green," Tony said.

The flicker of a smile came to Green's lips, then disappeared. He seemed momentarily pleased by the formality. He reached into his pocket and took out a business card. "When you're sixteen, you call me and we'll find you some part-time work that won't interfere with your school. But don't forget your school," he added. "It's the most important thing for you." Green glanced from Tony to his sister, taking in her small heart-shaped face.

"This is Carmela, my sister," Tony said. "This is Mr. Green, Carmela. And Mr. Levine."

The trace of a smile returned briefly, and Green reached out and cupped Carmela's chin in his hand. "She's a beautiful child," he said. "I have a daughter who's only a few years older than her." His eyes returned to Tony. "Take good care of her," he added. "Girls need someone to watch out for them."

Tony did not know what to say, but Green didn't seem to require an answer. He turned and walked toward a group of men who had formed near the door, Levine following him. Tony's eyes moved with the two men, and he watched as they stopped to shake hands and talk with the men near the door. Green appeared to say little, mostly nodding his head and uttering what seemed like terse replies. But the men hung on those brief words, and when Green moved away, Tony noticed that their eyes followed him out of the building.

The prayers were brief, punctuated by the sobs of Tony's mother, his aunts, and others who had joined the chorus of grief. But the priest, caught up in the solemnity of the loss of husband and father, droned out each prayer until Tony could feel the ache in his knees begin moving up into his thighs. When he had finished, Father Donato again came to the family and led them to the coffin as part of their exit ritual. Again Tony's mother burst forth, crying out for her husband to return, demanding that he not abandon her and her children. She threw herself forward, her arm across the body, the movement so quick and so violent that the coffin momentarily shook on its bier. The priest, assisted by Tony, eased her back as her sisters rushed forward, crowding in for support.

Tony felt helpless, uncertain what to do as his aunts elbowed their way between him and his mother. He looked into the coffin, noticing that his mother had forced his father's necktie out from under the fold of his suitcoat. His mother saw it, too, and she pointed and let out a wail as though the body had somehow been defiled. Tony stepped to the coffin and quickly slid the tie back under the coat. His hand froze when he felt the soft padding beneath his father's shirt. The word *crushed* came back to him, and he withdrew his hand slowly, as if any fast movement might cause the material to grab and hold him. His face had gone pale, and a shiver had begun at the base of his spine. He clenched his teeth and fought off a wave of panic.

"Kiss your father good-bye," his Aunt Marie said.

The words produced another cry from his mother, and his aunt turned back to her. Tony took his sister's hand and moved away from the coffin. He could feel the sweat along his back, but there was no sense of guilt at avoiding his aunt's instruction, only fear that she would notice and would force him to do it.

When they reached his aunt's car, they were forced to sit and wait for the others to leave, and for the coffin to be loaded in the waiting hearse. The car was cold, and the windbreaker Tony wore over his borrowed suit only protected his upper body and left his legs shaking beneath the thin material of the trousers, but he wasn't sure it was only from the cold. His teeth chattered, and he clenched them together again to keep the sound from the others. His aunt cursed the ineffective heater, banging a heavy hand against the dashboard, as if she could force the car to respond.

"It's got no respect for the suffering," she said. "I tell you, Angie, widows get nothing in this world. I know. *Madre mia,* how I know."

His mother sobbed agreement, and Tony wished he could reach across the seat and slap his hand over his aunt's mouth. Instead he sat and trembled.

Saint Francis Xavier Church was on the corner of Sixth Avenue and President Street, only two blocks from the funeral home, but the procession moved slowly, taken out of its way by the one-way streets, and more than ten minutes had passed before the cortege finally pulled up in front of the massive gray-stoned structure.

On the steps, Father Donato, who had gone ahead, stood in his funeral vestments, flanked by two altar boys Tony knew from school. They climbed the high stone stairs, his mother again supported by her sisters, followed by Tony and Carmela, then were led into the church and down the long central aisle to the first row of pews. Tony sat huddled next to his mother, his aunts behind them, and he prayed that the rest of it—the mass and the service at the cemetery—would go quickly. A funeral, he thought, had to be the longest thing that ever happened to a person, and the person it was for wasn't even there to see it happening. The thought dug at him. Jesus, was he denying his father the last thing anyone would ever do for him?

The graveside service, an hour later at Greenwood Cemetery, left him numb. His mother was no longer crying; she had settled into a steady moan, her body rocking slightly, each movement causing him to fear that she would topple forward and that his hand, clutching her arm, would be unable to support her.

The day, which had begun dark and overcast, had turned bright, and the sun caught the reflection of the highly polished wood of the coffin, creating flashes of light that forced him to lower his eyes. But he didn't mind. He didn't want to look at the coffin; he didn't want to think of his father inside it. He wanted to regard it as a thing that would simply cease to exist once he turned away from it. He no longer heard the priest's words, only the sound of his voice rising and falling as he read the final prayers.

The funeral director passed before them, handing each family member a solitary rose to place on the coffin at the end of the service. Only one more thing to do, he told himself. He would still have to go home and see the relatives who would gather for the food his aunts had prepared the previous night. But he knew he would be able to slip away without much trouble. And that was what he needed. To get away from them, from all of them, all the people who didn't seem to understand that he, too, felt pain.

They had taken paper plates of food and had gone up to the roof on the building. It was still cold outside, but the sun was high and warm, and the tar-paper roof seemed to hold the heat and radiate it up into their bodies. Tony and Petey and Joey sat in a tight circle, eating from the plates in their laps. In the distance, over the field of rooftops, rose the skyline of Manhattan, seeming impervious to everything other than its own false majesty. There were millions of people there, Tony told himself. And none of them knew anything about what had happened. He thought about that and drew a deep breath. Somehow it made life seem stupid.

"Man, this is good lasagna," Joey said. "I could eat this stuff until it came out of my asshole."

"Shut up, shithead," Petey said.

"Don't call me shithead," Joey snapped.

"Then don't talk like one," Petey snapped back.

Joey glared at him, then looked down at his plate. Petey was bigger than he was, and he knew he would whack him if he pushed it too far.

"Petey," Tony said. "When your father died last year, was the funeral as bad as it was today? I mean, was there all that crying and everybody bossing you around and stuff?"

Petey studied his plate. "I dunno, Tony. It was kind of military on account of my dad being a fireman killed in the line of duty. And the fire department handled everything. My mom and I kinda just got pulled along with it all." He looked up at Tony, seeming embarrassed by the question. "But she cried a lot, I guess. Just like your mom did."

"Heah, Tony," Joey interjected. "I don't mean no disrespect, but that's how Italian women are. They live for funerals. Shit, my mother goes outta her skull every time she goes to one, even if she don't know the person who croaked."

Petey swung his fist, catching Joey on his upper arm. "Heah, *scungil*, watch your mouth."

"I didn't say nothin'. Whatta you whackin' me for?"

Petey stuck his face forward. " 'Cause you're an asshole."

"Yeah, so's your mother," Joey snapped.

Petey started to lunge forward, and Tony stuck out his hand, stiff-arming him in the chest. "Come on. Not today, okay?"

Petey sat back and glared at Joey. "Just don't think I'll forget," he said.

"Yeah, yeah," Joey said. He dug into his plate again.

Tony stood and walked to the edge of the roof that faced First Street. There was a three-foot parapet, and he rested his arms on it and stared down into the street. Petey came up beside him and imitated the pose. After a few minutes Tony turned his face toward him.

"You mind if I ask you a question?" Tony asked. Petey shook his head. "When your father died"—he hesitated, uncertain how to phrase the question—"did they have the coffin open?" He paused again. "At the funeral home, I mean."

Petey nodded, then looked away. "Yeah. He wasn't burned, or nothin'. The building he was in, well, the floor fell out from under him, and a lot of stuff came down on top of him."

Tony hesitated, not certain he wanted an answer. He stuttered slightly as he began again. "I mean, did they have the whole coffin open or just the top part?" he asked.

"Just the top," Petey said.

Tony bit his lower lip, wondering if it was something they did when people were crushed. He turned his eyes back to the street. He could feel his emotion growing, twisting inside him. He could still see his father in the coffin; he could still feel the soft padding under his shirt. He wondered if he would always feel it.

"They shouldn't do that," he said at length.

"Do what?" Petey asked.

"Have the coffin open like they do." Tony felt his eyes filling, and he turned his head farther away and fought it. "That's the way I'm always gonna remember him now. And I don't want to remember him that way."

Petey was quiet for several moments. "My mom says it helps you understand that they're not gonna be around anymore," he finally said.

"Shit," Tony said. "It doesn't take a genius to figure that out. I saw my aunts packing his clothes in boxes."

"Yeah," Petey said, "I guess it *is* kinda stupid."

Joey sauntered up behind them. "Heah," he said. "Let's go up to Seventh Avenue and get an egg cream. Whaddaya say, huh?"

Tony turned around and looked into Joey's sharply pointed face. "Man, sometimes I think you could eat California. Besides, I haven't got any money."

"I got money," Joey said.

"Where'd you get money?" Petey asked. "You boost some old lady's purse or somethin'?"

Joey grinned. "I found it," he said.

"Yeah," Petey said. "Somebody forgot to nail it to the table and you found it."

Joey's grin widened. "Heah, what difference does it make? You wanna go or not?"

"Yeah, I'll go," Petey said. "How about you, Tony?"

Tony nodded. "Yeah, okay. Why not?"

Seventh Avenue was a steady flow of stores and shops with apartments above them, more diverse in nature and lacking the solidly ethnic feel of Fifth Avenue. At the corner of First Street stood P.S. 321, where the three boys were enrolled in the eighth grade. As they strolled by, Joey glanced up at the windows of their classroom.

"Man, I hope somebody looks out the window," he said. "They'll shit, they see us walking around like this."

Petey's eyes turned toward the window, and he found himself hoping Mary Beth Sweeney would look out. He would like her to see him like this, he thought. She'd probably think he was a wheel. Another thought crossed his mind. "Yeah," he said. "But what if the principal sees us and comes out and breaks our chops?"

"Break our chops for what?" Joey snapped. "Tony's father's dead, and our mothers sent notes about us goin' to the funeral. He can't do nothin'."

Tony's eyes darted to the windows; he found himself hoping no one would look out. For him the looks would be of pity, and he didn't want that. He never wanted that.

They turned the corner and headed toward the soda shop halfway down the block. A sharp wind, funneled between the rows of buildings, cut against their faces and turned their cheeks bright red. As they approached the shop Joey suddenly spread his arms wide, stopping them. He pointed across the street.

"*Madone.* Look at the size of the balloons on that one."

Tony and Petey followed Joey's gesture and saw an attractive young woman moving quickly along the opposite sidewalk, her hands clutching the collar of a thick imitation fur coat.

"Jesus," Petey said. "She's wearing a coat you could hide a St. Bernard in. How can you tell how big her tits are?"

"My old wazzoo tells me how big they are," Joey said. "And he says they're *big*."

"Shit," Petey said. "Now the asshole talks to his dork."

They entered the shop, found it empty except for the owner, and slid onto three stools at the soda fountain. The owner, a short, balding man with a deeply wrinkled face and holes in the elbows of his cardigan sweater, approached them with benign indifference.

"Three egg creams, Sam," Joey announced.

Sam looked at him levelly, not moving.

"I got the money," Joey said, reaching into his pocket and pulling out a wrinkled five-dollar bill. It was a rule of the shop. Money on the countertop before Sam's hand touched a glass.

"You robbed a bank?" Sam asked.

"I printed it in the cellar," Joey said.

"As long as the ink don't rub off," Sam said. He turned his face to Tony. "I'm sorry about your father. I would have come to the funeral, but I couldn't get anybody to mind the shop."

Tony nodded. "I know you would have, Sam. Thanks."

"How's your mother? She's okay?"

"She's okay," Tony said.

Sam began mixing the egg creams, keeping his eyes on the glasses. "You gonna haveta get a job now?"

"Yeah," Tony said. "Gino, at the grocery store, told me he could give me some part-time work. Stocking shelves and stuff. Deliveries. That sort of thing."

"You didn't tell me that," Petey said. "That's a good job. You can get tips on deliveries."

"I hope so," Tony said, looking at Petey and shrugging. Petey had a job hawking newspapers to help his mother support his three brothers and sisters. He worked Fourth Avenue, a main thoroughfare that fed approaches to the Manhattan and Brooklyn bridges, peddling the *Daily News* to cars stopped at traffic lights. Tony thought maybe he could do that, too, before school, if he could stake out a traffic light on Flatbush Avenue.

"Listen, I could tell you how to make some money," Joey said.

"No thanks," Tony said. He looked at Petey and they both began to laugh.

Three months had passed since the funeral. It was late March, and the weather had begun to change; people had taken to the stoops of their buildings, ending the winter solitude of being trapped inside their cramped apartments. Tony sat on the stoop of Petey Moran's building. He was reading a book on world history, underlining sections he thought pertinent. He was scheduled to take an entrance exam for Stuyvesant High School the following month, one of the city's schools for the exceptionally talented.

The door slammed behind him, and Petey bounded down the steps. "You finished yet?" he asked.

"Yeah, I just finished," Tony said.

"How much you make in tips at Gino's today?" Petey asked.

"A little over three bucks."

Petey whistled. "That's great. How much of that do you keep?"

"Nothing," Tony said. "Ma really needs the money right now. She's still got bills to pay from Christmas."

"Yeah. I know what you mean. The telephone company turned off our phone the other day. Boy, was my mom pissed. All those years my old man paid it like clockwork, and all of a sudden, whammo! No money, no phone. My mom told them to come and take it out." He grinned at Tony, then continued in a whisper. "She told them to shove it, too, but she didn't think I could hear."

"Sideways," Tony said. He stood and stretched. His back ached from carrying boxes of canned goods up from Gino's basement and from climbing flights of stairs with overloaded bags of groceries. But mostly he was worn out from the lack of time to himself. "Let's take a walk," he said.

"Sure," Petey said. "But I gotta be back in an hour."

They walked down Fifth Avenue, past the funeral home, and on until they reached Union Street. There they turned right, and began climbing the steep hill that led up to the park. Tony walked with his hands stuffed in the pockets of his jeans, the thumbs overlapping. He was a few inches taller than Petey but not as husky. He decided they probably looked just like what they were. Two kids with nothing to do and no money to do anything, anyway. It was not what he wanted. He knew that. And he began to wonder if he would pass the test for Stuyvesant and, if he did, if it would make any difference. At least he'd be out of the neighborhood for part of the day, he told himself. He'd be in Manhattan. And that had always seemed like a different world, almost a different country.

"You going to take any of the tests for high school?" Tony asked.

Petey shook his head.

"Why not? You're smart enough."

Petey shrugged. "I thought about it. But I could never sell papers and still make it into Manhattan in time."

"So get a different job," Tony said.

"Like what?" Petey asked. "You gotta be sixteen, or you gotta find somebody like Gino, who's willing to pay you off the books."

They continued walking, past rows of garbage cans that overflowed the alleys between buildings. They crossed Sixth Avenue, and up ahead they could see a group of firemen lounging in chairs outside a firehouse.

Petey raised his chin toward the men. "I used to kid my old man about the way firemen sat around on their duffs all day."

"Yeah, I know," Tony said. "Whenever my father came home with a case of booze or something, I used to kid him about it falling off the back of a ship."

The two boys glanced at each other, neither finishing his thought, neither willing to say he wished he had never said those things.

As they neared Seventh Avenue they heard shouts from around the corner. They hurried forward, then came to an abrupt halt. Ahead of them a short, fat man was struggling with Joey Gambardella. He had Joey by the collar of his coat and was trying to snap a pair of handcuffs on one of his wrists. Joey was fighting like a wild man, kicking at the fat man's shins and slapping his hand away each time he tried to get the handcuffs in place.

"Let go of me, you fat scumbag," Joey screamed. He spit in the man's face and received a sharp blow to his ear.

"I'll fix you, you fucking little thief. I'll have your ass locked up," the man shouted, his red face covered with sweat.

Petey raced forward, moving past the man and bringing his hand up sharply to hit the back of his head. He spun around, faced the man, and began dancing in front of him, barely out of reach. "Get me, too, you fat prick," he shouted.

Joey pulled back, trying to take advantage of the distraction, but the man held tight and slapped him again. "You

ain't going no place, you little dago bastard," he snarled.
He glared at Petey. "You, I'll get later."

"You'll get your mother," Petey shouted. "Just like everybody else does."

The man swung his free hand at Petey's head, but Petey moved easily out of reach, and the effort made the fat man stagger.

Joey twisted violently, trying to free himself, and from under his coat a whole ham popped free, fell to the sidewalk, and rolled a few feet away.

The man held Joey's collar firmly, and Tony lowered his shoulder and raced forward, slamming it into his kidney. The man grunted but still held fast to Joey. Tony bent down and picked up the ham, swung it away from his body, then drove it forward with one hand, smashing it into the fat man's face.

Blood erupted from the man's nose as the ham fell away, and his hands flew up to his face, freeing Joey. Tony grabbed Joey's arm and pulled him down the street, with Petey only a step behind. The man screamed obscenities at them, and Joey pulled his arm free and skidded to a halt. He spun around and grinned at the man, then raised his forearm, middle finger extended. He reached back into his coat and pulled out a prepackaged steak. "I'll think of you when I eat this, you fat prick," he shouted.

The man lurched forward in a lumbering run, and the three boys turned and ran. They raced along Seventh Avenue, turned into First Street, then cut across the playground of the school, and into Second Street. Halfway down the block, with the man still not in sight, they jumped the low iron gate of a brownstone and ducked behind a row of heavy bushes.

They remained there, listening for footsteps as their breath slowly returned.

"The fat fuck gave up," Joey said. He looked at Tony. "Man, you really gave him a shot with that ham," he said. "I think you broke his fucking nose."

Tony stared at him, incredulous. "What the hell did you try to steal a whole ham for?" he asked.

Joey shrugged. "What can I say? I like ham."

Petey started to laugh. "He likes ham," he said. "He likes fucking ham. Can you believe how stupid this asshole is?"

CHAPTER/SIX

April 1984

THE TAXI RACED up Madison Avenue, weaving from lane to lane, fighting for every foot of advantage it could gain. Pete turned his head abruptly and stared at Jennifer across the rear seat. "I'm not sure this is a good idea."

She thought she heard a slight note of tension in his voice. "I don't see what harm it can do," she said.

"If Tony sees us together, it could do a lot of harm. He'll know you're looking into areas he'd rather have left alone."

Jennifer brushed back a strand of hair, recalling her last meeting with Marco, when nothing had appeared glossed over or hidden. She thought he had been honest then, still thought so. About everything except his wife. She glanced at Pete and wondered why he was so tense. "We can go in separately and leave separately. There's no reason for him to think we're together."

Pete looked out the window. The taxi had slowed to a crawl, blocked now by the traffic ahead. "You mean, no one would think you'd take someone like me to a political

110

fund-raiser." A small smile came to his lips, then faded. "Only kidding," he said. "But I still don't see the point in it. And it won't seem natural."

"Don't cops go to cocktail parties for politicians?" she asked.

"Only the ones looking for political help in getting promotions."

"But not you."

"That's right."

"So everyone will simply think you've seen the light. Will your boss be there?"

Pete nodded. "And he'll be delighted to see *me* there, along with the other political flunkies who work for him."

Maybe that was it, Jennifer thought. It bothered Pete's ego that he would appear to be playing politics. She reached out and laid her hand on his. "The point *is*," she said, "that you might overhear something that might be significant, and that I might miss completely." She removed her hand and sat back.

That was only part of the truth, and a small part at best. She wanted to see them in the same room; see if the hatred Pete felt for Marco was mutual. It was part curiosity, but it also might tell her how much she could trust Pete's help. And, she hoped, after seeing Marco perhaps Pete might talk about it.

The taxi turned east on Sixtieth Street, then pulled to the curb in front of a red canopy that protruded from the grilled facade of the Metropolitan Club.

Jennifer began to open her purse, but Pete extended a hand, stopping her. "You go on ahead. I'll take care of this, then follow you in later."

"Shall we meet later?" she asked as she got out of the taxi.

"Go back to your apartment and I'll call you," he said.

When she entered the reception area of the Metropolitan

Club, Jennifer was greeted by a distinguished gray-suited man, wearing a nameplate that gave only his first name. He smiled and bowed slightly. "May I help you, madam?"

Jennifer explained she was attending the reception and, on request, produced her invitation, which was conspicuously stamped with the word *press*. The man glanced at the word, then back at her, a note of concern in his eyes that he quickly masked. It seemed the media was seldom allowed through the portals of the club.

He led her through the reception area, past a large screen, and into an enormous marble hall. He gestured with one hand. "If you will go through the Great Hall, madam, the reception is in the West Lounge at the opposite end."

After she had decided to attend the reception Jennifer had checked out newspaper files on the club. It had been founded in 1894 by a group of prominent businessmen, a group that included J. Pierpont Morgan and Cornelius Vanderbilt. The building, itself, had been designed by Stanford White and included among its present members the most influential of the world's business leaders, prominent American families, and a sprinkling of foreign royalty. Crossing the Great Hall, Jennifer marveled at the surroundings that members took as common occurrence. With the elegance of a Venetian palazzo, the ceiling, fifty-five feet above, was studded with rectangles of gold and red. The walls and floor were of highly polished marble, and the room was dominated by a massive stone fireplace and a sweeping twin staircase that rose to an encircling mezzanine.

When she entered the West Lounge, Jennifer again found herself in awe of the room's beauty. One hundred feet long and half again as wide, the room was dominated by two large marble fireplaces at each end; a row of floor-to-ceiling windows that looked out on Fifth Avenue;

and a frescoed ceiling, painted on canvas, in the Louis XIV style. Done in muted tones of crimson and dotted by crystal chandeliers and wall sconces, the room gave off a sense of Old World sedateness that Jennifer found both beautiful and overpowering.

There were slightly more than a hundred people in the room, and Jennifer scanned the group until she spotted Marco standing with a group of men near one of the fireplaces. Off to his left, talking with another small group, was Anne Mobray.

Jennifer accepted a glass of wine from a passing waiter, then moved slowly through the room, heading in the direction of Marco and Anne Mobray. She wanted to be close by when Marco saw Pete for the first time in order to gauge his reaction. The thought of approaching the group he was with crossed her mind, but she quickly rejected it. Not with Ms. Mobray so close. She'll sweep in and hurry him away, and you'll never get close again, she told herself.

Instead Jennifer positioned herself a few feet from the group Marco was with, attached herself to an elderly man who seemed to be both alone and safe, and kept her attention riveted on Marco as they spoke.

Marco laughed at the joke. It was not a funny joke, not even amusing, but he laughed, anyway, because it was expected. God, they were a dreadful group, he thought. Powerbrokers all, some more so than others, but each posturing to make himself seem more important than the next. But that was politics: the pretense of power, concern, intelligence, interest, knowledge. And the one who offered the best pretense usually came out on top.

A man on his left, whose name momentarily escaped him, was speaking to him, and Tony realized he had not heard a word he had said. He offered a slight smile and nodded, and the man turned away and started on someone else. Just agree with them and you're their friend for an hour, he told himself. Disagree and they'll hate you for the rest of their lives. No, not hate. They'll simply consider you unworthy of respect.

He shifted his feet and looked toward one of the windows, thinking how much he would prefer to be walking along Fifth Avenue, away from all the prattle. As he began to turn his attention back to the group, he saw Jennifer. She was only a few yards away, talking with a shipping company executive. He waited until she looked toward him, then smiled. She was dressed in a tailored business suit that accentuated the slender lines of her body, and it made her seem both businesslike and sensual, he thought.

Jennifer felt sudden elation as she saw Tony break away from the group and start toward her, then caught herself and glanced toward Anne Mobray to see if she had noticed. It would have been better, she told herself, if he had stayed with the group; it would offer less chance of a sudden interruption. Yet she felt distinct pleasure at seeing him move toward her, a nervous, satisfying sensation she had felt about few men.

As Tony came to her he smiled. "Nice to see you again," he said, then turned to the man beside her. "Nice to see you too. Mr. Jacobson, isn't it?"

The older man nodded abruptly. He was of average height, bald, with tuffs of white hair around his ears and a bushy white mustache. Earlier his blue eyes had seemed bright and friendly. Now they seemed hard, and his body stiffened.

Jacobson turned to Jennifer. "You must forgive me," he said, "but there are some people I must see." Without another word he turned and left.

Jennifer's eyes widened as she watched him stalk away. She turned back to Marco. "Was it something we said?"

Tony smiled and laughed softly. "I'm afraid Mr. Jacobson

is an executive with a shipping company. And I'm not on his socially acceptable list."

"You must have made his life very difficult," she said.

Tony's smile broadened. "Anytime we don't roll over and play dead when asked, they consider us difficult."

"Still, that was quite a reaction."

Tony repressed another smile. "You have to remember that Mr. Jacobson is British. And British executives tend to regard labor unions as one step to the left of Lenin."

Jennifer smiled and nodded. "We have some of those at the paper too."

"I'm sure you do," Tony said. "And is that why you're here? Covering this for the paper?"

"Just seeing if there's anything worth covering." She glanced around the room. "Looks like an interesting group."

"You'd be amazed how *un*interesting."

She looked at him with surprise. "I thought people with political interests found all politicians interesting."

"It's just me," Tony said. "Just tonight. I've even been forgetting the names of the people I know. I think I'd just prefer to be somewhere else."

"Too much of a good thing?"

"Too much of the same thing."

Jennifer allowed her eyes to roam the room. Pete was still not there. "Are most of these people members of this club?" she asked, buying time.

"I rather doubt it," Tony said. "I think a member has to sponsor the reception, but most of the people here are involved in Democratic politics. I doubt many Democrats belong to this club. One of its honorary members is Richard Nixon."

Jennifer glanced around again, this time concentrating on the opulence of the room. "No members from the Kennedy clan?"

"I seriously doubt it."

She turned back to him. "And Tony Marco is not a member."

"Ah, applying for membership might be interesting. Just to see how many votes I'd get from the Board of Governors." His eyes had brightened with the humor of the idea, but as he looked away from Jennifer they suddenly clouded.

She followed his gaze. Pete was standing at the opposite end of the room, his eyes fixed on Marco, his face hard and unforgiving.

She turned back to Marco in time to see him nod in Pete's direction. There was a look on his face, in his eyes, that she could not quite identify. Concern? Tension? She looked at him more closely. No, she decided, neither of those. It was more a look of regret. "Someone you know?" she asked.

He turned his attention back to her. "A friend from a long time ago."

Jennifer felt her pulse quicken. "Well, if you'd like to speak to him, I'll certainly understand."

The clouded look returned to his eyes, then evaporated. He smiled weakly. "We haven't been friends for a long time," he said.

"Oh, I'm sorry."

"So am I," Tony said.

Jennifer was about to ask why but hesitated. Then it was too late, as Anne Mobray moved to Tony's side.

She smiled at Jennifer with cold eyes as she linked her arm into Tony's. "Hello," she said.

Tony turned to her. "Anne, you remember Ms. Brady, don't you? She's a reporter for the *Globe*, and she was at your party last week."

Anne's cold smile returned. "Oh, yes, of course. Are you here reporting on the reception?" There was a slight cutting quality to her voice but one that only another woman would notice.

"If there's anything to report," Jennifer said.

"Oh, I'm sure there will be. One just has to know where to look for it." Anne raised one finger to her throat, stroking it lightly. "I understand you're interested in doing a story on Tony."

"Very much so."

Anne hesitated, almost as if timing her next line. She widened her eyes in innocence. "I do hope it will be a favorable story," she said.

"So far there's nothing about Mr. Marco that I've found unfavorable." She watched the line on Anne's jaw tighten almost imperceptibly, then looked up at Tony. "Well, I really should circulate," she said, looking back at Anne. "That's the only way I'll find out if there *is* anything to report."

"I hope we'll meet again soon," Tony said.

"I'm sure we shall." She smiled at Anne. "Very nice meeting you again." Jennifer turned and walked away.

Looking for Pete, she wandered to the far end of the room but still did not see him. Damn it, she thought. She glanced toward one of the bars and saw him turning, drink in hand. When their eyes met, he gave a discreet shake of his head, then moved away.

Okay, she thought, we'll play it your way. But I want to know what that look on Marco's face meant. She saw the shipping executive, Jacobson, again and walked up beside him. "I'm so sorry you had to rush off before," she said.

He looked at her, his face and eyes cheerful again. "Yes," he said, "so was I. I just don't particularly care for the gentleman who joined us."

Jennifer allowed her eyes to widen slightly.

"That surprises you?" he asked.

"Frankly, yes. I've heard only complimentary things

about Mr. Marco." She looked away for a moment. "In fact, I've even heard he's being considered for a post in the next Democratic administration."

"Then let us hope the Republicans win," Jacobson said in a clipped, annoyed voice.

"Why do you say that, Mr. Jacobson?"

Jacobson drew himself up. "Let us just say I have a great deal of admiration for your government, and I would find it regrettable if a position of authority was given to a thief and a scoundrel."

Jennifer's surprise was real now. "Why do you say that?" she asked, a bit too quickly.

Jacobson shook his head. "It's really of no importance."

"But it is."

Jacobson's eyes became wary. "Why does it interest you?"

Jennifer drew a deep breath. It was time to bite the bullet. "I'm a newspaper reporter, Mr. Jacobson. And I'm presently working on a story about Mr. Marco. So I'm very interested."

Jacobson's body became as rigid as it had earlier. "I'm afraid I have nothing to say, Miss Brady. And I'm afraid you'll simply have to attribute my previous remarks to having had too much to drink." Without further word he turned and walked away.

Jennifer watched him go, her mouth slightly open. A waiter passed with a tray of wine, and she quickly took a glass, needing it more than wanting it. She let out a deep breath. "Wow," she whispered to herself.

"So, you're wondering now if Anthony Marco's sainthood has been exaggerated."

She listened to Pete's voice over the telephone and felt slightly irritated by the smug tone. "Let's just say I'm very interested in finding out."

"I warned you, you might find out more than you bargained for."

"And maybe all I'll find is a shipping company executive who thinks a good labor contract is tantamount to theft," she snapped.

"If that's what you suspect, why bother?"

"Look, Pete, I just don't want to go off half cocked. But I do want to know."

There was a long pause on the other end of the line. "Well, get back to studying your clippings, then," he said. "In the meantime I'll try to set up that meeting." He paused again. "And I'll also find out which shipping company this guy Jacobson works for. You never know. You may have gotten a big break."

"What do you mean?" Jennifer asked.

"You may have found out where to start looking."

Tony sat in the corner of the large sectional sofa, staring out the window at the skyline of lower Manhattan. He drew heavily on a cigarette, trying to let the tobacco and the view calm his nerves. He glanced at his watch. Midnight and Shirley was still out.

He had had dinner with Anne after the reception, and the evening had become little more than another effort to smooth over her endless jealousy. Damn, it was all such a pain in the ass, he thought. The repetitive political functions, each one seeming identical to the one before. Shirley's nocturnal disappearances. Anne's continuous jealousy. All the bullshit you have to accept to get where you want to go.

He heard the sound of the door opening, then closing behind him.

"Oh, you're home already." Shirley's voice was a mixture of surprise and defiance.

"Obviously," he said. "Did you have a nice evening?"

He didn't turn, preferring to let her speak to the back of his head.

"Yes, I did. I saw a very interesting movie. It was about—"

His voice cut her off. "I'm really not interested in the movie," he said, refusing to listen to one of the regurgitated reviews Shirley used to cover her evening assignations.

There was a pause. "Bad day?" she asked.

"No more than usual."

Another pause. "Are you coming to bed?"

"I'm going to sit up a bit. I'll see you in the morning." He listened to the silence behind him, then the rustling of her clothing as she turned quickly and walked down the hall to their bedroom.

He leaned his head back against the sofa and took another long drag on the cigarette. His earlier thought returned: all the bullshit you have to accept to get where you want to go. He closed his eyes. *If* you really want to go. He thought about that, then shook his head. It was just the pressure, he told himself. The pressure of the union, of his ambitions, of everything he'd been forced to do to get where he was. The pressure of seeing Pete again. Damn, he thought, what wouldn't you give to go to a bar with him, sit and talk, have a beer together? Just have it the way it was when you were kids together. Tony crushed out the cigarette, then stood and walked to the window. But we're not kids anymore, he thought. And sometimes I wonder if we ever were.

CHAPTER / SEVEN

June 1966

TONY CLIMBED OUT of the subway at Brooklyn's Borough Hall, feeling a sudden tightness invade his stomach. He had grown taller in the past two years. Now, at the end of his sophomore year in high school, he was already six feet with a lean, quickly developing body that had left most adolescent awkwardness behind. He drew a deep breath, allowed his eyes to adjust to the sunlight that flooded Court Street, then opened his notebook and checked the address he had written there.

He started up the street, moving quickly, the low-cut gym shoes giving him a long, bouncing stride, the heavy blue jeans rubbing rhythmically along his inner thighs, the poor-quality sport shirt, starched and ironed by his mother, crackling with each movement. Halfway down the block a brass plate affixed to one of the buildings announced the existence of the longshoremen's union offices. Tony hesitated, checking the number of the building against the one he had written down, then started up the wide stone stairs.

When he stepped through the heavy oak doors, he found himself in a tiled foyer. To his right a wide staircase rose along one wall. Next to the staircase a woman was seated behind a small reception desk. She looked to be in her mid-fifties, and the heavy red lipstick she wore clashed with the red of her hair and the pale blue eye shadow; he could see that the thick makeup on her cheeks had broken into cracks at the corners of her eyes.

When Tony approached the desk, the woman glanced up at him, then turned her attention back to the magazine she was reading. "You want something?" she asked.

"I wanted to see Mr. Green," Tony said.

"Mr. Green's a busy man." The woman turned a page of the magazine with a long red fingernail.

Tony swallowed and shifted his weight from one foot to the other. "I called yesterday, and his secretary told me to come this morning."

The woman stared at him for several moments, as though her eyes would force him to admit the lie. "What's your name?" she finally asked.

"Tony Marco." He watched her write it on a message pad.

"What time's your appointment?"

"I was told to come at eleven." Tony shifted his books to his other hand and waited as the woman consulted her wristwatch.

"You're ten minutes early," the woman said. She motioned with her chin toward a sofa along the opposite wall. "Go sit over there."

Tony did as he was told, noting that the woman had returned to her magazine rather than use the telephone on her desk. Goddamn old bag, he thought.

When ten minutes had passed, the receptionist picked up her phone, dialed two numbers, then replaced the receiver and returned to her magazine. Five minutes later a heavyset man in a tightly fitted brown suit descended the staircase.

Tony watched him across the foyer and recognized him as the man who had attended his father's funeral with Moe Green. He struggled to remember his name, found he could not, and simply stood and smiled as the man approached.

"Hey, kid. Good to see you again," the man said, taking Tony's hand in a bearlike grasp. "You remember me, don't you? Paul Levine. I was with Moe at your father's funeral. How's your mother and sister?"

"They're fine, Mr. Levine," Tony said. He wanted to say more, especially that he remembered Levine, but the man stopped him.

"That's good," Levine said, taking his arm and leading him back toward the staircase. "Moe's upstairs in his office. He's going to be surprised to see how much you've grown."

When they reached the top of the stairs, Levine leaned toward Tony in a stage whisper. "How'd you like Gert?" he asked.

"Who?"

"The receptionist," Levine said.

Tony's cheeks reddened slightly. "Oh, she was fine," he lied.

"She's a dragon," Levine whispered. "That's why we've got her down there. Even the goddamn FBI couldn't get past her." They moved down a wide hall. "Her husband died on the job, like your father," Levine continued. "So we gave her a job here. Sometimes I think he did it on purpose, just to get away from her."

Despite his nervousness, the idea made Tony laugh.

Moe Green was seated behind an impressively large wooden desk, framed between two floor-to-ceiling windows. Tony had never seen anything like the office—the rich, paneled walls; the leather furniture; the carpeting that seemed to swallow half his gym shoes.

Moe Green came around his desk and squeezed Tony's arm, then waved his hand at the room. "How do you like it?" Green asked, his hawklike face showing a trace of a smile at the boy's reaction.

"It's really something, Mr. Green."

He gestured toward a leather sofa, directing Tony to sit there while he and Levine took matching club chairs opposite. "You probably thought we worked out of some crummy room in the back of a warehouse, like in the movies," Green said, his cold blue eyes hinting pleasure. "Believe me, in the old days we did. But now we have to have all this"—he gestured at the room again—"just to let those big shots in the shipping companies know they can't push us around." Green smiled, and the coldness of it made Tony twist slightly in his seat. "So tell me, how's your family? You all getting on okay?"

Tony swallowed hard. "Everyone's fine, Mr. Green. It's just that things are kinda hard with—"

Green cut him off. "Money. I know. It's hard even with a mother and father both working full-time these days."

"We're not complaining, Mr. Green." Tony's words were hurried, trying to make that point before Green got the wrong impression. "The union benefits really help, and we get social security, and my Mom and I both work. It's just—"

"What kind of work you doing?" Green asked, cutting him off again.

"I work in a market in the neighborhood. Delivering groceries, stocking shelves, and working the cash register on weekends. The man who owns it gave me the job right after the funeral, and he pays me under the table so there's no deductions, but it's still not very much." Tony hesitated, then rushed ahead. "My mother works too. She cleans other people's apartments. But she has to travel to Brooklyn Heights or Manhattan to do that, so she can't make an awful lot, either."

"Nobody in your neighborhood has people cleaning their houses, eh?" Green snorted, then nodded his head. "Nobody in my neighborhood could ever afford that, either." Green leaned forward in his chair. "So if things were tight, kid, how come you didn't come to us sooner?"

"Well, you told me when I was sixteen, you might be able to get me some work on the docks, and I'll be sixteen next week."

"I also told you to make sure your mother let us know if she was having any problems," Green said.

Tony wiped his palms on the knees of his jeans. "Things haven't been that bad, Mr. Green. I've been able to bring in enough money so we could get by." He hesitated and wiped his palms again. "It's just that with my sister getting older, and me in high school, things are getting more expensive. And I don't like to see my mother working so hard and having nothing to show for it."

Green sat back in his chair and began drumming his fingertips together. "I bet you don't like it that she's cleaning other people's houses."

Tony shrugged; his cheeks reddened. "She wouldn't stop doing it even if I could bring in more money. And she'd probably smack me if I told her I wanted her to."

Green let out a long laugh. "And she'd be right. It's good honest work. You should never be ashamed." He watched the color in the boy's cheeks deepen. "But you're right too. You should always want something better for your family. It's all right. You're not thinking of quitting school, are you?"

Tony shook his head. "No, sir. I want to go to college, even law school, if I can make it."

Green nodded. "How's your grades?"

"All A's so far. But it gets harder every year."

Green arched his eyebrows in appreciation. "Where do you go?" he asked.

"Stuyvesant High School."

"Isn't that one of the special schools you have to take a test to get into?"

"Yes, sir."

Green pursed his lips and nodded approval. "You must be a smart kid." He motioned with his hand toward a framed photograph on his desk that showed a pretty young girl with long dark hair. "My daughter Shirley," Green said. "She wanted to go to Music and Art High School, but I didn't want her going up to Harlem every day." He shrugged. "She's still mad at me about it. But she goes to a good private school over on the next street. Packer Collegiate. You ever hear about it?"

"It's supposed to be very good," Tony said.

Green snorted. "It better be, for the goddamned money they charge." He clapped his hands together. "But let's get back to you. I guess you want that job on the docks."

"Yes, sir."

"That I can do," Green said. "The day after your birthday you can go to work as an extra longshoreman. We'll make sure you get three or four hours every day. But if it starts to interfere with your school, you have to promise to let Paul know." Tony began to speak, but Green raised a hand stopping him. "Don't worry. If you can't work that much, we can still work out the money question. Trust me."

Green waved off Tony's thanks, returned to his desk, and, over the telephone, told his secretary to give the boy the forms that had to be filled out. When he replaced the receiver, Green gave Tony an abrupt nod. "Okay. You're set. You fill out the papers and get them back to us as quick as you can. Then you come here the day after your birthday and Paul will take you down to the docks and get you squared away." Green raised his hand as Tony again tried to thank him. "You run along now. You don't want to miss any time on your other job."

When the door closed behind the boy, Levine gave his friend a long, sideward glance.

Green acknowledged the look with a shrug of his shoulders, then returned to his chair behind the desk.

"You really went overboard for this kid," Levine said.

"You think so?"

"Yeah, I think so." Levine paused, studying Green, amused by his reticence about the special treatment. "Look, I don't give a damn. But normally, sure, we give the kid a card. But then he takes his chances like everybody else. And he works when the work's available." Levine allowed a small smile to come into his normally flat brown eyes. "Suddenly this kid gets a promise of three to four hours a day. I'm just curious about what makes him different."

Green raised his hands, then let them fall back to his desk. "How do they say it, those fancy goyim at the shipping companies? Maybe I like the cut of his jibe."

Levine let out a low laugh. "You do, huh?"

"Look, Paul. He's a nice kid. He's got good manners. But he's still got chutzpah. I'd like to see what else the kid's got." Green smiled at the foolishness of the idea. "Hell, he'll probably take one look at the animals who work down there and be back in his grocery store with his tail between his legs."

"But you hope not," Levine said.

"Let's just say I'm curious," Green said. "Let's say this boy reminds me of somebody I knew when I was a kid."

Levine smiled despite himself. "Really, Moe. And who was that?"

Green jabbed his thumb against his chest. "Me," he said.

*   *   *

Mary Beth Sweeney sat on the steps of the brownstone, her body positioned as close to Pete Moran's as possible. She was dressed in shorts that exposed every inch of her very attractive legs, and a T-shirt that delineated breasts that, although Mary Beth was only fifteen, would have caused envy among many mature women.

As Tony Marco came through the front gate she smiled and sent the fingers of one hand casually through her blond hair. Her blue eyes brightened when she first saw him but became slightly irritated now as Tony concentrated his attention on Pete Moran.

"So how'd it go?" Pete asked.

Tony shrugged, rolled his eyes, then broke into a grin and raised the thumb of his right hand.

"Fantastic," Pete roared. His face seemed to explode with pleasure as his slightly crooked smile spread across his face. Like Tony, he had grown considerably over the past two years. Now, an inch shorter than his friend but ten pounds bulkier, he had the look of a boy soon to emerge as a ruggedly handsome young man.

Tony leaned against the railing and shook his head. "I still can't believe it."

"So tell me what you can't believe," Pete demanded.

Tony shook his head and grinned. "The most I hoped for was that I'd get my name on a list and maybe get some work this summer." The grin widened. "Starting next week they're going to give me three to four hours a day as an extra."

"Jesus," Pete said. "You'll be knocking down real bread. So tell me what happened when you went there."

Tony described the meeting.

"Man, you really fell in it," Pete said, his voice filled with wonder over his friend's luck.

"Your mother is going to have a fit when she finds out," Mary Beth offered.

Pete gave her a look of disbelief. "Little Mary Sunshine," he said. "Aren't *you* filled with encouraging words."

Mary Beth lifted her chin and stuck out her lower lip. "Well, it's true just the same, and you know it."

Pete shook his head and began to laugh softly. He looked up at Tony. "What *are* you gonna tell her?" he asked.

Tony shrugged. "I'll tell her it's a job in the dock office, running errands, filing papers, stuff like that. That way she won't worry." He pursed his lips and blew out to emphasize his relief. "Man, we need the money. This is just too good to pass up." He turned to Mary Beth, a pleading look in his eyes. "Don't say anything about this or it could queer everything."

Mary Beth looked away. "I won't say anything. What do I care if you want to break your neck working the docks."

"Please," Tony said, bringing her eyes back to his.

"I *said* I wouldn't," Mary Beth snapped.

"I already told Gino the same thing," Tony said.

"Jesus, that's right. You'll haveta give up your job at the store," Pete said.

Tony leaned closer. "When I told him, I asked him if he was going to hire somebody else and I suggested you. He said if you want the job, you can have it."

"No shit," Pete said, the grin back on his face. "Hell, with the newspapers in the morning and that job in the afternoons and weekends, I could really knock down some dough. He really said that?"

Tony nodded, pleased he had been able to offer his friend something.

"That's great," Mary Beth said. "Now I'll never see you." Her eyes were sulky.

Pete slipped his arm around her and pulled her against

his side. "We'll find time," he said, nuzzling her ear. "Remember, your old man works nights and your mother goes to bingo three times a week."

"Sure," Mary Beth said. "And what do I do, lock my little brother in the closet?"

Tony looked away, hiding a smile. Mary Beth's main concern, he thought, was that she was going to lose some necking time. He glanced back at Pete and couldn't help feeling a touch of envy.

CHAPTER/EIGHT

PAUL LEVINE GUIDED Tony through the gates of the high cyclone fence that surrounded piers six and seven of the Red Hook Marine Terminal at the foot of Sackett Street. Tony carried a gym bag with his work clothes. Earlier Levine had asked about the bag, and Tony had explained it held clothes he hoped to leave at the docks.

Levine had smiled. "What kind of job did you tell your mother we gave you?"

Tony had blushed and had begun to offer a stuttering reply. But Levine had only said, "Just so she doesn't call up and start screaming at us."

Now, moving along the pier with Levine, Tony took in the organized chaos that surrounded him. At the ends of the piers huge gantries loomed above the berthed ships, their massive, floating cranes lifting containers as large as trailers from the ships' holds. Levine paused and pointed to the off-loaded cargo. "That's one of the best jobs down here," he said. "Working container ships. But it's also the most dangerous. If those containers shift, or if the crane fouls, the men in the holds don't have much of a chance."

Tony's mind jolted back to his father's funeral, to the padding that had hidden his crushed chest, and he wondered if his father had died in just such a ship. Levine's voice brought him back.

"But you don't have to worry about that. The work takes more training than you'll get as an extra. You'll probably start out in the warehouse until you get the hang of things. But eventually you'll end up in the hold of some break bulk ship." He paused again. "It's lousy work, but everybody does it. The loose cargo sweats, and you get a soup in the bottom of the hold that smells like five hundred Chinamen died in there. But you get used to it." Levine hesitated again, awaiting some reaction. "You still want the job?" he finally asked.

Tony nodded his head. "Yes, sir," he said, not sure at that moment if he was speaking truthfully.

"Okay," Levine said, smiling at the boy. "Let's go to the office and get you squared away."

The office was in the middle of the two piers in the front of one of the warehouses. Levine stopped outside the door and took Tony by the arm. "This is the office of the stevedore company that does the hiring for the shipping companies that use these berths." He hesitated to offer a cold smile. "But don't pay any attention to the blowhard who runs this place. He hires who we tell him to hire, or he finds out he doesn't have anybody to hire at all."

Levine entered the small, cluttered office with Tony at his heels. A secretary and several clerks looked up from their desks and waited expectantly.

"Would you tell O'Keefe I'd like to see him," Levine said to the secretary.

Moments later a burly, red-faced man with thinning hair and dull blue eyes emerged from the office and walked slowly to the counter that formed a barrier across the office.

"Hello, Paul. What can I do for you?" he asked.

"Let's step outside a minute," Levine said.

O'Keefe drew a deep breath. "Sure," he said as he started around the counter and followed Levine and Tony outside.

O'Keefe ignored Tony and squared his heavy shoulders toward Levine. "So, what's up, Paul?" he asked.

Levine nodded toward Tony. "This is Tony Marco," Levine began. "His father died on the job here a few years back, and Moe would like to see Tony gets some work after school and on the early part of the second shift. Three, four hours a day." Levine paused. "Guaranteed time. Five days a week. More in the summer and on school vacations if he wants it."

O'Keefe rolled his eyes and looked out along one of the piers. "Has he got a card?" he asked, still looking away.

"As an extra," Levine said.

"How old is he?"

"He's sixteen."

O'Keefe continued to stare along the pier. "You know there's only so many of Moe's contracts I can handle, Paul."

"This isn't a contract," Levine said. "He works for what he gets. We just want to make sure he works."

O'Keefe nodded and looked at Tony for the first time. "This isn't a Boy Scout camp, kid. You're gonna go home feeling like you did ten rounds with a heavyweight."

"I know, sir," Tony said.

O'Keefe nodded and turned weary eyes back to Levine. "When do you want him to start?"

"Today," Levine said.

O'Keefe exhaled heavily. "Sure," he said. He paused, then looked squarely at Levine. "While I got you here, Paul, we had a shipment of malt Scotch the other day. Real good stuff. Top dollar. And we came up thirty cases short."

Levine shrugged. "The manifest was probably wrong."

"There was nothing wrong with the manifest," O'Keefe said. "We just got some people around here with expensive tastes. I wish somebody would talk to them."

"It's those merchant seamen," Levine said. "They steal."

"Yeah, I know," O'Keefe said. "But if you could pass the word, I'd appreciate it."

Levine winked at him. "Always happy to help." He turned to Tony. "Okay, kid. You're set. You have any problems, you call me." He raised a hand, stopping Tony from thanking him. "I gotta talk to the men, make sure they're being treated all right." He turned back to O'Keefe. "See you around."

Tony and O'Keefe watched him go. Then O'Keefe took Tony's arm. "What you say your name was, kid?"

"Tony Marco."

"Okay, Tony. You got a good rabbi, and he gives you nice presents." O'Keefe motioned toward the yawning warehouse door with his head. "You follow me and I'll show you where your locker is."

Tony followed the hulking stevedore into the brightly lit warehouse, past rows of stacked crates and bags and into a long, narrow, partitioned area that held a line of battered lockers. O'Keefe approached one without a lock and pulled it open.

"Yours," he said. "If you're gonna keep anything in it, get yourself a good lock. There's people who steal around here."

"Yes, sir," Tony said, trying to suppress a smile.

"Change your clothes," O'Keefe snapped. "You'll start here in the warehouse. When you're changed, find a guy named Manny. He runs the warehouse. I'll tell him about your hours." He turned to leave, then stopped and looked back at Tony. "You seem like a nice kid, so watch out for yourself. We got animals working this place."

Manny Esposito was a small, hatchet-faced man with a humorless mouth and a wiry body that looked as though it were composed of steel bands. He looked Tony up and down with open contempt.

"You ever work before?"

"I worked in a grocery store, making deliveries and stocking shelves."

"That's pussy work. We don't have that kinda work here."

Tony clenched his teeth, vowing to keep his mouth shut. "I'll do whatever I'm supposed to do," he said.

"You will, huh?" Manny pulled a baling hook from a nearby crate and thrust it, handle first, at Tony. "We'll see what kinda work you do, grocery boy." He jabbed a stubby finger at the opposite side of the warehouse. "You see them guys loading bales on that truck over there? You go help 'em do it."

Tony glanced toward the men, then back at Manny.

"What are you, on a fucking coffee break?" Manny snapped. "Go."

Tony trotted across the warehouse, feeling as though he suddenly had been dropped on a strange planet. He had just shown up for work, and already these people were making him feel like he had committed some kind of crime. Jesus, he thought. Gino's had never looked so good to him.

When he reached the row of bales Manny had indicated, none of the men he had seen were in sight. Without waiting, he hoisted one of the bales on his shoulder, finding it much lighter than it looked, then moved across the loading ramp toward the open back of the truck. Inside he found a man sitting on a pile of bales.

"Heah," the man said. "You new?" He was short and pudgy with a round, happy face beneath a clump of red hair.

"Yeah. I just started today," Tony said.

"Just stack your bale the way I already started," the man said.

Tony did as he was told, and when he turned around, found the man facing him with his hand extended. "Name's Mike," he said as Tony took his hand.

"Mine's Tony."

"Listen," Mike said as they started out of the truck. "Don't work too fast. This is easy duty, and we can make it last the rest of the shift. If we finish too quick, they'll find something worse for us to do. Okay?"

"Sure," Tony said, not sure what else he could say. "I'm in no hurry."

When they exited the truck, another man stood facing them, one hand aimlessly scratching a protruding stomach that spread his shirt apart between the buttons. He was slightly taller than Tony and easily forty pounds heavier, with a two-day growth of beard and a nose that looked as though it had been broken in half a dozen places. When he opened his mouth, Tony could see that one of his front teeth was missing.

"Who the fuck are you?" the man growled.

"My name's Tony."

"My name's Tony," the man mimicked in a high voice. "And what the fuck are you doin' here?"

"Manny sent me over to help," Tony said, feeling his cheeks redden and hating himself for allowing it to happen.

"Yeah. Well, around here you do what *I* tell you to do." He stared at Tony for several moments, and Tony wasn't sure if he was sizing him up or simply trying to figure out what to say next.

The man ran a finger under his nose, as though clearing away something unwanted. "Right now I want you to work on my side of this stack," he finally added. "I need a fucking break, *capisce?*"

Tony shrugged. "Sure. Whatever you say."

The man glared at him for a long moment, then turned and swaggered out of sight behind a row of crates farther down the loading dock.

Tony exhaled heavily, hoisted another bale to his shoulder, and reentered the truck. As he dropped it into place Mike slid another bale beside it.

He nudged Tony with his elbow. "That was Sally," he said. "He's a fucking scumbag. And he's a mean mother, so you should watch your ass around him."

"Shit. I don't want any trouble with him or anybody else," Tony said. "I just want to make some money."

Mike inclined his head to one side. "With Sally you don't have to want trouble. He's fucking crazy." He shrugged. "Heah, you did all right. Don't worry about it." Mike grinned at him, something that made him look more like a teenager than a man in his mid-twenties. "He says somethin' to you, you do what you did today. You just say, 'Sure, Sally, anything you say.' And he'll feel like a big fucking man and he'll go away."

I wish he'd go all the way to New Jersey, Tony thought.

It was early evening, but the August air was still thick and oppressive as Tony made his way up First Street. Throughout the summer he had been working full-time on the docks, climbing into the stifling holds of the break bulk ships or struggling through the endless humidity of the warehouse. It had made him wonder, as it did now, about his father. He had worked the docks for twenty years, the same backbreaking work each day, with nothing to look forward to but more of the same. Tony shook his head. Not me, he told himself. Just long enough to get me through school, and then I'll never look at another ship, pier, or warehouse again.

At Gino's Market Pete was manning the cash register,

stuffing the purchases of an elderly woman into a paper bag.

"You almost through?" Tony asked.

"Ten minutes," Pete said. "You want to cash your check?"

Tony nodded and pulled the check from his wallet. He placed it facedown on the checkout counter and began to endorse it. A bead of sweat rolled from the tip of his nose and slapped down on the back of the paper.

Pete took the check, looked at it, and whistled softly. "Man, that's beautiful," he said.

"And I earned every penny of it," Tony said, his voice weary.

The old woman at the counter lifted her bag and stared at him. "You boys should have to work like your fathers had to work. You don't know what work is."

Tony laughed softly, almost weakly. "Yes, I do, lady," he said. "I really do."

The woman sniffed with derision and headed for the door.

"Old bitch," Pete said when she was out on the street. "She'd probably be pissed off if she knew you had the next two days off."

"I don't," Tony said. "I'm working tomorrow. They gave me six days this week."

"Man, you're gonna be able to buy those docks," Pete said.

Tony shook his head and closed his eyes in fatigue. "Right now, if I could buy them, I'd burn them."

Gino rumbled up to the cash register, his voice preceding him, his bald head glistening under the fluorescent lights. "Heah, moneybags," he said to Tony, "you wanna lend your old boss a couple hundred clams?"

"Listen to him," Pete said. "He takes his money home by the bagful and he wants to borrow yours."

"I'll give you bagfuls," Gino said, raising his hand in a

mock threat. "How much you take outta the cash register today?"

"Just enough to keep you in a better tax bracket," Pete countered.

Gino held out his hands, palms up in a gesture of helplessness. "Look at this," he said to Tony. "I give this goddamn mick a job, and he breaks my *cullions*." He turned to Pete. "Get outta here. And make sure you're on time tomorrow."

"*Addio*, Don Gino," Pete shot back, ducking another mock slap as he moved toward the door. "If you need help loading your money in the car, give me a call."

"I wouldn't let you near my money, you sticky-fingered Irish bastard," Gino shouted at Pete's retreating back.

Both boys were grinning as they hit the sidewalk, but the pleasure quickly faded as the heat struck.

"Jesus Christ," Pete moaned, his body in shock after three hours in the air-conditioned store. "It's still like an oven out here."

"Tell me about it," Tony said. "At noon I thought I was gonna die. By two I was afraid I wouldn't."

Tony stood atop a long row of stacked burlap sacks, gently easing them down to the waiting hands of two men working below. One of the men, a large muscular black man who was nicknamed Cherry, was humming a song Tony did not recognize.

"What's that song you're singing, Cherry?" Tony asked.

Cherry heaved a sack onto a waiting palette, then took a handkerchief from his pocket and wiped the sweat from his shaved head. He looked up at Tony and smiled, flashing a tooth capped in gold. "It's a West Indian song," he said. "Ain't got no name. 'Least none *I* know. My old lady sings it. She comes from Barbados."

"Were you born there too?" Tony asked.

Cherry's brow wrinkled into deep furrows. "Shit no, man. I was born here in Brooklyn. What make you think I come from some island?"

Tony shrugged. "I just thought if your mother came from there, you might have too."

Cherry let out a low, rumbling laugh. "I was talkin' 'bout my lady, not my momma. You think 'cause they call me Cherry that I is."

The rumbling laughter came again, and Tony felt his face redden but he smiled through it.

"They oughtta call you fucking Black Cherry."

The voice came from Tony's left, and he looked down and saw Sally standing a few feet away. His mouth was twisted into a snarl that seemed to match the unnatural curve of his nose, and his eyes remained fixed on the back of Cherry's head.

"Or maybe Midnight Cherry," he added, continuing his harangue.

Cherry glanced over his shoulder. "Heah, Sally," he said. "Why don' you go play the dozens on some white boy. Maybe you scare him good an' then you feel like a big man."

Cherry looked away, and as he did, Sally took two quick steps forward and slammed a work-gloved fist into the back of Cherry's head, just behind his right ear. The force of the blow sent Cherry staggering forward against the burlap sacks stacked on the palette.

Sally stepped in again and drove the steel-capped toe of his work shoes into Cherry's ribs. He swung his leg back, preparing to deliver another kick, but Cherry spun off the palette and drove a roundhouse blow to the middle of Sally's protruding gut, which sent him reeling back against the row of sacks.

The second man, who had been working with Cherry,

turned and moved quickly away. Tony watched him go, unable to move, knowing that he should.

Cherry sank to one knee, his left arm pressed against his damaged ribs, as he fought for breath. He eased himself up in a crouch as Sally regained his footing. Cherry kept his left arm pressed to his ribs and balled his right hand into a fist as Sally stepped forward.

Sally reached behind his back and withdrew the baling hook looped into his belt. He drew his arm back and swung the hook forward in a high arc, then drove it down toward the unprotected left side of Cherry's head.

Cherry jerked his head to the right, but the movement was too late, too slow, and the sharpened point of the hook plunged into the left side of his neck where it met his shoulder.

Sally's gloved left hand formed a claw and slammed into Cherry's face, holding it steady, as his right hand twisted the hook and pulled it back and forth in a ripping motion.

Tony heard Cherry scream as a fountain of arterial blood spurted into the air. The blood surged again and again, and Tony could feel his own heart pounding in his ears. His body, naked to the waist, was suddenly ice-cold, despite the heat inside the warehouse.

When the spurting stopped, Sally released the handle of the hook, and Cherry's body fell back on the concrete floor, arms and legs quivering in violent spasms, his wide, terrified eyes fixed blindly on the ceiling.

Tony stared at the body until the spasms slowed, then stopped. When he looked away, he saw Sally glaring up at him.

"You didn't see nothin', you understand me?" Sally growled. "That fucking shine had it comin'."

Tony stared into Sally's face as his mind tried to make sense out of the jumble of words. Sally repeated them again, and Tony nodded dumbly.

"Now get the fuck outta here," Sally growled.

Tony spun around and slid down the opposite side of the row of sacks. He was running when he hit the floor, and he raced across the warehouse toward the small battered desk occupied by Manny, the warehouse foreman.

Manny stood and came around the desk when he saw Tony racing toward him. "Whatsa matter?" he shouted when Tony was still several yards away.

Tony pulled up in front of him, breathless. "You got to call an ambulance," Tony panted. "Cherry's hurt."

Manny blinked, as though forcing the words to register, then pushed past Tony and ran back across the warehouse.

When he reached the body, Manny came to a skidding halt. He stood motionless for several moments, then slowly turned away, his face twisted and pained. Tony came up to him slowly, hesitantly, and Manny looked into the boy's face.

"He don't need no doctor," Manny said, his voice almost a whisper. "He don't need nothin' now, except a cop." The small, wiry foreman straightened his shoulders, then looked Tony straight in the eyes. "You see this happen?" he asked.

Tony looked away, saying nothing.

Manny's left hand shot out and grabbed Tony's arm, forcing him to look back at him. "You listen to me," Manny said. "You didn't see nothin', you don't know nothin'." He jerked his head back toward Cherry's body. "You can't do nothin' for him, but you can do a lotta harm to yourself. You understand what I'm saying?" He kept his eyes on Tony until the boy nodded in reply.

"Okay," Manny said, releasing Tony's arm. "Anybody asks you, you weren't here. You were off taking a shit, *capisce*?" He waited until Tony nodded again.

The detective held the notebook in front of him, a ballpoint pen poised in his other hand. He was a large

man in a rumpled suit with a flat, fleshy face and weary
eyes. A cigarette dangled from the corner of his mouth.

Tony stood before him, trying to keep his eyes from
straying toward the body. He had stood off at a distance
earlier, watching the police. One of them had put on thin
white cotton gloves and had carefully searched through
Cherry's pockets. Then another took a piece of white chalk
and drew an outline around the body while a third took
photographs from every conceivable angle.

They had stood around talking and smoking as Cherry
lay at their feet, the hook still imbedded in his neck, his
blood congealing into a sticky pool around him. It had
been as though Cherry didn't matter any more, had never
really mattered, as if his value had been replaced by the
fact that someone had killed him.

Tony looked up and saw Moe Green approaching from
the detective's left. He wondered what Green would do.

"Hello, Officer. What happened here, an accident?"
Green asked, stopping next to the detective.

"Who are you?" the detective asked.

"Moe Green. I'm president of the union that represents
these men." He gave the detective a cold smile. "How did
the accident happen?"

The detective stepped over to the body and pulled the
blanket back, revealing Cherry's head and neck. The eyes
were now dull and glazed. "The *accident*," the detective
said, "happened when somebody drove a hook into this
poor slob's neck."

Green ignored the sarcasm. "Sometimes the men carry
the hooks on their shoulders. Maybe he just fell." His
eyes moved to Tony, ignoring any reply the detective
might offer. He patted Tony's arm. "You look a little green
under the gills. You okay?"

Tony nodded his head, afraid his voice would crack if he
tried to speak.

He turned back to the detective. "You questioning the kid?"

"He was working with this guy."

Green turned back to Tony, his eyes hard, his mouth drawn into a tight line. "You see this happen, Tony?"

"No, sir," Tony said, forcing the words out. "I was in the bathroom."

A small smile began to form at the corners of Green's mouth, then disappeared. He turned back to the detective. "Don't be too hard on him. He's only a kid and he didn't see anything."

The detective snorted. "Nobody saw anything. Everybody was in the bathroom. You've got an epidemic of diarrhea around here."

Green shrugged his shoulders. "It happens," he said. "If I can help you, I'll be on the other side of the warehouse with the foreman."

Tony watched Green slowly walk away, then turned back to the detective.

"Give me your address and phone number," the detective said. Tony gave it to him.

Green stopped at Manny's desk and perched on the edge of it, then pulled down the lapels of his blue sharkskin suit, straightening them. "Who did it, Manny?" he asked.

Manny shook his head. "I don't know, and I don't wanna know."

"The kid see it happen?"

Manny nodded. "I told him to keep his mouth shut. But I think he would have, anyway."

Green stared across the warehouse at Tony. "How's the kid working out?" he asked at length.

"Good," Manny said. "He's a hardworking kid. I wish I had ten more like him."

"He get a hard time from the men?" Green asked.

Manny nodded again. "Sure. But he keeps his nose out of trouble. He handles it good. He's a smart kid."

Green stood and stretched his back. "You tell him to take a couple of days off, but put him in for the time so he doesn't lose any money."

Manny turned to Green. "I'm worried about the guy who did this. Maybe he'll get nervous about the kid seeing him."

"That's why I want him out of here for a few days," Green said. "I'll send Paul down tomorrow, and he'll make it clear nothing should happen to the kid. Paul's good at making people understand."

"You want me to do anything else?" Manny asked.

A thin smile came to Green's lips in appreciation of Manny's perceptiveness. "You know who the real bad-asses are," he said. "It was probably one of them, anyway. Keep all of them on the night shift for a while. And put the kid back on days."

"Sure," Manny said.

Green turned to go, then stopped and looked back at Manny. "And keep an eye on the kid. I want to hear from time to time how he's doing."

CHAPTER/NINE

September 1968

MOE GREEN WAS standing in front of his desk when Tony entered his office. He was in shirtsleeves, and Tony noticed how frail he seemed without the added weight of a suitcoat, but the cold eyes and hawklike face still sent a slight chill through him as they shook hands.

Green had not seen Tony in two years but had kept track of his progress. He directed him to the leather sofa and took the club chair opposite. "So, Tony," he began, "tell me what you've been up to."

"Just working and going to school, Mr. Green," Tony said.

"I heard you got a scholarship," Green said, leaning forward in his chair. "How do you like Columbia?" He watched Tony's jaw tighten; noted his momentary hesitation.

"It's hard," he said.

Green nodded. "It's a big change from high school. The work's a lot harder, I guess." He watched Tony closely, taking in the subtle hint of regret that came into his eyes.

"The schoolwork's not a problem. It's easier than I thought it would be. There's just a lot of it."

Green let the moment draw out. The boy obviously didn't want to explain. "So what *is* hard?" he finally asked.

Tony's jaw tightened again. "Just fitting in there," he said.

"You mean with the other students?"

Tony nodded. "Most of them look like they were born in Brooks Brothers. A guy from Brooklyn doesn't exactly feel at home."

"Not all of them," Green said.

Tony shook his head and smiled for the first time. "Except for the radicals, and they're so whacked out, I wouldn't want to be mistaken for one of them."

As a Jew who had grown up poor, Green knew what the boy was experiencing. Doubly so. His eyes narrowed. "So what are you going to do?" he asked. "You want to quit?"

Tony's jaw tightened. "No," he said, his voice harsher than he had intended. He shrugged, softened his voice. "I'll ignore it. There isn't much else I can do."

Green sat forward and jabbed a finger in Tony's direction. "You don't let them push you out, that's what you don't do."

Tony lowered his eyes and stared at the hands resting in his lap. "Nobody's going to push me out of anywhere, Mr. Green," he said. When he looked up, there was a smile on Green's lips, but it held no warmth and his eyes were hard and cold.

"There's always one thing you can count on from those people," he said. "They'll let you know you don't fit into their little club, and they'll keep doing it as long as they can. But remember, they can't keep you from taking anything you got a right to take. And that's what you're going to have to do. You're going to have to take, because they're never going to *offer* you anything. But someday you're going to find yourself on equal terms because of what's up here." He tapped his finger against his fore-

head. "And then you can show those schmucks that it's a
very different game."

Tony stared into Green's face, noting the quiet vehe-
mence, the hatred that seemed to boil just below the
surface. He knew the man was telling him what he, himself, had done. It made Tony feel he wasn't alone.

Green sat back again, reading the satisfaction he saw
now in Tony's face, pleased that it was there. "I want you
to promise me something, Tony," he began. "Whenever
some smart guy looks down his nose at you because of
your clothes, or anything else, I want you to ask yourself
how long he'd survive on the docks, doing what you've
been doing the last two years. I don't mean if he could do
the work. Anybody with a strong back could do that. I
mean, if he'd be tough enough and smart enough to survive with the men down there. Or if they'd just chew him
up and spit him out."

A small smile crept to Tony's lips as he thought of some
of the men he had worked with; the random violence and
brutality that had always seemed to be there, just waiting
for an excuse to be used—a wrong word, an accidental bump.

Green nodded. "You see, it depends on how you look at
it. Now, I've got a proposition for you. You've probably
heard the rumors about some layoffs. Well, they're true.
There's nothing we can do about them." He watched
concern flood Tony's eyes, then harden into something
else. "What I'd like you to do is take a job here at the
office. As a clerk. You'd work the same hours and earn the
same kind of money. . . ." He paused for effect, keeping
his eyes riveted on Tony's. "And you'd learn a helluva lot
more than you would pushing cargo around the docks."

Tony tried to speak, but the words wouldn't seem to
form in his mouth. The corners of Green's lips curved up
almost imperceptibly. "Look at it this way," he said. "If
you take the job, you won't have to hide your work clothes

from your mother anymore." He watched Tony's face flush. "You think we didn't know?" he asked. "Every day I expected a call from her, telling me she was putting a curse on my eyes."

Tony laughed, feeling his body flood with relief. "That would probably have been my Aunt Marie," he said.

"So, you'll take the job?"

"I sure will, and thanks. Thanks a lot."

Green waved away the appreciation. "You just do a good job. Come in around two tomorrow and we'll have somebody show you what to do." He stood up and took Tony's arm and walked him to the door. "Tell me something," he said as he pulled the door open. "What did you tell your mother you were doing all this time?"

Tony grinned at him nervously. "I told her I was working as a clerk."

"That makes you either a liar or a prophet." Green snorted, the closest he ever came to laughter.

When he closed the door behind the boy, Green walked slowly back to his desk and eased himself into his high-backed chair. He took a pack of cigarettes from his shirt pocket, withdrew one, and lit it with a desktop lighter.

Earlier in the day he had told Paul Levine about his plan to put the boy on as a clerk. Paul had shook his head and laughed, accusing him of trying to become a Jewish Father Flanagan.

But there was more to it than that. Times were changing. He had seen it coming for years now. And soon they were going to need smart young men who knew their way around. Smart young men who understood and who could back up men like himself and Paul. He wished Paul could see it, but Green knew he could not.

CHAPTER/TEN

THE LEAVES WERE beginning to turn, bathing Prospect Park with subtle hints of color. The change of seasons in the park always seemed slightly out of place, juxtaposed with the stark buildings beyond its low, encircling wall and the constant noise of nearby city traffic. But for the people who lived in its environs the park was a haven, an easy escape from the claustrophobic tensions that surrounded them each day.

Tony and Pete both felt that temporary sense of freedom as they walked slowly across a broad meadow, moving in the direction of the park's zoo. Their hands were stuffed into the pockets of their jackets, and their shoulders were hunched slightly, making them look like two brothers who had learned to imitate each other's movements.

"I think it's a mistake," Tony said, pausing to kick a small rock out of his path. Pete stopped to watch the rock skitter off to one side, and Tony took the opportunity to look at him squarely. "If you enrolled in City College for

150

the second semester, you could get a deferment, especially since you're supporting your mother. You'd never be touched by the draft."

Pete shook his head, turned, and started to walk on, forcing Tony to catch up to him. "City College is a madhouse. I'd never learn anything there. If I enlist now, I'll come out with a GI Bill, and I can go someplace decent."

"Sure. And in the meantime they'll send you to Vietnam and get your ass shot off," Tony said.

Pete looked at him sideways and grinned. "How do you know I won't end up in Germany or Japan or Hawaii? I might spend the next four years in a beer hall or a geisha house or flat on my back on some beach."

Tony glanced away at a dense clump of trees. "Fat chance. You don't have a father with the right friends." He looked back at Pete, leaving the rest unsaid.

Pete noted the distant tone in Tony's voice and decided not to pursue the reasons behind it. Not yet. They walked on until they reached the wide asphalt path that led into the zoo, then wandered along it, finally stopping before the three deep pits that housed the bears.

They leaned on the railing and stared down into the pit that held a battered-looking polar bear. There was a large pool at the pit's center, and rising rock ledges at its rear, complete with man-made caves. The bear—enormous with a dirty white coat—lay on its back near the pool, its two front paws sticking straight up.

"It looks like it's been shot," Pete said, making a gun with his finger and pointing it at the sleeping bear.

The gesture made Tony think again of his earlier warning about the war. He really didn't expect Pete to be killed, or even hurt. He wasn't even certain his friend would ever see a combat zone. What he feared was losing Pete's friendship, losing the one person he *could* talk to.

"So how're things going at Columbia?" Pete asked.

Tony shrugged, closing his eyes against the sun.

"You still feel out of place there?" Pete asked.

"Still."

Pete shook his head and turned his attention back to the sleeping bear. He knew how hard Tony had worked to get into the school, how obsessed he had been with the scholarship. "It'll get better," Pete said, knowing how false his words sounded.

"I feel like a jerk for even feeling that way. But, Christ, I can't help it." He turned to Pete. "Jesus, don't ever tell anybody about this. It's bad enough you know I'm a jerk."

Pete grinned at him. "Hey, I *always* knew that. And, anyway, it's not exactly a problem you can't solve. All you have to do is break down and spend a little dough on some new clothes."

"Yeah, sure," Tony said. "And what do my mother and sister do for money? Maybe I should start dressing up like the guys in SDS. An old army jacket is something I could afford."

Pete punched him lightly on the arm. "You better stick with the Ivy League look," he said. "The guys in the neighborhood see you in an old army jacket, they'll think you're a draft dodger and they'll beat the hell out of you."

Tony exhaled a short laugh. "Yeah. Besides, the ladies at Barnard like those button-down collars."

"See?" Pete said. "That's all you need and they'll be chasing your dago ass all over the campus. You'll still be a piece of shit, but all those little rich girls won't know it."

Tony tried to force a smile that didn't quite work, then looked away. "I don't give a damn, anyway. Like the man said, 'The hell with them if they can't take a joke.' "

Pete turned and stared down at the bear. Except that you really do care, he thought. You just won't let it show to anybody else. He watched the bear twist back and forth on its back, scratching itself. What the hell could Tony do?

He could live with it and try to work it out, or he could run away and hide. And Tony would never run. Christ, something like that shouldn't even matter, he told himself. But it's the type of thing that always does. Everybody always had to put on a show. A thought jumped to his mind and he started to laugh.

"What's so funny?" Tony asked.

Pete turned to him, grinning. "I just figured out how to solve your problem." He jabbed a finger against Tony's chest. "You take Joey up there and you show them all how Brooklyn guys look when they're really dressed up."

They both laughed at the idea.

"You'd also have to make sure he had all his shots," Pete said. "You might start a rabies epidemic."

"Don't give me any ideas," Tony said.

"Well, if you're gonna do it, you better do it fast. He goes up for sentencing next week."

Tony shook his head. Joey's latest arrest had been for hitting a cop with a baseball bat, and it had guaranteed him a long stay in a hotel with bars on the windows. "He's lucky the cops didn't kill him," he said, thinking of the week Joey had spent in the hospital after he had "accidentally" fallen down the stairs at the Seventy-eighth Precinct.

"He claims he did it to keep from being drafted," Pete said, laughing at the idea.

Shit, Tony thought. He wouldn't even have Joey to talk to. He hadn't even thought about that. "It's going to be weird without either of you guys being around."

Pete grinned at him. "You can write me letters."

"I'll let Mary Beth do that," Tony said.

"So you can visit Joey in the slammer."

"I'll let Mary Beth do that too," Tony said, grinning.

"You keep her away from that hump." He laughed. "She's already mad enough at me that she might say yes."

"How come?" Tony asked.

Pete shook his head. "She wanted to get married before I left."

Tony winced. "That's all you need. Another mouth to help feed."

Pete shook his head and grinned. "That's what I told her. I'd really like to marry her. Just not now. But even when I told her that, it didn't stop her from getting pissed. I even promised that we'd do it as soon as I got out, but it didn't help."

"She'll get over it," Tony said.

"Yeah, I suppose. Anyway, Joey will be safe behind bars."

"Don't count on it," Tony said. "He'll probably bust out."

CHAPTER/ELEVEN

TONY SETTLED INTO a job at the union that seemed little more than shuffling papers and running errands. Each week he would visit the various stevedore offices to collect work schedules and reports on work-related injuries and, once each month, checks for dues that had been deducted from the men's wages. In the office he handled reports and claims from the Longshoremen's Medical Center and the union's welfare fund, tasks that took little more than an hour each day and made him quickly realize he was being paid far more than the job was worth. He hoped no one else would notice and followed his mother's admonition to "always look busy. If they see you doin' somethin', they'll think you workin' hard, even if you not," she had advised.

Sitting in his small, cramped, closet-size office just off the reception area, Tony employed his mother's wisdom by reading through the multipaged document of the union's last labor contract.

"You must be the student from Columbia."

The slightly husky voice startled him, and when he looked up, he found it belonged to a young woman standing in the doorway. She was of medium height, well proportioned, and had long brown hair that seemed to accent her high cheekbones and large brown eyes. He recognized her from the picture on Moe Green's desk—Moe's daughter Shirley.

"Nobody's supposed to know about Columbia," Tony said through a smile. "It's a secret."

"Well, I know all about it. My father told me. He also told me you were smart. Are you?"

Tony's smile broadened. "Yes, I am."

Shirley pursed her lips. "I'm glad he didn't say you were modest. I'm Shirley Green, in case you haven't guessed."

"I know. I've seen your picture on your father's desk," Tony said. "My name's Tony. Tony Marco."

"My father will have to get a new picture. I've changed since that one was taken."

There was a note of defiance in Shirley's voice that made Tony feel she was daring him to say something. "I liked the way you looked in the picture," he said. "I thought you were very pretty."

"And now you think I'm not?" She had arched one eyebrow in mock severity.

Tony held up his hands as though fending off the accusation. "I didn't say that. I think you look great now too."

She gave him a small knowing smile. "Now I see why my father thinks you're smart," she said.

"How about you? Are you smart?"

Shirley tossed her hair and turned. "Smart enough to know when someone's flirting with me," she said over her shoulder. Then she was gone.

Paul Levine filled the doorway almost at once. "What's the matter, the job's not enough for you? Now you're after the boss's daughter?" He shook an accusing finger as he watched Tony's face redden. "Moe finds out, you'll be back on the docks wearing concrete overshoes."

"I'm just a poor kid from Brooklyn, trying to get ahead, Paul," Tony said.

Levine lumbered through the door. "You'll get ahead, wise guy. And you'll be holding it in your hands." He stared down at the contract on Tony's desk. "What are you doing with that?"

"I was just reading through it, trying to get an idea of the things it covered," Tony explained. "I never realized how complex it could be."

"I bet you thought only college boys could work something out like that, huh?" Levine winked at him. "We run the college boys around in circles when we negotiate."

"They probably all went to Yale," Tony said.

Levine closed his hand into a fist and held it before Tony's nose. "I'll give you Yale," he said. "You think some schmuck from Columbia would do better." He shook the fist. "He'd be chopped liver."

Tony laughed.

"Listen," Levine said, turning serious. "Moe and I have something new for you to do. You'll do it on a regular basis at different times of the month."

"Sure," Tony said, relieved to learn there would be something else to fill his time.

Paul took a sealed business-size envelope from his inside jacket pocket and dropped it on the desk. It was bulky and blank. Tony stared at the unaddressed envelope, then looked back at Paul.

Paul handed him a slip of paper with the name and address of a shipping company on it. "You go there. The office is on the twelfth floor. And you ask for Mr. Jameson. He'll be expecting you." Levine studied Tony's face, watching for any trace of concern. "He's going to give you an envelope like that one. You just take it and leave the office. When you're out in the hall, if there's nobody out there, you go straight to the fire stairs next to the elevators. Just inside the door you'll see a fire hose on a rack on the wall. You take the envelope Jameson gave you and you stuff it behind the hose. Then you go down to the eleventh floor, take the elevator down, and come back here." He kept his eyes on Tony's. "You got that?"

Tony nodded but said nothing.

"But if there are people in the hall, you go to the elevator and punch the button for the top floor. You stay on that elevator until there's nobody else in the car. When it's empty, you open the panel where they keep the emergency telephone and you put the envelope inside. Then you go down to the lobby and out."

Tony looked down at the envelope on his desk. When his eyes returned to Levine, he saw he was smiling.

"That's your insurance policy," Levine said. "What you'll be picking up is a little inside information. We have people in every shipping company we deal with who slip us information. Like what's going to be in cargo coming into the docks. Sometimes these companies ship in something hazardous but mark it as something else so they can beat the hazardous wage under the contract. Things like that. The shipping companies suspect this is going on, and every so often their security people poke their noses around. Sometimes the Waterfront Commission does too. It's not exactly kosher, what we're doing." He hesitated, watching Tony's eyes. "That bother you?"

Tony felt his stomach make a nervous turn. He shook his head.

"Good," Levine said. "Now, anybody stops you, you give them that envelope." He pointed to the one on Tony's desk. "It's got bullshit stuff in it that wouldn't cause anybody any trouble if they gave it to us." The smile had

returned to Levine's lips. "So let's say you get stopped."
He raised a lecturing finger. "This is what you tell them.
You work here. The other day you got an unsigned memo,
telling you to go to the shipping company and pick up an
envelope. They ask you how come no signature, you say
that's the way things are done around here. You just do
what you're told. If they ask you what you were supposed
to do with the envelope, you tell them that the memo
instructed you to leave it on the reception desk here in
the office." He raised his finger again. "In fact, that's just
what you do with this envelope." He patted the one on
Tony's desk. "When you come back, you leave it on Gert's
desk. That's so if anybody ever asks, she can say that's
what you do. You understand all this?"

Tony nodded, then forced himself to say "Yes."

"Okay, just one more thing. Anybody comes up to you
before you can stash the second envelope, you just drop
it." Levine grinned at him. "It would be nice if they didn't
see you drop it, but if it can't be that way, you just let it
drop. You don't know where it came from; you never saw
it before; all you have is the other envelope that Mr.
Jameson gave you. *Capisce?* But even that one you don't
hand over. It's union property. They want it, they have to
take it. Don't try to stop them, but don't offer it, either."

Tony nodded. "When do you want me to go there?"

"Tomorrow. Three o'clock," Levine said. "You take this
other envelope home with you tonight. Tomorrow you
wear a sport jacket and you put the envelope in the inside
pocket. The envelope you get from Jameson, you put up
the sleeve of your coat. That way, anybody comes up to
you, you can drop it easier." He noticed a sudden flash of
concern in Tony's eyes. He reached out and tapped him
lightly under the chin with his closed fist. "Don't worry.
Nobody's going to bother you." He stared into Tony's
eyes. "You don't have to do this. Moe thought you could

handle it, but if it makes you nervous, I'll get somebody else. No problem, no hard feelings."

Tony swallowed. "No, I can handle it," he said. "It just surprised me. It makes me feel like James Bond."

Levine laughed. "We'll call you 006½. Just remember, you don't know anything about anything. You're just a kid running an errand. Right?"

"Right," Tony said.

The building that housed the shipping company was located on State Street, overlooking Battery Park at the southern tip of Manhattan. Tony drew a deep breath as he entered the marble-walled lobby. His heart was pounding in his chest, and the palms of his hands were coated with sweat. He offered up a silent prayer that this new job wasn't going to end in trouble. Jesus, he told himself, don't let me wind up as Joey's cell mate.

On the elevator, which was far newer than the building, he stared at the box that housed the emergency telephone. There were two men in the car, and he resisted an urge to pull it open, to make sure he could if he had to. He could feel a slight tremor in his hands and quickly stuffed them into his pockets. On the twelfth floor he found the office without difficulty and stood outside it, staring at the words on the glass panel:

WATKINS SHIPPING LTD.
Main Office: 9 Grafton Street, London WIX 3LA
Telex 25511 WAT
M. Jameson, Managing Director, New York

Tony let out a long breath and opened the door. An attractive young woman seated at a reception desk smiled at him. "Can I help you?" she asked.

Tony tried not to stutter over the words. "I'm here to see Mr. Jameson."

"May I have your name?" The woman was still smiling.

"Tony Marco." He hesitated, then added, "I'm from the union. I'm supposed to pick up something." He quietly cursed himself as he watched the woman dial the telephone intercom. He had probably said too much, but he hadn't expected the receptionist, hadn't been sure what Paul had told Jameson or if Jameson had told the woman to expect someone with his name. Damn.

The woman stood, smiling again. "I'll show you the way," she said.

Tony found himself in a large, dark, paneled office that looked like a replica of Moe Green's.

Jameson stood up behind his desk as Tony entered, his body partially obscuring a large replica of a wooden sailing ship that stood on a table behind him. He was of average height and slender, with thinning gray hair and a bushy mustache that turned up at the ends. He held his chin erect, looking at Tony down a long, slender nose.

"You're the young man I was told to expect?" Jameson said in a voice as imperious as his manner.

Tony wiped the palm of his sweating right hand against his corduroy sport coat and offered his hand. "Yes," he said.

Jameson's hand did not move. He stared at Tony for several moments, as though pricing each item of clothing he wore. Tony felt his jaw tighten, and he stared at the man, holding back sudden anger.

Jameson opened a drawer in his desk and withdrew an envelope identical to the one Tony carried in his pocket, then extended it. Tony took the envelope and slid it into his right sleeve, causing Jameson to arch one eyebrow.

"My dear chap, I hope you won't lose that," he said. "It shan't be replaced if you do."

"Thank you. I won't lose it," Tony said, turning abruptly, wishing he had added "you asshole" to the end of the sentence.

"See that you don't," Jameson snapped at his back.

Tony made a half turn and stared into Jameson's eyes, then drew out each succeeding word. *"I won't lose it."*

Jameson's back stiffened, and his mouth hardened into a straight line, demonstrating his anger and contempt. "Cheeky young man, aren't you?" he said, his voice almost a hiss. "I shall have words with Mr. Levine about this," he added.

Tony offered him a small smile that didn't carry to his eyes, then turned, opened the door, and walked out without closing it behind him.

Tony moved past the secretary, down the hall, through the large open office, and out past the receptionist without looking at anyone. He stepped out into the corridor and glanced in both directions. It was empty. Quickly he moved to the stairwell, opened the door and stepped out on to the landing. The fire hose was to his right. He pulled the envelope from his sleeve, noting its bulk for the first time, and jammed it behind the hose.

Bastard, Tony said to himself as he started down the stairs. Acts like you were dirt. He was struck by the bulk of the envelope he had left at the fire hose, the feel and shape of a packet of money wrapped inside a few sheets of paper. I hope it is, he thought. I hope they're shaking down the creep for everything they can get. At the next floor landing he pulled the door open with such force it slammed back against the wall, filling the stairwell with an echoing crash.

Paul Levine picked up the telephone on his desk and listened to a familiar voice, deep and rasping.

"I got it," the male voice said.

"How'd the kid look?" Levine asked.

"When he went in, he looked like he was gonna piss his pants," the man said. "But when he came out, he looked like he was ready to tear somebody's head off."

Levine laughed into the phone. "Leave the envelope at the usual place."

"Of course," the man answered.

Levine leaned back in his chair, the hint of a smile still hovering on his lips. Jameson was by far the worst of a pompous lot who ran shipping interests in New York, and Moe Green had specifically picked him for Tony's first "errand." You're a genius, Moe, Levine told himself. The kid will think of all of them that way now. And what the hell, he thought, they were all the same, anyway.

The union Christmas party was held the following week in the St. George Hotel in Brooklyn Heights. The party took up two rooms on the lobby floor: a large banquet room, now filled with children and mothers; and the hotel bar, a massive, darkly lit room, now filled with the boisterous voices of longshoremen.

Tony stood at the bar, sipping a beer, and thought about the differences between this place and the crowded student bars that surrounded Columbia. The contrast brought a smile to his lips.

"What are you so happy about?"

He turned to see Shirley Green standing beside him. "I was just thinking about something," Tony said.

"Well, why don't you stop it and order me a drink."

Tony slowly shook his head. "Last week, when I smiled at you, Paul Levine told me I was going to end up with concrete boots. What do you think would happen to me if I got you drunk?" He smiled at her. "Besides, you're not old enough."

"Wrong again," Shirley said, offering him an imperious

tilt of her head. "I turned eighteen last August. And my father doesn't mind if I only drink wine."

"You sure?" Tony asked. "I don't want Paul breaking my legs over a glass of wine."

"Oh, stop it," she said. "Uncle Paul wouldn't hurt a fly. But if I told him you were mean to me . . ." She let the sentence die.

"Okay," Tony said. "I hope you know what you're doing." He turned to the bartender and ordered a glass of white wine and another draft beer. When he turned to hand it to her, Moe Green was standing next to his daughter, and the wineglass stopped halfway to her hand. Tony swallowed. "I hope this is okay, Mr. Green," he said.

Green nodded. "She's a fancy Vassar girl now," he said, slipping one arm around his daughter's shoulder and squeezing her to him. "You think I could tell her no?"

Shirley leaned over and kissed her father's cheek. "Tony says Uncle Paul threatened to put him in concrete boots if he smiled at me anymore."

Green laughed softly, then raised a finger to Tony. "Smiling I allow," he said. "But just smiling." He winked at Tony. "You two have fun, I have to circulate with the men and then go in the other room to welcome Santa Claus. A fat goy in a red suit."

Tony watched Green's departing back, then looked at Shirley. "You're dangerous."

"But I'm worth it," she said.

She had a beautiful face, he thought: the dark skin, accented by the high cheekbones; the large brown eyes; the soft hair. He didn't dare look at the rest of her, but he remembered enough from the previous week. There had been a slight sway to her hips as she had walked away. "It's a great party," he said.

She wrinkled her nose. "I wanted it to be someplace in Manhattan," she said. "But my father likes to keep it in

Brooklyn, because most of the men live here. They have another one in some clam house in New Jersey, for the men who work over there." She said the words *New Jersey* as though it were a foreign country.

"I like this place," he said. "I used to come here with my father when I was a little kid. I learned to swim in the saltwater pool downstairs. It's supposed to be the largest saltwater pool in the country. But that could be a Brooklyn fairy tale."

Shirley sipped her wine and looked up at him over the rim of her glass. "Did you bring anyone to the party?" she asked.

"My sister Carmela," he said. "She's in the other room, waiting for Santa Claus. She's only twelve."

Shirley leaned across him to place her glass on the bar and brushed his arm. "Show me the pool," she said.

"I don't know if it's open," he said.

Taking his hand, she pulled. "Let's find out."

The pool lay like a dead dinosaur, empty of water, its tiles cracked and broken, the diving board Tony had once loved to jump from long removed. "It's been a long time," he said, more to himself than to Shirley. "This pool looks like it would sink if they put water in it."

They were standing on the edge of the pool; its empty center sent Tony's voice echoing through the large, desolate room. Only the faint, residual odor of chlorine suggested it had ever been more than a broken hole in the floor.

"It's sad they don't fix it up," Shirley said.

"It's mostly old people who live in the hotel now. Old and poor. I guess they just didn't use it." Tony stepped back from the edge and turned to leave.

Shirley faced him, then took a step forward and slipped her arms around his neck. Before he knew what was happening, her lips pressed against his and her tongue was moving wildly against his own. He felt her pelvis pressing against him, and he immediately began to grow.

He eased himself back. "Jesus," he said. "You're going to get me fired or killed, or worse."

She smiled at him. "What's worse than being killed?"

"I'm afraid to even think about that," he said.

She brought a pout to her lips. "Don't you think I'm worth it?"

He hesitated. "Damn, I sure do," he said, bringing her mouth to his again. He felt her rub against him. You're out of your mind, he told himself, pressing back. He pushed himself away. "It's just too dangerous here."

She lowered her arms and smiled. "You're free weekends, aren't you?" She watched him nod his head. "Then after the holidays come up to Vassar some weekend." She tilted her head to one side. "Will you?"

Tony nodded again. "Yeah," he said. "I sure will."

CHAPTER/TWELVE

May 1970

THE AFFAIR WITH Shirley Green lasted only a few months,
little more than a scattering of weekends when long walks
in the countryside and quiet dinners at out-of-the-way
restaurants served as brief interruptions to long periods in
bed. Shirley had a private room at Vassar and assured him
that staying there would not cause her difficulties, but
Tony insisted on a room at a small local motel, stating
simply that he did not want to be the subject of sopho-
moric gossip. The true reason, of course, was an innate
dread of a surprise visit from her father, something that
sent a chill down his spine whenever he considered it.

But the affair ended at the conclusion of her freshman
year when Shirley left to spend the summer in Europe
with friends and remained in France for a semester's study
abroad. When she returned, it was obvious that passions
had cooled for each. Yet she and Tony remained friends,
and Shirley made a point of seeing him each time she
visited the union office.

For Tony the change in their relationship was accompa-

167

nied by a sense of simultaneous regret and relief. Shirley had approached him with an abandon that had been new and exciting, and the ever-present hint of danger had only heightened that feeling. But there had been more as well, though he had never consciously acknowledged it. The attention, the desire, had helped reinforce his sense of worth, his need to be valued for himself. It was something he had masked by taking pleasure in Shirley's sense of self-possession, even when it had crossed the line into selfishness, something he easily ascribed to the doting affection of a widowed father. The question of gratitude had never occurred to him.

But his relief, when it was over, could not be masked. He had played a dangerous game where the consequences had far outweighed the benefits—"thinking with your dick in your hand," as Pete had responded to a letter Tony had written describing his precarious situation. He had smiled then at the boyhood colloquialism but not at its accuracy, and in the months when he and Shirley were apart, he had decided he had no intention of repeating past dangers.

Seated in his closetlike office at the union, Tony stared at Pete's most recent letter. He had read it half a dozen times, as though the rereading might change the words somehow, or at least offer some hope. The word *Vietnam* pulsed in his mind, even though Pete had not used it. He had written with a resigned cheerfulness, like a small boy who had finally been caught in a repeated misdeed. That was the tone. The army had finally caught up with him.

Since he'd joined the army Pete had played a systematic game, one consistently used by army "lifers" to avoid unwanted postings. It was simple enough, or so he had been led to believe. After each course of training he had volunteered for even more selective training, gradually moving from one elite unit to another. Now, after completing advanced Ranger training in Germany, Pete had volunteered for Special Forces, only to find that the game had ended abruptly.

Tony reread the final paragraph. Pete's request for special forces had been denied. His battalion had been reassigned to Southeast Asia.

Tony ran his hand over the letter, smoothing it out against the desk. They finally nailed Pete, he told himself. The idea sent a wave of uneasiness through him, and as he stared down at the letter, he suddenly wanted it out of sight. He picked it up, folded it, and slipped it into the inside pocket of his sport coat, next to the "insurance" envelope he would carry on his errand to a shipping company later that day.

The pickup was in a building on Broad Street, directly opposite Fraunces Tavern, the lower Manhattan restaurant where George Washington had bid farewell to his troops. Like most of the buildings that housed the city's shipping firms, it was old and stately, intent on exuding the long standing affluence and importance of those it housed.

Tony walked quickly through the lobby, oblivious to the marble and highly polished wood. His monthly errands had become routine, in and out with as little conversation as possible. By now the receptionists and secretaries he dealt with simply smiled and announced his arrival, almost, he thought, as if he were somebody's kid who had dropped by to see Daddy at the office.

The thought crossed his mind as he opened the door to Whitehead Shipping Ltd. and moved across the comfortable reception area to the attractive middle-aged woman seated behind a desk.

The woman, whose nameplate identified her as Mrs. Sayers, looked up at him and offered a smile that never quite developed. Her eyes moved quickly to two men seated on a leather sofa, then back at Tony.

"It's Mr. Marco for Mr. Weathersby, correct?" she asked.

Tony nodded and watched her fumble with the telephone. He glanced at the two men on the sofa, but neither looked up from the magazines they were reading.

Mrs. Sayers stood, her lips drawn tight now, and asked Tony to follow her. They moved through a large, open work area toward a row of private offices along the far wall.

Weathersby's secretary was seated at a desk outside his office. She glanced up at Tony, then looked back at the papers on her desk. "You can go right in," she said without looking up again.

Tony felt his stomach tighten as he went through the door to Weathersby's office. Something was in the air. It was like walking on a dark street and seeing figures ahead, knowing in your gut that continuing on meant trouble. The clenched muscles in his jaw ached as he stepped into the well-lit office.

Weathersby was a short balding man who was normally affable and quick with a smile. Today his lips were drawn in a tight line, his eyes hard and unforgiving, and it seemed to make his entire face sag, as though it had sunk into the heavy roll of flesh beneath his chin.

"Beautiful day outside," Tony said, forcing a smile as he kept his eyes fixed on Weathersby's face. The office was cool and airy, but there was a thin line of perspiration along the man's upper lip.

Weathersby came out from behind the desk, picking up an envelope as he did. He glanced at a window. "I hadn't noticed how sunny it was," he said, and extended the envelope toward Tony. "Here you are."

Tony smiled at the short, sad looking man and turned toward the door, keeping the envelope in his hand.

As he stepped into the outer office Tony adjusted the envelope so it was cupped by the palm of his hand, its length running up along his inner forearm. He stepped quickly past the secretary's desk and started across the office. To his right there was an empty desk, and he veered slightly toward it, his body almost brushing it as he went past. With a quick move of his arm the envelope slid into an outgoing tray at the edge of the desk.

When he reached the reception room, only one of the men was seated on the sofa, and as Tony reached the front door, he could hear him move behind him.

Out in the hall Tony turned toward the elevator and saw the second man waiting there. As he started down the corridor the second man came toward him.

He was only a few feet away from the second man when he felt the hand on his shoulder. He turned to face the first man and saw that he had a credential case held open in his free hand.

"Morgan, Waterfront Commission," the man said. He had a broad, flat face beneath wavy brown hair that had gone gray at the temples. His blue eyes seemed to be smiling, but his mouth was firm.

Morgan nodded toward the other man, and Tony turned and saw the police shield in his hand. "This is Detective Gaffrey from the Manhattan District Attorney's office," Morgan said. "We'd like to talk to you, Tony."

Tony turned back to face Morgan and shrugged. "Sure," he said, feeling his heart pounding against his chest.

"You just get something from Mr. Weathersby?" Morgan asked.

"Yeah," Tony said.

"What'd he give you?"

Tony shrugged. "An envelope."

"What's in the envelope, Tony?"

"I don't know."

Morgan extended one hand and made several quick movements with his fingers. "Let me have it," he said.

Tony shook his head. "You'll have to check with someone at the union."

Morgan's face broke into a mirthless smile. "I don't have to check with anybody, asshole. You either give it to me or you're busted."

"For what?" Tony said, fighting to keep his voice level. "I'm just here running an errand."

Gaffrey took his arm and turned him. He had a hard, heavily veined face that looked like a road map of all the bars he had visited in his life, but his gray eyes were soft, almost tired. "You don't want trouble, kid," he said, his voice low and deep. He was shorter than Tony, and his thinning gray hair revealed a freckled scalp peeking out between the hairs. Tony kept his eyes on the freckles, avoiding the man's eyes.

"Look, I don't want to lose my job," Tony said. "You want to come back to the union with me, they say it's okay, I'll give you whatever you want."

Gaffrey shook his head. "Okay, kid, we do it the hard way. Put your hands up against the wall."

Tony did as he was told and felt Gaffrey's hands expertly roam his body. He kept telling himself it was like a bad television movie as he listened to the detective rattle off his Miranda rights in a bored voice.

Down the hall the elevator opened and two women got off. Tony felt his face redden as they started toward him, their voices lowered to whispers. He felt the handcuffs press against one of his wrists and snapped his head around toward Gaffrey.

"Regulations," Gaffrey said, pulling the handcuffed wrist away from the wall and bringing it behind Tony's back. The second hand followed smoothly and was snapped into place.

Gaffrey took Tony by the shoulders and turned him gently, then reached into the inside pocket of his suitcoat and withdrew a plain white envelope. He looked up at Tony with sad eyes.

"Is this the envelope you were given?" he asked. He watched Tony nod his head. "The assistant D.A. wants us to open it in front of him, but I'd like to be able to tell him you cooperated. He's a hard-ass, kid, but if you're straight with us, he'll go easy on you." Gaffrey offered a weak smile through tobacco-stained teeth. "Let me be honest with you. He wants bigger fish than you. But if you're all he can get, he'll take you. So don't be stupid, kid. Don't take a fall for the scumbags you work for. They'd sell you out like that." He snapped his fingers as he stared sadly into Tony's eyes.

"Come on. Let's take the little greaseball uptown," Morgan snorted. "We'll throw his ass in Rikers Island and let some spade bugger him for a couple of days. Then we'll see how much he wants to talk."

Gaffrey winced and turned to Morgan with one hand raised. "Take it easy, Jerry. He's just a kid. Give him a chance." He looked back at Tony. "How about it, kid? Just fill us in on how this went down."

Tony stared at the freckled scalp. "I have to talk to someone from the union first, Mr. Gaffrey. I can't do anything that's going to cost me my job."

Tony sat in the small, sparsely furnished interrogation room, struggling to quiet his nerves, trying unsuccessfully to stop reliving the events of the past two hours. He took a handkerchief from his pocket and wiped the palms of his hands and noticed it was already limp from the number of times he had used it. His stomach tightened, then turned. He tried to remember if he had said anything in Weathersby's office; if anyone might have seen him when he dumped the envelope. What if they had other people where he had made pickups? What if they had a room full of them, ready to line up and say they had given him envelopes?

Gaffrey and Morgan stood before the desk of the assistant district attorney. Barney Gottlieb was small and slender, with tight, curly brown hair that seemed bushy against his narrow, sharply defined face. Even the heavy-framed glasses he wore failed to hide the predatory look in his almost black eyes.

"What the hell is this?" Gottlieb said, his normally sallow complexion now a deep umber. He stared at the contents of the envelope spread across his desk. "You brought me shipping schedules. Goddamn shipping schedules." He glared up at Morgan, then Gaffrey.

"The kid must have been warned off the money," Gaffrey said. "This Weathersby guy must have tipped him."

"Bullshit," Gottlieb snapped. He jabbed a finger at both of them. "You guys blew this. Now I've got two detectives bringing Moe Green and Paul Levine down *here*." He jabbed his finger against the desktop. "Two of the most powerful labor people in this city." He picked up a handful of shipping schedules. "And look what I've got to wave in their faces. The man upstairs is gonna love this—"

"Look," Morgan interrupted, his own face red now. "It had to be this guy Weathersby or somebody else in that fucking office. There's no other way the kid could've known this was going down."

Gottlieb sat back in his chair and stared at Morgan. "I don't buy it," he said. "Weathersby had approval from his home office. We got our warrant based on their agreed cooperation. They're a foreign company, and they are not about to jerk around a U.S. law enforcement agency. And Weathersby's ass wouldn't be worth a nickel to that company if he did it on his own hook." He shook his head slowly. "No. You guys blew it. The kid dumped the cash and you missed it."

"No way," Gaffrey said, keeping his voice soft, even though his temper was rising. "That kid went through that office door with me waiting in the hall and Jerry climbing up his ass. He couldn't a dumped it without one of us seeing him."

"Listen, I worked this case for a month before I brought it to you," Morgan said. "I *know* how this scam is being worked. And we were on this kid tight."

"Don't misunderstand," Gottlieb said. "The District Attorny's office is grateful for the cooperation of the Waterfront Commission. In fact, I just can't wait to see the man upstairs to find out just *how* grateful he is." Morgan, his face deep red now, began to object, but Gottlieb raised both hands, stopping him. "The thing you do now is get back over to Broad Street. You talk to our friend, Mr. Weathersby, and anybody else this kid even breathed near. And you find that goddamn money. No matter what, you find the money." Gottlieb rose from behind his desk and ran a hand through his bushy hair. "I'll stall things here, and I'll sweat this kid myself. But I'm not going to have all day. Green's lawyer is going to be climbing up my ass within an hour. So do it now and do it fast."

Tony looked up into Gottlieb's smiling face, then watched him as he carefully seated himself on the opposite side of the small, green metal table that stood between them. Behind him a uniformed officer had placed himself in front of the door, his arms folded across his chest.

Gottlieb introduced himself, keeping his voice soft, in sharp contrast to his eyes. He placed a yellow legal pad on the table in front of him and withdrew a ballpoint pen from his pocket. "Have you been advised of your rights?" Gottlieb asked.

"Yes."

"Do you have any objection to talking to me?"

"I'd like to talk to someone from the union first."

Gottlieb leaned forward. "Why?"

"I just don't know what this is all about, Mr. Gottlieb. I tried to tell the other men that. I just ran errands."

Gottlieb studied Tony's face. It was a mask of innocence, but he knew the kid had to be bleeding inside. He had to be. He took off his glasses, studied them for a moment, then replaced them. "You know what a bagman is, Tony?"

"Yes, sir."

"That's what you are, Tony. And that means you're going to do some time unless you stop playing games with us."

Tony stared at Gottlieb for several moments, fighting the feeling of nausea that had suddenly hit his stomach. He drew a deep breath and forced himself to look into Gottlieb's eyes. "Can I make a telephone call, Mr. Gottlieb?" he asked.

Gottlieb was still seething when Tony returned to the interrogation room. He wanted the kid to bleed, and bleed openly. He wanted him to talk like his life depended on it. But even now, all he saw was that mask of innocence.

Tony was far more shaken than Gottlieb knew. He had called the union office and had been told, by Gert, that Green and Levine had left earlier with two detectives. She had called the union's lawyer and would call again to make sure he knew where Tony was, she had said.

Gottlieb leaned forward, searching Tony's eyes. "You made your call?" he asked.

"Yes, thanks."

"You're very polite, aren't you, Tony?"

Tony stared at Gottlieb but didn't answer. His hands

were in his lap, out of sight, the fingers interlocked and squeezed together.

"What did you do with the money?" Gottlieb asked.

"I don't know anything about any money, Mr. Gottlieb."

"I'm talking about the money in the envelope Mr. Weathersby gave you."

"Those other men took the envelope."

Gottlieb smiled at him, then shook his head. "Polite, but not very smart," he said. "I mean the other envelope, Tony. The one my men are out getting now. The one that's going to have your fingerprints all over it. The one that has marked money inside that Mr. Weathersby can identify."

Gottlieb waited for some reaction. When none came, he leaned back in his chair and began tapping his pen against the table. "We have Mr. Green and Mr. Levine in other rooms here." He smiled. "But you know that, don't you? I'm sure whoever you talked to on the telephone told you that." He shrugged. "Well, maybe one of them will tell us what you were supposed to do with the money." He leaned forward again. "But that'll be too bad for you, my polite young friend. Because whoever tells us gets to make a deal. That's the way these things work. Whoever talks, walks. Unfortunately, sometimes the bad guys talk first, and then . . ." He let the words fall off. "It would be too bad, Tony, if you really *were* just running errands and have to end up in a pile of shit because you're not smart enough to answer a few simple questions."

"That's all I was doing, Mr. Gottlieb. Just running an errand." He watched Gottlieb's face darken and felt his own pulse begin to pound.

There was a knock at the door. It opened, and a young woman poked her head in.

"Mr. Gottlieb, John Worthy is here. He says he represents Mr. Marco and would like to see his client."

Gottlieb nodded. "Show him in." He stared at the table for a moment, then up at Tony. "I feel sorry for you, kid. I think you're making a bad mistake."

When the door opened again, a heavy, round-faced man with a florid complexion walked briskly into the room and placed an overstuffed briefcase on the table. He smiled broadly at Gottlieb, adjusted the lapels of a well-tailored blue suit, then patted one side of his carefully combed hair.

"Barney," he said, still smiling, "what's going on? You seem to have half the union here today."

"It seems so, John," Gottlieb said. "And I may have the other half here tomorrow."

"Charges?" Worthy asked.

"Not yet," Gottlieb said. "Right now we're just looking for a few answers. But we're contemplating conspiracy to commit a felony."

Worthy raised his eyebrows. "To wit?" he asked.

"Extortion," Gottlieb answered.

Worthy nodded and smiled again. "May I have a moment alone with my client?"

Gottlieb stood, inclining his head to one side. "He's all yours," he said.

When Gottlieb and the uniformed officer had left, Worthy sat down quickly, every trace of joviality disappearing from his face.

"All right, Tony. Just tell me everything that happened." He watched Tony's eyes glance nervously around the small room. He raised a hand. "Not to worry. Nobody will be listening in."

Tony drew a long breath. "These two detectives, they just grabbed me when I came out of the shipping company office."

"What did they say?"

"They wanted an envelope Weathersby gave me. Then they searched me, handcuffed me, and brought me here."

"What did you tell them?"

"Nothing. Just that I didn't know what they were talking about. That I was just running an errand."

"But they took the envelope."

Tony shook his head. "They took the other one, the extra envelope I carry each time."

Worthy leaned forward, as though ready to climb out of his chair. "Where is the envelope Weathersby gave you?" he asked, emphasizing each word.

"I put it in a tray on a desk in the office."

Worthy raised one finger. "Inside the shipping company office?" He watched as Tony nodded, his finger still poised. "Did you say anything to anyone in that office that might in any way be construed as being illegal?" Again he watched Tony shake his head.

"The only thing I talked about was the weather."

Worthy sat back in his chair and began to chuckle. "The weather. My God, I love it."

Tony sat there, confused, watching the man's stomach shake with gentle laughter. "Look, Mr. Gottlieb just told me the detectives have gone back to find the other envelope. He said there's marked money inside, and if my fingerprints are on the envelope, I've had it."

Worthy leaned back and laughed, then sat forward and stroked his chin. "Tell me something, Tony. What made you get rid of that envelope?"

Tony twisted nervously in his seat. "It was just the way everything felt. Everyone seemed nervous, and the receptionist kept looking at those two guys who turned out to be detectives. I just freaked about it, and I figured, if nothing happened, I could go back and get the envelope later."

Worthy stared at him. "You might have looked foolish doing that," he said.

Tony gave a small shrug. "Yeah, well, I guess I didn't think about that."

Worthy leaned across the table and pinched Tony's cheek, hard enough to make him blink. "You have great instincts, my boy. Never, ever, stop listening to them."

"But what about my fingerprints on the other envelope?" Tony asked.

Worthy sat back and chuckled again. "Tony, they can find your fingerprints, traces of semen, saliva, and threads from your clothing on that envelope. If it didn't leave that office, none of it is worth a damn thing. You cannot extort something from someone if you never take it away from them. And that, my young man, is the law according to Worthy." He leaned back again and folded his hands across his ample stomach. "Do you remember what Mr. Levine told you to say about the unsigned memos directing you to run errands and about leaving what you picked up on the reception desk?" he asked.

"Yes," Tony said, then repeated the old instructions.

"Good," Worthy said. "Then let's invite Mr. Gottlieb back in and enjoy ourselves."

When Gottlieb returned, Worthy rose and offered him his chair. "Barney, my client is perfectly willing to answer any questions you have." He paused to offer Gottlieb a smile. "But before we start, please let me give you some background about young Mr. Marco."

Gottlieb stared at the money stacked neatly on top of his desk, the carefully opened envelope next to it. He raised his eyes slowly to the two detectives seated across from him. "Well, at least we recovered the money." His voice was soft, too much so for the look in his eyes.

"I still think somebody tipped the kid off," Morgan said, staring at the nails of one hand. "I can't prove it, but I'd bet my ass it was Weathersby. When we talked to him, he looked like he was gonna have a stroke."

"Wouldn't you, if you had just crossed Moe Green?" Gottlieb asked. He watched Morgan squirm in his chair, then leaned back in his own and continued to stare at him. "No, Jerry," he said. "You're looking for a scapegoat." He paused. "Not a bad idea, and Weathersby's handy. But it depends on how the man upstairs wants to handle it."

"How about the kid?" Gaffrey asked. "If Weathersby's not lying, he handled that envelope. So we get his prints off it and we go to work on him. Maybe even hold him as a material witness. And we lean on him . . . hard, until he admits carrying a bag for these people."

Gottlieb rocked his chair back and forth as he slowly shook his head in a counter-rhythm. "Let me tell you about this kid," he said. "His father died when he was thirteen—killed working on the docks as a longshoreman. From that day on the kid went to work to support his widowed mother and younger sister. First he worked in a grocery store, carrying packages of groceries up flights of stairs to old ladies who couldn't get out." Gottlieb's voice dripped sarcasm, and his rocking became more pronounced. "Then, at sixteen, he went to work on the docks himself, working the same job that killed his father; at the same time he was going to Stuyvesant High School—a place, in case you don't know, that's for gifted kids—and from which our friend graduated with a straight A average. Now, while he's still working his tail off to support his family, he goes to Columbia on a full academic scholarship."

Gottlieb leaned forward in his chair, resting his fore-arms on his desk. "The kid has no sheet, not even a juvenile record, which, based on the neighborhood he comes from, is a minor miracle." Again he slowly shook his head. "No, you openly lean on this kid and the newspapers will have him up for canonization within the week." He paused, looking from one detective to the other. "And in case you failed to notice, the kid does not rattle easily."

"So he beats us," Morgan snapped. "And we roll over like chumps."

Gottlieb stared at Morgan for several moments. When he finally spoke, his voice was soft yet threatening. "You think *I* enjoyed explaining this upstairs? You think *I* enjoyed explaining it to the judge who issued the warrant against one of the most powerful labor unions in the city, and whose political ass is now in a pile of shit? You think *I* enjoyed apologizing to Mr. Green and Mr. Levine for the unfortunate mistake that was made?" He continued to hold Morgan's eyes. "And all because we were outmaneuvered by a college kid?" He began tapping his fingers against the desk. "No, I'm not going to roll over, Jerry. But I'm not going to commit political suicide, either." He turned his attention to Gaffrey. "I want you on this kid's ass. At least once a week." He raised his hands and brought the palms together. "Ask some questions about him, in his neighborhood and up at the school. Maybe visit the dean. And pay him a few visits." He gestured with his joined hands, almost as if praying. "Yank him away when he's with some of his college friends. Nothing big. Just a little talk in the car. Who knows, maybe it will shake him up, lead to some little mistake." He leaned back in his chair, his palms still pressed together. "At least we'll let the son of a bitch know we haven't forgotten him. And I do *not* intend to forget Mr. Marco."

Tony sat with Moe Green, alone in his office. Green had poured him a small amount of malt Scotch. It was the first time Tony had tasted it, and he was surprised at how smooth and pleasant it was.

Tony had returned to the office with Worthy, the union

lawyer, and had been summoned to Green's office a short time later. Now that they were seated across from each other, Green seemed to exude a strange mixture of gentleness and simmering anger.

"I'm sorry this had to happen," Green said, offering a grimace, which, for him, passed as a smile. "I know it must have been humiliating for you, but"—he gestured in a circular motion with one hand—"sometimes these things happen. I want you to know I'm very pleased with the way you handled yourself, but I knew you would. For a long time now I knew you were that kind of young man."

Tony thanked him, and Green nodded, then drew heavily on the cigarette again. "Worthy thinks it might be good if I explained the circumstances to you. So does Paul." He hesitated, then added, "Is there anything you'd like to know?"

Tony shook his head. "I don't need any explanation, Mr. Green."

The grimace returned, and Green slowly nodded his head. "I didn't think you would, Tony. I don't like to explain. To me, people accept or they don't." He sipped his drink, watching Tony over the rim. "Let's just say this guy, Weathersby, or the company, or both, did something foolish." He shook his head almost sadly, but his eyes were hard and bitter. "They did the wrong thing, and I think someday they're going to be sorry they did."

"Now, for you, Tony," Green said. "From now on, no more errands. These people, once they get something in their heads, it stays there forever. There's no reason for you to be harassed, and we have plenty of other things around here for you to do."

"Yes, sir," Tony said.

"Good," Green said, standing and holding out his hand. He took Tony's arm and guided him toward the door. "My daughter's coming home from college this weekend. Why don't you come over for dinner on Sunday."

"I'd like that a lot," Tony said.

"Good," Green said. "You come around two o'clock."

Descending the stairs, Tony thought of the short, fat, perspiring Mr. Weathersby. He let out a long breath. You poor, silly bastard, he thought.

CHAPTER/THIRTEEN

THE YOUNG WOMAN hung on Tony's arm as they walked slowly down Broadway, toward a small Italian restaurant near the Columbia campus. The young woman was tall and slender, with long blond hair and a smile that looked as though it had come straight out of a toothpaste commercial. Her name was Samantha Richardson, and Tony had been dating her—among others—for several months, and as they walked together now, she looked at him with a sense of pleased possessiveness.

Over the past three years Tony had overcome his feelings of not belonging. He had put money aside and had gradually improved his wardrobe. Walking with Samantha now, Tony fingered the lapel of his lightweight blue blazer, which, together with the tan slacks, pale blue shirt, and solid yellow tie, gave him a sense of ease among his fellow students. He had even purchased, with difficulty, a pair of glove-leather Gucci loafers, and he smiled to himself at the conscious effort he had taken to make sure his dress was equal to his surroundings.

Samantha squeezed his arm against her side as she chattered on about their planned trip, the following day, to her father's closed summer house in Southampton.

"We'll have to rough it," Samantha said. "The cook and the maid are at the house in Greenwich."

Tony stopped and turned to her. "I don't know about that. I'm not used to primitive accommodations."

Samantha elbowed him in the ribs, then leaned her head against his shoulder and pulled him along. "You'll live," she said. "Just don't forget to remind me to check and make sure I have my key."

"Can you cook?" Tony asked.

Samantha shrugged. "I don't know. I never tried."

"My God," Tony said. "No cook and no key. I can see the headlines now: 'College Scholar Poisoned After Break-in at Weekend Retreat.' The *News* will have a field day. They'll probably have pictures of my body and everything."

"*I'm* going to have pictures of your body and everything," Samantha said. "And if there are going to be headlines, they'll read: 'College Scholar Strangled by Angry Cook; Rape Suspected.' "

"Only suspected?" Tony asked.

"It depends how badly you complain about the food."

At the door of the restaurant Tony heard his name called out, stopped and turned. His eyes hardened as he watched Gaffrey climb out of his unmarked car and walk toward him slowly.

When he was a few feet away, Gaffrey stopped, removed his shield from his suitcoat, and displayed it. "You remember me, don't you, Tony?" he asked.

"I remember you," Tony said.

Gaffrey looked at Samantha, then back at Tony. "You going to introduce me?" he asked.

Tony glared at him. Over the past few weeks Detective Gaffrey had questioned him several times, made visits to

Gino, to his mother, and to the dean of Arts and Science. He forced a smile. "No, I don't think so," he said.

Gaffrey returned Tony's smile. "We have to talk," he said.

"We were just going to dinner," Tony said.

"It won't take long. Why don't you have the young lady wait inside."

Tony turned to Samantha. Her eyes were wide and confused. He placed his hand on her arm. "I'm sorry," he said. "Why don't you go ahead. I'll only be a minute."

Samantha glanced at Gaffrey, then back at Tony. "Okay," she said.

"Have a nice evening, Miss Richardson," Gaffrey said, holding her eyes for a moment, enjoying the startled look at the use of her name, then taking Tony's arm and walking him to the car.

"Nice girl," Gaffrey said as he leaned back against the front fender. "I understand her daddy's a big-shot banker."

"I really wouldn't know," Tony said. "We only talk about sex and drugs."

Gaffrey laughed softly. "Not you, Tony. I hear you're a regular straight arrow." He paused to scratch his chin. "Although I *am* surprised to see you're not as polite as you were the last time I saw you."

Tony shook his head and looked away, then laughed softly. "We all have our bad days, Mr. Gaffrey," he said.

"Now that's better," Gaffrey said. "Tell me, Tony, you have a chance to think any more about what happened a few weeks back?"

Gaffrey was grinning up at him. Tony returned a half smile. "You know, I was starting to, Mr. Gaffrey. But then all these people started asking me about this guy from the District Attorney's Office who was coming around, and I was so busy answering their questions, I forgot about everything else."

Gaffrey's eyes hardened momentarily, then softened to match his returning smile. "That's a shame, kid." He paused, taking time to look down the street. "You know what else is a shame?" he asked at length.

"No."

"It's a shame a kid like you, who's got the world by the balls, should be heading for so much trouble."

Tony looked at him levelly. "Mr. Gaffrey, anything I've got, I worked my tail off to get. And there's nothing in my pocket that belongs to anybody else."

Gaffrey scratched his nose, bending his head slightly, so the freckles on his scalp looked out between his thinning hair. "Sure, kid. You just look the other way while other people steal."

Tony forced his face to remain impassive. Then he excused himself, saying that he had to join Samantha.

Gaffrey decided he wasn't going to get a rise out of the kid and took a step toward the door of the car. He stopped. "By the way, you hear about that guy Weathersby?"

"No."

"Last week. They found him in a parking lot. Two broken legs and a concussion."

Tony looked away. His voice softened. "That's too bad," he said. "He seemed like a nice guy."

"Yeah," Gaffrey said. "Nice but dumb. Have a good time with your girlfriend, kid."

Samantha was seated at a window table where she had obviously watched Tony's conversation with Gaffrey.

"That's enough cops and robbers for today," he said as he slid into the seat opposite her.

"What was that all about?" Her eyes were still wide, still confused.

Tony shook his head in mock sadness. "It was about the bank job I pulled last month. The one where I raped the cashier and then shot it out with the cops before I made my getaway."

Samantha stamped her foot under the table. "Tony!"

"It's nothing *really*. Last month there was some stuff missing off a ship. The shipping company insists it was stolen by the longshoremen who were working that day."

"But what does that have to do with you?"

Tony held out his hands in a gesture of helplessness. "I'm the clerk at the office. I keep the records of who was working on a given day. This cop wants those records, but I can't give them to him without a warrant."

"So why doesn't he get a warrant?"

Tony shook his head. "You ask him. He's talked to my mother, a guy who runs a grocery store in my neighborhood, and even the dean. He's just trying to get me to give him what the courts *won't* give him."

"But that's not fair."

"You're telling me," Tony said. "After I fill out those records they go into a locked file cabinet. And I don't even have a key. I keep trying to tell him that, but he doesn't want to believe me."

"But how did he know *my* name?"

Tony looked at her warmly. Now we get down to the real question, he thought. "He probably saw us together and asked somebody. It's just another needle he can stick in me to try to get what he wants." He inclined his head toward the window and the street outside. "Look, you were sitting here and you must have seen us talking. He was just pushing for information that I couldn't give him, even if I wanted to."

She sighed, then toyed with her knife and fork. "Do you think those longshoremen took those things?" she asked.

"Probably," Tony answered.

Samantha's face registered surprise. "Really?" she asked. Tony began to laugh, partly from his surprise at her reaction and partly out of relief at being able to make his first true statement in the past five minutes. "Longshoremen steal," he said. "So do the stevedores who run the piers and the seamen who work the ships. They find things that fall off the back of a truck."

Samantha's face screwed up in confusion. "What?"

"It's a saying," Tony explained. "Somebody comes home with a television set he didn't buy, or a case of liquor, and somebody asks where he got it. He says it fell off the back of a truck. You understand? He found it. No questions asked."

"That's terrible," Samantha said.

"I know," Tony said, "but it happens." He smiled wickedly.

Samantha cocked one eye. "You never did that, did you?"

Tony sat back in his chair, feigning surprise. "Never," he said.

CHAPTER/FOURTEEN

THE NEWS ABOUT Pete came the Friday before the Labor
Day weekend, the final respite before the start of Tony's
senior year at Columbia, a weekend where there would be
nothing for him to do but sit and wait it out.

The union offices had closed early to give everyone a
running start into the long three-day weekend. To Tony it
simply meant time to himself. He had rented a cabin in
the Catskill Mountains for his mother and sister and Aunt
Marie, and they had left that morning, his aunt's car
loaded like a gypsy wagon, each of them burdened with
far more than they could ever unpack, let alone use, in
seventy-two hours.

He smiled, thinking back over it now: the yelling and
bickering over what should or should not be taken; the
oaths to the saints over the slowness or stupidity of one or
the other. And finally his mother's decision, after the car
was packed, that they should wait until evening so Tony
could go with them.

He had escaped that, but only just, and now the week-end lay ahead with time to think and sort things out.

He was just about to enter the apartment building when he heard his name called out in a high, agonized wail. He spun around, his body defensively tense, and saw Mary Beth running toward him across the street, her tear-streaked face a mass of fear and pain.

She threw herself against him, sobbing into his shoulder, and he took her arms and pushed her back, searching her face and body for some sign of attack, some physical injury.

"What happened, Mary Beth? What happened?"

"It's Pete," she sobbed. "They killed Pete." The flood of tears began again, and she fell back against his shoulder and sobbed uncontrollably.

Tony felt his stomach tighten, the bile rise to his throat. A cold chill ran down his back, and his hands began to tremble. "What are you talking about? How do you know?"

Mary Beth struggled to catch her breath, and the words came out in gulping sobs. "His mother got a telegram. Just an hour ago."

"What did it say?" He waited, and when she didn't answer, he took her arms and shook her. "What did it say?"

Mary Beth trembled, both from the pain she felt and the violence in his voice. "It said he's missing in action and presumed dead." She choked on the final word; her body seemed to buckle.

He slipped his arm around her waist and pulled her to him, supporting her, the word *presumed* playing over and over in his mind. Not dead, he told himself, only "presumed." Not the same thing. He felt his own breath coming in gasps, the trembling in his arms moving to his legs. "Let's go upstairs," he whispered. "I think we both need to sit down."

He seated Mary Beth in one corner of the large over-stuffed sofa. She huddled there, legs drawn beneath her, body still trembling. The room was dimly lit, the shades drawn against the day's heat, and her pale complexion seemed ghostlike. Tony went to the kitchen and gathered a bottle of wine, two glasses, and a dampened washcloth. When he returned, he sat next to her and wiped her face, cleaning away the streaks of mascara that had formed dark, cracked lines across her cheeks. He poured them each a glass of wine and handed her one, watching as she held it in both hands in an effort to subdue the tremors that engulfed her body.

"They'll find him," he said at length, his own voice shaky and uncertain. "I know they will."

Mary Beth looked at him, then lowered her head, eyes closed, and slowly shook her head back and forth.

They sat in silence, sipping the wine, lost in their own thoughts. Absently Tony refilled their glasses, his mind reliving all the days with Pete. They had grown up together from childhood; had been closer to each other than to members of their own family. There was nothing, not a pain, not an ambition, not a failure they had not shared with each other. His thoughts came to an abrupt halt. Except in the past few years, he reminded himself. He closed his eyes, wishing he had been with Pete when it happened. The idea jolted him. Pete was dead. No matter how much he wanted to believe otherwise, no matter how much he continued to resist the idea, it was true. He turned to Mary Beth. "I want to go up to the church," he said. "Do you want to come?"

Her lips trembled, then she shook her head. "I don't think I could walk that far, Tony."

He reached out and stroked her cheek. "Stay here if you want. I won't be very long."

St. Francis Xavier Church was dark and cavernous, its

Gothic arches rising high above, the only light filtering in through the soot-coated stained-glass windows. Tony knelt in a pew halfway down the center aisle, his nostrils filling with the scent of beeswax from the rows of votive candles that lined either side of the long altar rail. In a front pew an elderly woman knelt and prayed, her arthritic hands fumbling with a pair of rosary beads, her face raised toward a statue of the Virgin Mary. She wore a black dress with a black scarf tied tightly around her head, and Tony knew if she stood, he would see the sturdy black shoes he had seen on neighborhood women all his life.

He looked up at the altar, the gold tabernacle its center-piece, placed beneath a massive crucifix of the dead Christ. He and Pete had received their First Communion there and, years later, had walked to the altar to kneel before an auxiliary bishop to be confirmed. Tony had taken the name Francis, and Pete, Xavier. It had been a joke between them, naming themselves jointly after the church itself. He looked toward the side aisle where confessionals had been placed every twenty feet along the wall. He recalled the Saturday evenings they had spent sitting and waiting, trying to determine which priest occupied which confessional, fearful they would choose incorrectly and find themselves faced with one who would scream out at them for their adolescent sins.

No more sins now, Pete, he told himself. No more sins ever again.

Mary Beth was still huddled in the corner of the sofa when he returned, the bottle of red wine empty on the coffee table before her. He went to the kitchen and opened another bottle. Better to dull the pain as much as possible, he told himself. To be numb is to be free. At least for today.

She looked at him as he filled her glass. The sobbing and shaking had stopped now, and the puffiness around her eyes had begun to subside. She was dressed in shorts and a loose-fitting scoop-neck jersey, and despite her well-defined figure, she looked very small and very frail.

"You know it's true, too, don't you?" she asked.

He sat back and rested his head against the back of the sofa. "I don't want to think about it, Mary Beth. Not now."

She moved toward him and placed her head against his shoulder. He slipped his arm around her neck and stroked her arm.

He raised his head and looked down at Mary Beth. The scoop neck of her loose-fitting jersey had fallen forward, exposing the soft white skin of her breasts. She shifted her weight against him and he could see she was not wearing a bra. It caused a sudden stir within him, and he looked away.

"Are you okay?" he asked.

She nodded her head against his shoulder. "It was just the shock," she said. "It was like someone hit me in the stomach. I couldn't even breathe. I better go," she said. "Your mother will be coming home, she'll see us here, she'll see the wine, and she'll think—"

"Not today," he said. "They all went away to the mountains for the weekend." He squeezed her arm. "You hungry? My mother made up a pan of manicotti so I wouldn't starve to death while she was gone. All I have to do is heat it up."

Mary Beth nodded. "I don't ever remember being this hungry before. It makes me feel so stupid, so gross. But I can't help it."

Tony understood. He felt the same inexplicable hunger. He eased himself up from the sofa, then turned back to Mary Beth with a weak smile. "Bring your wine," he said, "and Chef Anthony will start getting his act together."

They stood side by side in the kitchen, leaning against a

196 William Heffernan

counter. Mary Beth sipped her wine, using only one hand now, her eyes still distant and thoughtful. "It all seems so stupid," she said. "We've all been together since we were little kids. Just playing and growing up and trying to figure out what we were going to do next. You go to college, Pete goes into the army, and I get a job as a waitress." She turned and stared up at him. "I don't even know what that shitty, stupid war is about. I never cared what it was about. I was just waiting for Pete to come home so we could get married. What a stupid joke," she whispered. "What a shitty, stupid joke."

After dinner they returned to the living room and sat facing each other from opposite ends of the sofa, a third bottle of wine between them. They talked about the neighborhood, about growing up together, and the crazy and funny things that had happened to them all, both individually and together, all of it somehow returning to Pete in the end.

It was like a private wake, Tony thought, the way friends and relatives gathered after a funeral and spoke only of the good times they had known with the one person who was no longer among them. A sweet melancholy, a time of acceptance before going on.

Mary Beth reached into the pocket of her shorts and withdrew four poorly rolled joints of marijuana and held them out in her open palm. "Dessert," she said.

Tony nodded and moved next to her, taking one of the proffered joints and lighting it. He sucked the harsh smoke into his lungs and held it there, passing the joint to Mary Beth, who did the same. On the third hit a tingling sensation began at the base of his skull, then pushed a mellow haze up into his brain. He closed his eyes, enjoying the feeling of numbness that began to flow through his body, relaxing each muscle in turn until he felt limp and loose.

When they had finished the third joint, Mary Beth placed her head against his shoulder, and Tony again encircled her with his arm. Slowly, with just the tips of his fingers, he stroked her arm and shoulder, which, under the dulling quality of the marijuana, now had the feel of fine silk. The room seemed shrouded in a dull, quiet haze, and he closed his eyes, enjoying the sensation of Mary Beth's fingers softly stroking his upper thigh. Without thought his hand moved into the loose-fitting scoop of her blouse, cupping and stroking each breast in turn, allowing his fingers to play gently against each nipple, enjoying the sensation of hardness, of distension to what seemed an impossible length.

Mary Beth groaned softly and twisted her body with pleasure.

"We shouldn't, Tony. It's not right," she said.

"There's nothing wrong with it," he said. "Not anymore."

He continued to run his hands along her body, stroking, caressing, and she turned her body toward him and began imitating each touch he offered her. She raised herself up and placed her mouth against his, her lips softer than he had thought lips could be, her tongue playing languorously against his own, in a lazy, slow, erotic dance.

He eased her back on the sofa and, still kissing her, slowly removed her shorts and blouse, then his own clothing. He ran his lips over her neck, then down to her breasts, lingering over each with a slow, unhurried determination, then back to her neck, her face, her eyes.

Mary Beth let out a low, pleasurable groan, and when she opened her eyes, Tony was staring down at her, his face filled with desire, need.

She opened her legs, and he slid between them and felt her hips twist, undulate, until she seized him and drew him inside. She closed her eyes and gasped, then placed her face against his, her mouth pressed to his ear.

"Make me forget," she whispered. "Please, Tony, make me forget."

Tony was seated in his small, cramped cubbyhole of an office, trying to keep his mind attuned to the monotonous task set before him. He had spent this Tuesday, following the Labor Day weekend, registering for the semester's classes, moving like a somnambulant through the boring ritual, his mind still fixed on the weekend.

The guilt he felt was overpowering, yet he continued to dismiss it. He had spent the weekend in bed with Mary Beth, each of them taking turns exhausting the other, each exploring new ways to give and take pleasure. He had lost count of the number of times they had made love, the hours they had simply held each other, each trying to avoid the one thought that kept creeping back.

He drew a deep breath and massaged his eyes with his fingertips. His mother and sister were back now, and Mary Beth was gone. But he knew he would be with her again. There was no way to avoid it, and he knew he didn't want to avoid it, even if he could.

"No sleeping on the job. Or are you just hung over?"

He turned to the sound of the voice, his eyes slightly blurred at first, then gradually focusing on Shirley Green's smiling face.

"What the hell are you doing here? I thought you'd be up at Vassar, fighting over classes with all the other little rich girls."

Shirley inclined her head to one side, then casually raised the middle finger of one hand.

"Nice," he said. "You can take the girl out of Brooklyn . . ." He let the line die without completing it.

Shirley crossed the tiny room and perched on the edge of his desk. "No more Vassar," she said.

"How come?"

"I got bored with country life. So I transferred."

"To where?"

She smiled mischievously. "Barnard. Now we can be roommates."

"Hey, that's great." Tony forced himself to become serious but only barely. "But forget that roommate stuff. I'm too young to be packed in a crate and shipped to Australia."

She shrugged. "Your loss," she said. "But I've decided to be nice to you, anyway."

"That sounds intriguing. And just how, pray tell?"

"I've gotten you the afternoon off." She paused, watching Tony's eyebrows go up in mock surprise. "But only if you spend it showing me around the new campus. Interested?"

"Beats the hell out of work," he said, ducking away as she swung an open hand toward his head.

"I missed you, Tony." Shirley drew out the words, then exhaled with pleasure as she arched her back, pressing against him and drawing him deeper inside. "I want you," she said, the words coming out in a hiss of satisfaction. "I was crazy to let you get away from me." Her body thrashed beneath his, each movement demanding more of him, each groan, each thrust driving him to a higher level of excitement.

The daybed in Tony's dormitory room was long and narrow and substituted as a sofa during the day, one not suited to impassioned lovemaking, and Shirley's acrobatic vigor had nearly thrown him to the floor several times.

The "tour" of the campus had lasted little more than ten minutes when Shirley had asked to see his room. Once there she had simply undressed and led him directly to bed. Her blatant desire for sex was one of several things about her that excited him. Another was her honesty about that desire. Once, earlier in their relationship, he had asked her about it. She had simply smiled at the idea. "There's nothing about screwing I don't like," she had said.

Tony struggled now against her ever-intensifying movements. Shirley had already reached orgasm several times and now was approaching a near frenzy of pleasure. Her legs tightened around his waist, and her back arched again, until only her head was supporting her. She let out a long, low moan that broke into small, weak gasps with each rhythmic thrust, until finally Tony could contain himself no longer and, with a low, almost painful cry of his own, exploded within her.

They collapsed on top of each other, each still moving with a gradually slowing pace, like two powerful machines that suddenly had been turned off but whose impetus demanded continued movement beyond natural restraint.

Shirley held him tightly against her, her lips caressing his neck and shoulder, her breath still hot and fast against his skin. He could feel the muscles of her vagina contracting, squeezing and pulling against him, drawing out each last vestige of pleasure.

"You've got to stop forcing your intentions on me," she said, punctuating each word with a light, gentle bite. She flicked her tongue against his ear. "At least you could give me time to make myself safe," she said.

Tony raised up and stared down at her. "You're kidding me," he said.

Shirley bit her lip fighting back laughter. "What's the matter? Wouldn't you marry me if a little Tony suddenly started to grow?"

He lowered his head and kissed the tip of her nose. "Of course I would," he said. "Then I'd strangle you with your own brassiere."

She giggled at the thought. "Don't worry. It's the per-

fect time of the month. You should have learned all about
that from the pope."

"The pope's celibate."

"Poor baby," she whispered.

Tony slipped down next to her and drew her against
him. Her body was soft and sensual and comforting to
touch. He kissed her forehead and the top of her head,
taking in the delicate scent of her rich, dark hair. Lying
there, his mind drifted to Mary Beth. There was the
unavoidable comparison, although he was not certain why.
Shirley was the far more vigorous of the two; far more
aggressive, more impulsive, with an instinctive desire for
sex that he found constantly exciting. It was hard to think
of Mary Beth in terms of Shirley. They had used each
other, had needed to at the moment. There had been a
sweetness, an innocence, about it. They had helped each
other through a terrible moment, and that was something
he could not bring himself to regret. Yet it was something
he knew he should not continue. It was odd. He had
never before thought of Mary Beth in a sexual way. She
had belonged to Pete. Even now, when he thought of
what had happened, it was with gratitude, not passion.
But he would have to see her again. She did not deserve
the hurt of rejection. He knew too well the pain rejection
produced, and it was not something he would care to
inflict on someone else. It would have to be done over
time, with tenderness and affection, until Mary Beth understood they had only helped each other recover from
the loss of Pete. He closed his eyes and pushed the
thought away.

"You seem very far off." Shirley had pulled her head
back and was staring into his eyes.

He smiled weakly, then kissed her forehead. He suddenly wanted to tell her about Mary Beth, but it certainly
didn't seem the time or the place.

"If I told you I was thinking about someone else, would it make you angry?" he asked.

"I'd only kill you," she said. She studied his face again, then, seeing the pain in his eyes, shook her head. "Tell me," she whispered.

He pulled her close to him, and slowly, quietly, told her what had happened. He told her about Pete and how one thing had seemed to wash away the other.

When he had finished, Shirley lay quietly in his arms for several minutes, her fingers absently stroking the hair on his chest. "I'm sorry about your friend," she said at length. She raised herself up and brought her face close to his. "As far as your friend, Mary Beth, is concerned, she's crazy if she lets you get away. Anyone who let you get away would have to be." And *I* don't intend to, Shirley told herself.

Shirley brought her mouth to his, open and hungry. Her tongue filled it, lashing violently against his own, searching out every corner. Her hand moved slowly down his body, until she found what she sought, her fingers moving gently but firmly, bringing him back to life.

CHAPTER/FIFTEEN

ON THE DAY before Thanksgiving Mary Beth told Tony she was pregnant. She had been taking her birth control pills, she had insisted, but something had gone wrong. Now something had to be done, and Tony had to help her do it.

They had talked quietly in his room at Columbia, tears welling up in Mary Beth's eyes at the mention of an abortion. His relationship with Mary Beth had dwindled over the past month, just as his closeness to Shirley had steadily grown. But he and Mary Beth had remained friends; up to this point, it had gone as he had planned, a gradual separation without unnecessary pain. Now all that had changed.

The conflict had torn at him, but he had known his choices were limited. *Doing the right thing.* The philosophy of the close-knit society in which he had been raised had played over and over in his mind. Marriage, he had decided, was out of the question. He could see no point in a lifetime of mutual sacrifice for a mistake that had been made jointly. The choices, they had finally both agreed, were limited to two. Mary Beth could have the child and Tony would support it, or she could have an abortion and Tony would bear the expense. The final decision would be hers. If she chose the latter, it would have to be done surreptitiously but with great care, for although a movement existed to legalize abortion in New York, it could be years before it became a reality. What had frightened Tony about that choice had been that many of those practicing beyond the law had reputations as virtual butchers. And when Mary Beth had decided on that option, Tony had spoken to Shirley about it and had been urged to go to the one person he could trust to help.

Moe Green stared at him across his desk, his normally cold blue eyes now colder than Tony had ever seen them. He leaned forward as though ready to leap across the barrier that separated them. "I suppose you're doing the same thing with my Shirley," he said, his voice little more than a hoarse growl.

Tony's body tensed, and he felt perspiration wash his palms. He shook his head. "I really care about Shirley, Mr. Green. A lot more than I've ever let you know. I think she feels the same about me. At least I hope she does."

Green sat back in his chair, his eyes still hard and angry. "So how did this happen?" he asked.

Tony told him. He told him about Pete, and how he and Mary Beth had stumbled into an affair out of mutual need, mutual grief. And he told him how it had ended when he had begun to see Shirley again. It had simply not ended soon enough.

"Are you sure it's your kid?" Green asked.

The question startled Tony. It was a thought that had never entered his mind. "She said it was, and I know it could be. I don't see where I have any other choice." He drew a deep breath; the hands in his lap were clasped tightly together. "What scares me," he continued "is that she'll end up with some butcher, and I don't want that to happen. I just don't know anything about this sort of thing. I don't know how to pick someone who's safe. And I can't go to anyone in the neighborhood for advice, because then they'd find out about Mary Beth." He shook his head. "Where we live, a person could never live that sort of thing down."

"You care about this girl?" Green asked.

"Not in the way you mean. But we grew up together, and she meant a lot to Pete. I just don't want to see her hurt."

Green nodded, then paused to light a cigarette. "Okay, kid." He paused again. "There's somebody we know, through the union, who we use from time to time. Sometimes some of the men get their women into this kind of trouble, and it's better to have somebody who can take care of things than let them do it themselves and really screw it up." He stared at Tony for several seconds. "You. I thought you were smarter than this."

"So did I," Tony said.

"You have the girl here next Monday at ten o'clock. It'll be set up by then, and we'll have somebody take her there and bring her home."

"I thought I should be with her," Tony said.

"No!" Green snapped the word out so sharply, it made Tony jump. "You stay away from the whole thing. And you stay away from her. Be smart this time. Think with your head, not your . . ." He motioned with his head toward Tony's crotch and let the sentence die.

Tony twisted in his seat, then finally nodded. Green's help, he knew, would depend on doing as he was told.

"Don't worry, Tony," Green said. "We'll make sure there's a woman with her, and that she's looked after in every way."

When Tony left, Green called Paul Levine into his office.

"Seems our boy, Tony, has gotten himself in some trouble with a young lady," Green explained.

Levine chuckled over the news, then shrugged his shoulders. "He's young," he said. "It happens."

"Well, we're going to help him out this time, with our doctor friend in Jersey."

Levine said nothing.

"You set it up," Green continued. "The girl will be here at ten on Monday, and I'd like you to take her there and then bring her home. And I'd like you to take a woman with you. Someone the girl will trust."

"No problem," Levine said.

"There's more," Green said. He waited for some comment and, when none was forthcoming, continued. "Afterward I want word about this to get around the girl's neighborhood. Then later I want you and the woman to go to her. Tell her you heard she's having a hard time about the whole thing and offer her a job and some money so she can get away and get a fresh start someplace else."

Levine stared at his friend for several moments. "You're going to a lot of trouble over this, aren't you, Moe?" When Green did not respond, Levine leaned forward in his chair. "How come, Moe?"

"Let's just say I have plans for Tony, and they don't include having some little chippie around who can't keep her legs together."

Levine sat back in his chair and nodded. His face had become a mask. He didn't at all like what he was hearing.

It was early January when Mary Beth came to Tony's room at Columbia to tell him she was leaving the city to take a job she had been offered in Las Vegas. The neighborhood was just too much for her: the looks, the snide comments, the way some people simply turned their heads away.

"They make me feel like that woman in the book everyone had to read in high school," she said.

Tony nodded. *"The Scarlet Letter,"* he said.

"They're such bastards," she said, then insisted it didn't matter. She wanted to get away. She hated the neighborhood, felt stifled by it, and had wanted to leave for years.

Tony offered to help in any way he could; he explained he had never wanted to hurt her and would do anything if he could reverse what had happened.

Mary Beth smiled at him and inclined her head to one side. "We had our chance," she said. "We just couldn't go through with it." She reached out and stroked his cheek. "But I'll always love you for being willing to. You just think about me from time to time. And love me a little too," she said.

Tony put his arms around her and drew her to him. "I will," he said. "I always will."

In May, one month before Tony's graduation from Columbia, he received a telephone call from Pete's mother, and it left him with a mix of emotions he had never before experienced.

Pete was alive. He had been wounded, captured by the Viet Cong, and held prisoner for five months before escaping and finding his way back through the jungle. He was now hospitalized in San Diego and would be there for several months.

When the call ended, Tony sat in numb silence. Pete was alive; the fact itself seemed like a miracle. He would see him again, speak to him again. He felt an enormous sense of relief and happiness, and with it, an enormous dread. He would have to tell him what had happened with Mary Beth, try to make him understand. It struck him in a wave. Never in his life had he felt such revulsion toward himself.

A week after his graduation from Columbia, Tony asked Shirley to marry him. He had decided, after considerable thought, to specialize in labor law, an area where he could combine his intellect and background to best advantage. He cared for Shirley, was more in love with her than any of the others he had dated, and the promise their marriage held for his rise in the labor movement was, at best, only an ancillary consideration.

It was a decision applauded by Moe Green, who, to Tony's surprise, greeted the news with enthusiasm, asking only that they agree to a civil ceremony rather than cross the bounds of either of their religions.

Even Tony's mother was pleased. The idea of a civil ceremony caused her her only concern, and he thought he detected a shrewdness in her that he had never noticed before. She liked Shirley; that had never been in question since they had first met. But she had always held a parochial view of life, in which marrying one's own kind had always been an essential tenet. Now that view seemingly had disappeared.

"She'll be good for you, Tony," his mother had said. "She's a good girl, and she'll help you make a good life for yourself."

Two weeks later Pete Moran returned home to Brooklyn.

It was a hot, miserable day, common to the first week of July in New York. Tony was seated in his minuscule office, the door open to gain what comfort he could from the air conditioner that cooled the reception area.

He was on the phone, trying to arrange delivery of additional furniture to the Brooklyn Heights apartment he had moved to the previous week. He was about to express that frustration when a voice from the reception room stopped him. Without another word he replaced the receiver and rose from his desk.

Pete was standing in front of Gert, his weight supported by the cane he held in his left hand. There was a jagged scar on his left forearm, still bright red from recent healing, and the short-sleeved polo shirt he wore clearly showed an extensive loss of weight.

Tony called his name and started toward him. As Pete turned, he saw the haggard, hollow face, an older face than he had known, one etched with lines of pain, with eyes that now poured out deep hatred.

Tony stopped short as Pete hobbled toward him, and he could feel the eyes of the longshoremen, waiting in the reception area, bore into his back.

Pete stopped in front of him. "Tell me why, Tony?" Pete's voice was soft, but still cracked with emotion as he spoke.

"Let's go into the office, Pete. We can talk alone there."

"Fuck your office. Just tell me." Pete's eyes were shot with red, as though he had not slept in several days, and there was a nervous tic at the corner of his mouth.

Tony wanted to throw his arms around him but knew he could not. He lowered his eyes. "It just happened, Pete. It was my fault, not hers."

The blow caught Tony on the right cheek as Pete swung his right hand, backhanded, with all the force and purchase he could gain. He staggered against the cane, then swung the hand back, bringing it hard against the opposite cheek.

Tony heard Gert screaming for Pete to stop, then shouting for help. His hands remained at his sides.

"You bastard," Pete growled. "You rotten bastard." His right fist drove into Tony's jaw and sent him staggering back against the wall. Blood filled Tony's mouth and came in a steady stream from his nose.

"Pete. Don't, Pete. Listen to me."

Pete hobbled after him, raising the cane across his body, readying himself to smash it across Tony's head.

One of the longshoremen grabbed Pete from behind, one arm around his throat, his free hand restraining the cane. Another moved in front of him and sent a fist crashing into his stomach. Pete buckled forward in pain, but the man hit him again, then a third time.

"Leave him alone," Tony shouted, grabbing the second longshoreman and spinning him away.

"That's enough." The voice came from the staircase, harsh and demanding. Tony turned to the sound and saw Paul Levine standing there. His eyes met Tony's and held them. There was a small smile on his lips. He turned his attention back to the longshoreman who was still holding Pete. "Get him out of here," he snapped.

The longshoreman bundled Pete toward the front door, his arm still tight around his neck. Tony stared in disbelief, unable to move or speak.

Pete's words filled the reception room as he was pushed out the door. "I'll get you, Tony. No matter how long it takes, I'll get you."

Tony slumped back against the wall and stared at the now closed door. Gert was at his side, dabbing at his face with a piece of tissue. He raised his arm and gently guided her hand away.

Paul Levine appeared in front of him. "What was that all about?" he asked.

Tony shook his head. "Personal problem," he said. He stared past Levine toward the empty doorway.

"Well, if you ever had any plans on being a heavyweight contender, kid, I'd forget them."

Tony's eyes met Levine's, anger flashing for the first time.

Levine met the gaze with contempt. "You better get

yourself cleaned up," he said, then turned abruptly and headed back toward the stairs.

Half an hour later Tony was summoned to Moe Green's office.

Green was pacing the floor when Tony entered, and rounded on him immediately. "What the hell's the matter with you?" Green raged. "You let some goddamn cripple come in here and slap the shit out of you in front of the men. Everybody on the goddamn docks will know about this in an hour. How the hell do you expect to have their respect if you let something like *that* happen?"

"It was Pete. Pete Moran," Tony said. His voice was low and soft and filled with shame.

"I thought he was dead," Green said.

"So did I," Tony said. "I found out a couple of months ago that he was alive."

"And you didn't expect him to come after you? You didn't do anything to cover yourself?" Green's voice was incredulous.

"I didn't know he was back," Tony said. "I wanted to see him, tell him myself. But I didn't know he was here until today, just now."

"But you let him whack you around. Paul said you didn't even raise your hand to him, didn't even try to stop him."

Tony glared at Green, his eyes blazing. "I got what I deserved. I'm sorry if I embarrassed you."

Green continued to stare at him in disbelief as Tony spun on his heel and walked quickly out of the office.

Green returned to his desk and sat heavily, shaking his head. "And this is going to be my son-in-law?" he asked aloud. "This is the kid I've made plans for?"

He stared at his desk for several moments, then absently withdrew a cigarette from the pack in his shirt pocket and lit it.

Something had to be done, he told himself. Something had to happen to change the image Tony had just created for himself. And if he couldn't do it, he was no use to anyone. Paul was right. If the kid didn't have balls, there was no place for him in the union. And there was no place for him as Shirley's husband.

Green reached for the telephone, dialed the number of the warehouse on piers six and seven, and asked for Manny Esposito.

"Manny, this is Moe Green. I've got something for you to do, and nobody else is to know about it. *Capisce?*"

CHAPTER/SIXTEEN

TONY ARRIVED AT the warehouse at twelve-thirty the following day. He had hardly slept the previous night, his mind constantly returning to the hatred he had seen in Pete's eyes. He had agonized over that hatred; had thought about calling him to explain that he and Mary Beth had never intended to become involved. But it would have done more harm than good. It would have changed nothing and would only have added to the pain. He had betrayed his best friend, no matter what the circumstances had been. And what he had done could never be forgiven.

As he stepped through the wide double doors Tony's senses were assaulted by the humidity trapped inside the aging building. The men had just returned to work after their half-hour lunch break, and he found Manny Esposito seated at his battered desk, poring over a stack of shipping manifests.

Tony perched on the edge of Manny's desk. "I always forget what a hellhole this place is in summer," he said.

"That's what happens when you get to be a union big

shot," Manny responded. He stared up at Tony, taking in
the swelling on the right side of his mouth. "Nice lip you
got there," he said. When Tony only nodded, he added,
"I heard about it. Everybody heard about it."

"I'm glad everybody's ears are working," Tony said.

"I figured you had your reasons," Manny said. "Nobody
who survives two years down here could be afraid of a guy
with a crutch."

"It was a cane," Tony said.

"Whatever," Manny answered.

It hurt to smile, but Tony smiled at him, anyway. He
had always liked Manny, had always thought of him as a
man who, despite his gruffness, watched out for the best
interests of others.

Manny handed him the work and accident reports he
had been sent to collect, and Tony noticed there were
hardly enough of either to have made the trip necessary.

Manny shrugged. "It's been slow," he said. "But there
are a couple of accident reports in there, the guys will
want to collect on."

Tony nodded and rose to leave. When he turned, he
saw Sally hulking toward him across the warehouse floor.

Tony had only seen Sally a few times over the years
since the day he had murdered Cherry; their paths had
seldom crossed.

Seeing him now, Tony felt a familiar sense of revulsion
and loathing. Sally lumbered toward him, naked to the
waist, his hairy body glistening with beads of sweat, his
two-day growth of beard darkening the already evil expression on his face.

"Well, if it ain't tough Tony," Sally growled. "You get
your ass kicked by any fucking gimps yet today?" A mo-
ronic grin spread across Sally's face, and he glanced around
to see if anyone appreciated his humor.

Tony stared at him, allowing his eyes to move down to the baling hook stuck in Sally's belt, and the vision of Cherry's body rushed to his mind.

Sally extended his hands to the side. "Hey, we don't care about no fucking cripples. No fucking cripple is gonna get to tough Tony. He's got the boss's daughter now. He can just go hide behind her sweet little pussy."

"Fuck off, Sally." Tony's voice was low and soft, but the blood had surged to his face, and he could feel his heart pounding out his anger in his chest.

"Hey, don't get mad, big shot. You got problems with any cripples, you give Sally boy a call." He was grinning at Tony with his wide, malevolent mouth.

"Can't do that, Sally." Tony paused to return the smile. "This cripple would put his foot up your fat ass."

Sally's face became twisted with rage; his smile changed to a snarl. "But *you* won't, you fucking little shit."

Sally lunged forward, one hand extended, clawlike, reaching for Tony's throat.

Tony slipped to the side, away from the outstretched hand, then his right fist shot out, straight from the shoulder, and hit, with all his weight behind it, directly between Sally's eyes.

The punch stopped Sally's forward movement, and he staggered back. Tony struck out again, a looping left to Sally's liver that raised him to his toes.

Sally fumbled for the baling hook in his belt, and Tony quickly moved inside to grab Sally's ears in his hands. Pulling Sally's head forward, Tony drove the top of his own head into Sally's face, splintering his nose and smashing his front teeth.

The baling hook clattered to the floor as Sally reeled back and fell. In a second Tony was on top of him, straddling his chest, his left hand around Sally's throat, squeezing with all his strength, his right hand smashing down repeatedly in his face.

Two men grabbed Tony from behind and lifted him away as Manny jumped in front of him. "Easy, Tony. For chrissake, you'll kill the stupid bastard."

Tony's breath came in gasps through clenched teeth, and his eyes were wide and wild. Gradually his breathing slowed, and he stared down at Sally's unconscious body. Tony looked at Manny. He was calmer now but still spewing anger. "You tell that son of a bitch if he ever opens his mouth to me again, they'll take him home in a box."

Manny looked down at Sally's battered face, then back at Tony. He was grinning. "Don't worry, kid. The only person he's gonna be talkin' to for the next couple of months is his dentist."

Paul Levine stood at the large window behind his desk and stared down at the rain-slicked street. His hands were balled into fists, his shoulders hunched like those of a fighter ready to move to the center of the ring. He had spent the previous half hour in Moe Green's office, listening to his friend describe the beating that damn kid had handed out to Sally at the pier six warehouse.

Levine's jaw tightened, the muscles dancing along his cheek. The kid had bounced back. Better than bounced back. Tony had won the kind of respect that only he and Moe had had. Now, with the recording secretary due to retire in September, Moe had decided to put Tony in that slot, a position only two rungs below Levine, himself, on the local's executive committee.

Levine turned his back to the window, away from the depressing weather. The hell with you *and* your new son-in-law, Levine thought. Promises had been made. Throughout all the struggling and fighting it had always been understood that Paul would take over when Moe decided to step aside. And no snot-nosed little dago bastard was going to change that.

He sat heavily in his chair and began drumming his fingers against the desk. Slow and easy, he told himself. He still has to play your game. And nobody plays it better than you.

CHAPTER/SEVENTEEN

May 1984

JENNIFER THOUGHT MICKEY MAXWELL looked like a weasel in human form. He had a long straight nose that seemed to run halfway up his narrow forehead. His hair was thin and slicked back, and his eyes were small and set wide apart. Even his mouth, with lips constantly parted to expose yellow teeth, added to the impression.

He was sitting on a sofa in Pete's loft-apartment, his feral eyes darting between Pete and Jennifer, as if he were expecting an attack.

"I don't know why I agreed to come here. You didn't say I was gonna be talkin' to no woman." He was speaking to Pete, but his eyes remained on Jennifer. The way he studied various parts of her body sent a shiver down her spine.

"What is it, Mickey, you turn gay or something? You don't like women anymore?" Pete spoke in a soft voice, but somehow the words still sounded threatening. He was dressed in a T-shirt and running shorts, and it emphasized his muscular body. Jennifer thought it was intended as a suggestion of potential threat.

"I don't like to talk business with women," Mickey said. He paused to leer at Jennifer, as if that would negate Pete's question. "Other things—okay," he added.

The revulsion Jennifer felt for the man was almost unbearable, and she had an overpowering urge to throw something in his face, even if it meant an end to her story. His clothing disgusted her: a herringbone suitcoat worn over checked trousers; a brown shirt and striped tie. He looked like a circus clown. Even his shoes were scuffed.

The wall of windows behind her were open, sending a fresh spring breeze against her back, and though it blew in Maxwell's direction, she could still smell the heavy scent of his cologne.

"Are you worried what we say here won't remain confidential?" she asked.

Maxwell grinned with his yellow teeth. "Yeah, I'm worried about that. You think I wanna end up with a shiv in my back?"

"Nothing goes out of this room, Mickey. You have my word." Pete made the last statement sound like a threat, almost as though refusing to accept it would be an insult.

"I ain't worried about you," Maxwell said. "Just her." He leaned back in the sofa and looked Jennifer over again. She was wearing baggy blue slacks and a loose-fitting white blouse. Trying to hide all the good stuff she's got, Maxwell thought.

"Only three people will ever know what was said here, Mickey," Jennifer said. She gave him time to count the three she meant. "If I do a story and you decide you want to be quoted, we'll write out exactly what you want to say and we'll both sign it. Otherwise, I've never met you in my life."

Maxwell tilted his head to one side; his face became a sneer. "What guarantees do I have?" he asked.

Jennifer drew a deep breath. They had chosen Pete's loft because it was located on a short, dead-end street that had few pedestrians and almost no vehicular traffic. "We've been careful so far, haven't we?" She waited but received only a shrug from Maxwell. "Pete's given you his word, and so have I. If I tried to go back on it, and you both denied we had ever met, I'd look like a fool. Besides, I'm going to need you again before this is over."

The final statement seemed to mollify Maxwell, and it also seemed to plant a seed in his feral brain. "And what's in it for me?" he asked. "If I run against Tony next year, you gonna do a nice story about me?"

Jennifer winced. "No promises," she said. "But if it's worth a story then, I'll recommend it to the city desk."

Maxwell's sneer deepened. He looked at Pete. "Somebody oughta explain the facts of life to this lady," he said, jerking his head in Jennifer's direction.

"Those *are* the facts of life, Mickey," Jennifer snapped. "You talk to us because it's the right thing to do and because you're a good citizen."

Maxwell let out a high-pitched laugh. "That's me," he said. "Citizen of the Year."

Jennifer stood and walked toward the window. She was wasting her time. No matter what he told her, she would find it hard to believe, and she certainly wouldn't want to end up in the middle of a libel suit with Mickey Maxwell as her star witness. She turned back to face him. "Okay, Mickey. Thanks for coming by."

"Heah, wait a minute." Maxwell stared at her, then looked at Pete. "What's going on?"

"Maybe the lady's tired of your bullshit," Pete said.

"Look," Maxwell snapped. "I just wanna make sure I'm covered."

"We told you you were. What do you want us to do, tattoo it on your forehead?" Pete's voice brimmed with disgust. "All we're asking is that you point us in the right direction, if you know what that direction is. If there is anything going down."

"I know," Maxwell snapped.

Jennifer decided to let Pete push Maxwell, irritate him into talking. She wondered if it was always like this for Pete—having to deal with the dregs of society to get at those who were even worse. No wonder most cops were as hard and cold as the people they chased.

Pete stared at Maxwell for several moments before speaking. "So what *do* you know?" Pete asked.

"I know about kickbacks from shipping companies. I know how they wash the money, and I know who gets it."

"You talking about yesterday or today?" Pete asked.

"It's the same thing," Maxwell said. "It never changed."

"You have names, dates?"

Maxwell rolled his eyes at the ceiling. "You think I'm crazy? You think I go around digging into records, then go down and work the docks? You think I wanna float to New Jersey?"

"So you don't know anything. You're just guessing."

"I know," Maxwell said with a sneer. "I keep my ears open. It ain't that hard to hear things, if you know who to listen to. I got the names."

"So, you want to tell me the names?"

Maxwell's yellow teeth flashed. "Maybe," he said.

Pete stared at him with disgust, then rubbed his thumb and index finger together. "What is it, Mickey? You want a taste first?"

"I don't want no money," Mickey said. "I just wanna make sure you and this"—he hesitated, debating as to which word to use—"this *lady* reporter are gonna follow it through before I stick my neck out."

"So what does that mean?"

"That means I give you a little something now, and if you follow it up and it works out, maybe I'll give you a list of names." He jabbed a finger at Moran. "Give *you*. In the mail. In a brown paper envelope, like they say. No more meetings, no more conversations."

Pete leaned back in his chair and stared at him. "So, give."

Maxwell's grin widened, and his eyes darted from Pete to Jennifer and back again. He raised his chin to Pete. "Can you get into the files of old investigations in the Manhattan District Attorney's Office?" He watched Pete nod. "Even when no arrests were made?"

"Yeah, I can get them."

"Look up an investigation that involved Marco, back when he was in college. It also involved Paul Levine, Moe Green, and a shipping company called Whitehead."

"What am I going to find, Mickey?"

Mickey's thin lips spread across his narrow face. He shrugged. "Who knows? Maybe you'll find out that Tony Marco used to be a bagman."

"Do you believe him?" Jennifer stood facing Pete in front of the massive window.

"I don't think he'd tell us if he didn't know for sure."

Jennifer shook her head, then turned and stared down at the traffic moving along the FDR Drive and the river beyond. "He's such a sleaze. I think I'd find it hard to believe him if he told me he was born of woman."

"He probably wasn't," Pete said. "But right now he's *our* sleaze, and he's the only one we've got."

She turned back to him. "Can you get a copy of that report, if it exists?"

Pete nodded. "But if you ever use it, and they figure

out where it came from, I can kiss my little blue uniform good-bye."

"I know," Jennifer said. "I'm not sure it's anything I could use, anyway, especially if he was only *suspected* of doing something. Maybe there will be some kind of statement from the shipping company. At least that would give me a basis to go to them and maybe get more. Can you get it without anyone knowing you even looked?"

Pete laughed. "You don't want much, do you, lady?"

"It isn't possible?"

"It depends. If it's on microfilm, maybe. There was a stabbing on one of the piers last month. I'll use that as my excuse to check union members." He shrugged. "I'll go Friday afternoon. Everybody's in a hurry to get out of the office then. Maybe they won't watch too closely."

The small neighborhood bar in the Bay Ridge section of Brooklyn was filled with the smell of stale beer, sweat, and the cloying perfume of a half dozen aging hookers. Paul Levine stepped through the single door and stopped, waiting for his eyes to adjust to the dimly lit room. Gradually the purple neon behind the bar revealed a row of backs bent over drinks. A woman turned and smiled, but Levine ignored her and moved slowly toward the back, where a scattering of battered tables sat in even dimmer light.

He slid into a chair and stared across the table at Mickey Maxwell. "So, how did it go?" he asked.

Maxwell grinned. "They sucked it up, just like you said they would."

Levine nodded. When Maxwell had called to tell him about the approach from Moran and the reporter, Levine knew immediately that somebody was investigating Tony's act. Somebody who was out to show that Marco wasn't the

savior he claimed to be. And, even more important, somebody who could be fed just what he wanted them to know.

"You told them you'd give them more later?" he asked.

Mickey nodded. "I told Pete. He did most of the talking. But you shoulda seen the broad. I thought she'd come
in her pants."

"The reporter's a woman?" Levine asked.

"Yeah, and a real piece to boot."

Levine sat back in his chair, thinking. Marco would
charm the hell out of her. He had seen him do it too many
times to doubt it. But you can't charm someone who's
scared to death of you, he told himself. And he knew just
how to scare her when the time came.

"You said Moran did most of the talking. How did he
seem to you—his feelings toward Tony, I mean?"

Maxwell shrugged. "Pete don't show his feelings that
much. But you don't have to worry about him. He wants
Tony's ass, and he wants it bad. If I said something good
about him, he'd probably choke me."

Levine leaned forward and smiled at Maxwell. "You did
good, Mickey. Now you just lay low until they come back to
you, and then you come to me and I'll give you what you
need."

Maxwell hesitated, as if he were uncertain how to continue. "Listen, Paul," he began, "you sure this ain't gonna
blow up in our faces? I mean we don't want them to find
out too much, right?"

"Don't worry, Mickey. They're not going to find out
anything that will hurt anybody but Tony and his friends."
He paused, allowing himself a small smile. "And what
they find out is going to hurt them bad. You can count on
that."

Mickey let out a soft, high laugh. "It'll be nice next
year. Running against a bunch of guys who got the law
breathing down their necks."

"I don't think it will even go that far, my friend. I think you're going to see a lot of resignations long before that."

"Heah, whatever works," Mickey said.

Levine studied Mickey's face. It was too bad you had to use slime like this to help you, he thought. But that's only temporary. Mickey would only be around as long as he was needed.

"Mickey, you're going to like being on the executive committee," Levine said. "You're really going to like it there."

CHAPTER/EIGHTEEN

PETE WAITED IN the Chinese-style gazebo perched atop a rock promontory that overlooked a small, man-made pond just north of the Children's Zoo in Central Park. His eyes searched the stretch of parkland below, already dotted with sunbathers and playing children, for the sight of Jennifer. She arrived dressed in tight-fitting jeans and a baggy rugby jersey and despite her casual appearance, she looked sensual to him. She wore little makeup, and her hair was pulled back into a short ponytail. That, and the freckles along her nose, made her seem much younger than she was.

"I never would have recognized you," he said. "Now I know what you looked like when you were a high-school cheerleader."

"I was never a cheerleader," she said. "And besides, I thought that was the idea—to blend in." She looked down at the well-traveled path that crossed in front of the promontory. "Not exactly inconspicuous up here, are we?"

Pete smiled at the rebuke. "People in New York seldom

look up," he said. "Their predators are at ground level, and that's where they keep their eyes."

Jennifer thought about it and nodded. "They teach you that in cop school?" she asked.

"There and other places," he said.

She sat down next to him. Pete, too, was dressed in jeans, with a lightweight blue windbreaker over a red T-shirt. "Aren't you hot in that jacket?" she asked.

"Unfortunately it's needed to keep the gun concealed."

She wrinkled her nose. "Even on your day off?"

"Department rules," he said. "Like they say in those phony TV commercials, 'Don't leave home without it.' "

Jennifer shrugged, thinking the gun was a burden she would not like to bear. She looked at the manila envelope on the seat next to him. "Is that the report?"

Pete nodded and picked it up but did not hand it to her. "It seems our little sleaze knew what he was talking about."

"No arrest?" she asked. She watched Pete shake his head slowly. "What was the basis for them picking him up?"

"A statement from a guy named Weathersby, the head honcho for the Whitehead company's New York office. Claimed Tony made regular pickups of money demanded by the union as bribes."

"So why didn't they arrest him?"

"No evidence. According to the report, they think Tony smelled a rat and dumped the envelope before he left the office."

"Wasn't this Weathersby's statement enough to hold him?"

Pete shook his head. "His word against Tony's. A charge by management, denied by the union. It wouldn't survive one day in court."

"Maybe that's all it was," Jennifer said.

"Could be," he said. He stared out across the park. "A few weeks later Weathersby was found in a parking lot with two broken legs and a concussion. The company shipped him home to England."

Jennifer grimaced, then reached for the envelope, opened it, and began reading. The report included information on Tony's background, his support of his family, his scholarship to Columbia. "The background report makes him sound like a Boy Scout," Jennifer said. "No wonder they didn't push it. The newspapers would have crucified them."

"Yep," Pete said.

"Of course, it's possible he didn't know what he was picking up. In fact, it seems logical they wouldn't tell him, especially since he was just a kid."

Pete looked at her, a slightly hard cast to his eyes. "You looking for excuses for him or what?"

"Just trying to anticipate reactions," she said.

"Look, Tony may be a lot of things, but stupid was never one of them." Jennifer began to object, but Pete placed a hand on her arm. "I'm not saying he wasn't roped in. At least in the beginning. But he stayed. That's the bottom line."

Jennifer turned her attention to a group of children racing along the path, trailing balloons behind them. Maybe he'd needed the money, she thought. She caught herself. It was a lousy excuse, no matter how you looked at it. "Okay," she said. "What do you think the chances are of confronting the company with this statement?"

"Zilch. Less than zilch." Pete stood and stretched, then walked to the other side of the gazebo before turning back to face her. "There's no percentage for them in starting the whole thing up again. The statute of limitations is past, so all they can do is buy themselves trouble they don't need." He paused, rubbing his chin. "You have any vacation time coming to you?"

"Yes. Why?"

"That report gives Weathersby's age as fifty-four at the time. If he's still alive, he should be retired now. Who knows, maybe he'd be willing to talk. And maybe he knows even more than he told the cops when the whole thing went down."

"You mean, go to England to talk to him?" Jennifer's voice was incredulous. "How would we even find him?"

"I have some friends in Scotland Yard who can do that," Pete said. "If he has national health insurance, all they'll have to do is punch up the computer, and we'll know if he's alive and well and where he is."

"Expensive trip for a story," she said. "I'd have to cover it out of my own pocket."

Pete raised a questioning eyebrow. "I didn't think your paper was that cheap."

"I haven't told them about the story yet," she said. "I wanted it to be solid before I let anyone know." She watched Pete's eyes and decided to add something that was at least partially true. "People at newspapers have big mouths." She watched his concern ease and wondered what his reaction would have been if she had told him, "Sorry, Pete, but if I let them know, they'll tell me to be a good little girl and go write another story about a gorilla."

"So, are you willing?" Pete asked.

Jennifer nodded quickly, forcing herself to accept the decision. "If you can find him, I'll go."

"If I can find him, I'll go with you," he said.

Jennifer looked at him with surprise.

"Don't get nervous," he said. "Getting answers out of people who don't want to talk is the one great expertise of my job. Besides, I've never been to the U.K., and I'm overdue for a vacation."

Jennifer studied his face, noting the serious line of his

mouth. It forced her to smile. "It will be the first time I ever traveled with a bodyguard," she said.

His expression remained unchanged. "You better get used to it. In the weeks to come, you may need one. Let's not forget what happened to Weathersby."

The statement sent a chill down Jennifer's spine. She thought of Marco, of the last time she had been with him. It seemed impossible he could be involved in something like that. There was too much compassion, too much caring. Yet he accepted violence as part of his world. She wondered if he could also order it. "I'm meeting Tony tomorrow," she said. "He's going to introduce me to his mother and sister."

An unpleasant smile came to Pete's lips. "Taking you into the holy of holies, eh?" he said. "Tony always knew good PR when he saw it. You'll be ready to propose him for canonization when his mother gets through talking about him."

Jennifer ignored the sarcasm. "I still haven't met his wife and son. He seems reluctant about that."

"He should. At least as far as his wife is concerned."

"Why?"

"Because she climbs into every available bed she can find."

Jennifer felt jolted again. "How do you know that?"

"Everybody who knows Tony, knows that," he said. "Shirley doesn't make a big secret about it. You see, I'm not the only one who hates Tony Marco's guts."

Pete Moran slept on the sofa, his arm dangling over the edge, his fingers still touching the report that lay on the floor next to him. He had reread the report before dozing off and had noted again the time period, a time when he, too, had undergone questioning. The irony of it had almost made him laugh: Tony, sweating it out in an interrogation room at the Manhattan District Attorney's Office while he lay bound and battered in that rat-infested hooch twenty-five miles northwest of Da Nang.

He had fought to force the image away, but it had returned with a will of its own. He had kept himself sane then by thinking of the old neighborhood. Thinking of Tony and Joey and Mary Beth; of his mother and Gino, and sitting on the stoop on hot summer evenings. The smells of the stores along Fifth Avenue, the cooking odors wafting from the open windows of houses on First Street. He had concentrated on it, putting himself there, keeping his thoughts away from the small, hard-eyed men who questioned him between beatings. Walking in Prospect Park with Mary Beth, her body leaning into his, soft and lithe, their arms encircling each other, not a problem in the world, just enjoying each other and the day. He almost had been able to feel it, to put himself there, replace the stench of the hooch with the smells of the avenue; change the trembling of his body to the nervous excitement he felt when he held Mary Beth in his arms. Lying on a blanket on the roof, the lights of Manhattan glowing in the distance. Her hands moving over his body, stroking him, arousing him. It had worked. It had kept him sane. At least until the small men returned.

Sweat broke out on his forehead, and his body twisted in fear on the sofa. Outside, the sound of the traffic along the FDR Drive became the rhythmic beating of a crude drum, the sound he always heard as they returned to question him again.

Pete awoke to the sound of his own screams, his body bathed in sweat, his arms and legs trembling with uncontrollable violence. He jerked himself into a sitting position, his eyes darting around the room, wide with terror, searching for the three men who had been there only moments before. He heard the blast of an automobile horn outside and, in the distance, the sound of a siren wailing its mournful cry. Through the open window the cool, night, spring breeze brushed against his chest, and he took long, panting breaths, drawing in the air. He buried his face in his hands, waiting for the trembling to subside.

It was only the dream, he told himself. Just the dream. His body continued to shake.

Jennifer stood in front of the large, black-painted door and stared at the gleaming brass knocker. It was mid-afternoon, and the warmth of the day was already beginning to fade, a cool breeze rippling through the leaves of the trees that lined the street. She used the knocker and waited. Behind the door she heard the sound of running feet, and when the door swung open, she found herself looking down at a small boy with brown hair; large, searching brown eyes; and a mouth held open in a circle of expectant curiosity.

"Hi," she said. "I'm here to see Mr. Marco. Do I have the right house?"

The child remained immobile and continued to stare up at her, as though he were seeing some strange new creature for the first time.

It was her red hair, she knew. The color seemed to mesmerize young children who were unaccustomed to seeing it.

"It's okay, Josh." The voice came from behind the child, and Jennifer saw Tony moving toward her down a long hall.

He stopped behind the boy and ruffled his hair. "This is my son, Josh, and he already seems quite taken with you," he said.

"It's the red hair," Jennifer said. "Kids usually stare or start crying when they see it for the first time."

Tony smiled at her, then looked down at his son again. "In a few years, if he has his father's tastes, he'll start following women with red hair."

Jennifer felt color rising to her cheeks, and she bent toward the child to hide it. "This one can follow me anytime," she said.

The boy stepped behind his father and began peeking out behind his leg.

"How old is he?" Jennifer asked.

"Almost six. But he's still a bit shy." He took his son's hand and stepped aside. "Please come in."

As Jennifer stepped into the foyer her eyes moved from Tony to the child. The boy didn't look anything like his father, and she thought it regrettable that he didn't. She studied Tony, acknowledging her attraction to the man. It was the first time she had seen him dressed casually: he wore tan slacks and a dark green Lacoste shirt that emphasized the trim lines of his body.

Tony led the way through a pair of double doors and into a large, formal sitting room, dominated by a black marble fireplace. The furniture was oversize and comfortable, and there were doilies covering every conceivable surface that could collect dirt. It was an old ladies' room, almost a cliché of what Grandma's house should look like, Jennifer decided.

"My mother and sister are downstairs attacking the dishes," Tony said. "She was disappointed you couldn't join us for dinner."

"I was disappointed too," Jennifer said. "It's been a long time since I had a homemade meal." She had declined because she knew people were more reserved over dinner, especially with a new and unknown guest, and she very much wanted to deal with them in a relaxed manner and to get Tony's mother and sister alone if she could.

Almost on cue, Angie Marco burst into the room like an

overweight whirlwind. A stout woman with gray hair and a round, cherubic face, she wore a shapeless black dress patterned with white flowers.

Her grandson rushed to her as she entered, and she bent to kiss his head. "I'm sorry I keep you waiting," she began. "My daughter and me, we was cleaning up the dishes. How come you didn't come to dinner? You shoulda. I made lasagna, Tony's favorite. You woulda liked it." She hesitated a breath and looked Jennifer up and down. "You should eat more 'talian food. It would put more meat on your bones."

Tony let out a low, rich laugh, his eyes glistening with pleasure at his mother's monologue. He turned to Jennifer. "My mother believes that if you're not twenty pounds overweight, you're destined for intensive care."

Angie Marco stared at her son and raised a warning finger. "You don't laugh at your mother," she said. She turned back to Jennifer and gave her a quick wink. "He thinks, 'cause he's the boss of the union, that he's the boss here too. But I'm the only boss in this house." She looked back at her son and watched as he raised his hands in surrender.

"That's why I don't let her come to the office," Tony said.

His mother frowned playfully, then broke into a smile. "Come," she said to Jennifer, "let me show you the house."

"I'd love to," Jennifer said as she rose from her chair.

Angie Marco put a hand behind her grandson's head. "You come too," she said, then, looking at Tony, added, "You stay here." They left the room to the sound of Tony's laughter.

They went through a second set of double doors, which led from the sitting room to a second parlor that had an identical marble fireplace. The room was smaller than the first, but the furnishings were similar, the only difference being a large console television set.

"Tony, he's give me that TV last Christmas," Angie Marco said with obvious pride. "He give his sister this house too. It was a wedding present. My daughter, Carmela, she's divorced now." She rolled her eyes toward heaven. "Everybody gets divorced now. Except Tony."

They moved out into the hall and walked toward the stairs. "Is Tony's wife here?" Jennifer asked. "I've never met her."

There was a slight tightening to Angie Marco's mouth. "No," she said. "She had something else she hadda do. She's a very busy person."

Jennifer was shown through the two upper floors, which consisted of bedrooms and a small sewing room. The rooms were tastefully decorated, but the presence of religious statues and votive candles clearly marked the background of the people who occupied them.

As they descended the stairs to the lower level, which housed the dining room and kitchen, Angie Marco continued her running monologue.

"The house is really too big for us," she said. "When my daughter got her divorce, I wanted to make an apartment and rent it out, but Tony, he said no. He didn't want no strangers in the house. I suppose he's right. You never know about people no more."

"Do you still go down to your old neighborhood?" Jennifer asked.

"Oh, sure. I go down to the old block every day. And I still go to the old church." She shrugged. "There's not too many of my old friends there no more. Young people, they buy up most of the old houses and fix them up. Useta be everybody was poor there. Now everybody seems to have lotsa money to do things."

"It must have been a nice neighborhood to grow up in," Jennifer said. "For Tony and your daughter, I mean."

"Yeah, it was nice," Angie Marco said. "They had nice friends." Her eyes brightened as they entered the kitchen. "One of Tony's friends, Joey Gambardella, he works for Tony now. He got in a lotta trouble when he was a boy, but I asked Tony to help him, and now he's gotta good job with the union."

A woman in her late twenties turned away from the sink as they entered the kitchen, pushed a lock of hair from her forehead, and moved toward them with a smile. "Hi," she said. "I'm Tony's sister, Carmela. You must be Jennifer Brady."

Jennifer extended her hand, then glanced at a child seated in a high chair. "Your little girl?" she asked.

Carmela smiled. "Yes," she said. "My daughter Angie. She's named after Mama."

"It's the way it should be," Angie Marco said. She lowered her eyes to her grandson, who was standing at her side. She looked up at the ceiling and rolled her eyes. "But some people don't think that way." She leaned closer to Jennifer and whispered. "Who's ever hear of a 'talian boy named Joshua?"

"Ma!" Carmela interrupted. "You got a one-track mind about things sometimes."

Angie Marco shrugged and rolled her eyes again. "I know what I know."

Carmela shook her head and quickly changed the subject. "What were you saying about Joey Gambardella?" she asked.

"Just how nice the old neighborhood was, an' how Tony and Joey and Petey Moran was such good friends."

"Does Petey Moran work for the union too?" Jennifer asked, jumping at the chance.

A look of resigned regret came over Angie Marco's face.

"No," she said. "Tony and Petey don't see each other no more. I guess that happens when boys grow up. He was a nice boy, Petey. Him and Tony, they was like two brothers when they was kids."

"That's too bad," Jennifer said. "Did he move away?"

"No," Carmela said, a little too quickly. "Petey was in Vietnam, and when he came back, he was a little strange. They just never got close again."

Carmela's eyes had become tense and suspicious, and Jennifer decided to back away from the subject. It was like a conspiracy, she thought. Something no one would talk about.

"Why don't we have some coffee," Carmela said, in an obvious attempt to change the subject. "Why don't you get Tony, Ma? Then we can all sit and talk."

"Sure," she said. "We have some coffee and some good 'talian pastry. You like 'talian pastry?" she asked Jennifer.

"I love it," she said.

"Good," Angie said. "It'll put some meat on you."

It was after five when Jennifer finally excused herself and explained she had to leave. It had not been a highly productive afternoon and had raised more questions than it had answered about Pete and Tony. But it had revealed obvious tensions, both about Pete Moran and Tony's wife, Shirley. It had also offered a glimpse of Tony Marco's background, one that fully meshed with everything Jennifer had read about him.

And there was something more. Tony exhibited a total lack of concern about his background. Something, Jennifer knew, that she, herself, had never been able to achieve. Or was it an act, she wondered, as Tony walked her to the front door? Was his ethnic pride just something he used because he knew it worked so well for him right now?

"I'm sorry you have to leave," he said as he opened the door for her.

"So am I," she said, smiling up at him. "But I think I'm going to have to see you socially again very soon."

Tony cocked his eyebrows. "I'm delighted to hear that, but why?"

"It seems I owe you a very expensive dinner."

Tony's brow furrowed momentarily, then he broke into a smile. "You found a bookie at the paper," he said.

"I sure did," she said. "The *Globe* pays him a salary, and all he does is take bets."

They stood in the doorway and laughed.

CHAPTER/NINETEEN

JOEY GAMBARDELLA LET out a low, mirthless laugh. "Pete Moran, huh? Jesus, Tony would shit if he knew Pete was sniffing around."

"All the more reason he shouldn't find out," Paul Levine said.

They were standing on the Promenade in Brooklyn Heights, their elbows on the railing as they stared out across the river at the Statue of Liberty rising in the distance.

Joey shook his head and laughed again. "It's almost too funny," he said. "Pete actually getting the hook to bring Tony down." He turned his face toward Levine. "You sure you can count on him? You better be sure he only gets what you want him to get. He's still a cop and I don't trust him. He gets too much, he might take everybody down."

"That's why it's time for you to clean up your accounts, Joey. He can't prove what he can't find."

Joey thought about that. There wasn't a great deal to find, nothing like what Paul had promised if and when they forced Tony out. It was too bad Tony had to get it in the neck, he thought. But that was what the world was all about—take or get taken. And that's the way Pete would look at it, too, he thought. That was what worried him. If Pete found out too much, he wouldn't stop with just Tony.

"I'd feel better if I was sure we could keep him pointed in one direction," Joey said. "Pete's a hard-ass. Even as a kid he was like that."

"Hatred's a wonderful thing, Joey. It's like having a fire in your living room. As long as it's burning, it occupies your full attention. It doesn't give you time for anything else." Levine smiled at his own metaphor.

Joey's coal-black eyes narrowed. "Heah, it's been a long time since Tony and Pete had that problem," he said. "People forget."

Levine raised himself off his elbows and turned to Joey. "When the hurt's deep enough, they never forget." He inclined his head to one side. "But you never know. That's why I want you to take a little trip to Las Vegas, Joey. I want you to bring somebody back who can throw a little gasoline on Pete Moran's fire."

"You're kidding," Joey said. He watched Levine slowly shake his head. "I thought you told me she was a real bust. On junk, the whole thing."

"She is, Joey. And she should be ready to do anything she's told, just to get what she needs." Levine's false smile returned. "And that makes her a three-alarm fire, my friend."

"When do you want me to go?" Joey asked.

"Let's give it a couple of weeks. We'll let our friends develop the information we want them to have, and then we'll bring her in and practice a little arson. I think that will help keep Mr. Moran's attention focused where we want it. Don't you, Joey?"

Joey let out a soft grunt. "Yeah. I think that'll do it. Especially if she says what we want her to say."

"Oh, but she will, Joey. And you're going to make sure she does."

Joey nodded slowly and smiled at the idea. There could be unexpected benefits in this, he thought.

"To Gloucester. Suddenly I feel as though this entire story is becoming Shakespearean." Jennifer felt slightly nervous about the whole idea, and she chewed on her lower lip as she thought over the various ways it could fail. "Can we be sure he's there? I'd hate to go driving halfway across the English Midlands and find he's off in Italy on vacation."

Pete leaned back against the sofa and stretched. "He's there. My friend at the Yard checked very discreetly with the local constabulary. Seems Weathersby's health isn't too good, and he seldom travels."

"Why discreetly?" Jennifer asked. "Why don't we call him first and see if he's willing to talk?"

Pete shook his head. "I don't want to give him time to think about it and get cold feet. Or call his former employers and have them talk him out of it."

Jennifer bit her lip again. She knew Pete was right, but it still seemed like a large gamble, and a damn expensive one.

"Think of it as a vacation," he said. "One where you put in a day or two of work. Then it won't seem so bad."

She stared at him across the sofa, wondering if his talents as a detective included mind reading.

She reached for the bottle of wine on the cocktail table and filled her glass, then refilled his without asking if he wanted more or not. This was Pete's first visit to her apartment, and she had wanted to treat him as graciously as possible. She had hoped he would admire the apartment, in some way acknowledging all the effort she had put into it. But he had said nothing. He had simply settled in on the sofa and gotten directly to the matter at hand. Damn insensitive cop, she had told herself.

"Okay," she said, with more than a little surrender in her voice. "When do you want to go?"

"I've already checked with my people. I can leave anytime next week. Do you think you can arrange it?"

"It shouldn't be a problem. The heavy vacation schedules haven't started yet, and I'm not working on anything special. At least nothing they know about."

Pete picked up his glass and sipped the chilled white wine. "You haven't told me how things went with Tony on Sunday," he said. "Did you find out anything?"

Jennifer kept her eyes averted. Only more questions about the two of you, she thought. "Just that he seems to be the ideal son and father," she said.

Pete laughed, a little harshly she thought. "I told you it was perfect PR."

She turned to face him, struggling to hide her annoyance. "I liked Mrs. Marco, Tony's mother. She mentioned you, by the way. She told me how close you and Tony were, and how nice you were as a kid."

Pete's eyes hardened. "How did I come up in the conversation?"

"Purely by accident," Jennifer said. "We were talking about your old neighborhood, and she started telling me what nice friends her children had had there. You were just one of the ones she mentioned."

Pete took another drink of wine. "She was a nice lady," he said. "She was always good to me, to all of us."

Jennifer sensed regret in his voice, and she wondered if it was because he knew that by hurting Tony he would be hurting his mother as well. "She's still a nice lady." She was goading him, and she wasn't certain why.

He nodded his head, almost imperceptibly. "And you met his son too?"

"Yes," Jennifer said. "A cute little boy."

His eyes became distant, then hardened again. "They say the kid means everything to him," he said at length.

"I guess that's only natural," she said.

He looked at her, his face expressionless. "If you say so," he said.

They sat on a bench against the wall, listening to the staccato sound of a dozen tennis balls being battered back and forth across the other, still occupied indoor courts. It had been a vigorous game, even though they had not bothered to keep score, and Tony could feel every muscle in his body—tired, yet enlivened. He wiped his face with a towel, then draped it around his neck and rolled his head to loosen the muscles.

Anne was carefully dabbing the sweat from her face, trying not to smear her makeup. Tony took a moment to enjoy the sight of her, the long slender legs beautifully tanned and sleek in her short tennis dress. It had been a pleasant time with her, one without the pressures that seemed, lately, to mark their days together.

He exhaled and rolled his head again. No talk of politics, or leaving the union, or of his planned divorce from Shirley. It was foolish, he knew. He wanted all those things, intended to have them. He simply wanted to avoid the endless discussion of them.

Jennifer Brady came immediately to mind. They had talked about his future, his plans too. But there was something more to the conversations as well, something that relaxed him, made him look forward to the next time they met. She had called that afternoon, explaining that their "very expensive dinner" would have to be delayed. She was taking a week off for a vacation in England. He realized now that the postponement had disappointed him. It was foolish, he told himself.

He had met Anne in England, at a party outside London. Years ago now. He remembered how much their meeting had meant to him, how it had overshadowed everything else about the trip.

"You're so quiet, darling," Anne said. She was smiling at him, that beautiful, sensuous smile that always gave him pleasure.

"I'm afraid you wore me out," he said.

"Don't say that. I plan to take you home when we leave here, and I certainly don't want you to be worn-out." She thought she detected a sense of weariness come into his eyes and then disappear. She wondered if he was becoming tired of her or if it was just the tennis that had brought it on.

She stood abruptly. "Well, I think I'll shower and change. Then let's have a drink in the bar."

"I can use the drink. And the shower," he said.

She tossed her hair and turned. "I'll see you there in about twenty minutes," she said.

The woman's locker room was empty. Anne sat on the bench, before the open locker door, staring at her clothes without making any effort to reach out for them. It was coming apart. They were coming apart. She could feel it.

Her jaw tightened. Just as everything came apart for her, no matter what she chose to do; no matter who she chose to be with. She had always had everything. But it had never been enough. And when it had seemed to be, she had always lost it.

She thought of people and how they looked at her when they realized who she was. What thoughts they must have when they read about her in society columns. The perfect life. God, it was all such a bad joke. The troubles, the pain, the hurting were all the same. The same needs; the same frustrations; the same failure. Even the parties didn't satisfy her anymore. Her one great talent, giving parties. Perhaps that was what they would put on her tombstone: ANNE FINCHWORTH MOBRAY, 1954–???? SHE GAVE GOOD PARTY. She tried to smile at the self-imposed joke but found she could not.

And now even Tony seemed to be resisting her. He seemed to be holding back, almost as though everything she wanted to do for him had no value. No, she told herself. He was just tired, just feeling the pressures of his work, his life. She would have to try to ease those pressures, help make his decisions easier. That was what she would do. Then it would all be so simple. He would see what she was offering, see the value of it, see how much it would mean to him. And then he'd take it without hesitation, without doubt.

She reached for her clothing, then paused, thinking it out again. First she had to get him away from the union. Other things could wait. Once he was out, their affairs would come more easily. He would come to her more easily. And once he came, he would stay. She could see to that. God, she wanted him. He was everything all the others never were.

She wondered how she would have reacted to Tony if she had known him when they were children; when they were teenagers or college students. You would have rejected him out of hand, she told herself, then wondered if he realized that as well. But he had to know she wouldn't reject him now. She wanted him too much; needed to have him. She would show him how much it could mean to him. Yes, that would be the beginning, that would make it all work. And she wouldn't wait. She couldn't wait. Not now.

James Giuliani came from behind his desk smiling in open appreciation as Anne Mobray entered his New York

City office in the World Trade Center. Like most New York governors, he spent as much time as possible here, rather than Albany, in order to enjoy the excitement the city offered. As he guided Anne Mobray to a couch set before a wall of windows that overlooked New York harbor, he acknowledged that she was very much a part of that excitement—beauty and great wealth and power, which, he reminded himself, she offered generously to those she favored.

"Well, I must confess, I was a little surprised by your call but very, very pleased as well. Is there something I can do for you?"

Anne crossed her legs, knowing the gesture would produce a favorable reaction. "There *is* something, Jim," she began. "I just don't know if you can."

Giuliani nodded seriously, playing her game, but aware that because of the size of her past political contributions and the level of her friendships, he would make every effort to help her in any way he could. "Oh, you'd be surprised at some of the things I can manage," he said. "Why don't you tell me what you need."

Anne smoothed the skirt of the green silk suit that hung appealingly upon her body. "It's not for me, actually. It's something I hope you can do for Tony Marco."

"That would delight me," he said. "What do you have in mind?"

Anne leaned slightly forward, her eyes more direct and businesslike. "I'd like you to offer him a political appointment. Something he would find difficult to refuse, and something that would force him to step away from the union, at least temporarily."

Giuliani laughed softly, unable to control himself at the brazenness of the request. "That's not as easily done as one might think," he began.

Anne pushed ahead, ignoring him. "It would not have

to be a paid appointment," she said. "But it would have to be prestigious."

Giuliani was intrigued, and he, too, leaned forward, creating a conspiratorial atmosphere between them. "Do you have something specific in mind?"

Anne turned her head and looked pointedly out the window. "New York Harbor," she said.

Giuliani laughed softly. "Do you want to buy it?"

"No, I want Tony to save it." She watched Giuliani's eyes widen and his head nod slightly, urging her to continue. "What I had in mind was a commission to study and recommend ways to revitalize the port," she began. "A commission of *very* prominent people, with Tony as its chairman." She toyed with her skirt again. "He would, of course, have to step away from the union. And, if he did, I think I could assure you that he'd never have to go back." She paused again. "I think we both would like to see that."

Giuliani nodded, then leaned back in thought. "Both ideas—of Tony stepping away from the union and of a commission—certainly appeal to me," he began. "And I think it would appeal to the people I have to convince." He rubbed his chin absently. "Yes, I like the idea. Let me sound some people out and then call the top editors at the city's newspapers. They've all been clamoring for some action, on and off, about the port's decline." He snapped his fingers suddenly. "In fact, I could ask one of them to serve on the commission. That would almost assure support." Suddenly he frowned. "But would Tony be agreeable? Especially since it would mean stepping away from the day-to-day operations of the union?"

Anne also sat back, imitating the governor's meditative pose. "I think I could guarantee that, Jim. In fact, I'm sure I could."

Giuliani looked at the woman closely and wondered

what it would be like to have a powerful woman as firmly behind him as Anne Mobray was behind Tony Marco. The price tag might be much too high, he decided.

When Tony entered the governor's office a few days later, he was already aware of what would be offered. It was Anne's way—doing extraordinary things for those she cared about but making certain they were fully aware of the origins of their good fortune.

Tony listened as the governor outlined what he had in mind, aware that Giuliani was working very hard to sell him the idea. If he only knew, Tony thought. If he only realized how little choice I have. The appointment had suddenly become a condition for getting everything else he wanted. Oh, it hadn't been put that way, but the underlying message Anne had delivered made it very clear that it was not something he could turn down.

It was odd, he thought. The appointment was something he would have coveted; would have sought out himself had he thought of it. But somehow, offered under pressure, it had lost a great deal of its glitter. But he would do it, and in time, he knew, he would come to want it very badly.

"So what do you think?" the governor asked.

"I think it's a great idea," Tony said. "I'm just not sure I'm the man for the job." Tony smiled to himself again, amused by the game he could not resist playing, even when it was pointless.

"No one would be better," Giuliani insisted, a slightly worried look in his eyes. "Of course, you'd have to take a leave of absence from the union. Just to avoid any accusations of conflict."

"That wouldn't be a problem, Jim. It would just take a bit of time to make sure I had the right person lined up to take over temporarily," he said, adding to himself that the "right person" would be anyone but Paul Levine, and anyone who would let him continue to run things at his newly imposed distance.

"It's going to take a bit of time for me as well," Giuliani countered. At Tony's lifted eyebrows he raised a hand. "No problem. Just bureaucratic red tape and a few political steps to get the major New York papers behind the idea."

"Do you think they'll go for it?" Tony asked.

"Completely. Especially with what I have in mind. By the way, can you give me a list of favorable stories the various local papers have written about you?"

"Sure. And there are a few others coming up. A piece in *Manhattan* magazine, naming me one of the bright young men of the city, and a feature story in the *Globe*."

"Who's the reporter at the *Globe*? I might want to mention that when I talk to Bill Diesart over there."

Tony gave him Jennifer's name and listened as Giuliani discussed the advantages the appointment would provide; the prestige of being chairman of a blue-ribbon commission, which could be used in his future political résumé. Tony registered each word as though it came down a long tunnel. The savior of the Port of New York, he told himself. It was truly appropriate. He closed his eyes, thinking how welcome it would be to have even a small chance to ease a problem he had helped create, no matter how unwillingly.

He looked across at the governor and smiled. "I guess we have a deal, barring any unforeseen problems from your end," Tony said. "And thanks, Jim."

The governor waved off Tony's thanks and found himself wondering if his friend knew the source of his sudden good fortune. Well, if he doesn't, it's not for me to tell him, Giuliani thought. But I wonder what the price tag will be.

*   *   *

When Jennifer was summoned into William Diesart's office, she had no idea what was in store for her. A summons to the executive editor was uncommon enough that it might mean trouble.

Diesart waved her to a chair, declining to rise when she entered the room. His large, paunchy body remained fixed to the executive chair that his broad back all but obscured.

Diesart was in his late fifties, with steel-gray hair and a rubbery face that would have served a character actor well. The horn-rimmed glasses he wore added a look of intelligence, something the majority of the staff was quick to question.

"I understand you're doing a story about Tony Marco," Diesart said. "What's it about?"

Jennifer stammered, uncertain what to say. "I've really just started gathering things together," she replied.

"Does it look as though it will be favorable?"

Jennifer felt her stomach tighten. There was no way she could lie to the man and then expect his support later if she had to fight the story past Twist. "I'm not sure," she said softly. "It looks as though the union may be just as corrupt under Marco as it was under the gangsters who ran it before."

"Who else knows about this?" Diesart asked.

Joe Walsh flashed to Jennifer's mind, but she decided to keep that to herself. "No one."

A slow, steady grin appeared on Diesart's mouth. The governor had called only an hour before and had done a first-class selling job of his plan for a commission. Then the governor had dropped the other shoe, the fact that he had asked Diesart's counterpart at the *New York Times* to serve on the newly planned commission. Diesart was smarting under the blow to his ego. This sort of thing happened all too often. The *Globe* sold three times as many newspapers daily as the *Times*. But whenever the prestige was handed out, he and the *Globe* were always found at the bottom of the list.

He stared across at Jennifer. "Can we prove it?"

"I think so, but it will take a little time, and part of the evidence is in England." She quickly detailed the British end of the story and her plans to follow it there on her own time.

"Do it," Diesart snapped. "And we'll pay for it. Just two conditions. First, no one here knows about it except you and me. *No one.* We can't afford to let anything leak out, and there's nothing leakier than a newsroom." He raised a second finger. "Second, you have a hard deadline, and I expect you to meet it." There was a note of threat in his voice. "The governor tells me he plans to announce Marco's appointment to a commission studying New York Harbor at the end of next month, and I want us to be ready to nail Mr. Marco, *and* the commission, as soon as that announcement is made." He leaned forward and smiled again. "Not before but immediately afterward. Can you be ready to do that?"

"I think so."

Diesart let the note of threat rise to his eyes. "Don't just think so, young lady. Do it. Do we understand each other?"

Jennifer sat straight in her chair. Getting the story could mean more now than she had ever hoped. It could be her ticket. She felt a chill go through her. Of course, if she failed, it could be a ticket right out the door. "I understand," she said. "I can do it."

CHAPTER/TWENTY

JENNIFER AND PETE stayed at a small tourist hotel in London on a narrow dead-end street abutting the University College Hospital, just off Tottenham Court Road. They had arrived in London at Heathrow Airport at nine A.M., which was four A.M. New York time, and had gone immediately to their hotel where they had collapsed in adjoining rooms. When Jennifer awoke, it was mid-afternoon, and Pete was already gone. He had left a note with the hall porter asking her to meet him "as close to five-thirty as possible" at the Magpie and Stump, a pub located next to the Old Bailey Criminal Court.

Jennifer arrived shortly before six, having been unable to resist a stroll through the gardens of Regents Park, only a few blocks from the hotel. The walk had revived her, even more than the five hours of sleep. The taxi ride through the clean, well-ordered London streets made her feel pleased she had come, despite the new pressure Diesart had placed on her.

The pub was dimly lit and crowded, making it difficult

to get more than the impression of dark, polished wood and venerable age. Jennifer eased herself through the crowd and found Pete standing at the bar, talking with a tall slender man with sandy brown hair, a long, straight nose, and exceptionally soft blue eyes. Pete saw her approaching, reached out and took her arm, and guided her past the crush to stand next to them.

"I was afraid you were still sleeping it off," Pete said, then, glancing at the man, added, "The jet lag, I mean."

"No, five hours was enough," she said. "I even had time for a walk in Regents Park." She turned and smiled at the man, whom Pete promptly introduced as Mark Haversham, "the gentleman who got us our information about Weathersby."

The man from Scotland Yard. Jennifer looked at him closely and decided he failed to fit the image conjured up in various British mysteries.

"A pleasure to meet you, Miss Brady," Haversham said. "Can we get you something to drink?"

"A lime shandy. And please call me Jennifer."

A small smile came to the detective's lips. "I see you've been to our country before," he said as he signaled the bartender and ordered the mixture of lime soda and lager.

"After college," Jennifer said, "I managed to scrape up enough money to do the traditional grand tour, complete with backpack and traveler's checks in very small denominations."

Haversham smiled more broadly as he handed Jennifer her drink. "It's still being done that way, I assure you," he said. "The only students traveling first-class are the Arabs, and they are either traveling on daddy's oil riches or on terrorist expense accounts."

As Jennifer glanced around the pub she noted for the first time that most of the clientele was dressed in business suits and carried attaché cases. "Is this a favorite spot for the legal profession?" she asked.

"Very much so," Haversham said. "It's the reason I suggested it to Pete, in fact. I spent most of the day waiting to testify in court. Much to no avail, I'm afraid."

"It looks quite old," Jennifer said. "What I can see of it."

"Actually it was rebuilt in 1931, although the original goes back quite a bit. Used to have a lovely view of Newgate Prison, which is gone now, of course. The barristers and judges gathered here to view the public executions through the windows. Enjoying the fruits of their labors over a pint, so to speak." He watched Jennifer wrinkle her nose. "Quite," he said. "But the pub survived rather well, even lacking that rather ghoulish entertainment."

"Nothing like a hanging to make the customers thirsty," Pete observed.

"Nothing like the compassion of a New York City cop," Jennifer remarked to Haversham.

"An attitude among police the world over," he observed. "So tell me, will this be your first trip into the countryside?"

"Yes," Jennifer said. "I never got out of London the first time. I was in too much of a hurry to get to Paris and beyond."

"You're in for a bit of a treat, then. You'll be so near to the Cotswolds, a truly lovely place, you shouldn't miss. And then it's not far to Wales, which is also worth a visit. Charming people, the Welsh, despite what most of my countrymen have to say about them."

"Tell me about Weathersby," Jennifer said. "I really don't know what to expect."

"I'm afraid I can't offer you much more than a bit of gossip from the local constable," he said. "Moved there

quite some time ago. Lives in a cottage on the Thames.
Part of a family farm inherited by his wife. Seems they
rent out the land to neighboring farmers and live a rather
quiet life, mostly keeping to themselves. The old boy,
himself, is a cripple. Came back from the U.S. that way.
The constable believed it was some sort of accident, but
Pete tells me he ran into a few of your bashers in a car
park. Seems not to be something he wanted the locals to
know about, though." He offered a slight shrug. "Afraid
there's not much more I can tell you, other than he's had
no trouble with the authorities. Quite a model citizen,
actually."

Crippled, Jennifer thought. And perhaps bitter about it.
And all because he pointed a finger at Tony Marco and the
union. She stopped herself, realizing she was exaggerating
Marco's involvement. He had only been a college student
working a part-time job, not someone who sent out orders
for legs to be broken. But she wondered if Tony had
known about it when it happened.

"When are you leaving?" Haversham asked.

Pete glanced at Jennifer, realizing he hadn't had time to
tell her about the plans he'd made that afternoon. "Tomorrow, if Jennifer agrees," he said. "I thought we'd take a
train to Oxford, have lunch there, then rent a car and
drive to Weathersby's cottage."

"It's a lovely drive. Weathersby's cottage is about halfway between Buscot and Lechlade." Haversham held out
a slip of paper. "Here, I've drawn you a bit of a map. If
you have trouble, the constable in Buscot can direct you.
He's the chap I spoke to."

Flat marsh and farmlands spread out on both sides of
the River Thames, broken only by hedgerows that grew
along the snaking path of the river. The route was bucolic,

and the small villages they encountered seemed fixed in a century long past.

Jennifer insisted on driving, arguing that earlier experience in Bermuda, with its left-side-of-the-road regulations, made her the expert. She did not explain that her experience had been limited to a motor scooter, nor that her real reason was to maintain some control over where the car went.

At Buscot, Pete located the constable and received exact directions to Weathersby's cottage. A few miles later they crossed the Thames and entered Gloucester, then turned down a long gravel drive that led back to the river.

The cottage was a small stone affair, surrounded by a white picket fence, which seemed to have no other purpose than the support of climbing roses. Inside the gate, precisely arranged flower beds filled the area on each side of the path leading to the front door, showing a great deal of care and effort and time, Jennifer thought. But perhaps that's all Weathersby and his wife had now. Perhaps that's all that had been left to them.

A woman came around the side of the house when they were halfway down the path. She was tall and slim, dressed in a gardening hat, gloves, and a heavy canvas apron covering a simple white dress. She smiled at them as she approached, her blue eyes friendly but questioning. She looked to be in her early sixties, but her movements were vigorous and youthful.

"Hello. May I help you?" she asked.

Jennifer offered a smile. "I hope so," she said. "We're looking for Mr. John Weathersby."

The woman cocked her head to one side. "You're American, aren't you?" she said. "I'm Diana Weathersby. You must forgive my surprise. We're not used to having visitors, and certainly not those from abroad. It's been so long since I've even heard an American accent." She did not finish the statement and simply extended her hand to Jennifer. "John's resting at the rear of the house. May I ask what you wish to see him about?"

Jennifer explained briefly, offering as little information as possible, but as soon as she mentioned the union, the newspaper, and Weathersby's accident, the woman's mouth formed a tight line, and her eyes became hard and protective.

"I don't think that's anything John would care to talk about," she said in a brisk voice. "I wish you had telephoned first. It would have saved you a long journey."

Jennifer began to work around the objections but was stopped almost at once. "My dear young woman," Diana Weathersby began. "John went to your authorities about that union once, and it cost him the reasonable use of his legs. It is *not* something we wish to have repeated."

Jennifer began to explain that anonymity could be guaranteed but was stopped by the sound of a man's voice. She looked behind Diana Weathersby and saw a short, heavy-set man turning the corner of the house, supported by two canes. She stared at his legs, unable to stop herself. They were twisted at obscene angles, dragged forward behind the canes only by the strength of the man's shoulders.

John Weathersby smiled as he approached them, but the strain in his face was apparent, and there were beads of perspiration along his bald pate.

"What have we here?" he asked. "Visitors, no less. This is a surprise."

His wife turned quickly and stepped slightly to the side, as though creating a shield between her husband and his visitors. "John, you should be in your chair," she said.

"Nonsense, my dear. I heard voices and naturally wished to see who was here."

Jennifer could see Diana Weathersby's back rise under

a deep breath, then listened as she explained, in the most negative terms, the purpose of Jennifer's and Pete's visit.

John Weathersby's face changed from exuberance to cold dispassion. "I see," he said. "Then I think it only proper we invite our guests back to the rear garden where we can be more comfortable."

"John," his wife snapped. "You shouldn't."

"But I want to, my dear," he said, his voice soft and soothing. "It's something I've wanted to talk about for a long time now. I simply never had anyone who was willing to listen." He paused to smile at his wife. "Except you, of course, my dear."

The rear garden sloped gently toward the river, a wide expanse of lawn, broken by beds of perennial flowers. Jennifer and Pete sat in wrought-iron chairs, a low table set between them and Weathersby, who was seated in a wheelchair.

"It's beautiful here," Jennifer said.

"Yes, it is," Weathersby said. He inclined his head toward the house where his wife had gone to prepare refreshments. "It was part of a farm my wife's father operated. This cottage was used as a summer retreat by the family." He smiled. "We always intended to retire here. It just happened a bit sooner than we planned."

"What did happen?" Pete asked.

"It was all rather simple, really. My firm decided to seek help from the authorities to put an end to a rather long-standing system of bribery, imposed on it by the union. It fell to me, as head of the New York office, to carry it out." Weathersby paused to light a pipe and get it going properly. "Well, I failed miserably," he began again. "But I had warned home office that I probably would and that the results could prove disadvantageous." He chuckled slightly. "I hadn't, of course, realized exactly how personally disadvantageous it would be." He offered a

weak smile. "I had thought we'd simply suffer some unpleasantness on the docks. I hadn't anticipated this." He
gestured with the stem of his pipe at his nearly useless
legs.

Jennifer felt herself shudder inwardly. "And Tony Marco
was the person who collected the bribes?" she asked.

"Yes," Weathersby said. "But only during the last year.
Before that there was rather a grim fellow who did the
job. Let me see, now. Oh, yes. Name of Morgenstern.
Unpleasant fellow, as I said. It was a relief, actually, to
have young Marco coming by."

"Why was that?" Pete asked.

Jennifer noted a slight tightening along Pete's jaw, and
he leaned forward, almost as if challenging the statement.
She reached out and touched his arm.

"Well, he was rather a nice lad. Well mannered, well
groomed. That sort of thing. Actually I felt rather badly
involving him, but I had no choice in the matter."

"Did he know there was money in the envelopes he
collected?" Jennifer asked.

"I have no way of knowing," Weathersby said. "But I
assume he did."

"Nothing was ever said during any of his visits to indicate he might?" Pete asked. "Either by you or Marco?"

"Heavens no. Not the sort of thing one discusses. Of
course, I have no idea if any of the others did."

"The others?" Jennifer asked.

"The other shipping firms," Weathersby said. "It was
common knowledge that we were all in the same kettle of
fish, so to speak. Actually spoke about it from time to
time. Just to make certain we were all being charged the
same rates, don't you see?" He smiled. "The shipping
industry is like a large club in many ways."

"And it was just straight payoffs. Cash money," Pete
said.

"Yes. Although I understand it's changed since my day. A bit more complex now."

"How do you know that?" Pete asked.

"Chap from the office who came by for a visit," Weathersby said. "Of course, he didn't go into detail. No need for me to know, you see."

"How did Marco know to get rid of the money?" Jennifer asked.

Weathersby smiled at her. "Same question the police asked," he said. "Actually accused me of warning him off. Bloody fools. Implied as much to home office. Didn't even retract it after I was attacked. I suppose they thought I had myself crippled to avoid detection." He shook his head, then jammed his pipe between his teeth. "I suspect the police made a cock-up of it. Silly sods. Anyway, young Marco must have suspected he was in for it, because he dropped the lolly into a tray on one of the desks in the outer office. And since there were no witnesses, other than myself, there wasn't much could be done."

"And then you were attacked," Jennifer said.

"It was a week later, actually. We had had some difficulties on the docks, some unusually long delays and some suspicious damage. Frankly I thought that would be it, that the troubles would continue until we returned to the old scheme. I was simply awaiting word from home office." He stared off toward the river as though remembering his error; there was a sad, distant look in his eyes. He looked back at Jennifer and gave her a wan smile. "They were waiting for me in the car park. One of those multistory, concrete monstrosities a few blocks from the office. They were rather large chaps, and I was certainly no match for them. One of them grabbed me from behind, with his hand over my mouth. The other simply used a lead pipe. Took both my kneecaps first." He shook his head. "Excruciating pain. Then he started on the legs.

Fortunately I lost consciousness. When I awoke, I was in hospital and was told they had broken the bones several times, in both the upper and lower legs. Apparently gave me a few kicks about the head as well, since I was concussed rather badly." He shook his head again. "There were several bits of surgery, but the damage was simply too extensive."

Jennifer fought back an urge to look at Weathersby's mangled legs and turned her attention to the river. Pete's earlier warning about the danger that surrounded a story about the union seemed all too real now.

"Did they say anything to you?" Pete asked. "Tell you it was because of the business with the police?"

Weathersby shook his head. "No need," he said. "It wasn't robbery. They didn't take a thing. And I was never the sort of chap to get involved in things that would lead to a punch-up—chasing other men's wives or getting into difficulties over gambling losses. There was simply no other reason. And, of course, there was also the immediate end to our difficulties on the docks."

"So the bribes started again," Jennifer said.

"I suspect so. They're being paid now, in any event. Or so I'm told."

"Why just suspect so?" Jennifer asked.

"Well, I was called back to home office when I left hospital and removed from the firm a few weeks later."

"You're joking," Jennifer said, astonished.

"Oh, not at all. The managing director who instigated it all needed someone to—how did you say it in the States?—oh, yes, take the rap, so to speak. And I'm afraid I was the logical choice."

"But you had warned them," Jennifer said.

"Yes. Well, it seems my memo was never received at home office, and my copy, in New York, couldn't be found." He looked back toward the river. "Oh, they gave me the golden handshake. Rather a nice settlement. And invested in an annuity it gave me a comfortable income until my pension began to come in. But still . . ."

"The bastards," Pete said, then, noticing that Mrs. Weathersby had returned with a tray of tea and biscuits, offered a quick apology.

Placing the tray on the small table, then taking a seat next to her husband, Diana Weathersby looked at Pete levelly. "A very apt description of that whole lot," she said. "Not one of them even visited John in hospital. Treated him as though he were a leper."

Weathersby reached out and patted his wife's hand. "There, there, my dear. It's too long past for bitterness." He looked back at Pete. "It could have been worse, you know. I was never what could be described as an athletic chap. Books and my garden were my sort. And I can still do that quite well. I do miss the long walks Mrs. Weathersby and I used to take. But we go by car now, and the Cotswolds are quite close. You should give it a go before you leave the region. Most lovely this time of year."

Jennifer closed her eyes. The thought of life in a wheelchair terrified her; the vision of a mangled, twisted body, even more so.

"How do you feel about Tony Marco?" Jennifer asked at length.

"Hard to say," Weathersby said. "I haven't actually thought about him in a long while. As I said, he seemed a nice lad. Actually visited me in hospital, you know."

"What?" Jennifer said.

"Yes, quite so. Seemed very disturbed about what had happened."

"Cheeky little beast," Diana Weathersby added.

Weathersby patted her hand again. "Now, now, my dear." He turned back to Jennifer, his eyes far-off, as though recalling days past. "I was touched, actually. I suspect he could have got himself in a bit of a stew if his masters had found out. But, as I said, he was always a well-mannered lad."

"He kept on working for them," Pete said, his voice holding more than a little condemnation. "Did you know he's president of the union now? And he's being considered for a federal cabinet appointment somewhere down the line?"

A look of genuine concern came to Weathersby's eyes. "Dear Lord, what a shame," he said.

"What do you mean?" Jennifer asked.

"That he should have been so corrupted," Weathersby said. "That he wasn't able to escape them."

The Coln River joined the Thames at Lechlade, and Jennifer and Pete followed it north into the Cotswolds, choosing the narrow winding roads that meandered alongside the tributary, passing through lush green hills and thick forests, villages removed from the hurry of the outside world. They stopped for the night in Coln St. Dennis, at a small inn nestled in a coppice on the banks of the river, a few miles south of Chedworth Woods.

It had been a quiet drive, with little said about their visit with Weathersby. Comments seemed reserved for the scenery, but thoughts, for each, kept returning to the small, mangled man seated in his wheelchair.

They ate in the inn's small dining room overlooking the river, choosing typical British fare: roast beef with Yorkshire pudding and horseradish sauce for Pete; grilled Dover sole for Jennifer. Lingering over poorly brewed coffee, Pete decided to broach the subject.

"You've been quiet all afternoon. Are you still trying to sort out what Weathersby had to say?"

"There's not much to sort out, is there? And I'm still not sure just how much we really have."

"So let's look at it objectively," Pete said. "We know that cash payoffs were taking place years ago, and that Tony, knowingly or unknowingly, was involved. It's really a moot point, since the statute of limitations is long past." Pete picked up his coffee, stared at it, then replaced it in its saucer without drinking. "We also know things have not changed in recent years, only become more complex, as Weathersby put it. Tony's been running the union for the past six years; he's a lawyer, and a good one, and that points a circumstantial finger right at him."

Jennifer turned her face to the window and stared at the river, which moved swiftly here, crashing through a small rapids. "Do you think it would do any good to approach any of the shipping companies in London?" she asked.

"It could only hurt us," Pete said. "If they won't let Weathersby know what's going on, they sure as hell aren't going to tell us. But they might get word back to the union, just to cover themselves."

Jennifer continued to watch the river, her thoughts returning to Weathersby. She felt a small shudder along her spine. The last thing she wanted was exposure. She looked back at Pete. "You weren't kidding when you said they could be violent, were you?"

He shook his head. "All the more reason to be careful. And to stay close if we think they've caught on."

She closed her eyes momentarily. "I find it hard to believe Tony's involved." She stared evenly at Pete. "It's just an uneasy feeling that there's something we haven't come across, something that will explain it."

Pete returned her stare. "If it's there, we'll find it," he said. "But I wouldn't count on it. Tony wouldn't be the first golden boy with clay feet. He's been living in a nest of rats for a long time, and he always knew how to adapt to his surroundings. He's a born survivor. And you better learn how to be one too," he added. "From now on things could start to get rough."

"I can handle it," she said.

"I didn't mean that you couldn't," he said. "But with these people, being overconfident can be as bad as being inept. Let's just stay close and watch each other's backs."

Jennifer stared at her coffee, trying, without success, to keep her mind off Weathersby. She looked up at Pete. She felt protected being with him, she told herself. Protected against physical danger she had no way of controlling. She hated the idea of needing it, but there damn well wasn't any way of providing it herself.

"Do you think they know we're here?" she asked.

"I doubt it, but who knows how close they're checking on you? A lot depends on how careful Maxwell was, and how much we can depend on him to keep his mouth shut."

Maxwell's weasel face flashed in Jennifer's mind, and she shuddered at the idea of trusting her safety to his sense of discretion. "Then I'd feel safer assuming they already know," she said.

Pete nodded. "So we'll start being careful now."

Jennifer drew a deep breath and thought of their rooms upstairs. They were next to each other, but the old structure's thick plaster walls now seemed far from a guarantee of safety. She looked at him and acknowledged the attraction she had felt in recent weeks. But the thought of sleeping with him had only been a fleeting one, and she wasn't at all certain even that had been reciprocated. "We better stop talking about this," she said. "Or I'm going to be afraid to be alone in my own bed."

"It might not be a bad idea if you stayed at my place when we get back to New York—until this is finished," he said. He caught her look but couldn't be certain what it offered, other than surprise. "The sofa opens into an extra bed," he added, wanting to say more, but not certain exactly how.

Jennifer placed her hand over his, feeling a sudden rush of relief. "I think that's a good idea," she said. "But we could alternate between your place and mine." She smiled at the line. "Sounds like something dreamed up at a singles' bar, doesn't it? But at least that way I wouldn't be a bother."

"You wouldn't be a bother," he said.

She studied his face, the deeply etched lines around his eyes; reminders of past pain, she thought. She wondered what it would be like being with him and realized she was about to find out. "I'm glad I wouldn't be," she said. "You won't be, either."

She had left her hand on his, and he took hold of it now. "I have nightmares sometimes," he said. "A holdover from the war. Just so you know in case it happens."

She nodded but said nothing. And I have my own nightmares, she thought, but decided it wasn't something she could talk about. Her thoughts drifted to Marco. And what happened to him? she wondered. She recalled the look in Weathersby's eyes when Pete had told him about Tony. And his words: *What a shame . . . that he wasn't able to escape them.*

CHAPTER/TWENTY-ONE

FROM HIS FIRST day on the union's executive committee Tony Marco found himself in a constant struggle with Paul Levine. It was a game of control, a maneuvering for position and power. It was a game Tony did not seek, but it was also one he could not avoid. In the end Tony Marco played the game better, and all the advantages proved to be in his favor.

This resulted, in part, from the advanced age of several members of the executive committee, but also because of Tony's instinctive political talents, which seemed at their best whenever he was challenged.

Over the next three years two members of the executive committee retired, and despite the opposition of Paul Levine, Tony's growing influence with Moe Green allowed him to bring his own handpicked men into those positions.

What followed was a political *blitzkrieg*. In 1973, at the age of twenty-four, Tony had himself named business administrator of the union's medical center and representative of the welfare fund—jobs no one wanted because of the excessive work they entailed. But they also included power. In short, they gave Tony unobtrusive control of the primary source of the local's investment capital and, with it, the local's purse strings and the subtle influence that conferred.

Two years later Moe Green suffered his first heart attack, and though it was mild, was ordered to curtail his activities. Tony met the opportunity by creating a new position on the executive committee, that of organizational director of the local. In effect, the new post, to which he was later elected by the membership, made him Moe Green's assistant and the number-two man on the executive committee. Paul Levine, as vice-president and business agent, suddenly found himself number three, with only one hope of ousting Tony Marco—by opposing him in the next union election. It was a battle Levine knew he could not win.

By then Marco was twenty-six years old and had just passed his New York State bar examination.

Tony's evaluation of those years lacked any degree of euphoria. There were private union matters from which he was excluded by Green, and life with Shirley was not what he had expected.

The first year of their marriage was all Tony had hoped for. Shirley's natural effervescence and sexual eagerness provided excitement and passion, and their time together lacked any of the tensions normal to newly married couples. And her influence with her father also grew as did Moe's concern that she live as well with Tony as she had at home with him.

It was something Shirley used to Tony's advantage. For Tony it was the impetus for his rise in the union, a guarantee of support from Moe Green for his political maneuverings, something Shirley termed her part in his future. It also gave Shirley a power over their relationship to know that his continued success was largely dependent on her continued happiness. And while her support of him grew, so did her sexual aggressiveness. She had a series of brief affairs that she made little effort to conceal.

When Tony had objected, Shirley had only smiled and insisted her involvements with other men were nothing more than casual flirtations. She was bored, she explained, with the endless hours he devoted to union activities by day, combined with evenings spent poring over law books. So he accepted it and tried to improve their relationship. He had no choice. He could leave, or he could keep struggling to change it. Something—his love for her, he told himself—made him stay.

The situation was not much better within the union. Tony had his power base and his own people on the executive committee, but it was little more than a pro-logue. Final power—the power to force decisions—still flowed from Moe Green with Tony as a conduit that could occasionally direct the flow. Still, direct opposition to Green's decisions was not possible. Tony's major strength lay in his control of the medical center and welfare fund, and those were positions held at Green's pleasure. Basically, the same tactics Tony had used to box out Paul Levine had been employed by Green to keep Tony under thumb.

The degree of that control became even more apparent in September 1975, when Tony was summoned to Green's office to discuss proposed investments of welfare fund assets. Recently Green's appearance had shocked him. He seemed to deteriorate daily, his always-thin figure shrink-ing even more into the folds of his suit, his skeletal face accented by ever-darkening patches beneath his eyes.

Seated across from him, Tony noticed the recent tremors in Green's hands had intensified. There had been speculation that, in addition to a chronic heart ailment, Green also suffered from Parkinson's disease. But it was something that could not be confirmed. Green kept his health a closely guarded secret, reminding Tony of an aging predator that remained close to its lair to keep rivals from discovering its vulnerability.

"How are you feeling, Moe?" Tony asked as he opened a leather-bound financial folder on his lap.

"How do I look?" Green responded.

"Overworked," Tony said.

Green snorted. "I've been overworked for forty years. It's about time somebody started to notice." He waved a hand, dismissing his own remark, then stared across the desk. "How are things with you and Shirley?"

Tony kept his face impassive. "Fine. We're both busy and don't see as much of each other as we'd like, but aside from that, we're okay."

Green kept his eyes fixed on Tony's face, searching for some flaw in his words. "Shirley's impetuous," he said at length. "She always has been. You just have to be patient with her."

So even you know, Tony thought. And you want to make sure I'll tolerate it. He nodded in response.

"A child would be a good idea," Green said. "Nothing like a kid to settle people down."

Tony smiled at the paternal interference, not because it was benevolent but because of the ruthless self-interest that directed it. "All we need is the time to work on it," he said.

"I think I found the time for you," Green said. "I want you to make a trip to Las Vegas for me. You can combine it with an impromptu vacation and take Shirley along. It'll do you both good."

"Vegas?" Tony questioned.

Green nodded. "The question of casino gambling in Atlantic City is scheduled to come up before the New Jersey legislature next year. Some of the casinos out there are talking about opening branches if the legislation passes, and they're looking for investment capital. I thought it might be something we should look into."

Tony let out a long breath. "We'd have to be careful of the legalities. We'd also want to be careful about who else was tied into it, so we wouldn't be linked to the wrong people."

Green waved his hand in disgust. "If we invested in the Vatican Bank, we'd be criticized," he snapped. "As far as the legal problems go, that's for you to work out." He picked up a pencil and began tapping it on the desk. "I want you to look at it from the standpoint of personal investments too. For you and me, and anybody on the executive committee who might be interested."

"I can look into it for you and the others," Tony said, "but I don't have the kind of capital they'd be interested in."

Green stared at him for several moments. "Yes, you do. Right now you've got about two hundred and fifty thousand bucks in a bank in Grand Cayman."

Tony sat forward and stared at Green with disbelief. "How?" he asked.

"You remember years ago, when you used to run errands to shipping companies?" He waited until Tony had nodded. "Well, we both know what was in those envelopes. Let's just call it gratuities." He gestured with both arms. "Well, those gratuities have continued, and since you joined the executive committee, you've had a share in them."

Tony's jaw tightened. Five years on the executive committee, at fifty thousand dollars a year in bribes he never knew existed. Five years of class-A felonies. "Why wasn't I ever told?" His eyes bored into Green, but he fought to keep his voice and manner calm.

"Call it a testing period," Green said with a shrug. "There was some concern about whether we could be sure of you. Whether you'd last."

"How is the account set up?"

"A Grand Cayman Corporation with you, Shirley, and myself as officers. It requires at least two signatures to release the money."

"But I never signed anything."

"Shirley signed. For herself and for you, as your wife. Their laws allow it down there."

Tony stared at the folder in his lap. And what court would ever believe I didn't know? he asked himself.

Green smiled at him, his face cold and mirthless. "Let's just say it's a belated wedding present. You're becoming a wealthy man, Tony. And it's going to get better. Security for you and Shirley."

Tony kept his eyes averted, struggling for control. And firmly trapped, he told himself. Tied to you and your daughter whether I like it or not. "It's quite a surprise, Moe. I never suspected."

"Don't thank me," Green said. "Just invest the money wisely."

Tony held the smile. No, he thought, I'll spend the next years figuring a way to get out of it. "You bet, Moe," he said.

He did not mention the conversation to Shirley. He saw no point in it. What could he ask, other than why he had not been told? And he already knew the answer to that. It was another hold over him, one that, this time, included Moe Green as well. Shirley and Moe, the only witnesses who could testify that I never knew about the money, he told himself. If the idea wasn't so sickening, it almost would be cause for laughter.

Instead he had cabled the bank in Grand Cayman and confirmed the balance in the account. That cable, at least, would be confidential, given the island's banking laws. The account, itself, in fact, would be reasonably secure. But he knew he had to get out from under it, or it would hang over him indefinitely. And until he could, the account would continue to grow. There was nothing he could do to stop it. The great danger was exposure of the bribes, themselves. That would lead to a paper chase that would eventually uncover the foreign bank accounts. Something had to be done, he knew, to keep the bribes safe from disclosure. A better system. He shook his head at the idea. New felonies to keep old ones hidden. It was like falling into quicksand.

The suite at the Las Vegas hotel was provided compliments of the house, as were the fully stocked bar, all meals, and tickets to the shows. Tony had little doubt that, had he arrived alone, one of the casino's approved prostitutes would also have been sent to his room. It was Las Vegas sleaze at its best, or worst, depending on how one viewed it.

Shirley wasted little time finding her way to the casino, her purse stocked with complimentary chips and a healthy amount of her own money as well. Tony went straight to a meeting with casino officials and listened carefully to a scenario that included everything from lobbying strategies, to licensing, to actual construction design.

The costs, both for construction and operation, were staggering. But the projected revenues, based on a statistical draw from New York, Philadelphia, and Washington, were even more so. By the end of the meeting there was little question in Tony's mind that it was a sound investment. His only remaining reservation was the type of partners with whom the union would find itself in bed. But that, he knew, was not information the casino would offer. It would require independent inquiries, something he would have to convince Moe Green to initiate.

When the meeting ended, he declined an offer to visit a private club within the casino, choosing instead to move about on his own. He decided to avoid the casino in the hotel and not risk being dragged into Shirley's gambling adventures. It was his first visit to Las Vegas, and he left the hotel and joined the crowds on the Strip, moving past the endless array of neon, which, even in daylight, continued to blink out its ever-present promise of undeserved riches.

Within a block the afternoon heat drove him inside again, into another hotel with yet another casino, its rows of slot machines and gaming tables, and its swarm of people whose eyes seemed too intense for pleasure. He noted the layout of the hotel with a mixture of admiration and amusement. Like his own hotel, it was impossible to go anywhere—a restaurant, a bar, a public rest room—without passing by the gaming tables. No opportunity was lost, he decided, and each frustration was met with the promise that next time one would win.

He watched the play at several of the tables without much interest, other than the amounts of money people were willing to risk. There seemed to be a pervading disdain for those who played small amounts, by those who gambled more recklessly, and he found himself wondering if condescension was needed to justify the amounts that repeatedly slipped through their fingers. You're an asshole because you're only losing five bucks, while I'm losing two hundred. He thought a psychologist could do an interesting study on the needs and practices of rationalization.

After watching a woman play roulette—placing several

hundred in chips on red for each spin of the wheel, then tipping the croupier fifty dollars when she lost and a hundred when she won—he decided he could spend his time better over a glass of Scotch. The cocktail lounge was large, yet intimate, with dim lighting and quiet corners artfully arranged for privacy. Unlike the casino, where lights blazed in unending daylight, here there was perennial night, soft and muted, a resting area before the return to dazzle.

He slid onto a stool at the bar and ordered a drink. He was just about to pick up the glass when a woman slipped into the space next to him.

"Tony Marco," a soft, highly feminine voice said.

He turned to find himself facing a beautiful woman in a low-cut cocktail dress, perfectly coiffed blond hair, and makeup that accentuated large blue eyes. A glimmer of recognition flashed in his mind, then disappeared. He began to speak, then stopped himself, and just stared.

"You don't remember me," the woman said.

"I do, but . . . oh, Christ. Mary Beth."

Her smile filled her face, and she reached out and took his hand. "I almost fell down when I saw you walk in here. I thought I was back in Brooklyn."

They both laughed, kissed each other's cheeks, then moved to a table, away from the crush.

"I knew you came out here, but I thought, by now you would have moved on. Gotten married or just decided to find someplace that had trees."

Mary Beth laughed at the remark. "We get used to sand and cactus. And we actually have a few trees." A waitress stopped at the table, and Mary Beth ordered a Perrier with lime. "Never when I'm working," she said, then continued before he could question the statement. "And I was married. For all of nine months. He was tall and handsome and had a great personality. Unfortunately he was also a louse." She shrugged, then asked what he was doing there.

Tony explained with as little detail as possible about the business trip, his involvement with the union, and the presence of his wife.

"Have you seen Pete at all?" Mary Beth asked.

Pleasure flowed out of him, and his eyes became distant. "Once," he said. "But it didn't go too well."

Mary Beth lowered her eyes. "He took it hard, I guess. I'm so sorry about that." She looked up at him. "And I can see you are too." She shook her head. "He wrote to me after he got home. But I never had the guts to write back. Maybe I should have. I might have been able to explain and set things right between you two."

"No. There was no way to set it right," Tony said.

"I suppose not. But, dammit, we were just kids who were hurting because we thought he was dead." She smiled weakly. "I never regretted it, even though it shouldn't have happened."

Tony returned the smile. He wanted to change the subject, get away from painful memories. "You said you were working here. What exactly do you do?"

Mary Beth glanced away, then back at him. "I work as a hostess for the casino." She waited, watching it register, allowing him to sort out the term, put it in its proper perspective. A look of hurt came to his eyes. "Heah, it's not that bad, and I do pretty well financially. I just entertain the high rollers. In any way they want to be entertained." Her eyes became flinty. "And I'm damn good at it."

"I'm sorry," Tony said. "I wasn't being judgmental. I was just surprised."

She reached out and took his hand. "It isn't as bad as it sounds, and besides, I won't be working for the hotel much longer."

"Why?" he asked.

"I'm twenty-six, and that's getting a little long in the tooth for the high rollers. They like young little lollipops. But I'll still be allowed to work the casinos if I want to. I just won't work for them."

"Why don't you get away from here?" he asked. "What ever made you decide on Vegas, anyway? I know someone arranged a job, but you never told me who."

Mary Beth stared at him, her face incredulous. "You really don't know?"

"Know what?"

"Boy, those people are like the Mafia," she said.

"Who are you talking about?" Tony asked.

"The union," she said. "Your union. They got me the job out here when things got bad in the neighborhood. Except they were the ones who made sure things got bad in the first place."

"Mary Beth, what are you talking about?"

"The woman who took me to the airport—a woman from the union—she told me about it. I guess she felt sorry for me or something. Or just wanted to make sure I knew the score, so I didn't try to come back and find myself in the same mess all over again."

"I still don't understand," Tony said.

Mary Beth let out a long breath. "You remember how after the abortion the whole neighborhood seemed to know what had happened and how they made my life miserable? Well, they knew because somebody in the union made sure the story got around. Then the union offered to help me out by getting me a job here, and I jumped at it. Well, this woman who took me to the airport, she explained how it happened. How they wanted me out of the way so there wouldn't be any more trouble. She was the same woman who took me for the abortion, and I guess she felt sorry for me." She stared at him for several moments. "I always thought you knew."

Tony stared at the table, his mouth drawn in a tight line, the muscles jumping along his jaw. "No," he said, his voice hoarse. "But I should have. I should have known they'd be behind it. That *he'd* be behind it. You just didn't fit into his plans."

"Who's 'he'?" Mary Beth asked.

Tony looked across at her. "A man who I'm going to repay, no matter how long it takes. Along with the people who helped him."

Mary Beth took his hand again. "Tony, it's not worth it. I'm okay here."

"It's worth it," he said. "It's worth it to me."

Tony Marco proved himself a patient man. For three years he continued to consolidate his influence within the union, using and manipulating his ties to Moe Green to put himself in a position of unquestioned strength. And as Green's health consistently deteriorated, so did his influence among the members of the executive committee. Only Paul Levine resisted Tony's growing authority, and in each case Levine found himself politically outmaneuvered, often to the point where his own authority came into question.

At home Tony also proved patient. Shirley's flamboyant life-style continued, her repeated disappearances becoming more frequent, excuses no longer even attempted. Tony iced himself against it, no longer hoping to resolve the problem; no longer caring how many men she chose to see. When the time came, he decided, he would act.

In 1978, Shirley gave birth to their son, Joshua. Standing before the large glass window in the maternity ward, Tony stared at the tiny, red, shriveled child, its small hands clutching its blanket as though it offered some tenuous hold to life itself. The infant turned its head and stared sightlessly in his direction. Tony smiled at the helpless figure. This was a child, he told himself, who would not grow up without a father. And he would also, Tony vowed, not be raised by a mother who moved from one bedroom to another at will.

Shirley's power came to an abrupt end the following year, when a massive coronary closed out the final chapter of Moe Green's life. On the day after the funeral Tony took control of the main office, and also laid out the ground rules under which his life, and Shirley's, would be lived.

She had raged at the idea that her position of power had come to an end and had threatened to go to her "Uncle Paul."

Tony had only smiled, explaining in a quiet voice that Paul Levine was hanging on to what he had by his fingertips.

"And there's nothing I'd like more than to chop them off," he said.

She glared at him. "There's still the money you know." She stopped, waiting for him to respond. "I know you know about it. Don't pretend you don't." Still he said nothing. "You can't touch it without my signature," she added. "You know that too."

"The money's yours, Shirley. We'll transfer it into an account in your name tomorrow."

Her face blazed anger, then uncertainty, then anger again. "I'm sure you wouldn't want word to get out about that account, would you, Tony, dear? It could be arranged, you know."

Tony looked at her levelly and said, "When Moe died, you also became the surviving partner in a bank account in Curaçao. Her mouth opened but nothing came out. "Oh, yes, Shirley, I made a point of finding out about that. I also know it was never reported as part of Moe's estate.

But that really couldn't be done, could it? So, you see, if you point a finger at the account in Grand Cayman, I'll just have to do the same for the one in Curaçao. And then, Shirley, you'll end up with exactly nothing."

He watched her face turn pale and her lips begin to tremble.

"So, for the time being, you'll take care of our son and you'll stop making a public spectacle of yourself. I don't care who you see, but you *will* be discreet."

"What do you mean, 'for the time being'?" she asked.

"Right now Josh needs you. In a few years, when he doesn't, he and I will leave you and your money behind. Until then you'll just have to behave yourself."

"You can't leave me," she shouted. "You can't."

"That's not even a point in question," Tony said. "The only question is what you'll have when I do. And that's entirely up to you."

CHAPTER/TWENTY-TWO

THE FIVE MEN took their positions around the conference table, Tony Marco at its head, a yellow legal pad with his notes set before him.

"First let's talk about some organizational changes that will have to be made," Tony began. He watched Paul Levine's hands tighten into fists. Levine was the only man in the room who did not know what was coming, and he feared the worst.

"As you know, we have union elections coming up in September. With Moe's passing, we have a vacancy on the executive committee, and we're also faced with Frank Malboa's plans to retire." He nodded toward Malboa, a fat, round-faced man with a bald head, a cigar fixed firmly in the center of his mouth. Malboa nodded through a cloud of cigar smoke.

Tony tapped a pencil against the legal pad as he appeared to study his notes. "Now, this means the positions of organizational director and recording secretary will be open." He paused. "*If* we choose to have them open."

"I don't understand what you mean," Levine said. His eyes were hard and searching. There was no question in his mind that Marco planned to eliminate him. It was only a question of how and when.

"What I'm thinking of is fairly simple, Paul." Tony smiled at him. "First we can keep the position of organizational director or we can drop it. It was really only necessary because of Moe's incapacitation." He allowed the irony of the statement to drop of its own weight, then continued quickly. "Myself, I like the idea of keeping it. It gives us a five-member committee, which avoids tie votes and the misunderstandings they produce.

"Now, the logical thing to do is to move you, Paul, into that position and find somebody new for your spot on the ballot."

Levine nodded, his eyes narrow and suspicious. He glanced down the table and raised his chin toward the man seated next to Tony.

Tony glanced at Joey Gambardella. Joey's narrow, hawklike face was set in a permanent scowl, the years, if anything, having made his features crueler and more threatening. He was there now, not because Tony wanted him, but because Tony had yielded to a plea from his own mother to get Joey a decent job.

Tony looked back at Paul and shook his head. "I'd rather have Joey take Frank's spot." He hesitated again. "Except I'd like him to do it after the election."

"Why?" Levine asked.

"Joey's had a few 'difficulties' with the law. So we'll need time to straighten that out. To give us that time I think it best if Frank stands for reelection, then retires afterward for health reasons. Then we can appoint Joey and give him a few years in the job to establish himself. In the meantime he can work with Frank as a consultant and learn the ropes."

Levine studied Tony's face, looking for something not being said. "If we put him on the ticket, he's part of the package. He goes in with the rest of us. As far as I know, there's no opposition."

Tony nodded. "But there's a public relations problem. I want to present our ticket as a *reform* administration to the media. And I don't want to give them anything to dispute that concept. Next time around, when Joey's been part of the committee, it won't make any difference."

"What are you planning to reform?" Levine demanded.

Tony smiled at him. "Nothing, Paul. It's just an image I want to project."

Levine sat back and studied his hands, noting for the first time that his fists were clenched. He opened them, palms flat on the table. "And if I move up, who do you have in mind as a replacement?"

"Manny Esposito," Tony said. "He's a warehouse foreman, and he's a proven hand with the men."

Levine nodded but said nothing. And one more *gumba* for the committee, he told himself. Four wops and a token Jew.

When Levine failed to comment, Tony moved quickly on. "Just one more item. The 'donations' we receive from the shipping companies."

All eyes turned toward him, and Tony had to struggle to keep his expression impassive. Nothing like talking about people's bank accounts to get their attention.

"The way we do it now is simply too dangerous," he said.

"It's always worked in the past," Levine interjected.

"That doesn't mean we can't do it better."

"What do you have in mind, Tony?" Vince Albanese's square jaw jutted forward with interest. He was dressed in a neat blue suit but still had the look of a man who had worked the docks most of his life.

"It's very simple," Tony began. "We form a number of service corporations. Food services, a small building company that specializes in shipyards, a shipping consulting firm. Things of that type. The officers of those companies will be friends or relatives." He glanced at Frank Malboa. "After Frank's retirement he'll be on the board of directors of each one. In effect he'll run them. The shipping companies we deal with will then hire these companies to do work for them. At least on paper. Later, if it seems worthwhile, we might even have these companies doing some legitimate work for other concerns."

"What about taxes?" Levine asked. "Right now we don't face that problem. With corporations there'll be corporate taxes to pay. City, state, and federal. That's a big chunk of money for safety."

"First, each of our corporations will do business with the others. Purchasing their services on paper. It will create a trail of expenses that will be very hard to follow and will also provide each company with deductions that will sharply reduce their profit. Whatever profit is left over in each company will then be covered by loans to create the additional deductions necessary to eliminate tax payments." He watched Paul Levine raise a questioning eyebrow.

"As you know," Tony continued, "the union welfare fund has the right to make loans, as an investment of excess capital. In the case of our companies the fund will make short-term loans to them each year. But only on paper; no money will actually change hands. The interest on the loans will be in the exact amount of any leftover profits. In the meantime the corporations will invest those profits in tax-free bonds and will pay the interest earned back to the union. In the end the welfare fund's books balance, and the corporations have nice, clean, laundered money that even the feds can't question."

"And when it's passed to us?" Levine asked.

"Same as before," Tony said. "A choice of personal preference. It can be passed through the casinos in Las Vegas and declared as winnings, or simply funneled to individual corporations in the Netherlands Antilles or the Cayman Islands."

No objections came from the others. Finally Paul Levine nodded. "I don't see any reason why the shipping companies wouldn't buy it."

"Neither do I," Tony responded. "They'll have straight-out tax deductions without any need to juggle their books to cover their losses, and they'll also be sidestepping any potential problems with the law."

"Have you talked to them?" Levine asked.

Tony shook his head. "If no one has a problem with this, I plan to go to Europe next month and meet with them individually."

When no objection was forthcoming, Tony pushed himself away from the table and stood. "I have one other thing for you," he said, indicating a wrapped package leaning against the wall behind him.

He undid the wrapping and held it up. It was an oil portrait of Moe Green, the eyes staring out with the same cold cruelty they had offered in life.

"Shirley had this painted several years ago," Tony said. "We decided it belonged here, in the conference room, to remind us all of everything Moe did for the local."

Tony smiled at the approving nods. What he did not tell them was that he had told Shirley he wanted her father's sinister face out of his home.

CHAPTER/TWENTY-THREE

TONY MET ANNE MOBRAY for the first time in London. It was at a dinner party, a black-tie affair at the home of an English earl. Lord Chetworth sat on the board of one of Britain's major shipping firms. He was a short, plump, red-faced man with an unintelligible manner of speech who was referred to by his friends as Bumpy.

The estate, located off Hampstead Lane in the northern environs of London, was—like those of many of Britain's nobility—partially opened to the public, both to defray costs and to make available its extensive art collection.

Tony walked slowly through the music room, admiring the paintings hung there, works by Gainsborough and Reynolds, an overpowering seascape by Turner, and the pride of the collection, a self-portrait by Rembrandt, placed alongside another work once attributed to the master but later discovered to be the work of one of his students.

"Incredible difference, isn't there?"

He turned and found a woman slightly behind him to his right. She was tall and slender with sculpted, long blond hair that framed the delicate bones of her face. She was looking at the two paintings, not at him, and Tony took advantage of her inattention to study the floor-length white silk dress she wore, noting it clung appealingly to her sensual figure.

Anne raised her chin toward the portrait of a woman, now attributed to Rembrandt's student. "It amazes me that they ever thought it was a Rembrandt," she said. "When you see it next to his work, the difference is so striking."

"It's still very good," Tony said.

"Mmm." The sound of agreement came from deep in Anne's throat. "But one is poetry and the other is just very good descriptive prose." She turned and smiled at him. "I sound as though I really know what I'm talking about." She said it with a laugh in her voice, then extended her hand. "I'm Anne Mobray."

"And I'm Tony Marco." He took her hand and smiled.

"I know," she said. "I've seen your picture in newspapers."

"And I've seen yours," Tony said. "Is your husband with you?"

"My husband and I are never together anymore," she said.

"I'm sorry."

"Don't be. Life is far more interesting without him." She started toward another wall. Tony walked with her, stopping, when she did, before a Vermeer. The painting showed a girl playing a guitar, the fingers so delicate and lifelike, it seemed as though they would move at any moment.

Anne looked at Tony, her pleasure obvious in her eyes. "Do you enjoy art?"

"Very much," he said. "I took an art history course in college and became addicted. I've just recently begun buying art. Although almost all of it is contemporary. Paintings like these are very much out of my league."

"Out of almost anyone's league," Anne said, laughing. "Most of these were bought in the 1880s and '90s, when prices were reasonable and taxes didn't devour one's funds."

"It must be nice to come from a long line of people who could afford to collect," Tony said.

"Not so long," Anne said, smiling like someone prepared to give away a choice piece of gossip. "The first earl didn't become the first earl until the 1890s. He was given the title for building the family's brewery into an economic giant. The family made a great deal of its present money by smuggling beer into the United States during Prohibition. Not unlike the way Joseph Kennedy put together a great deal of his fortune."

Tony laughed. "I just assumed there was a long line of earls, going back centuries."

"Apparently beer barons qualified. Not very Victorian of Queen Victoria, was it?" Anne smiled at him, and Tony found he liked her ironic sense of humor.

As they continued around the room, Tony wondered about the husband who made life more interesting by his absence. Charles Mobray was chief executive officer of one of the largest steel companies in the United States, the same industry in which Anne's family had built their own enormous wealth. A marriage made in the boardrooms.

As they left the music room Anne slipped her arm in his. "Let's stop by the dining room," she said with a smile. "If you're not seated next to me at dinner, I want one of the maids to switch the name cards so you will be."

They met again the next evening for dinner. Tony's business in the United Kingdom was finished. His meetings in Edinburgh, Liverpool, and London had all con-

cluded with satisfactory results. He was due now in
Marseilles but found he was in no hurry to get there.

When Anne expressed her love of Indian food, it had
made the choice of a restaurant easy. The hall porter at
the Savoy, where Tony was staying, recommended the
Strand on Bedford Street, only a short walk from the
hotel, and, according to the porter, one of the finest
Indian restaurants in London. It proved to be that and
more: a small, intimate room with service excellent and
polite, in the best London tradition.

It was almost eleven before they finished their meal,
and they were about to fall victim to Britain's antiquated
drinking laws when barmen across the nation announced
the eleven P.M. curfew by calling out: "Time, gentlemen,
please," then allowing ten minutes for customers to gulp
down what remained in their glasses.

"It's the only thing about London that I hate," Anne
said about the curfew as they walked along Trafalgar Square
en route to an absent friend's home on St. James's Street
where she was staying. Her offer of a nightcap had been
accepted happily.

They walked casually along Pall Mall, their arms linked,
passing by the formal, almost forbidding facades of the
gentlemen's clubs that lined the broad avenue. Pall Mall
ended at St. James's Palace, and they turned right into St.
James's Street, which ran north to Piccadilly and had a few
elegant homes and still more clubs.

"That's Boodles," Anne said, indicating one of the clubs.
"It was a famous gambling club in the days of Beau
Brummell. Farther along is the Carlton Club, supposedly
the most prominent club in London." She rolled her eyes.
"At least according to my husband, who is a member."

She squeezed his arm against her side, and Tony could
feel the lithe, sensual flow of her body against his own. He
thought of V. S. Pritchett's view of London clubs: "Those

mausoleums of inactive masculinity . . . places for men who prefer armchairs to women."

In her suite, they sat on a long sofa before a gas fire in the hearth, lit more for effect than for heat. Anne was turned toward Tony, her arm draped along the back of the sofa, her eyes steady on his face as she sipped a snifter of cognac.

"Why the labor movement?" she asked. "Why not a good law firm or industry? I'm sure those opportunities were open to you."

Tony wondered if she truly understood how little was open, and to what a limited degree. He inclined his head to one side. "Power," he said. "And the ability to effect change."

"Power?" She said the word as though savoring it on her tongue. "Like Machiavelli's views of the politician and the merchant?"

Tony smiled wryly at the idea, recalling the line: *The politician seeks power to achieve wealth; the merchant, wealth, to achieve power.* He nodded. "Something like that."

"And which are you after?"

"Both."

Anne laughed. "Aren't we all," she said. She studied him closely, enjoying the look of him, the feel of him being near. "And is the power there?"

"Politically," he said. "At all levels."

She raised her eyebrows. "I have a home in New York, and I spend a great deal of time there, but I've paid very little attention to its local politics."

"The power is there for organizations that can provide the politicians with money, campaign workers *and* votes," Tony said.

"The unions," Anne said.

Tony nodded.

She sipped her cognac thoughtfully. "And bright young union leaders who don't carry the tarnish of the back alleys and the barrooms are especially appreciated," she added.

"Especially," Tony said.

She traced the back of the sofa with a long fingernail, still watching him closely. "Do you have political ambitions yourself?"

"Not to elected office."

"Why not?"

"It's too demeaning. To do what it takes to get elected. And I don't care to expose myself to the kind of scrutiny that's required."

"But you expose yourself to that already."

He shook his head. "Only to the degree I choose, and when and where I choose."

"So, appointed office, then."

"Perhaps. Someday. But I'm years away from thinking of that."

"Secretary of labor?" There was no laughter in her voice at the idea.

"It has a nice ring to it," Tony said.

"And your personal life?"

"I try to keep that as much in the present as possible," Tony said.

"And at the present?"

He smiled, his eyes steady on her own. "At present I'd like very much to make love to you."

Anne raised her chin, her head tilting slightly to one side, a small smile forming on her lips. "I think that's a wonderful idea," she said.

They traveled together to Marseilles, taking time after Tony had completed his business to wander through that most polyglot of French cities. Anne reveled in the chaos, the cacophony of voices, people shouting more often than speaking their native tongues, bodies moving at a speed that would make New Yorkers seem indolent by comparison.

They stayed at Le Petit Nice, Marseilles's finest hotel, located just off Corniche Kennedy on an isolated strip of rocky coast set between two coves and overlooking the Mediterranean which stretched out to the horizon.

They ate breakfast on a terrace above the sea, washed by a gentle breeze that felt warm and comforting. It was hard to imagine, Tony thought, that in winter the driving mistral would make the city gray and frigid, though only slightly more than one hundred miles away people would luxuriate in the sun of Cannes, and, in Nice, walk along the Promenade des Anglais beneath the gentle sway of palm trees.

"You seem lost in thought," Anne said, bringing him back.

"Lost in ideas of how to avoid work," he said.

"Mmm. That sounds delicious. Tell me."

He sat back in his chair, turning his face to the sun. "I was thinking how it would be to travel up the coast to Nice and Monte Carlo."

"I'll vote for that." She was wearing a soft silk blouse that clung to her body, accenting the lines of her breasts, unencumbered beneath the sheer cloth.

So would I, if I could, he thought, recalling their love-making earlier that morning, the eager insatiability she brought to their bed. He shook his head with genuine regret, noticing the pout that came to her lips.

"I have these meetings that I've already postponed once." He watched the pout spread to her eyes, secretly pleased by her disappointment but also amused by her need to have every whim pampered.

"What I thought we might do . . ." He paused to draw out the speculation, taking time to look out at the sea. He looked back at her. "You could go on to Nice, and I could take care of the meetings in Italy and Greece. It would be only five days, a week at most. Then we could meet in Venice. I was planning to stop there before returning home, and I'd much rather see the city with you."

Her face brightened, the smile instantaneous, her eyes distant with plans already being made. "Mmm, Venice," she said. "We could stay at the Danieli. It's one of my favorite hotels in the world. And in the morning we can take a water taxi out to the Giudecca for breakfast at the Cipriani." She reached across the table and took his hand in both of hers. "You've never been to Venice before?"

Tony shook his head. He and Shirley had spent their honeymoon in Europe—a gift from her father—but their time in Italy had been limited to Rome.

"Then I'll show it to you," Anne said. "If you think you enjoyed the art at Bumpy's house, wait until you see the Scuola of San Rocco. The Titians and the Tintorettos will make you think you've never seen art before. And the city, itself—you'll never want to leave it."

He reached across the table and gently stroked her cheek. "With you there I know I won't," he said.

Tony went on to Livorno and Naples, then to Athens and north again to Trieste. The meetings went as he expected. His plan was presented as a new business arrangement, one of mutual assistance between the union—and its new favored companies—and the shipping firms. To the executives he dealt with it was business as usual, and the less heavy-handed approach seemed appreciated, along with the tax and legal advantages. Only in Athens had a problem arisen, when an executive for a major Greek line thought he detected a hint of weakness in Tony's more businesslike suggestion.

The Greek businessman had balked at the idea, insisting

his firm had already decided to end its long-standing financial arrangement with the union. Tony had simply nodded, then had gathered his papers into his briefcase and had risen to leave. "It's regrettable," he had said, looking down at the aging Greek, his voice soft and even. "But I'm sure your captains are familiar with the Ports of Philadelphia and Boston."

"We will go to the Port of New York," the Greek had said.

"Your ships will not be unloaded there."

The Greek had looked at him coldly. "Then we will have men on board who will unload them."

Tony had smiled at him. "Our men will not like that," he had said.

The Greek had shrugged.

"If you choose to do that, may I make a suggestion about your first cargo?" Tony had asked. The Greek had simply stared at him. "Medical supplies," Tony had said, then he had turned and left the office.

The Greek had telephoned his hotel that evening, and the arrangement had been struck.

It was late morning when he left for Venice, and traffic was light, the few cars on the road screaming past him as their Italian drivers indulged their love affair with the speeding automobile. Tony allowed his mind to wander, his experience with New York City drivers having somewhat prepared him for Italian roads.

Business had gone well and, with the exception of the minor incident in Athens, far more smoothly than he had anticipated. He had felt a tinge of guilt before his first meeting in London, but it had quickly dissipated, and he had fallen back on the explanation Moe Green had given him years before.

It was a part of the shipping industry, a practice that existed throughout the world, and the costs to each individual company were simply passed on, made a part of the cost of shipping cargo. And it was far less venal than the bribes paid to Liberian politicians and others, who then allowed unsafe ships to be registered and sent to sea.

He knew it was a rationalization; recognized it; accepted it for what it was. You don't change the way the world operates. You content yourself with changing the few things you can. For himself, for the local, that would involve the lot of the membership. And in helping those people, Tony Marco would also carve himself a place in this world.

His mind turned to Anne, awaiting him in Venice, and then to Shirley at home in New York. She had wanted to come with him; had been furious when he had rejected the idea. He was glad now that he had. Anne had told him in Marseilles that she would not be returning to her home in Pennsylvania, but instead would go to her house in New York. He would continue to see her, and if possible, she, too, would become a part of the place he sought for himself.

The hell with you, Shirley, he told himself. A cold smile began to form on his lips. When the time comes, you can have your money and your hobby—trying to screw every man in the Manhattan telephone directory.

The water taxi moved slowly down the Grand Canal, and Tony sat in the stern, marveling at the buildings, the gothic palazzos with columned arches and intricate lattice-work, and balconies overlooking the blue-green water.

The Grand Canal meandered in an inverted S, beginning at the Santa Lucia Railway Station at the foot of the Ponte della Liberta causeway and ending at the Plaza San Marco. Along the route gondolas, black and sleek, glided past water buses and taxis, each moving leisurely through the endless competition between domed churches and proud palazzos, many bearing colorful mosaics or sculptured facades, each with its own docking area and doorway facing the canal.

Tony felt a surge of pleasure course through his body as he surveyed the living museum. The bridges that crossed the canal were alive with people, hurrying to complete daily tasks, surrounded everywhere by centuries of beauty and art. Anne was right, he told himself. It was a place that would be very hard to leave.

The water taxi pulled into the San Marco landing platform at the foot of the Calle Vallaresso. Tony had spoken to Anne by telephone before leaving Trieste and had agreed to meet her at Harry's Bar. He entered the renowned café and found himself in a large, open area with a bar to his left and clusters of tables along the remaining walls, the entire room straining with the sound of laughter and eager conversation.

The maitre d' took his suitcase and spirited it off to the cloakroom, then guided him to a table where Anne was waiting. He bent and kissed her, longer than appropriate for a public place, then slid into the chair opposite.

"I missed you," she said.

"And I missed you. But here we are now."

"You look wonderful, more relaxed than I expected." She gave him a taunting look. "Are you sure you were working?"

"Every minute."

"Did it go well?"

"Exceptionally well."

"Good. Now, I don't want to hear any more about business, or anything else that doesn't involve just us."

"Word of honor." He smiled at her. She looked radiant, her face and arms tanned from the week in Nice, her blond hair a shade lighter from the sun. "You look beautiful."

"I feel beautiful," she said. "Now." She tossed her hair back to one side and smiled. "Are you hungry?"

"Starved."

"Good. The food is wonderful here, so we'll have a long, leisurely lunch."

"And after lunch?" he asked.

Her eyes glistened with pleasure. "Everything in Venice closes for the afternoon siesta—the shops, the offices, the government buildings. Everyone goes home for a couple of hours. It's the custom."

"It's a wonderful custom," he said. "I think it should be observed."

"So do I," Anne said.

CHAPTER/TWENTY-FOUR

SITTING ON A bench facing the model yachting pond in Central Park, Pete watched the small boats skim across the water as the children and adults who launched them moved along the edge to keep pace with their crafts.

"So you found what I told you you'd find," Maxwell said.

Pete kept his eyes away from Maxwell's weasel face. "It's not enough. We still have to know how the money is being passed."

"Heah, I can't do it all for you," Maxwell said. "The two of you—a cop and a reporter—you oughta be able to do some of it."

Pete snapped his head around and stared into Maxwell's grinning face. "Listen, shithead, you want this to go down or not?"

"Heah, let's not get nasty."

"You want it or not?" Pete's voice was low and gravelly, and his body language indicated he was ready to bolt and leave Maxwell sitting there.

"Sure, I want it. I just have to be careful, that's all."

"Then where can I find what I need?"

Maxwell looked out at the pond. "Maybe you should find out what companies the union has been lending money to," he said. "The loans are legal, but the names might prove interesting."

"Come on," Pete snapped. "We haven't got a chance in hell of getting our hands on those records. We'd need a court order, and we'd have to have a helluva lot of evidence before we'd get a judge to even consider one."

"Maybe something could be arranged," Maxwell said.

"Don't play games with me," Pete warned. "Can you get a copy of loan records or not?"

Maxwell stood and stretched. "Keep a watch on your mail. You never know what might turn up." He looked back at the pond, then pointed at the elaborate boats. "Look at what kids got to play with today," he said. "When I was a kid, we used to make boats out of popsicle sticks and sail them in the gutter."

And you never moved far away from it, Pete thought.

Jennifer and Tony walked down the steps of the union's office building and headed for his car.

"I hope you don't mind meeting me here," he said, "but I wanted our wager paid off in a Brooklyn restaurant."

"Why Brooklyn?" Jennifer asked. "I expected you to collect in Le Cirque or La Lavandou. Someplace that would force me to sell the family jewels to pay the bill."

He laughed as he opened the rear door for her, then slid in beside her. "If I did, your story would say that this humble man of the people dines on pheasant while his men eat hamburger."

"Never," Jennifer said, laughing in a way that said she might. "Where *are* we going?" she asked.

"A nice Italian restaurant in a nice Italian neighborhood. It's called Monte's Venetian Room."

Jennifer's heart was pounding as they were led to a booth in the restaurant, and she fought to keep the nervousness from her eyes.

"This was always a favorite place for neighborhood people when I was a kid," Tony said.

I know, Jennifer thought. You and Pete used to come to the back door for leftovers. She forced a smile. "The food must be good if it's been around that long."

"It is," Tony said. "And the family jewels will be easily preserved."

Out of the corner of her eye she saw a waiter approaching, and her eyes darted nervously toward him. Her heartbeat increased. Damn. It was the same man.

"Heah, Tony, it's about time I see you again," the waiter began as he stopped at the table.

"It hasn't been that long, Al."

"Too long," Al said. "But you look good. How's your family?"

"Couldn't be better. How about yours?"

"Good, thank God." He turned toward Jennifer, hesitated, then smiled. "You musta liked it here last time, huh, lady?"

Jennifer looked up at him, fighting to keep her lips from trembling. "Yes, very much," she said.

"You didn't tell me you'd been here before," Tony said. He was smiling at her, as if he had been caught in some elaborate joke.

"Sure," Al said. "She was here three, four weeks ago with Petey Moran and some other guy."

Tony's smile faded, and he stared across the table. "I didn't know you knew Pete. We grew up together."

"I know," Jennifer said. "I found that out later. From your mother, in fact." Jennifer tried to keep her voice light but knew she was failing. "I met Pete here with another reporter."

"Well, that's certainly a coincidence," he said. And he just happened to be at the fund-raiser at the Metropolitan Club, too, Tony added to himself. He turned to the waiter. "Well, what do you recommend, Al?"

Jennifer watched Tony's eyes. They were cold and flat and filled with something she couldn't quite identify. She thought it was disappointment.

Paul Levine worked a nail file around the edge of one finger, keeping his attention on its progress as he spoke. "So you think our little reporter and her detective friend are primed and ready?"

"More than ready," Maxwell said. "Hungry."

Levine carefully placed the nail file on the table next to his chair and turned his attention to Maxwell's narrow, grinning face. He hated having the man in his apartment; hated seeing him in the large overstuffed chair that Moe Green used to occupy whenever he visited. Levine had lived contentedly in the apartment for over twenty years now, but this man's presence made it feel shabby and unclean. Levine picked up a large manila envelope from the coffee table set between them and handed it to Maxwell. "The printouts on the loans we want them to know about are in there. If they're not fools, they should be able to tie the companies back to the union without much trouble."

"Aren't you worried about being involved yourself?" Maxwell asked.

Levine's fleshy face creased into what passed for a smile. "Our friend, Tony, did such a good job of boxing me out, I can't be tied to anything," he said. "And besides, Tony's connection at the newspaper will undoubtedly keep the story out of print, anyway." He watched a note of concern flash across Maxwell's face. "But it will be enough to force his resignation. And then *I* just might call for an investigation. How do I strike you as the union's new reformer?"

"You look like a reformer to me," Maxwell said. He turned the envelope over in his hands, then looked back at Levine. "This is sealed," he said.

"And make sure it stays that way," Levine said. "In fact, you just address it and I'll mail it."

"Whatsamatter, Paul, you don't trust me?"

Levine's face creased again. "I don't trust anybody. That's why I've been around so long."

When Maxwell had gone, Levine walked to a small antique desk, picked up the telephone, and dialed.

"How'd you like to go to Las Vegas and bring our friend back, Joey?" He heard Joey laugh on the other end of the line, then agree eagerly. "And as soon as you do, there's one other thing to take care of." He paused, then continued. "It's our friend, Maxwell. I think it's time that something heavy fell on him." He listened again to Joey's response. There was a pleasure in Joey's voice that would have been hard to describe.

When he returned to his chair, he stared down at the manila envelope Maxwell had addressed in his own hand. Inside, along with the union printouts, was a typewritten note, supposedly from Maxwell, claiming he had been found out while obtaining the material.

The door bell rang, and he eased himself up from his chair. When Levine pulled back the door, he reached out immediately and drew the woman into a warm hug. "You look wonderful. I'm glad you could come."

Shirley Marco stepped back and stared into his eyes. "I wouldn't miss the chance for anything," she said. "I can't wait to play my part in this."

Jennifer sat on the edge of the sofa, wrapped in a heavy terry-cloth bathrobe, her hair, still wet from a shower, tied up in a towel. "I hope Maxwell delivers," she said. "It would make this whole thing a lot easier."

"He'll deliver," Pete said. Like Jennifer, he wore a robe; his body felt loose and relaxed from the long shower they had taken together. His mind was far from relaxed, however.

"What's bothering you?" Jennifer asked. When they had made love earlier, he had seemed tense and distant. Now he was merely distant. "You should be pleased," she said.

"It bothers me," he said.

"What, for heaven's sake? We're finally getting the break we needed."

"That's just it. Who's giving it to us?"

"Maxwell is," she said, her voice slightly irritated.

He shook his head. "Maxwell doesn't have access to that information. Somebody's giving it to him. And that means we have a player we don't know anything about."

Jennifer slid next to him and cupped his chin in her hand. "Listen," she said. "To get this story I'll take the information any way I can get it."

"I guess I just don't like to be led around by the nose," Pete said. "I know what Maxwell's angle is, but I don't know what's in it for the other player or players."

"Somebody just doesn't like Marco," she said. "I didn't think you'd find that hard to understand." Jennifer regretted the words as soon as they were out. She watched Pete's eyes harden momentarily, then soften again. They reminded her of Marco's eyes earlier that evening when the waiter had mentioned Pete. It was the look of someone who had been betrayed. Marco had masked it well, but it had been there, if only for a moment.

She pulled herself closer to Pete and wrapped her arms around his neck. She felt his arms come around her, and she thought about the "players" they knew nothing about.

He was right: They should know who was involved. It was risky not to know. And could even be dangerous. But she couldn't let it stop the story. "Who do you think is behind Maxwell?"

"I don't know," he said. "But we better find out before you print anything."

Jennifer nodded absently, then leaned over and kissed his cheek. No way will I put off printing this story, she told herself. It's too big, too important to risk losing. The image of Marco's face returned to her. Damn, it hurt to have him look at me that way, she told herself.

She pushed herself back and stared into Pete's face. "Why do you hate Marco so much?"

He stared straight ahead for several moments. "Sometimes I wonder if I do."

She stared at him, her look questioning.

"I guess old habits are hard to break," he said.

CHAPTER/TWENTY-FIVE

"WHAT THE HELL is this story you're working on about Tony Marco?"

Jennifer sat across the desk from Martin Twist in his glass-walled office off the newsroom. There was a sneer on Twist's round, flushed face. His necktie was pulled loose from his collar and lay twisted on a protruding paunch. His blue eyes were slightly glazed, and he looked argumentative, something that usually happened when he drank.

Jennifer stared at him, wondering if he was angry or had just had too many drinks at lunch. It was five-thirty, and the effect of lunch should have dissipated, but with Twist it was difficult to gauge. She recalled the executive editor's warning to keep the Marco story secret. "Just something I've been looking into. There *is* no story yet."

"And who the hell assigned you to look into it?" He leaned forward, putting on his best bullying posture.

"It was enterprise. I was at a cocktail party and I overheard talk about him being named to a future cabinet post, so I decided to find out more about him. At best I felt I'd have a good feature story."

"Enterprise, my ass," Twist snapped. "You go crashing around, stirring up all kinds of crap, and then—"

Jennifer stopped him short. She, too, had leaned forward, and her face was red with anger. "Just a minute, Marty. You're always bitching and moaning about reporters not picking up on things on their own time or, if they do, not following up on them. You preach enterprise as if it were the ninth wonder of the world, but when *I* exercise some, you chew me out."

"Don't give me any of that crap. You should have come to me and gotten my okay. Then I wouldn't be getting phone calls about stories I don't know anything about."

"There was nothing to tell you," Jennifer said. "When I had something solid, I planned to come to you, not before."

"And what have you got so far?" he demanded.

Jennifer fought to control her voice. "I'd rather not say until I'm sure."

"Oh, you wouldn't, would you? Well, I'll tell you something you can be sure about. You're off this story. You don't look into anything else. And you go back to your desk and do what I tell you to do. Understood?"

"No, it's not understood," Jennifer snapped, her own mouth twisting with contempt. "I've been doing this on my own time, and I'll continue to do it on my own time. And when I'm finished, I'll bring you the results, and if you don't want it, I'll sell it to someone who does."

Twist glared at her, putting forth every ounce of intimidation he could muster. "You might find yourself working nights if you don't have a *very* fast change of attitude," he warned.

Jennifer stared at him for several moments, then stood abruptly. "That's fine," she said, her voice soft and even. "It will give me more time during the day to work on this." Twist started to speak, but she cut him off again. "It will also give me time to work up a very thorough grievance. About this *and* the sexual harassment I've had to put up with." She started for the door.

"You're buying yourself a lot of trouble, lady," Twist growled.

Jennifer turned back to face him. "You bet I am. And it's all going to be hanging around your neck."

It was almost seven-thirty when Pete pushed his way through the front door, a trench coat slung over his shoulder, his hand clutching the mail from the downstairs mailbox. He looked tired, but there was an expectant smile on his lips.

"Hi," he called. "Why so glum?"

"Just my editor, Twist," Jennifer said. "He tried to order me off the Marco story."

"And?" Pete's eyes narrowed.

"I told him to stuff it."

Pete sat next to her on the sofa and gazed out the loft window toward the river. "How did he find out about it?"

"He said he got a telephone call. He didn't say from whom. But that's not hard to guess."

"Did you tell him what you have?"

"No. Just that I was working on a story, nothing specific." She bit her lip.

"And he still wanted to kill the story without even knowing what it was about?" Jennifer nodded.

"Did you go to Diesart? After all, he okayed everything." Jennifer nodded again. "And what did he say?"

"He told me not to worry. He said that when the time came, he'd handle Twist. In other words, keep taking his crap and keep the faith. And if the story goes bust, he'll pat Twist on the back as he kicks me out the door." She smiled coldly at Pete. "The boys never take sides against each other."

"Damned bad luck," Pete said. He held up a manila envelope, and the hint of a grin appeared on his face. "But it may be too little, too late, for our friend Mr. Marco, and *his* friend Twist. This is from Maxwell. I opened it downstairs."

Jennifer grabbed the envelope, pulled out the contents, and spread it on the cocktail table. Quickly she scanned the computer pages, then looked up at Pete. "It's a list of company names and one individual."

He pulled a sheet of paper from his inside jacket pocket. "This was with it."

Jennifer took the note and stared at it, her eyes returning to the underlined, typewritten words: "This is the Laundromat." She turned back to Pete.

"It looks as though these are the companies and the individual Maxwell was talking about," Pete said. "And the loans are the way they wash the profits."

"My God," she said. "If he's right, we could have it all within a week or two." She stared back at the note. "Maxwell says he thinks somebody found out he got this information. What should we do?"

"Just stay away from him. Let him lay low. There isn't much else we can do."

Jennifer dismissed Maxwell from her mind. She was too excited about having the information, about having what she needed to prove the story. And to shove it under Twist's nose. Suddenly even Marco didn't matter. She looked up at Pete. "I think we've got him," she said.

He nodded, but there seemed to be a hint of concern in his face. "What is it?" Jennifer asked.

"Did you notice the envelope?" he asked.

Jennifer picked it up and looked at it again. "It's a union envelope."

"And stamped with a postage meter. That's not something Maxwell would have. This was mailed from the union office. At least that would be my guess."

"So somebody's helping him. So what?"

"So I'd like to know who, and why."

"I don't care if it's the ghost of Lee Harvey Oswald," she said. "The important thing is that we have it and we can nail down the story."

Pete stood and walked to the window, then turned to face her. "Something they taught me in cop school," he said. "Always investigate the people giving you information. If you know why they're doing it, then nobody can lead you down a garden path. We don't know who, and we don't know why, and it makes me nervous."

"Well, it doesn't make me nervous," Jennifer said. "If this information checks out, we'll have all the documentation we need. I'll leave the reasons to the sociologists and settle for a Pulitzer Prize."

"I suppose," Pete said. "It's not a criminal case yet. There'll be time to check those things out if it gets that far."

"If?" she said, and laughed. "They won't have much choice if these printouts show money was loaned to companies that exist only on paper. Companies who also do make-believe work for shipping companies with union contracts. Even the feds will want a piece of that." She tapped the papers spread out before her. "I can't wait to find out who this guy is, this Frank Malboa."

"He used to be recording secretary for the local," Pete said. "He's retired now."

"Then he has to be the front, the connection to the phony companies."

"It's a good bet," Pete said.

Jennifer threw herself back against the couch. "Then we've got it all," she said. "If it proves out, we can tie it all back to the local. *And* Mr. Anthony Marco." She spoke the final sentence triumphantly.

Pete turned and looked out the window again at the Queens shoreline. "It looks that way," he said. He stared down into the river, watching the fast-moving water carry a small boat rapidly downstream. When the boat had left his view, the wake still remained, set in motion, now continuing. Yes, they had Marco if everything proved out. But still, something about the information bothered him. He tried to dismiss the worry as something all cops felt, especially when they were getting close. And he was close to Marco now, so close to getting him he could almost taste it. He wondered why he didn't feel better about it.

Martin Twist sat in his glass-walled office sipping straight Scotch from a coffee mug. His shift was over; the night city editor had already taken charge of the rim. But he was not ready to leave. He needed time alone, time to think. He needed a way to find out what was in the story that little red-haired bitch was working on.

The call had come from Marco that afternoon, and with it, the chips had been called in. He shook his head, finished off the remaining Scotch, then poured more from the bottle in his desk drawer.

It had all happened years ago, and he was still paying for it. The drunken traffic accident in which the child had died, the sudden fear that his career would be destroyed. He had been a reporter then, covering labor for the paper, and he had gone to Moe Green for help. And the help had come by way of Green's association with a corrupt Brooklyn district attorney. Reports had been altered, witnesses ignored, and the parents of the child had even been browbeaten out of filing a civil suit.

Twist drank heavily from the cup. It had been an easy

step then to do small favors for Green—and accept the money in return. Now, for the first time, he was being called on to make a heavy repayment on his debt. And there was nothing he could do. The canceled checks he had received were still sitting in the union's files.

But he could do it and he would. If the story looked like it would stir up trouble, he could find a way to discredit it and Jennifer Brady. The stupid little bitch deserved it. In the meantime he would keep her busy on other things, and then he'd fix her once and for all.

CHAPTER/TWENTY-SIX

"HOW DO YOU like it, babe?" Joey took Mary Beth's elbow and ushered her around the hotel suite. "Nothing but first class, just like I promised."

Mary Beth looked around the sitting room without interest. She had dark circles beneath her eyes, and her face seemed haggard and much older than her thirty-five years. "It's nice, Joey," she said. She looked at him nervously. "Is the stuff here?"

He smiled at her. It was a crooked, knowing smile that held no warmth. He patted his jacket pocket. "It's right here. And more to come whenever you need it."

She stared at his jacket pocket, noting the lack of a bulge. "But you said eight ounces. A whole eight ounces." Her eyes were wide now, almost frightened.

Joey reached out and pinched her cheek, harder than necessary. He watched her wince with pain, and he smiled again. She was just like all the junkies he had ever known. Always frightened, always worried they wouldn't get their shit; willing to do anything to make sure they did. Just like Mary Beth would do what he wanted.

"Don't worry," he said. "A taste now, the rest later. Just as soon as you deliver your part of the action."

"You wouldn't stiff me, would you, Joey?" Her eyes were still frightened.

"Never, baby. Never. After all, we grew up together."

She smiled at him, her concern eased. "That's right. Those were really good days, weren't they, Joey?"

"Better for some of us than others," Joey said.

Mary Beth cocked her head to one side. "What do you mean?"

"Well, for Petey and for Tony they were a little better, weren't they? After all, they were the ones getting into your pants. Now, Joey, he never got any of that, did he?"

Mary Beth looked at him, her eyes nervous again. "Come on, Joey. Don't talk like that."

"Like what?" He reached out and ran a hand along her breast.

She stepped back instinctively. "Please, Joey. Don't treat me like that."

Joey let out a long, mirthless laugh. "Don't *treat* you like that? If I handed you a couple of hundred bucks, you'd have your mouth around my joint before I could get my pants down." His eyes hardened. "Is that what you need, Mary Beth? You need an incentive?" He reached in his pocket and pulled out a clear glassine envelope containing an ounce of white powder. "Is a little nose candy good enough? Or maybe, for Joey, you need more than that." He stepped forward and drove his fist into her stomach.

Mary Beth doubled over, then staggered back and fell into a chair. She fought for breath, gagging on words she could not speak. He cupped her chin in his hand, digging his fingers into her cheeks. "Please don't," her voice sputtered out.

He stood over her, shaking his head, then dropped the glassine envelope on the table next to her. He looked at his wristwatch and realized he would have to delay his fun for a few more hours. "You enjoy your nose candy, babe," he said. "I have a little job to do, and when I get back, you be ready to pick up where we left off." He forced her chin up, until their eyes met. "And if you want to see the other stuff, you be ready to be nice to Joey. *Capisce?*"

"Sure, Joey," she said. "Anything you want, Joey."

He looked down at her and smiled. "Those are my favorite words," he said. " 'Anything you want, Joey.' " He stared into her eyes and laughed again.

Joey stood on the end of the pier, just off West Tenth Street in Manhattan. The pier was deserted, unused by ships for many years, a place now occupied only late at night when the area's homosexuals turned it into a trysting ground. He had chosen it partially for that reason. Paul had said to make it messy and to make sure it was discovered quickly. Joey smiled at the idea of some fags finding more than they bargained for when they wandered down to the pier later that night.

Joey turned and looked out across the Hudson. There was a mild breeze off the water, carrying the earthy, decaying smell of the river, but the night was clear and calm, and the lights off the distant New Jersey shore glistened off the water in long, wavering strands. Slowly he buttoned the cheap plastic raincoat over his suit and slipped on a pair of surgical gloves before thrusting his hands in his pockets. In his right pocket his hand ran along the shaft of the baling hook he had placed there, probing with his finger for the needlelike point. Messy, he thought, then smiled at the idea.

He heard the footsteps before he saw the outline moving toward him. As the footsteps drew closer the figure materialized, and he could make out Maxwell's crooked yellow smile.

"This is a helluva place to meet," Maxwell said. "Whatsamatter with a nice bar somewhere?" He walked up to within two feet of Joey and stopped.

"Paul thinks Tony's getting wise. He just wants to be extra careful."

"Yeah, he told me," Maxwell said. "He also said there was another package I should get to Moran. You got it?" He watched Joey nod, then noticed the plastic raincoat. "What, you expecting rain?"

"It's just that these places get so dirty," Joey said. And messy, he added to himself. "I don't want to get my suit all screwed up."

Maxwell grinned at him with a touch of amused contempt. "So where's the package?"

"Right here," Joey said. He withdrew his right hand from the pocket. There was a cold smile on his face, and his eyes held Maxwell's as he took a step forward.

The speed of Joey's looping, upward thrust made any defense impossible, and Maxwell's eyes simply bulged as the hook imbedded itself into his stomach. Reflexively his hands reached out for Joey's throat, then froze in midair as Joey pulled up on the handle of the hook. The sound of ripping flesh and cloth filled the silence, then disappeared under the gasping, gurgling noise that began deep inside Maxwell's body and rose slowly to his throat. The hook jammed, and Joey took it in both hands and pulled harder, raising Maxwell to his toes as the hook moved up under his sternum, sending a spray of arterial blood over the front of Joey's raincoat.

Joey stared at Maxwell's face, watching as the eyes gradually went blank; the color drained from his face, and his body sagged back, supported only by the hook. Joey let the body fall, watching as it rolled on its side, a gray mass of intestines flowing out of the gaping hole and onto the dock. He bent over the body and unzipped the trousers, then took a knife from his pocket and began to cut. Within seconds he had his prize. Finally he unbuttoned his raincoat and dropped it into the water, his eyes never leaving the still-twitching body that lay before him. "Messy," he said aloud. "Very, very messy."

Paul Levine picked up the telephone and listened. "That sounds good, Joey. Very good. Now you just have to deliver Mary Beth to Moran, and then you can arrange a little visit to our reporter friend." He listened to Joey's question. "No, Joey, just what I told you to do, nothing more. We can handle the reporter and her newspaper, so we don't want to go too far right now. We just want to put a little pressure on the young lady," he said. "The kind of pressure that will make her think Tony Marco is out to hurt her. To hurt her very badly." He listened again. "Yes, I agree, Joey. People do believe more strongly when they actually get hurt. But that may come later. You'll just have to be patient. In the meantime you enjoy yourself with Mary Beth. Just make sure she's in good shape for Pete Moran."

Levine replaced the receiver, then walked to a side table and poured himself a drink. It amused him to think of Marco being destroyed by the friends of his own childhood. His only regret was that he couldn't take a more active part in it himself. But I'll be there at the end, he told himself. I'll be there, and I'll see his face when he knows that he's lost. And then I'll watch him die.

CHAPTER/TWENTY-SEVEN

PETE MORAN STROLLED along East Seventy-second Street, heading back to his apartment. It was his day off, and he had planned to while away the afternoon at a movie. Those plans seemed unimportant now as he read, for the second time, the *Globe*'s account of Mickey Maxwell's gruesome death.

He tried not to feel responsible, but the hard truth kept returning. He had gone to Mickey, had pressured him to get the information that was needed. Mickey Maxwell, he thought. A sleazy, rotten little lowlife, the kind of person cops use and then forget about. Except you can't, no matter how hard you try. It was one thing the police department hadn't been able to teach him.

He folded the paper and put it under his arm, checked the traffic on York Avenue, then hurried across. He noticed a woman standing in front of his building, but he paid little attention to her. He moved quickly, anxious to get back to his apartment and the telephone.

He turned into the entrance of his building, ignoring the woman, who had now taken a step toward him.

"Hi, Pete."

He snapped his head around to the sound of the female voice, momentarily confused. When he looked into her face, he stopped. It was an older face, well worn, and very much different from the one he remembered. But it was one he had never forgotten.

"Mary Beth?" he said.

She smiled at him, a warm, giving smile. "It's nice to be remembered. How are you, Pete?"

It was hard for him to speak, but he forced himself. "What are you doing here?"

"Looking for you." She laughed, pleased by his surprise. "I was in New York for a few days, and I decided to look up some old friends." She paused. "Well, one old friend, anyway. They told me in the neighborhood that you lived in Manhattan, so I checked the phone book and here I am. Actually, I was just leaving. I thought you were out, and I was looking for a piece of paper to leave a note."

Pete stared at her. She was speaking rapidly; too rapidly, he thought. The dark shadows under her eyes and the pallor of her skin told him she was on something and had been for a long time. He took her arm gently at the elbow and guided her toward the entrance. "Let's go upstairs."

He sat across from her in an easy chair. She curled up in the corner of the sofa, tucked her legs beneath her, and took the coffee he handed her. He noticed her hand was trembling.

"So Tony just walked away from you," he said.

Mary Beth twisted slightly in her seat. "Well, things got kinda unpleasant, you know. With people in the neighborhood and everything."

"His union got you a job in Vegas. And that's when you started hooking. Right?" Pete looked at her levelly, showing no emotion. The lack of animation seemed to intensify her uneasiness, and she began toying anxiously with the coffee cup.

"Look, that's what it's like out there." She gave a short, mirthless laugh. "I don't sing and dance, and it's the kinda place where everybody's on the hustle in one way or another." She gave a slight shrug to her shoulders. "I did what I do best."

"And you still hold it against Tony." It was a question spoken as fact.

She shook her head, then hesitated, as if deciding if that were the correct answer. "Well, only a little." She caught herself again. "Look, it hasn't been that bad. I've done all right for myself. And I like it out in Vegas. I like the action."

Pete looked at her for several moments without speaking. She was struggling to explain herself so he would accept her, but she was also trying to do something else. He wasn't quite sure exactly what. The only thing he was sure of was that the two efforts were in conflict. "How long have you been on drugs?" he asked, deliberately trying to shock her.

It worked, and her body stiffened. "What are you, a narc or something?" She tried to laugh the question away, but failed.

"No, just an old friend who knows the signs."

She shrugged again, even more weakly than before. "I do a little coke now and then, that's all. It's practically the national pastime, you know."

Pete continued to stare at her, watching her nervousness grow. She was thirty-five, but she looked ten years older, and even the professionally applied makeup couldn't hide all the damage. "You do a lot of coke, Mary Beth.

And you've been doing it a long time." He had kept his voice soft and gentle, but the words had still seemed to jolt her.

"Okay," she said. "So maybe I do a little too much. But it's nothing I can't control." She stared at him, her eyes begging for belief. "Really, Pete."

"What are you doing in New York, Mary Beth?"

Her body gave off another twitch. "Just shopping," she said. "For clothes," she added with emphasis.

"They don't sell clothes in Vegas? I know they do in Los Angeles, and that's a lot closer. Why New York?"

Mary Beth put the coffee cup down and held her hands in her lap, trying to control their nervous movements. "Let's just say I was homesick."

"Who sent you to see me, Mary Beth?"

She stared at him, her eyes wide, her lips moving slightly. "What do you mean?"

"Who sent you to see me?"

Mary Beth lowered her gaze, and her hands began to tremble noticeably. Tears started to form in her eyes, and she brought her palms to her face. "Damn it, I couldn't even do this right." She looked up at him, her breath coming fast. "Tony never knew the union arranged for me to go out there. He didn't know who did."

"What did Tony know?"

She shook her head. "Only that I was pregnant and wanted an abortion."

"So why didn't he help you afterward?"

She shook her head again, violently this time. "He did everything he could for me. It was people in the union. They wanted me out of the way. They even managed to get the word about the abortion around the neighborhood. Just to get rid of me."

"Does Tony know it happened that way?"

"I told him about it nine, ten years ago. He was out in

Vegas, and I ran into him and told him about it. He never knew until then." She shook her head. "I never saw anybody so mad. I mean, he didn't scream and shout or anything. You know how Tony is. But it was like he was ready to explode."

"Who sent you to see me?"

"The same people. People from the union."

"What were you supposed to tell me?"

"Just that I was hooking and everything. And to let you see that maybe it was Tony's fault everything turned out this way." She stared down at her lap, and the tears started again. "I'm sorry, Pete," she whispered. "I didn't have any choice."

"Who are they?"

She looked up at him, her eyes truly frightened. "Don't make me tell you that, Pete. These people really scare me. I'm not sure what they'd do if they found out. And they've got friends out in Vegas. I wouldn't be safe even if I got away from here."

Her hands were trembling again but not from nervousness. Pete thought about Mickey Maxwell, about the way he had died. He nodded his head slowly. "Tell them you did what they wanted. Tell them I was furious. Tell them just what they want to hear. And then get out of here as fast as you can."

"I will, Pete. I will." She started to rise from the sofa. "And I'm really sorry, Pete. I really am. I always cared about you."

He looked at her with sad eyes. "I know you did, Mary Beth."

Tony Marco laid the newspaper on the desk in front of him, then pressed the intercom button. "Ask Paul Levine to come in here, please."

When, moments later, Levine ambled into Tony's of-

fice, he was in shirtsleeves—the way he preferred to work—
and his tie was pulled away from his collar. His face was
impassive.

"Did you see the paper?" Tony asked. "About Mickey
Maxwell?"

Levine nodded. "Sounded pretty bad."

"There are going to be questions. I hope nobody here
knows anything about it."

"I don't," Levine said. "Look, it was a known fag area.
Maybe Mickey went that way. Who knows these days?"

"Homosexuals don't kill people with baling hooks. Peo-
ple on the docks use them that way." He was watching
Levine's eyes, looking for any crack in his demeanor.
There appeared to be none.

Levine's face creased into his Buddha-like smile. "I
don't think we have to worry too much. He was one
member of a large union, and he got knocked off a long
way from work. He was on his own time, and it had
nothing to do with us."

"Except that he was making noises about running in the
next union election," Tony said.

"Coincidence," Levine said.

"That's what I'd like to believe. You don't think Joey got
carried away, do you?"

"Joey's been in Vegas on vacation," Levine said.

Tony nodded, almost imperceptibly. "Okay. Let's send
the usual flowers and find out when the funeral is, so we
can be there. Did he have any family?"

Levine shook his head. "I already checked. Nobody.
Maybe he *was* a little funny."

"Well, he's not laughing now," Tony said. He spun in
his chair and looked out the window. Something's wrong, he
thought. And it's going to get worse very soon. He could
feel it in his gut.

* * *

Jennifer cornered Eddie Rogers as soon as he came into the office. Her stomach had begun to churn when she had read the story about Maxwell and it hadn't stopped since.

Rogers was a short, elfish man with long gray hair, a bushy gray mustache, and baby-blue eyes, which gave him the appearance of someone's uncle.

"Eddie, what do you know about this Maxwell murder, the one on the Tenth Street pier?"

She perched on the edge of his desk when he sat down, hovering over him for an answer. Rogers leaned back in his chair and grinned. "He's dead," he said. "And I got that exclusive. What are you doing for lunch?"

"Come on, Chief," she said, using the nickname she knew he preferred. "You're our top police reporter. Tell me what you know."

"How come you're interested?" Rogers asked.

"I met Maxwell once—on a story I did a couple of years ago."

Rogers drummed his fingers on his desk. "Not much to it," he said. "Two fags found him while they were out looking for love. Somebody gutted him with a baling hook and then cut off his genitals. They're still missing."

Jennifer grimaced, despite herself. "Do the cops think it was somebody involved with the docks?" she asked.

"Hard to tell," Rogers said. "The baling hook would indicate that, but who knows, maybe he was having it off with another longshoreman. Most mutilations turn out to be homosexual murders, especially when certain parts turn up missing."

"A gay longshoreman?" Jennifer said, her voice skeptical.

"Longshoremen, pro football players, truck drivers, you can't be sure about anybody anymore." He winked at her. "Except me."

"That's comforting to know, Eddie," she said. "Whenever I get depressed about the availability of straight men, I'll try to remember that."

"What memories I could give you," he said.

"But I wouldn't respect you in the morning," Jennifer said.

"Respect I can live without," Rogers said.

She breathed deeply again, tired of his game. "So the cops think it was sex-related?" She thought about Maxwell, about the last time she had seen him in Pete's apartment; she found it hard to believe even another man, no matter how desperate, would find him attractive.

"They're not sure. Maybe somebody just wanted to make it look that way. If they did, it was clumsy using a hook. That would take it back to the docks, or somebody who worked there. You see, the hook was left in him. It wasn't even tossed in the river."

Jennifer felt a shiver course through her body. "Thanks, Eddie. Let me know if you hear anything else."

When her telephone rang an hour later, Jennifer was still thinking about Maxwell. She had tried not to dwell on the description of his death, but it had been difficult. She had told herself it had nothing to do with the story, not something Marco would have ordered. It was too gruesome. She had tried to convince herself the connection didn't make sense, but deep down she knew it might.

"Did you hear about Maxwell?"

She recognized Pete's voice and lowered her own, so others in the office wouldn't hear her. "Yes. It's all I've been thinking about for the last hour."

"We're going to have to talk to the guys handling the murder investigation," Pete said.

"Why?" Jennifer snapped. "We don't know that it had anything to do with what I'm working on."

"And we don't know that it didn't," Pete said. "Christ,

Jennifer. I'm a cop. I can't conceal evidence, even evidence that may turn out to be nothing."

"Well, I don't have to reveal a source. And I damn well don't intend to until I'm ready." She drew an exasperated breath. "Pete, I've been digging through records for two weeks now, checking out what Maxwell gave us. And I'm almost there. I've almost got it all together. I'm not going to screw it up now."

"Your source is dead, Jennifer. He's a murder victim, and no court is going to guarantee your First Amendment rights for a corpse."

"Damn it, Pete, I'm too close, and I've worked too damned hard to get there. I don't want some cop turning the information over to every newspaper in town before I even get it into print. Diesart would have me writing obits for the rest of my life."

"Jennifer, they're not going to pass around leads on a murder investigation. And, besides, there's something else."

"What?"

"A woman came to see me today. Somebody I knew when I was a kid—who knew Tony *and* me. She was sent by someone in the union—she was too frightened to say who—but whoever it was wanted to be sure I was very mad at Tony Marco."

"Who was she? What does she have to do with the story?"

"It was a personal thing, nothing to do with the story. But, don't you see? Somebody knows I'm helping you, and they want to make sure I keep after Tony; keep *you* after Tony. It's all just too convenient. Just like Maxwell's murder. The baling hook, the material we were sent. Somebody is pointing us in Tony's direction. And it's coming from inside the union."

"Are you sure?" Jennifer snapped. "You could be talking about coincidence too. It doesn't have to be a part of what we're working on. Please, Pete. Just give me a few more days. Then we can go to anyone you want."

There was a long silence on the other end of the phone. "Jennifer, the people I work for are not going to like the fact that I was helping a newspaper reporter on my own time. I'm in the soup with that alone. But, dammit, I'm not going to top it off by committing a felony of withholding evidence. I'm sorry, I just can't do that."

"Just two days, Pete. That's all I'm asking."

"I'm sorry. I'll tell them as little as possible, but I'm going to talk to them this afternoon."

Jennifer could feel her heart beating in her chest; her face became flushed. "Damn you, Pete Moran. Damn you." She slammed down the phone, trying not to think about what her executive editor would do if the whole story blew up in her face. So close, she thought. So damned close.

CHAPTER/TWENTY-EIGHT

IT WAS SEVEN o'clock when Jennifer finally reached her apartment. Under the schedule they had arranged she was supposed to spend the night at Pete's, but she had decided against it. She did not even want to hear what he had told the homicide detectives that afternoon, and she had no intention of answering her door to anyone.

She dropped her briefcase on an occasional chair. The briefcase was heavy—stuffed with photostats of the records she had been searching. Only that afternoon she had found even more interesting information about the companies on Maxwell's list. In just a few more days she would have all she needed, and until then, she intended to avoid Pete, and the police, and anyone else who could throw a wrench into the works.

Rolling her head to loosen the tightened neck muscles, she walked to the kitchen and withdrew an already opened bottle of white wine from the refrigerator. She poured herself a glass and leaned against the counter, sipping it. The wine felt cool and relaxing, and she kicked off her shoes and walked back into the living room, carrying the wine bottle.

The room was neat, neater than she usually kept it. It was something Pete's regular presence had brought on, a need for order, to at least appear to be a well-ordered person. But he never even noticed, she told herself; he never offered the slightest recognition, the smallest compliment.

Settling on the sofa, she poured herself another glass. Her anger at Pete was irrational and she knew it. He was doing what he had to do. He was simply doing it sooner than she would have liked. And asking him to wait could be wrong; it could leave her looking foolish, even unprofessional, if Maxwell's death was eventually tied to the story. But it won't be, she told herself, unable to believe her own forced conviction. If only it had happened a few days later. She shook her head at the crassness of her own thoughts, then realized she meant them. She would have completed her work by then, satisfied Diesart's deadline, and the entire story could even have been tied to a murder. The dramatic impact would have been overpowering, and even Twist could not have gotten away with an attempt to kill it.

She thought about Twist for a moment. There was something there, something that went beyond mere annoyance at not being informed about a working story. Maybe he owed Marco, and it was something that made him jump when Marco asked a favor. Someday she'd find out and then . . .

The sound of the telephone interrupted her train of thought, but she made no move to answer it. She stared at it, thinking Pete was probably calling. Or worse—the detectives he had spoken to that afternoon. They would want a statement from her, and they would insist on taking copies of the documents she had gathered. And then it would be over. One loose word from a cop trying to curry favor with someone in the media—hoping it would give him a little press when the case was finally solved—that's all it would take. Cops loved to see their names in the paper. They were convinced it was the short route to commendations and eventual promotion, so they seldom missed a chance to "get themselves some ink."

The telephone finally fell silent, and she rested her head back against the sofa and closed her eyes. God, she was tired. Every muscle in her body felt as though she had run a marathon and was now near collapse.

A bath, she told herself. A long, hot, lingering bath. Then something light to eat and a quiet evening in bed. Slowly she eased herself up from the sofa, almost as though her body were too weak for any vigorous movement. She looked down at her stockinged feet and realized she had left her shoes in the kitchen. The hell with them, she thought. Let them stay there until morning.

She went into the bathroom, then turned on the water and tested it with her hand until it reached the desired temperature. She raised the wineglass to her lips, then stopped halfway, distracted by her reflection in the bathroom mirror. You look haggard and beaten, she told herself. The pressure is getting to you. She ran the fingers of one hand through her hair, trying to put it in some semblance of order. It felt lank and gritty, filled with the filth that floated through the city's air. She closed her eyes until she was facing away from the mirror, then walked down the short hall to her bedroom.

The bedroom was dark, the curtains drawn against the heat of the day. She fumbled for the light switch, flooding the room with the dull, muted light of two small bulbs in a heavy ceiling fixture. Jennifer took a step toward the bed, then stopped. Staring at the object in the center of the bedspread, she tried to force her mind to focus on it. The wineglass slipped from her hand and crashed to the floor, shards of broken glass spraying out, the cold wine splashing against her legs. The gagging sound started deep in her throat, rising in choked spasms, cutting off her breath, until her eyes bulged in her head. She stared at the bed, unable to move, and her body began to tremble, then finally shake.

The penis had been impaled on the tip of a baling hook, the point driven up the shaft, the hook laid on its back so the organ was held suspended several inches above the bed. The skin enclosing the testicles had stretched, forcing them to hang at an obscene length, the flesh tinged purple from the trauma and encrusted with black blood.

Jennifer's hands flew to her mouth as she felt the bile rise from her stomach, and the vomit spewed forth between her fingers, racking her body with convulsions even after there was nothing left to release. She staggered back, her hands spread out before her, as if trying to fend off some advancing threat. When she backed into the hall, she turned and ran, her body crashing against the wall as she stumbled toward the telephone. The receiver fell from her hand, and she grasped it again, then dialed the number with jerking, trembling fingers.

When Pete's voice answered on the fourth ring, she could hear her own cracked, screeching voice explode into the receiver.

"Pete. Get over here. Oh, please, God, get over here."

She heard him ask what was wrong, panic in his own voice now, but she only repeated her begging request, over and over again, until she realized he was no longer on the line.

It took Pete twenty minutes to reach Jennifer's apartment, and when he opened the door with the key she had given him, he saw her sitting in the corner of the sofa, her body drawn tight, legs against her chest, her eyes wide and terrified. He hurried to her and slid next to her on the couch.

Her body drew back, almost as though she were afraid he might touch her.

"What is it? What happened?"

Her lips began to tremble as she fought to speak, then her arm extended from her side and one finger began jabbing toward the hall. "In . . . there . . . In . . . there," she stammered, then closed her eyes and mouth tightly, as though trying to force away unwanted reality.

Pete entered the bedroom, his revolver out. He saw it at once, acknowledged what it was, then looked away. He walked to the telephone next to Jennifer's bed, took out a handkerchief, and carefully lifted the receiver to avoid smudging the fingerprints he knew would not be there. When the call was answered, he asked for the detective he had spoken to that afternoon.

"This is Pete Moran," he said to the low, tired voice that answered. He gave him Jennifer's address. "You better get over here right away," he added. "I think I just found the rest of Mickey Maxwell."

Pete held Jennifer in his arms, stroking the soft skin along her back. They had returned to his apartment once the detectives had finished questioning her, and it was only now, two hours later, that she had finally stopped trembling. The bed was in a corner next to a window, and below, the sound of sporadic traffic along the FDR Drive seemed to vibrate through the room. Her breathing still came in long, hard breaths, and as he looked down at her face, nestled in the hollow of his shoulder, he could see that her eyes were tightly closed. It would take time for her to get over the shock, he knew, and there was nothing he could say or do that would make it any easier.

When he had brought her back to his apartment earlier, he had given her a stiff drink, helped her undress, and hurried her into bed. When he had begun to undress himself, she had reached out and grabbed his hand.

"Leave your shorts on, please," she had said, then turned her head to the pillow and violently shook her head. "I'm sorry," she said. "I just can't help it. I can't stand the thought of seeing a man naked right now."

She had continued to fight the fear over the next hour, then had finally drawn against him, as though struggling to overcome something that repulsed her.

Now, lying next to him, she tentatively ran her hand along his chest, gently stroking, feeling her way, as though making sure nothing would reach out and harm her. Slowly, carefully, she allowed her hand to reach his stomach. It seemed to freeze there, almost as though frightened to move on.

He reached across his body and stroked her cheek. "It's all right," he said. "It was a terrible shock. It will just take time to forget. Don't force anything."

"No," she whispered, her voice hoarse. "I can't stand letting myself be afraid of anything. I just can't." She forced her hand down and took hold of him tentatively. Her body shuddered again, but she forced her hand to remain.

He continued to stroke her face, gently moving her hair away from her eyes. "Facing things can be hard. And even when you do, sometimes you still never forget." He stared up at the ceiling for several moments before continuing. "When I was in Vietnam, I was captured by the VC. They held me in a small village, and every day they came and beat me, trying to get me to tell them things I simply didn't know. Between beatings they'd leave me alone for hours, letting me worry about the next time they'd come. It was after about a week that I managed to loosen the ropes that held my wrists and ankles, and I slipped out and found a machete. But I didn't run away. I went back into the hooch and waited for them. And when they came back, I went crazy. I killed all three of them." He paused again and closed his eyes. "When our people found me in the jungle, I didn't remember any of it, and it took two months with an army psychiatrist before I could. Even now, when I dream about it, I only dream about the torture. I never dream about killing them. I guess I'm just not able to deal with that yet, and that was almost fifteen years ago."

Jennifer pressed her face against him. "I'm surprised you became a cop after that."

"A shrink I saw since told me it was all part of recovering. He said something inside made me take a job where I had to carry a weapon every day." He paused again. "I've never had to use it," he said at length. "And I'm not really sure I could, if I had to."

They were quiet for several minutes before Jennifer finally spoke.

"Pete, why do you hate Tony Marco?"

He tightened his arm around her. "It goes back to that same time I was telling you about. Something happened then that made me feel he had betrayed me. We had been like brothers—closer than most brothers, really. And at the time it all seemed magnified and very much out of proportion, and all the hatred I felt, for everything, just suddenly centered on him."

"Did he betray you?"

Pete remained silent, listening to the sound of traffic float in through the window. Finally he shook his head. "No, Jennifer," he said. "I don't think he ever did."

CHAPTER/TWENTY-NINE

THE TWO DETECTIVES had spent more than an hour in Tony Marco's office. They had been courteous and direct, but the implications had been clear. Mickey Maxwell was now tied to a story Jennifer Brady was developing—a story that could allegedly prove damaging to both Marco and the union.

Tony had grimaced when he had heard about the supposed attempt to frighten Jennifer off. The macabre warning left on her bed could be perceived as another message from the union, the detectives had said, but they had conceded it also could have been arranged simply to make it appear that way.

It was too neat, too pat, and as a lawyer, Tony knew it was circumstantial. Yet it was hurting him, putting pressure on him, and if it went further, the mere involvement with a murder investigation would damage his future.

He stared out the window as his car sped across the Brooklyn Bridge, heading into Manhattan. The day was overcast, and a dark pall seemed to hang over the imposing skyscrapers of the lower island. He shook his head. It didn't make sense to tie him to a murder investigation when there was no hope of providing anything more than innuendo. It could harm him, but it couldn't benefit anyone else; certainly not enough to warrant murder. The other explanation was equally disconcerting. Someone in the union had panicked. Someone had learned about Jennifer's probing, and Maxwell's involvement, and had dealt with it as it would have been handled in the old days. He ticked off the names in his mind. Only Joey was crazy enough to react that way. Had Joey been in Las Vegas?

He looked back toward the river as the car moved up the FDR Drive in light traffic. When Anne Mobray's call came an hour ago, she had sounded almost hysterical. He couldn't imagine she could have heard about the murder, or about the police questioning him. No, he told himself. It was some minor disaster, one of the many Anne so adeptly turned into imaginary catastrophes. He rested his head back and ran through the Mickey Maxwell possibilities again. Nothing fit. Nothing warranted such insane reactions to problems that could be dealt with easily. And anyone who could have learned about Maxwell, or Jennifer Brady, would have known that. None of it fit. It simply did not fit.

Anne was pacing the living room when Tony arrived, and she quickly dismissed the maid who had shown him into the room. Her face was tight and nervous, and her movements seemed jerky, uncontrolled.

He stood in the center of the room and stared at her. "What's wrong?" he asked. "You look frantic."

Anne stopped in front of the marble fireplace and turned to face him. Her mouth seemed an angry contrast to eyes filled with hurt, and she fought to control the movement of her hands, finally clasping them in front of her. "Your wife was here," she said.

"Shirley?"

"Unless you have another," she snapped.

He drew a breath and returned her level gaze. "What did she want?"

"A little chat," Anne said. "Oh, not the type you would have expected. No leave-my-man-alone nonsense."

"Then what?"

"She talked about bank accounts. Foreign bank accounts and how certain people were very close to catching up to you about them."

"Did she say who?" Tony kept his voice even, but he could feel his anger rising.

"No, she didn't. But who else could it be but some federal agency?"

"I don't have any foreign bank accounts," Tony said.

"But she said you did," Anne insisted, stamping one foot.

"I used to," he said. "But I don't anymore, and there's no record of my ever having had one." He explained quickly what had occurred: the account that had been opened without his knowledge and put in his name on Shirley's signature.

He continued to stare at her, annoyed by her concern, knowing it was essentially directed toward herself. "Several years ago, after a great deal of complex maneuvering, I convinced the bank to remove my name from the account, and all traces of it ever having been there. Since the money wasn't leaving the bank, and since it also involved some rather healthy deposits from the union's welfare fund, they finally decided it was something they could do."

"But you knew this money came from bribes and you did nothing about it."

"That's right," Tony said. "I knew, and I didn't do anything except plan to get myself out."

"But why?" Anne's face was a mask of incredulity.

"First you have to assume there was something I could do," he said. "And that would involve nothing short of sending my wife and father-in-law to prison." He paused a beat. "*Providing* anyone was even willing to believe I knew nothing about what was going on. And that's not very likely, is it, given the union's past? And over the last few years I did know, didn't I?"

"Your damned union," Anne said, folding her arms across her chest. "It's like an albatross."

"That's right," Tony said. "But it's my albatross, not yours."

"Oh, really," Anne said angrily. "And if this hits the newspapers, no one will connect me to you at all."

"Not legally, certainly."

"And what about the people who *know* us? What about the people I've introduced you to, people I've known all my life; the same people who realize how close we are, who couldn't help but realize it."

Tony stared at her for several moments. He felt like shouting, like verbally striking out at her. But when he spoke, his voice was calm, almost soft. "You tell them you made a very unfortunate social error. Tell them how you tried to help someone from a lesser social level, so he could use the talents you had recognized. Tell them how you obviously made a serious mistake and how much you now regret it." He offered her a cold, steady smile. "They'll believe you, Anne. They'll believe everything you say, because it's something they'll want to believe."

He turned abruptly and headed for the door. Anne stared at him in disbelief, her mouth slightly open.

"Tony," she called. "Where are you going? Please, don't."

There was no conviction in her voice. He opened the door to the hall and continued out the front door.

Shirley was seated in the living room when Tony arrived home. He hardly glanced at her. He moved slowly through the living room and into his small study, opened the center drawer of his desk with a key, and withdrew two legal documents bound in blue wrappers.

When he returned to the living room, there was a small smile on Shirley's lips, and her eyes bore into him with reserved amusement. He walked slowly toward her and placed the two documents on the cocktail table in front of her.

Shirley looked down at the blue-bound documents, then back at him. "What's this? The start of our soon-to-be-heralded divorce?" Her eyes turned cold. "Forget about it, darling. You'll get over the Ms. Mobray affair. I should know. I've gotten over enough of them myself."

"This is better than a divorce, Shirley," he said, dropping a pen on top of the papers. "In the first document you're signing over all the Cayman Island money to Josh, without restrictions. In the second you're granting me full custody over him, and in the event anything happens to me, you're awarding that custody to my sister. Now pick up the pen and sign both of them."

She stared up at him, her eyes wide. Then she began to laugh. "You're mad."

He reached down and took her by the throat, his fingers digging deep into her windpipe. "There were two police detectives at my office today," he said in a voice little more than a whisper. "Questioning me about a murder. A murder they think I may have been involved in." He fixed her with his eyes and felt her body tremble. "Don't do anything that will make them come back, Shirley. Just pick up the pen and sign the papers."

Shirley reached out, took the pen, and did as she was told, then watched as Tony gathered up the documents, slipped them into his pocket, and headed back toward his study. "That will never stand up in court," she screamed after him. "It never will. They're not even notarized."

"They will be, Shirley," he said. "I promise you they will be."

"That's illegal," she screeched.

"Then it's something that will fit very nicely into our lives," he said. "Won't it, dear?"

Within seconds after Tony left the apartment with their son, Shirley dialed Paul Levine's private number.

"Don't panic," Levine's rough voice offered, after she had blurted out her story. "He's not going to take little Josh away from you. He's not going to take anything away from you at all."

"But he said . . . he said—"

"It doesn't matter what he said," Levine interrupted. "I'm going to take care of everything, and when I finish with Tony, he'll come crawling back to you begging you to tear up those papers."

"But, Uncle Paul, you said—"

"Never mind the buts," Levine said, silencing her. "I know what I'm doing, Shirley. All you have to do is keep quiet about all this and let me handle it. Do you understand? You don't say anything. Not to anybody, but especially not to Tony."

"I understand," Shirley said. "But are you sure?"

"I'm sure," Levine said. "You just trust your Uncle Paul and you'll have nothing to worry about."

When he returned the receiver to its cradle, Levine stared at it for several seconds. How could a man like Moe Green have raised such a stupid child? he asked himself. But she'll be taken care of. She won't have a thing to worry about. Except how to live her new life as a very wealthy young widow. Levine began to chuckle at the idea, then gave way to a full-throated laugh.

He caught hold of himself and sat back in his chair. Shirley's visit to Anne Mobray had certainly sent Marco into orbit. But that reaction, he told himself, was what he had intended the visit to do. Part of his plan involved pure vindictiveness. He recognized that. But Tony's reaction also showed some very irrational behavior. After all, he asked himself, what kind of man would try to take his child away from its mother? He hadn't even considered the part about the documents. Tony had done that for him. And now it would be just one more indication of his erratic state of mind. Poor Tony, he said to himself, thinking how he would soon say the same thing to the police, who would be investigating Tony Marco's death.

Tony strolled quietly through the zoo in Prospect Park, Josh's hand held loosely in his. The boy's eyes darted from cage to cage, taking in, with quick delight, the sight of the animals housed there.

It had been a long time since Tony had been to this zoo. Normally he took Josh to the Bronx or Central Park zoos, not here. How long had it been? Not since he and Pete had walked there so many years before. He pushed the thought away, not wanting to interrupt his time with his son with painful memories. There were enough of those already, he thought. Far more than he needed.

He bent down and lifted Josh up, holding him against his chest. "Which is your favorite animal?" he asked.

"The lion," the boy said. "I like the lion best."

"Why is that?"

"I like the way it sounds when it roars," Josh answered, finishing off with a squeaky imitation that was far from ferocious.

Tony laughed and kissed him on the cheek. "Do you like lions better than ice cream?"

The boy thought for a moment, then grinned at his father. "I like ice cream better."

Tony nodded, keeping his face solemn. He made a humming sound with his lips. "I don't know if the lion will be pleased to hear that. But I bet we could get some ice cream when he isn't looking."

Josh glanced back over his father's shoulder. "He's not looking now," he said, pointing toward the lion's cage.

"Then we better hurry," Tony said. He put the boy down and took his hand again. Immediately Josh pulled at him, trying to make him go faster. "What's the matter? You afraid the ice cream will melt before we get there?"

"Come on, Dad," the boy said. "Let's hurry."

Tony quickened his pace, allowing himself to be pulled along in the boy's wake.

Josh looked back at him again and grinned. "Hurry, Dad," he said.

Tony smiled back at him, realizing how much he enjoyed just the sound of the boy's voice, the sound of Josh calling him "Dad." "I'm hurrying," he said, feigning a more exaggerated stride. "You're just too fast for me."

The boy laughed with delight, and Tony hurried past him and began pulling him instead.

CHAPTER/THIRTY

JENNIFER'S TAXI FOLLOWED the funeral cortege up a long, winding drive in Brooklyn's Greenwood Cemetery. On either side of the roadway elaborate marble statues stood guard over well-tended graves—angels, their wings spread, some with heads and fingers pointed to the heavens, others looking solemnly at the graves themselves; Greek and Roman women clothed in flowing robes; images of the dead themselves; obelisks; domed and columned tombs. It was an architectural marvel dedicated to death.

Ahead, the hearse carrying Mickey Maxwell's coffin slowed to a halt, creating a chain reaction among the two dozen cars that followed. Pete had told her not to attend, not to risk any confrontation, but she had refused, knowing full well she had to go, had to do it alone, just to show them she couldn't be frightened off. And to prove it to herself.

She had not gone to the funeral home but had joined the funeral at the church instead. Marco had been there, along with other members of the union. There were not many in attendance; no one who seemed to be a member of Maxwell's family, and no women, other than herself. A vision of Mickey Maxwell's life had struck her at once, one of a lonely little man who had only acquaintances, not friends, and whose funeral was attended, at least in part, by the men who had killed him.

The thought sent a shudder through her, and she remained at the back of the church, slipping out the door and into the waiting taxi before the others emerged.

It was a cowardly gesture that had defeated her own intentions. But now, at the grave site, there would be no hiding from the others. She would be out in the open, exposed, and, she hoped, defiant.

Standing at the far edge of the grave site, away from the group of men, Jennifer saw that little mourning was taking place. The faces were stoic and reserved, some openly bored, eyes glancing off in various directions. Marco stood at the center of the group, dressed in a dark suit and black tie. He carried an umbrella against the threatening skies, and his dark eyes seemed to be concentrating on the casket, covered now with floral arrangements that gave off a sweet, sickly odor.

As she watched him, Tony's eyes rose and met hers. There was no expression on his face, neither anger, nor hate, nor the pleasure she had once seen there. Jennifer felt her nerves tighten, but she forced herself to return his gaze. The sense of regret she felt was overcome by revulsion and anger. There was no question in her mind he was behind Maxwell's death; no question he was the person who ordered the mangled genitals left on her bed. The cold, calculating viciousness made her want to strike out at him, to produce in him the fear she had known herself. But it wasn't possible. At least not yet. Her story would have to appear, and the noose would have to tighten. Until then he would remain calm and cool and unaffected.

The voice of the priest droned on as he recited, without emphasis or emotion, the prayers for the dead, and she recalled the same prayers being said for her mother several years earlier and how she had ignored them then as well, concentrating instead on looking for her father, who had never arrived.

Joey Gambardella also ignored the prayers as he studied the long, lithe lines of Jennifer Brady's body. She was wearing a loosely tailored black suit and a wide-brimmed black hat that made her red hair seem even more dramatic than it had the other time he had seen her.

He thought about that now: how he had waited outside her apartment, watching every woman who entered, then watching Jennifer's windows, waiting for the lights to go on. He had known it was she as soon as she passed through the lobby doors. It was the way she walked, the purposeful stride, the slightly arrogant upturn of her chin. She was one of those bitches who thought she was too good for any man on earth. One who thought that place between her legs was made of gold. He wished he had been there when she had found Mickey's prick on her bed. Just to see that she knew how unsafe she really was. How somebody could get to her anytime they wanted. And even do more than just leave a little present on her bed.

A small smile came to his lips. There was still more fun to come with her, he told himself. And the sooner it came, the better he would like it. He had his own ideas about that.

Paul Levine was standing next to him, and Joey gently nudged his arm. Paul leaned his head down. "The broad," Joey whispered. "That's the reporter."

Levine allowed his eyes to steal a furtive glance at Jennifer. He had noticed her before but had assumed it was some friend or relative of Mickey's. He looked at her again and realized how wrong he had been. Mickey never could have had a blood relation, or even a friend, who looked that good.

And gutsy, too, he thought. A little too gutsy. He leaned back toward Joey, keeping his voice at a whisper. "I think the lady should have some more trouble. And I think it should be as soon as possible. But not from you," he added. "It has to be someone who she won't see if she walks into the union office with the cops." He raised his chin, indicating two other men at the grave side. "You take care of it." He looked at Joey again and noticed a look of disappointment that bordered on anger spread across his face. "Don't worry," Levine added. "There'll be another time. And when it comes, it will belong all to you."

"I can't wait," Joey said, his voice louder than Levine would have preferred. Joey looked back at the tall, slender body and began to think about her, about what he would do. He wasn't certain exactly what it would be, but he knew when the time came, he would take a long time doing it.

Once the priest gave his final blessing, Jennifer hurried back toward the roadway. The taxi that had brought her had refused to wait, and she now faced a long walk to the front gate and the Twenty-fifth Street subway station just beyond. She moved as rapidly as she could, but her high-heeled shoes sank into the damp turf, forcing caution. The last thing she wanted was a broken heel, and a clumsy, hobbled walk as she made her exit. Thunder rolled overhead, and she felt the first drops of rain strike against the brim of her hat. She reached into her purse for the collapsible umbrella she kept there and quickly opened it.

"Do you have a car?"

The voice came from behind her, and she recognized it at once; with it came a chill of fear and anger. She turned and stared into Marco's face. "No. But I can manage quite well."

"If you'd like, I can have my driver take you to Manhattan. And it might give us a chance to talk."

Jennifer cocked her head to one side. "What is this, *Mr*. Marco? Are you showing me your Dr. Jekyll side today?"

Tony's eyes remained flat, regretful. "I know what happened to you. Two detectives who paid me a visit told me about it. I had nothing to do with it, and I don't think anyone in the union did, either."

"Oh, you don't? Well, I'm afraid I don't share your sense of innocence. Not about that—or about the little bribery scheme you and your friends operate."

Tony's expression did not change. "I don't receive any bribes, Jennifer. I'm not saying I'm surrounded by angels. I'm just telling you that you're not going to connect me to any illegal money."

"Is that a warning?"

"Just a statement of fact. I don't want to see you hurt by writing something that's going to blow up in your face."

Jennifer felt her cheeks redden. "Oh, it will blow up, Mr. Marco. But it won't be in *my* face. And you can keep your warnings. I already received one, and I wasn't impressed."

"Jennifer. Think about it. If I wanted to exert pressure, if I wanted to try to stop your story, don't you think I'd have better means at my disposal?"

"You mean little Martin Twist?" she asked. "But you tried that first and it didn't work. So then it was time for the goons, wasn't it?" She began to turn away, then stopped. "You know Mickey Maxwell didn't have to die. He had already given me everything he could, and I had already developed it. Now the police have copies of it, and there's nothing that can be done about that, either. So you can call off the goons. They can't do anything for you."

Tony stepped forward to block her way. "They were not my people. But if I'm wrong, and they *are* somehow connected with the union, it won't matter to them who has what. I'm just telling you that so you'll be careful. And, yes, I am trying to frighten you. But for your own good."

Jennifer's face reddened again. "I can take very good care of myself, so keep your warnings to yourself."

Tony stepped back and allowed her to pass. He watched her begin the long walk to the front gates. It was all going wrong, he told himself. And if Jennifer Brady wasn't careful, something was going to happen *very soon*.

CHAPTER/THIRTY-ONE

THE N TRAIN to Manhattan was just pulling into the platform as Jennifer descended the subway stairs. She fumbled in her purse for a token, then hurried through the turnstile and boarded the next-to-last car, only to have the train sit there, doors ajar, in no apparent hurry to depart.

She took an empty, two-person seat next to a rear door and settled in for the ride back to her office. The car was nearly deserted, her section completely so, and she closed her eyes and relaxed, trying to will away the tension her conversation with Marco had produced.

She heard the doors close with a rush of air and a banging rattle, then felt the first lurch of the train as it headed out of the station. She opened her eyes and saw that a man was standing over her, holding on to the metal strap rather than occupying the empty seat next to her. Instinctively she tightened her grip on her purse and kept her eyes from looking directly in his face. Indifference and an absence of fear—those were the cardinal rules for riding New York's subways.

The man shifted his body, positioning himself so he cut off Jennifer's view of the rest of the car. His legs had moved closer to the empty seat next to her, reducing her ability to move. Jennifer felt penned in, and when she moved, as though to rise from her seat, the man's body inched closer, keeping her in place.

An uneasy feeling began to grow inside her, and she watched the man's hand move slowly, then slide into his raincoat pocket and gradually withdraw again. His fingers were closed around something, and she looked away, not wanting to see what it was.

As a sharp clicking sound brought her eyes back she found the blade of a knife only two feet from her face. The man bent over to bring his face closer to hers, and as he spoke in a low, guttural voice, she was washed by the rancid smell of his stale breath.

"Some people should learn to take warnings," the voice said.

She looked up at his face for the first time and saw only the cold, malicious eyes of someone enjoying the fear he produced. Jennifer opened her mouth as if to speak or cry out, and the knife moved quickly to a point just below her throat. She stared up at the face again, this time seeing the flat, hard features; the slightly crooked nose; and the small scar on the left cheekbone.

"You open your mouth and you're dead," the man said.

Jennifer pressed her lips together and closed her eyes, then opened them again as she felt the point of the knife trace a slow line from her neck to the top button of her blouse. The blade slipped under the button, remained still for a moment, then, with a quick twist, sliced the button free and sent it flying to the floor of the train.

Jennifer stared at the falling button, almost as though a part of her body had been cut away. The button bounced, spun momentarily, then rolled away toward the rear of the car. She let out a small cry of alarm and immediately felt the blade prick the skin on her chest.

Looking down, she saw a small drop of blood glistening on the point of the knife and heard the man's voice say, simply, "Don't."

He had cut her. Not deeply, but he had still cut her, and she was suddenly aware that he could easily push the blade forward and end her life with one simple act.

Jennifer began to tremble. She fought to control it, but it was impossible. The tremors began in her legs, then moved up to her arms and body, and finally to her lips. She closed her eyes tightly and clenched her teeth. The knife began to move again, a slow, steady descent along the flesh between her breasts.

She was not wearing a bra, and she could feel her breasts quiver as the trembling along her body intensified. The knife stopped at the next button, toyed with it momentarily, then cut it free. She looked down at the knife again as the man began moving it from side to side, spreading her blouse apart until her breasts lay nearly exposed.

Jennifer hunched her shoulders, trying to force the material together, and the knife jabbed at her again, more gently this time, warning her to stop. Her shoulders sagged; her body felt drained of strength. When she looked up at the man again, she saw he was smiling at her with crooked teeth.

The train began to slow as it approached the next station. Jennifer's eyes darted around as the train came to a halt. Suddenly a second man positioned himself next to the first. Her heartbeat began to quicken, and she looked up into the newcomer's face, praying he would help her. He was younger than the first, with dark wavy hair, but the line of his mouth was equally cold, and his dark eyes bore down at her without compassion.

He bent forward, as the first man had. "You got nice tits, lady," he said. "It's too bad you also got a big mouth. Mouths are for sucking on things. Not for talking to the wrong people."

Jennifer squeezed her eyes closed again and felt tears run down her cheeks. She felt fingers fumbling with her open blouse but kept her eyes closed as they moved roughly from one breast to the other. She knew it was the second man, could still feel the point of the knife held by the first. She shuddered as fingers closed over one nipple, then squeezed it roughly, making her gasp with pain.

"You like that?" the voice of the second man asked. "Sure you do. But this nipple, here—the one I got between my fingers—I think we're gonna have to cut it off, unless you learn to mind your own business. You understand what I'm saying, lady? You understand what we're gonna do to your tits if you don't listen?"

Jennifer nodded her head. She wanted to speak, to beg them not to cut her, but she knew her voice would be only a broken wail if she attempted it.

The knife slipped lower, along her midriff, and she could feel another button fall away, laying her blouse open from neck to belt line. The men kept speaking to her in turn, but she fought to block the voices out, allowing only the occasional word to slip through. She continued to tremble, her hands began to ache, and she realized that she was gripping her purse so tightly that her muscles had cramped.

The train came to a halt again, jolting her in her seat. There were no hands on her now, and she wondered if they were just waiting to begin again or simply daring her to try to move; to say something so they could cut her again.

She heard the doors close, and the train begin to move again. Slowly she opened her eyes. They were gone. She looked quickly at the other passengers, her eyes wide and gaping, searching for the faces that had stared down at her. Across the aisle an old man stared back at her, a slight, unpleasant smile on his lips, and she remembered that her blouse was completely open. Quickly she grasped the material with both hands and pulled it together.

Gradually the trembling began to ease, then started again as she realized they simply might have moved to another car, to wait and watch for her to leave, and then to follow her. The train pulled into another station, and she looked for the sign that would tell her where she was: Union. She was in Manhattan at Fourteenth Street. Union Square. She had been on the train for nearly half an hour. The thought of it sent another chill down her spine.

When the doors opened, she rushed out, ran through the turnstile and up the stairs, and quickly crossed the sidewalk to the curb. Her eyes searched for a taxi, the hand holding her purse waving above her head. A yellow blur slid to the curb next to her, and she opened the door and jumped into the rear seat.

"Where to, lady?" the driver asked.

She stammered for a moment, then gave him the address of her apartment. As the cab sped off, she turned and stared out the rear window. There was no one there. No one had followed her.

When Jennifer reached her apartment, she rushed past the doorman and hurried into the elevator. Once the elevator began to rise, she felt the tension finally ease. She was in her building, she was safe, and soon she would be behind her own door, with it bolted and locked. The fear rose to the surface again: They had gotten in there before, hadn't they?—gotten in and left that foul thing on her bed. She shook herself as though casting off her own fears. The police had warned the doorman, questioned him. Security would have been tightened. Even the doorman, himself, and the building superintendent had assured her of it.

The elevator came to a stop and the door opened. She stepped out and hesitated, holding the door ajar with one hand, then glancing down the long hall that led to her door. It was empty.

She started down the hall, telling herself she could rely on Pete to stay with her.

The man stepped through the emergency exit door, halfway down the hall, and stood facing her—the same flat, hard features, the slightly crooked nose, the small scar on the left cheekbone—only this time he was smiling, cold and mean, something he had not done on the subway.

Jennifer staggered back and watched, horrified, as he slowly started toward her. She turned and ran back to the elevator and began slamming her hand against the call button. She looked back down the hall. He was still coming, slowly, deliberately, in no hurry to reach her. His hand slid into the pocket of his raincoat. She stared at the hand, waiting for it to withdraw as she continued to pound against the call button, willing the elevator to return, to give her a way out, a way of escape.

He was only four steps away when the elevator doors opened, and she jumped inside and drove her hand against the lower buttons on the panel, hitting more than the one she wanted. His wide-shouldered body filled the opening, and the hand came out of the pocket, the blade of the knife flashing as the elevator doors began to close. The last thing she saw was the smile on his face; the last words: "I'll be back."

The elevator stopped at the fifth and third floors, but the floors were empty, no one waiting, no one who might provide the simple safety of another human being, the simple deterrent of a witness.

When the doors opened onto the lobby, Jennifer raced

from the elevator, her high heels clattering against the tile floor, her damaged blouse open, the fear of her flight causing her to forget the need to hold it closed. She shouted at the doorman as she passed him, telling him there was someone on her floor, someone after her. She did not stop but pushed through the front doors and ran into the street, wildly waving her hand for another cab, her eyes darting back toward the building entrance. As a cab pulled to the curb she jumped into the rear seat and blurted out Pete's address, then began fumbling through her purse to make sure she had the keys he had given her.

At Pete's apartment door she was out of breath, and fumbled again with the keys until the door finally yielded. She had stepped inside and turned to close the door when she saw the second man move toward her from the shadows of the landing.

"I came to give you some more," he said, heading toward the door.

Jennifer slammed it shut; threw one bolt, than another; and finally placed her back against it as a human blockade. Through the door she could hear his soft laughter, only inches away on the other side. Her body trembled violently as the words filtered through.

"It's okay, baby. We know where to find you."

Jennifer's entire body trembled as she sank down to the floor.

Pete arrived fifteen minutes later and called to her through the closed door. When Jennifer telephoned him, he told her where his spare pistol was kept, and even now, as he opened the door, he stood away from the opening, afraid she might fire.

Stepping into the loft, he saw the weapon trembling in her hand, her normally pale face whiter than ever before.

"Put the gun down," he said softly, then waited as she lowered it to the cocktail table.

He was beside her a moment later, pressing her to him, his hand stroking the back of her head. "It's all right. There's nobody out there."

"One of them was at my apartment too," she said, her voice almost gagging on the words. "Waiting for me."

Pete continued to stroke her head, keeping his voice soft, doing everything he could to calm her.

He listened quietly as she told it all, and though he remained calm, Jennifer could feel his body tense with anger as she explained what they had done to her.

"We'll have to call the detectives working the Maxwell case," he said when she finished.

She pushed herself away. "No, I won't. Not this time. Not again." She began to shake her head violently. "Even if I did, it wouldn't help. They couldn't help me."

"All right," he whispered. "I can take some time off. I can stay with you. You won't be alone until it's over."

She lifted her head and stared at him, her lips trembling. "Can you?"

"Yes," he said, pulling her close again.

"If it continues, it's going to blow up in somebody's face, and nobody—*nobody*—is going to escape the fallout."

Tony stared across his desk at Pete Moran. He hadn't been surprised by Pete's call, asking to see him. It was something he had expected since Maxwell's murder. What he had not expected was the tone of the conversation—the absence of animosity, of accusation.

"I had nothing to do with Maxwell's death. Or any of the assaults on Jennifer Brady."

"Somebody in the union did." Pete watched Tony's eyes; he could almost see the thought process as he tried to figure out who that somebody was. "And whoever it is, is doing his damnedest to make sure you look guilty."

Tony nodded slowly, then abruptly shook his head. "It

doesn't make sense, Pete. There's nothing that Maxwell could have given Jennifer Brady—no matter who helped him—that could have produced any criminal action against me. It may look like it on the surface, but I assure you, there's nothing that will hold up." Pete started to reply, but Tony held up a hand, stopping him. "I'm not saying I can't be hurt by it all. It's no secret I have ambitions outside the union. And what's happened so far has already damaged those pretty badly. And more publicity, more scandal, will probably kill them for good. But that's why it doesn't make sense. If somebody in the union is out to get me, it's because they want me out. But doing it this way only guarantees I'll be forced to stay. I won't have any other place to go."

"What about the possibility that someone else in the union might face criminal charges?" Pete asked.

Tony thought about it, wondering how well others had covered themselves. Then he dismissed the idea. "I don't know. But even if that were the reason, why do it in a way that pointed a finger back at the union? And hell, Pete, it couldn't have been done more blatantly if they put up signs."

"I know it's people inside the union," Pete said. "They sent somebody to me, somebody they thought would keep me after you, keep the hatred going. I don't know who they are, but they knew the right buttons to push."

Tony winced slightly at the word *hatred*, then pushed it away. "Who? Who did they send to you?"

Mary Beth flashed into Pete's mind. "I can't tell you. I wish I could but I can't. It's still a murder investigation."

"And I'm still a suspect," Tony said, completing Pete's statement.

"Somebody's worked very hard to make sure of that."

Tony sat back in his chair. It had to be political. But that, in itself, was madness. You don't kill innocent bystanders and terrorize reporters to stop political appointments. He shook his head again. "What do you want me to do?"

"I want Jennifer protected," Pete said. "I can't offer you any promises about the story she's working on—"

Tony waved him off. "That doesn't matter. I'll survive that. Not as well as I'd like to, but I'll survive it. But I don't know what I can do to protect her."

"Just get the word out. Make noises that you're out to find who's behind this. It might scare them off, it might not. But it's the only damned thing I can think of, short of getting my hands on them."

"I'll do what I can, Pete."

"Do something else too," Pete added.

"What?"

"Watch your back."

CHAPTER/THIRTY-TWO

PAUL LEVINE TAPPED his fingers on his desk, then broke into a broad smile. He had seen the near panic in Marco's eyes. Oh, Tony had masked it as anger, as determination to stop the attacks against the reporter. But there had been fear there as well; a knowledge that he couldn't stop what he couldn't find. And who did he come to? Who did he ask to find what he couldn't find himself? Levine released his pleasure in a low chuckle. The one man who would never interfere with his plans to leave the union: good old beaten-down Paul Levine.

Levine swiveled in his chair and stared out the window. The sky had turned dark, and a slow, steady drizzle had begun, giving every indication it would continue throughout the day. A good day to finish it, he told himself. You can't count on Tony playing the fool much longer.

He turned back to his desk and, picking up his telephone, punched out Joey Gambardella's internal number. "Joey, this is Paul. I'm going to need you tonight. Late. Meet me at my office at eleven." Then he punched the

button for his private line and dialed an outside number.
When a man's voice answered, he spoke without identify-
ing himself.

"I need you on Marco today. All day and all evening. I
need to know where he is so I can reach him when I have
to." He waited as the man grunted agreement. "Then I
want you at my office before ten tonight." He paused
again. "And bring your partner with you."

Levine replaced the receiver, stared at it, then picked it
up again and called one more number.

"Shirley, this is Uncle Paul. I have some good news for
you. . . ." he began.

As Tony Marco sat across the table from James Giuliani,
he saw a hint of pain flicker through the governor's eyes.

"Can the newspaper story be scotched?" Giuliani asked.

"I don't know," Tony said. "If this killing is solved and
there was no union involvement, probably. Everything
else is conjecture, at least as far as I'm concerned."

"I don't like the way that sounds, Tony. It's too
open-ended."

They were seated at a corner table in a small, dimly lit
French restaurant on Manhattan's Upper East Side, and
Tony looked around to reassure himself they were far
enough removed from other patrons to be overheard.
"That's the problem," he said. "It *is* too open-ended, and
any story is going to throw a great deal of mud in my
direction, and probably result in some type of investigation."

"What about eventual criminal charges?" There was an
uneasiness in Giuliani's eyes now, and it gave him the look
of a man ready to bolt from the table.

Tony thought back over his years of involvement, the
phony corporations he had created, the arrangements he
had made personally with the foreign shipping companies.
His name appeared on nothing incriminating; he, himself,

was clear of any ties to the money, and he doubted that distance could be broached. It was also unlikely anyone in any of the shipping companies, or the union, would offer any damaging evidence against him, and within a few months, the statute of limitations would be in effect. In those respects he felt safe. Still, looking back on it all gave him a sense of despair, a dirty feeling he knew was deserved, one that no amount of cosmetic legal cleansing would remove.

"I have no problems in that area," he said.

The governor sat back in his chair, looking somewhat like a prizefighter resting between rounds—relieved but still aware more blows might come his way.

Giuliani drew a deep breath, privately grateful no announcement had been made about Tony's appointment. He had received a call from Anne Mobray withdrawing her support. He understood that now, but he still wanted Tony in the post, wanted his talent and the future union support it would guarantee, but not at the expense of being painted with the same brush that might bring Marco down.

"How bad will the mud be?" he asked. "Give me a worst-case scenario."

Tony drummed the fingers of one hand against the table. He had asked for the meeting with Guiliani to give the governor a way out, expecting him to take it. It was a courtesy, an obligation to a friend; nothing more. Now he found himself hoping he could avoid that obvious necessity, find some way to pull himself back.

"All the claims we've made—that *I've* made—about turning the union around." Tony stopped and shook his head. "They'll be badly damaged." He raised both hands, palms up, then let them fall. "My excuse will be that there's still work to be done, that it's ongoing and always will be. I'll paint it as a holdover from the past, and I'll brazen out all the innuendo. But it won't work, and it will take several years to get back to where we—where I—am now. That's the worst case."

"And you think it's likely." Giuliani's words were statement, not question.

Tony hesitated, then looked at Giuliani and nodded reluctantly. "Yes, Jim, I do."

The governor rubbed his hand across his forehead. "Well, we'll wait and see, of course," he said. "But if the worst case comes out, or if an investigation is even started, there's no way I can go through with the appointment." He looked up at Tony with weary eyes. "You understand that, don't you? You understand that it's not a condemnation, only facing a political reality?"

Tony nodded. "I understand, Jim. It's the reason I'm here."

Giuliani lowered his eyes. "And I appreciate it. I'll get the word down to the right people, to keep your name out of this murder case, if at all possible. But that's the most I can do." He shook his head with regret. "The power of high political office is largely illusion, I'm afraid. Especially when the newspapers get involved."

"I'll work it out, Jim."

The governor looked across the table and nodded, but without conviction. "I hope you can," he said. "I really hope you can."

Paul Levine picked up the telephone on the first ring and listened to the low, almost growling voice he had been expecting.

"He's just leaving the restaurant now. You want us to keep following him?"

"No," Levine said. He glanced at his wristwatch. Nine-thirty. "Get back here right away, as quickly as you can."

He eased himself up from behind his desk and began

pacing his office. He had been worried about having to telephone Tony at the restaurant and risking the possibility he might mention the call to whomever he was with. Everything was working perfectly. He walked back to his desk and gave the mobile operator the number for Tony's car.

"This is Paul Levine," he said to the driver. "Is Tony with you?" Levine waited until Tony came on the line. "Tony, it's Paul. I've come up with something on Maxwell's killing. Some good news and some bad. But mostly good for us, I think."

He could hear the anxious anticipation in Tony's voice as he asked for clarification.

"Not on the phone," he said. "You know how I am about phones. I'm at the office. Can you get here by ten?" He recognized the eagerness in Marco's voice. "I'll be waiting in my office."

After all these years it would finally be over. All the humiliation repaid, all the forgotten promises overcome. And, best of all, Marco would be on his knees, broken and beaten, with no hope of changing anything. Levine's eyes glistened. Marco was already a walking corpse. He simply didn't know it. But very soon he would. And then he would have to sit and wait for it to happen. Sit and wait for Paul Levine to do it. Those would be the best moments, Levine told himself. That, and the look on his face. He crossed the room to a side door that led to an adjoining office, opened it, and stood there nodding to himself. The sight of the sleeping form in the chair comforted him. It made him certain everything would work as planned.

When Tony entered the office, Levine was seated behind his desk, his face partially hidden in shadow from the lone desk lamp that illuminated the room. Levine smiled as Tony entered, but the lighting made the smile appear on only half his face, the intense look of what seemed like expectant pleasure coming from only one eye.

"You said good and bad news, Paul," Tony began.

Levine sat back in his chair so all of his face, above his chin, was now in shadow. "Yes, I did."

Games, Tony thought. "It's been a long day, Paul, and not a very pleasant one. Tell me the bad news first."

Levine remained in shadow, but Tony could almost feel him gloating. He's enjoying himself, he thought. And a lot more than he should. Levine was still silent. "Can we get to it, Paul?" Tony tried, but failed, to keep the irritation out of his voice.

Levine moved forward, bringing his face into the light. It glowed with all the hatred Tony had always known was in the man, but which he had never before seen. Levine seemed to sway slightly, and the hard smile spread fully across his mouth. "The bad news, Tony, is that the killings aren't over. There'll be more tonight." He paused, staring at Tony with eyes that seemed almost glazed. "The good news is that they'll be blamed on you, and then it will all be over."

Tony stared at him. "You," he said, the sound of his voice as incredulous as his thoughts. "I thought of you, almost from the start, but there never seemed to be any percentage in it." He studied Levine's Buddha-like face, the creases of flesh folding in on each other under his smiling grimace. "And there still isn't. You'll never be able to tie me to any of this."

"I won't have to. You'll do that yourself. You see you're going to write out a little confession. Or maybe we should call it what it will be. A sort of suicide note."

"You're out of your mind," Tony said, and started to rise.

Levine's hand came up from his lap and leveled a small, snub-nosed revolver at Tony's chest. He watched Tony ease back into his chair. "Yes, you will, Tony. You'll do exactly what I tell you."

"Not very smart, Paul. Shoot me now and it sure as hell won't look like a suicide, even if you try to forge a note."

Levine looked at the gun and shrugged. "Oh, this isn't what's going to make you do it, Tony. This is only going to make you wait until you *see* the reason." He inclined his head toward the door to the adjoining office. "The reason's in there. You go take a look and I think you'll understand."

Tony sat motionless, returning Levine's stare, his mind spinning with possible alternatives, calculating what he might do and how. But right now he had to buy time, he told himself. Buy as much time as you can.

Levine jerked his head toward the door again, more emphatically this time. "Go look," he snapped. "Now!"

Tony walked toward the door, and when his hand was on the knob, turned back to Levine. "When I open it, maybe I'll just keep going, Paul."

Levine let out a low laugh. "No, you won't, Tony. You'll just come right back here and sit down. And then you'll do whatever I want you to do."

Tony continued to stare at him, then pulled the door open. Two men stood on either side of the large chair—one older, with a scar on his cheek; the other younger, his face fixed in a sick smile. The men, he knew, were the ones Pete had described to him. He looked down at the occupant of the chair, at his sleeping son, the boy's small chest rising and falling, his legs curled up in a fetal position. Slowly Tony turned, closed the door behind him, and walked back to the chair facing Levine's desk. "How did you get him here?" Tony asked. There was a slight trembling in his voice, partly rage, partly fear.

Levine's eyes glittered at the sound. He had waited a long time to hear it, and now he wanted to enjoy every second of it.

"I said, how did you get him here?" Tony repeated.

The revolver was back in Levine's lap now, and he sat back in his chair, obscuring his features again. "It wasn't hard. A little sleeping pill in his milk after I picked him up. You see, Shirley's been very worried about the legal papers you had her sign." He shook his head in reproach. "Taking a boy away from his mother." He leaned forward and smiled. "Of course, I don't think she gave much of a damn about that. But the money? Well, that's a different story. Signing the money over to Josh, then signing Josh over to your sister's custody . . . well, for Shirley, that just boiled down to giving your sister *her* money. And she didn't want that at all."

Levine's voice sounded bored. "I set up a meeting with a lawyer for her and offered to take care of Josh. Keep him overnight, in fact. The lawyer is young, very good-looking, and very, very willing. I knew I could count on Shirley to take me up on the offer. I'm sure you understand that much, at least."

Tony felt the bile rise in his throat, but not from any sense of humiliation over Levine's words. He had long ago overcome any sense of shame about Shirley. The shame was because of the helplessness he felt, the fact that his son was being used, and that he could do nothing to stop it, nothing to remove the threat against him, except buy more time.

"You didn't have to go to that much trouble with Shirley," Tony said. "I'm sure if you told her you wanted me shot, she would have pulled the trigger herself."

Levine was annoyed by the cold calm in Tony's voice. "I'm afraid I've known her too long to trust her," he said. "Except to follow her natural instincts." He watched Tony's eyes, looking for some sign of pain. What he received in return was a hard, unemotional stare.

"So what's next?"

Levine folded his hands in front of him, like a child on opening day of school. "We wait for Joey to arrive. That should be in about thirty minutes."

Tony walked to the window behind Levine. The older man did not move. He knows you won't try anything, Tony told himself. Not with the boy in the next room. "What's Joey's part in this?" he asked, staring down into the street.

"Joey's going to kill the reporter and, if necessary, your friend Moran. It seems Ms. Brady is staying at his apartment on East Seventy-second." Levine swiveled his chair and stared up at him. "A little less dramatically than the way he killed Maxwell, I hope."

Tony had been watching Levine over his shoulder and now turned back to the window and closed his eyes.

"And what do you need me here for? For the meeting with Joey, I mean?"

"Just insurance," Levine said. "Joey's still intimidated by you, although he'd never admit it. He might balk at killing Moran, or even the reporter, if he thought you'd object. But we can put his mind at ease, can't we, Tony?"

"You're crazy, Paul. You know that? You're crazy."

"You can refuse, Tony. But then, the boy doesn't go home. And, as far as you're concerned, nothing will change. You'll still be dead."

"All nicely wrapped up, isn't it, Paul?"

"I think so." Levine tapped one finger against the desk. "So, what will it be?"

Tony remained silent for several moments. "It will be whatever you want." He turned back to face Levine, longing to put his hands around the old man's throat.

Tony stood in the shadows by the window as Joey received his instructions from Levine. There was an unreality to it all, the cold, indifferent way it was done, as though human lives were not even being discussed. Before Joey arrived, Levine had removed his suitcoat so he could give the orders in shirtsleeves, like some foreman issuing instructions to a laborer.

Joey hesitated momentarily, and Levine had turned to Tony to solicit his agreement. Joey had been unable to see Levine's eyes, but they had been cold and defiant, filled with unspoken threat. Tony capitulated, the words almost choking him; then he turned back to the window, hiding his rage again in the shadows.

And Joey was gone.

"He'll do a good job," Levine said. "It's the type of thing he does well."

"Yes, he'll do it," Tony said, thinking that all his life Joey had been headed in this direction. It had only been a question of who would point him.

Tony walked to the side of the desk so he could see Levine's face. He wanted to see the pleasure he knew was there, wanted to see the cold madness in his eyes. "He seems to know exactly where to go. You didn't even have to give him an address."

Levine smiled with his lips, a thick, heavy, self-satisfied smile. "We've been keeping watch." The smile faded. "You don't have to be a college boy to know how to plan things. But that's something you never understood, is it?"

Tony ignored the remark. "So what happens now?"

The mirthless smile returned to Levine's face. "We wait to make sure it's done. I think it would be a nice touch if your suicide is done with the same gun Joey uses."

"And you expect Joey to just stand around and watch that?"

Levine let out a long, harsh laugh. "Joey won't be standing around watching anything," he said. "He'll be another victim. If and when they find him." He shook his head in mock sadness. "You're not very sharp today, are you, Tony?"

Tony closed his eyes. The man talked about killing people the way an exterminator talked about ridding a house of insects. Cherry flashed into his mind, his throat ripped open, sprawled on the floor of the pier six warehouse. He hadn't thought of that poor black man in years, of how he had been speaking to him only moments before he was killed, laughing with him. Now it's you. And maybe your son, Josh. He shook away the final thought, telling himself he could never let that happen. Levine's voice came from a distance, unintelligible. Tony focused on his face again.

"I said I want you to call your driver and tell him to go home. He *is* waiting outside, isn't he?" He watched Tony nod. "Well, he's served his purpose. He's seen you come in, and he's seen Joey come and go. So get rid of him. We don't need him anymore." He allowed the rest to go unsaid. The look on his face said it without words.

As Tony stepped toward the desk and reached for the telephone, he saw Levine's hand go to the pistol in his lap. Grasping the receiver, Tony lifted it and began to draw it toward him. Halfway there he pivoted and, with all the force he could bring to bear, drove the receiver into the center of Levine's face.

The blow sent Levine back in his chair, and the chair against the wall. Blood poured from his face, and his eyes were momentarily dazed, but his left hand was still firmly fixed to the revolver.

Tony jumped forward and grabbed Levine's wrist with his right hand; his left dug, clawlike, into Levine's throat, squeezing his windpipe. Levine forced himself to his feet with such strength he virtually raised Tony off the ground.

Muffled rage burst from Levine's mouth as he pressed his bulk against Tony, his left hand twisting against Tony's grasp, inching the gun slowly toward his body.

Tony fought back, perspiration already running freely

along his body. Despite his age, Levine's strength was awesome and now, fed by the rage that pulsed through his body, seemed practically unstoppable. Tony reared back and drove the top of his head into the center of Levine's face, feeling the soft flesh, bone, and cartilage crush under the force of the blow. But it was like trying to move a tree planted in front of him. Tony could shock him, stun him, force his body to sway slightly, but Levine was still there, unmoved.

With a grunt of effort Levine jammed the gun against Tony's stomach and fired. The sound of the shot was muffled by Tony's body, but the impact hit like a hammer, doubling him over, shocking all his senses. His mind blurred, turned blank, then refocused again. Tony grabbed the revolver with both hands, the adrenaline pulsing, and twisted the barrel away and up until it jammed under Levine's chin.

The second shot exploded up through Levine's skull, popping out his left eye and sending a red spray of blood, bone, and mangled brain tissue against the ceiling in an obscene, Rorschach-like blot. Levine collapsed, falling to the floor like heavy, wet cloth. Tony fell atop him, the revolver now clasped in his hand, the searing pain in his stomach working outward in hot electrical flashes to every extremity.

Behind him, the door to the adjoining office crashed open, and as he spun, automatically, to the sound, Tony found the two men facing him, their eyes wide and unbelieving.

He leveled the revolver, moving from one to the other. "Paul's dead," he said, his voice little more than a wheeze. "You want to join him, move an inch."

The two men stood motionless, hands raised, both sets of eyes riveted on the remains of Levine's body, the skull gaping open like a broken and ravaged egg, the blood and fluid oozing onto the carpet in a growing pool.

Tony struggled to his feet. "Take your guns out and throw them over here."

The men did as they were told, but instead of guns, each threw a knife in his direction.

"No guns," the older one with the scar said. He opened his jacket as proof, an action imitated by the younger man.

Tony moved around the desk, using one hand against it for support. "Get against the wall."

The two obeyed, each staring at the blood that trickled through the fingers of the hand pressed against Tony's stomach.

"You're hurt," the older one said, a trace of hope in his voice.

Tony pointed the gun squarely at his head. "And the last thing I'm going to do before I drop is blow your face off."

The two men stared at him, accepting his word, as Tony moved slowly toward the door to the adjoining office. Stopping there, he looked inside and saw his son still asleep in the chair.

"He's okay," the younger man said. "Nobody touched him."

With the gun Tony gestured toward the door to Levine's office. "Get out of here," he said. "And if you want to live, don't stop."

The two moved slowly at first, then quickly, out the door. Tony leaned against the doorjamb of the adjoining office, listening to their footsteps beat a tattoo on the stairs. When the front door slammed behind them, he turned and walked to the chair holding his son. He reached out and felt his cheek with the back of his hand and listened to his slow, steady breathing. Then, clutching his stomach, he walked unsteadily to the desk and picked up the telephone to call his driver.

A minute later, when his driver came rushing into the

room, he gestured toward the sleeping child with his chin. "Call a cab and take him to my mother's house," he said. "I'll need the car."

The driver stared at Tony, at the growing stain on his shirt. "You need a doctor. Let me take you to the hospital."

Tony shook his head vehemently. "There's something I have to do. Myself. Just do what I told you. Please. Just do it."

Jennifer sat on the edge of the sofa, her legs tucked beneath her. She had just come out of the shower and was dressed in a loose shift that clung to her still damp body. She was tired, mentally exhausted, and even the beating hot water had been unable to revive her.

Across the room Pete sat in a chair, going over the notes she had given him. His forehead creased as he turned to the outline of the story she would write about Tony. The facts were there, clear-cut and direct, and as presented, they offered a damning portrait of continued corruption within the union. It was clear, even to the unsophisticated reader, that the bribes paid by shipping companies had never stopped when Marco "reformed" the union. They had simply become payments made to paper corporations headed by a retired union official, who then undoubtedly funneled the money back to union officials, while the union, itself, obscured that money with loans to the corporations.

There was no hard evidence against Tony, himself, nothing that would cause him immediate legal problems. But the circumstantial evidence, the innuendos, was enough to end any hopes he had for a political future. Pete shook his head slowly, almost imperceptibly. There was nothing wrong with the facts, nothing he did not believe to be true. Yet somehow it bothered him.

"What do you think?" Jennifer's voice cut through his thoughts.

"It will nail him to a wall," Pete said. "It won't put him in jail unless somebody comes up with something harder, but for all practical purposes it might as well. He'll never get out of that union now. Not to anyplace that means anything."

"You sound disappointed. You don't like it, do you?" There was a trace of hurt in Jennifer's voice.

"It doesn't tell me why," Pete said.

"It's not supposed to tell you why. It's a newspaper story. It's just supposed to tell you the facts."

Pete nodded, saying nothing.

Jennifer stared at him, then shook her head in frustration. "What do you want me to do? Talk about the poor Brooklyn boy? The scholarship student who scratched his way through college and law school, taking care of his widowed mother?"

Pete looked at her. "No, I guess not."

"The trouble is, that's what I feel I should have written," she said, her voice low and soft. "Maybe I could have if I didn't believe he was behind all these threats."

The sound of a knock at the door stopped her, and she shifted her gaze to stare toward the sound.

Pete pulled himself from his chair and walked toward the door. When he pulled it open, Joey stood there grinning at him.

"Hello, Petey. How you doing?"

The grin remained on Joey's face, as his eyes shifted to Jennifer, and Pete felt himself stiffen. "What are you doing here, Joey?"

Joey turned to face him with wide eyes. "Is that any way to greet an old pal, Petey?"

"What do you want, Joey?"

"I got some information for you. About our old friend, Tony Marco. If you're not interested, maybe your reporter friend will be." He looked past Pete at Jennifer.

"What kind of information?" Jennifer said almost defi-
antly, as she raised herself from the sofa.

Joey's grin gradually turned into a leer as he appraised
Jennifer's body. "Something you don't have, don't know
about, and never will unless I give it to you."

Jennifer felt her skin crawl under the look Joey gave
her. She recalled the things Pete had told her about this
man—his blind, witless cruelty. She repressed a shudder.

"Let's hear what he has to say," she said to Pete.

"How come, Joey?" Pete asked. "How did Tony suddenly make your hit parade after all he's done for you?"

Joey looked at him with a pained expression that slowly
returned to a leering grin. "I suppose if I told you I
wanted to be a good citizen, you wouldn't believe me."

Pete stared at Joey without expression, then stepped
around him and closed a single dead-bolt lock on the door.
"Not even if you gave me letters of commendation from
the mayor, the governor, and the pope."

Joey let out a high, nasal laugh as Pete started back
toward the sofa.

When Pete's back was turned to him, Joey moved slightly
to his left, using Pete's body to obscure Jennifer's view,
then reached for the automatic tucked into the rear waist-
band of his trousers.

Jennifer's voice froze in her throat as she watched Joey's
hand rise up behind Pete and come crashing down on the
back of his head. Pete's shoulders hunched as he staggered forward and fell to the floor.

Eyes darting from Pete's body to Joey, standing behind
him, Jennifer's voice finally came in one long, steady gasp,
then froze again when she saw the flat, dark automatic in
Joey's hand.

"Where does he keep his handcuffs?" Joey snapped.

Jennifer's mouth moved, but no sound came out.

"Answer me, you stupid cunt. Where does he keep them?"

Jennifer pointed a shaky arm toward the nightstand beside the oversize bed in the corner of the loft. "In the drawer," she said, barely able to recognize her own voice, her eyes unable to leave the gun in Joey's hand.

"Get them."

Jennifer did as she was told. She stared momentarily at the pistol lying next to the handcuffs, closed her eyes, then walked back to face Joey over Pete's unconscious body, extending the handcuffs toward him.

"Put them on him," he snapped. "His hands behind his back."

Jennifer stared at the handcuffs, her face clouded with confusion. "How do they work?" she asked in a trembling voice.

"Just press them against his wrist. They'll snap around and lock automatically. And squeeze them tight when they do."

Jennifer knelt next to Pete and, for the first time, noticed the stream of blood moving down his head to the back of his neck. She looked up at Joey. "He's bleeding," she said.

Joey jabbed the gun in her direction. "Put on the handcuffs, bitch. You can worry about his fucking head later."

Jennifer lifted one of Pete's arms behind his back, surprised at how heavy it felt, then, following Joey's instructions, snapped the handcuff in place and repeated the act with the second arm.

When she stood, she could feel her legs trembling, and as Joey stepped toward her she lurched back, staggering under unsteady legs.

As Joey squatted next to Pete, checking the handcuffs, a wave of dizziness hit him. He had stopped for a drink before coming to Pete's apartment, and he realized now he had had one more than he should have. He felt his nerves tighten. Just kill them and get out of here, he told himself.

He dropped one knee to the floor to steady himself, and as he started to rise, Jennifer raced past him, heading for the door.

Jennifer threw back the dead-bolt lock and was just turning the doorknob when Joey's hand grabbed her hair and yanked her head. She staggered back, her arms flailing, trying desperately to hit him, to hurt him somehow. His fist lashed out, striking the side of her face, sending a flash of bright light across her eyes. She staggered back, her feet hitting Pete's body, and then, when he hit her again, she fell to the floor and lay there, gasping for breath.

Joey stood over her, his face twisted with rage. "You bitch," he growled. "You stupid, fucking bitch." He reached down and grabbed the front of her shift and yanked her up to a kneeling position, the thin cloth ripping in his hand from neck to waist.

"Leave her alone."

Joey stared down at Pete. He was on his side now, his eyes glazed as he struggled to right himself. Joey lashed out with his foot, digging it into Pete's side.

Pete groaned and slumped back to the floor, then struggled up to a sitting position. "You're going too far, Joey. Think. It's not too late." He looked behind Joey. The door to the loft was slightly ajar. If you raise your voice, he thought, somebody might hear you. You have to keep him talking.

"It's already too late for you, asshole. And it's too late for your bitch too." He looked down at Jennifer. Her torn shift was spread open, exposing one breast. Joey stared at it, noting how white her skin was, how even whiter it seemed contrasted with the deep red of her small nipple.

As he looked, Jennifer pulled the cloth together, covering herself. Joey glared at her, then reached down and ripped the shift again, the violence of the act tearing it open to her knees.

Pete lunged at him, slamming his shoulder into the side of Joey's knee. But the blow had no force, and Joey slapped down with the pistol, catching Pete on the side of the neck, knocking him to the floor again. "Try that again and I'll kill her now."

Pete lay on his side, glaring up at Joey. "Don't be stupid, Joey. You can still walk away from this."

Joey looked down at him and laughed. It was a high, harsh, grating sound that seemed to border on madness. "Oh, I'll walk away from it, Petey boy. Just like I walked away from that asshole Maxwell. But you won't walk away, Petey. And neither will your little slut here." He looked back at Jennifer and smiled, watching her body tremble as he did. "But maybe you will, lady. Maybe if you do me a little favor, you can walk away from all of it." Jennifer had closed the torn cloth again, and Joey moved her hands away with the barrel of the pistol.

"Joey!" Pete's voice was loud and harsh, bringing Joey's eyes back to his. "Tony will get you if you do this. You know that."

Joey let out another long, high laugh. "He already knows, Petey boy. But Tony doesn't give the orders anymore. Tony's finished. You and your girlfriend saw to that." He laughed again. "With a little help from Tony's friends."

"What do you mean?" Jennifer's voice came out in a shaking, stuttering timbre.

"Everything you got, baby, we gave you. It was a setup, right from the start. Both of you were just too stupid to see it." Joey looked back at Pete. "Even Mary Beth was a setup, Petey boy. But don't worry. I gave her a good fuck for you, just for old times' sake." He saw Pete's eyes harden, and he laughed again, then looked back at Jennifer. "I think I'll do something nice for you too. How would you like that?"

"Why don't you do something nice for me, Joey?"

The voice came from behind him, hard and threatening, and Joey recognized it at once. His body stiffened at the sound. He turned his head slowly. Marco stood in the doorway, a revolver in his hand, and Joey could see it was pointing directly at him. "What are you doing here, Tony?"

Marco's eyes flashed with a violent anger Joey had never seen before. It sent a chill down his spine.

"I've been standing here, listening to you talk like some stinking animal," Marco said. "But I guess that's what you've always been. I just wanted to think you'd changed."

"Heah, Tony, don't talk like that," Joey pleaded, his voice a whine. "I'm just doing what I was sent to do. You know that."

"I'm canceling Paul's order," Marco said, his voice as flat as his eyes. "Now drop the gun. I don't want to hurt you, Joey. But I will, so just do it."

A weak smile came to Joey's lips. "Heah, Tony, it's too late for that. It's gone too far. They even know about Maxwell now."

"That was a stupid thing to do, Joey. And this was even more stupid."

"Heah, wait a minute. You were there. You agreed to it. At least this time you did."

"Paul had my son, Joey. I didn't have any choice." Marco extended the weapon a little farther in Joey's direction. "Now I do. So drop the gun, Joey. Right now."

Joey's body tensed, the muscles springlike, ready to move.

"Watch him, Tony." Pete's voice was like a warning growl as he struggled up to his knees. His eyes snapped toward Jennifer. "The keys for the handcuffs are in my pocket. Get them and get me out of these."

Joey's head turned to Pete, then back to Tony. "Don't do this, Tony. You're selling me out."

"I'm not going to let you kill them, Joey. You can drop the gun and take your chances with Pete. But that's all I can do for you." Tony watched Joey's face fill with confusion. His eyelids began to flutter, and a tic appeared at the corner of his mouth. Tony held himself erect, with more difficulty than he allowed himself to admit. He had buttoned his suitcoat over the growing red stain on his shirt, but inside he felt the fire growing, and his knees were getting weaker by the moment.

Finally Joey shook his head and offered Tony a pleading stare. "Please, Tony. Don't do this."

"Drop the gun," Tony snapped, the harshness of his voice nearly doubling him over.

"Heah, what's the matter with you?" Joey asked.

Tony leveled the pistol at him again. "This is the last time I'm offering."

Joey dropped the gun and moved slowly toward Tony, his hand held in front of him in a defensive gesture. "Paul's not gonna like this, Tony. You're selling him out too."

"Paul won't mind. He's dead." Marco hunched his shoulders in pain and bent forward slightly.

Joey noted the movement, then stared at Tony's free arm, pressed to his abdomen. "Looks like he didn't die easy," he said, taking a step forward. Tony cocked the hammer on the revolver and stared into Joey's face. "I don't want to, Joey, but I will, damn you, I will."

Joey held his hands in front of him as though they could ward off the bullet. "Okay, Tony, okay." He began inching toward the door. "You don't want to do the right thing by me, but that's okay." He hesitated. "But I don't

think you're gonna shoot me if I just get out of here. Not
your old friend Joey." He stared at Marco's eyes and
realized he was right, then gritted his teeth and rushed
through the door.

Tony watched him go, dropping the revolver to his side.
Go and run, Joey, he told himself. Run like an animal
until they catch you. When he looked back across the
room, Jennifer had removed the handcuffs from Pete's
wrists and was helping him to his feet.

Pete staggered slightly and brought a hand to the wound
at the back of his head.

"I'll get you a cold towel," Jennifer said, and hurried
toward the small kitchen.

Pete walked unsteadily across the room and stopped in
front of Tony. "You shouldn't have let him go." There was
no recrimination in his voice, only a weary sadness.

"I didn't have any choice," Tony said. He winced, fighting to keep the pain from his face.

Pete reached out and opened Tony's suitcoat, then closed
it again. It was a bad wound. He wondered how Tony was
still on his feet. "Did Levine do that?" he asked.

Tony nodded his head. The perspiration was forming
heavily on his forehead now, and he was losing color in his
cheeks. "And then you shot him?"

"We were fighting for the gun," Tony said. "This one."
He extended his hand, and Pete took the pistol.

"Is your kid okay?"

Tony nodded again and leaned against the doorjamb.
"My driver took him to my mother's house."

His knees seemed about to give, and Pete reached out
and took his arm.

"I'm okay," he said, forcing a smile.

Pete noticed there was a film of blood on his teeth.
"You better let me get an ambulance."

Tony reached out and grabbed his arm with surprising

strength. "No, Petey. I want to go see Josh. Then I'll get myself to the hospital. I promise."

Pete shook his head. "You won't make it," he said softly. "I don't think you'll even make it with the ambulance."

"Yes I will. And then I'll go to the hospital in the old neighborhood." He forced a smile. "I've been heading back there for a long time," he said. "All my life, really."

Pete closed his eyes and nodded, and when he opened them again, Jennifer was standing next to him, a damp towel in her hand.

Jennifer pressed the towel against Pete's head, then looked at Tony. She was still trembling, and her face was pale. Her eyes were filled with regret. "Thank you," she said, her voice hoarse, almost choked.

A smile came to Tony's eyes and he nodded, then he turned and walked out the door.

Jennifer turned back to Pete. "Where's he going?"

"To see his son," Pete said.

"B-but . . . but," Jennifer stammered. "Are you sure it's safe for him?"

Pete looked down at the revolver in his hand, the one Tony had given him, then past it to the small, dark pool of blood on the floor. "It never has been," he said.

Jennifer followed his eyes. "That's blood, isn't it?" She looked up at him. "His blood." She watched Pete nod his head. "How badly is he hurt?"

"Bad. Very bad."

Jennifer squeezed her eyes shut. "Oh, God," she said.

Pete slipped his arm around her waist. "I'm afraid there's no story now," he said.

Jennifer stared at the floor, then slowly shook her head. "Yes, there is. There's the story I should have written from the start."

"I don't think your paper will want it."

"I won't write it for them," Jennifer said. "I'll write it for myself. It's something people should know about. Something they should understand."

Pete looked at her for a long time and realized that he liked her very much. Very, very much. He reached out and ran one finger along her jawline. "Wouldn't it be nice if they could," he said.

The black Chrysler turned onto First Street and came slowly to a halt against the curb. Tony hunched forward against the wheel, breathing deeply. He eased himself up and stared out the windshield. His mother's house was still three blocks farther up the street, but he knew he wouldn't make it. He smiled weakly to himself. It doesn't matter, he thought. You never belonged up there anyway. The smile broadened, then faded under the pain.

He leaned back against the seat, trying to ease the fire in his stomach. He turned his head to the left and looked up at the building in which he had been raised, allowing his eyes to move up to the windows of his old apartment, then to the roof where they had all played as children.

Kids aren't supposed to know that they're poor, he told himself. But you knew. You always knew. He closed his eyes, wondering now why it had always mattered so much. But it always had, and there was nothing he could have done to make it different.

He smiled at the idea. You get what you're born with. It comes like a gift you didn't ask for. But it's there, all the same, and there's nothing you can do about it. You can manipulate it. Use the good things; try to overcome the bad. But they're all still there, and it's something you can never change.

He opened his eyes and looked across the street to the building Pete had lived in as a kid. He could almost see himself, sitting there on the stoop with Pete and Mary

Beth. It was a long time ago, and yet, not really so long at all.

Up the street, Josh was in bed now. He was sleeping and safe, without any knowledge of what lay ahead. But it would be better for him. Somehow it always had to be better for the ones who followed. He wondered if it ever was.

The pain seared through him, and he bent forward against it. As he coughed, blood slid over his lips and ran slowly down his chin. He should wipe it away, but he was too tired to try. He put his head back against the seat, his breathing slow and steady. Josh would be all right, he told himself. Everything would be all right now.

His breath began to come in quick gasps, and he could feel his body weakening, a slow, steady draining of strength. God, you tried so hard, he told himself. All your life you tried so hard. It just didn't work. You just couldn't make it work.

He sat up abruptly and stared out into the street. But you almost made it. He grasped the steering wheel tightly in his hand, and there was a look of fear on his face.

"There's never enough time," he said aloud. "Damn it, if only there was enough time."